TAKING
INITIATIVE

ELLE M. STEWART

First paperback edition June 2024

Cover design by Ana Grigoriu-Voicu
Interior design by Alison Cnockaert

ISBN 979-8-9903212-1-2 (paperback)
ISBN 979-8-9903212-0-5 (ebook)

Library of Congress Control Number: 2024906992

Published by the author
www.ellemstewart.com

TAKING
INITIATIVE

For The Inhumans—Lia, Makara, Mia, Milo, Svartül, and
Tallow—and the wonderful humans who brought them to life.
This book would not exist without you.

AUTHOR'S NOTES

This story deals with an unhealthy past relationship. It includes mentions of criticism and ridicule, guilt-tripping, pet theft (no animal harm or death), and sexual coercion. I have tried to treat these topics with compassion and respect and to focus the story on growth rather than trauma. If the inclusion of these topics means that this story isn't for you, that's okay. Take care of yourself first and foremost.

This book also includes a number of words and phrases in Spanish. Traditionally, non-English words within English works are italicized for "clarity." I've chosen not to do this. This practice of italicizing has been called into question more and more recently, especially by those who feel othered seeing their languages treated as exotic or confusing. Because English is my primary language, I have chosen to listen to the voices of those who are most impacted by this practice and treat all languages equally within the text. My sole goal with this choice is to minimize harm. If you find unfamiliar words in this book—in any language!—go ahead and look them up. There's never a wrong time to learn more about the world around us. *insert The More You Know gif here*

1

A LIBRARY HAD never seemed so daunting.

It shouldn't have. It's not as if it were some massive Renaissance-Era edifice, domed and imposing. It wasn't the New York Public Library, flanked by two stone lions acting as silent, judgmental guardians. It wasn't even that spaceship-looking monstrosity in San Diego, all hard corners and glass walls and angular concrete supports.

No, the Ashville Public Library was a single-story brick rectangle on a quiet corner in a quiet town forty minutes outside Wichita, Kansas. That corner is where Jo Rainier stood on a Tuesday evening in late April. For nearly five minutes, she'd been staring at the front doors, psyching herself up to go inside.

"You're being ridiculous, Jo," she muttered to herself. "It's going to be *fine*."

A middle-aged white woman emerged from the library, paperback in hand. She had seen Jo and smiled at her on her way inside. Now, she smiled again—and then did a double take. "You lost, sweetheart?"

Jo shook her head, about to toss out an "I'm good!" before she remembered she wasn't in California anymore. It might be rude not to give an actual answer. "No, I'm just…" She scrambled for a valid excuse. "I'm waiting until the event starts."

The woman's eyebrows raised with interest. "Is there a new book club or something?"

"No, it's, um, a game night?" Jo said, twisting the statement into a question.

"Ah," the woman replied. "Not for me, sweetie, but you have fun." She waved like she and Jo were old friends.

Leaning on her newfound manners, Jo waved back as the woman headed toward the parking lot. "Have a lovely evening, ma'am!"

Her phone buzzed. She slid it out of her jean jacket pocket, half-hoping she was suddenly needed to cover a shift at White Hills Senior Living and Care Center, where she was the newest member of the nursing staff. No such luck. Just her calendar app with one final reminder.

> MnM night
> 6:30 p.m. – 8:30 p.m.
> Ashville Public Library

Sure enough, it was six thirty on the dot. Jo silenced her phone, took a deep breath, and finally walked into the library. She'd been here a handful of times in the three weeks since she'd moved to Kansas. Ashville's library was tiny compared to the ones she frequented back home in Orange County, but there was a decent variety of titles and plenty of cozy spots to read. And since moving so far from home was ostensibly about saving money, she was trying really hard to borrow books instead of buying them.

Now that she'd made it into the lobby, Jo's nerves eased. It was hard to feel anxious surrounded by that familiar old dusty-book smell. She glanced around, but there were no signs indicating where to go for the game. The flyer she'd seen on the events board hadn't listed a specific spot either. She approached the front desk, where a young Asian American woman gave her a crooked grin. Jo had seen the librarian once or twice but had never spoken to her. She had long black hair dyed blue at the tips. Her name tag read "Leni," and above it, she wore an enamel pin that said "Ask me what I'm reading."

"Evening, hun. Can I help you find something?" Leni asked.

"Yes, where's the Monsters and Mythology game happening?"

"Oh, yeah, Felix's thing." She pointed to a set of stairs across the lobby. Jo hadn't been to the basement yet, though she'd noticed the stairs on her first trip to the library. It was impossible to miss the large, caution-tape-yellow sign that read "Tornado Shelter" with an arrow pointing down. She suppressed a shudder. She'd take California's earthquakes over tornadoes any day.

"The community rooms are downstairs so that it stays quiet up here," Leni continued. "I'm not sure which room it's in, but it's the only event tonight. It'll be the room with the light on."

"Thanks." Jo started to turn away but paused. "What are you reading?"

Leni lit up and pointed at her pin. "Hey, it worked! I just finished a sci-fi book called *A Circle of Stars* about two guys trapped in an adrift spaceship who fall in love. It's so good. We have it here if you're interested."

"I love sci-fi. I'll grab it after the game," Jo said, relaxing into a smile.

"You won't regret it." Leni's grin grew even bigger and more crooked. "Tell Felix hi for me."

Jo's heart beat a little quicker as she started down the stairs, a strange mix of excitement and nerves flaring up. *It's going to be fine, Jo. It's only one game.*

THE FLUORESCENT LIGHT on the ceiling buzzed loudly in the quiet meeting room. Seated at an otherwise empty table, Felix Navarro double tapped his phone screen. It was six thirty-three.

How long should he give it? Ten more minutes? That sounded fair. He would wait another ten minutes before officially declaring Monsters and Mythology Night a failure. Warren, the library's director and Felix's boss, might not be too pleased about that, but what else could Felix do if no one showed up?

Absently, he adjusted the stack of twelve giant hardcover books that sat next to him, aligning their corners just so.

The soft thumping of footsteps on the carpeted stairs made him sit up straight. He folded his hands on the table in front of him, just in time for someone to step into the doorway.

"Are you Felix?" the woman asked. She was of average height and build, with a generous curve of round hips. She wore black leggings with a high waist and a cut-off yellow T-shirt with a strange geometric shape on it: a hexagon filled with triangles, with the numeral "20" in the center. Her auburn hair was curled, the ends barely brushing the collar of her denim jacket.

"How did you know my name?" Felix blurted. Not his finest moment of customer service, but that question wasn't one he'd anticipated.

The woman's lips twitched up at the corners. She was wearing dark red lipstick that contrasted with her fair skin and complemented her hair. It was a pretty color on her. Perhaps a bit bolder than one might expect for a Tuesday night at a library, but he found he liked it.

"For one, Leni mentioned it," she replied. "She says hi, by the way. But also, you *are* wearing a name tag." She raised perfectly arched brows above her pale brown eyes, giving him a playful, teasing look. It made her look even prettier than the lipstick did. "Did you forget?"

"No," he said, and that expression on her face encouraged him to tease her right back. "But if you can read my name tag from there, why did you ask?"

The woman laughed—a clipped, brazen "ha ha" that filled the room, echoed in Felix's chest, and then was instantly gone.

"Fair enough," she said with a shrug. "It seemed as good an opening as any. I'm Jo."

"I'm still Felix. Hello."

"Hi." She glanced around the empty room. "So... I guess I'm the first one here?"

Felix could feel a blush creep up his neck. What the hell had come over him? He was here to host an event, not tease cute patrons. He sat up even taller.

"Yes, welcome," he said, more reserved now. He gestured at the chairs around the large table. "Feel free to have a seat anywhere. We'll begin shortly."

Jo took the middle seat on one side of the table and removed a few things from her purse: a mechanical pencil, a small drawstring bag, and a piece of paper folded in quarters. She unfolded the paper and smoothed it out with a delicate touch. Trying not to stare at her, Felix grabbed the top book from the stack beside him. He opened it to the first chapter and skimmed over paragraphs of nonsense proper nouns and verbs that surely did not mean what the author seemed to think they meant.

"Um, sorry, are you using that setting?" Jo asked.

Felix looked up. "What setting?"

"The Marshlands." She pointed at the book. Felix looked more closely at the front cover, which read, *The Marshlands: A Monsters & Mythology Campaign Setting.*

"My character is set up for the Sibylline Wastes, but it's okay. I can make some changes," she continued. "Or, actually, should I roll up a character in front of you? Some GMs are picky about that with players they don't know. I used point buy, so you can check it if you want."

Felix glanced at the creased paper she held out, an indecipherable mix of printed ink and handwritten notes and numbers. His stomach clenched as several curse words ran through his mind. Just like that, everything he'd been dreading about that night seemed to be coming to fruition.

"No, that's fine," he said carefully, keeping his expression neutral. "I don't need to see it."

She shrugged, picked up her pencil, and started erasing.

"We can do the other one you said." Felix rotated the stack of books so he could see the spines. "You don't have to change your... thing. Your paper. What was it you said?"

"The Sibylline Wastes?"

"Yes, that one." He wrestled a book out from the bottom of the stack: *An Adventurer's Guide to The Sibylline Wastes.* It was almost twice as thick as the *Marshlands* one.

Fuck.

Jo opened her mouth and inhaled. She paused, regarding Felix with narrowed eyes that twinkled with amusement. Felix's attention snagged on those dark red lips, parted to reveal a pink tongue. Her next words came out as if she'd figured out a juicy secret. "You don't know anything about Monsters and Mythology, do you?"

"I... know that it's a game," he said in a futile attempt to retain a shred of dignity.

"Mm-hmm. What kind of game?"

He glanced at the stack of books. "A game with a lot of rules."

That crisp laugh of hers echoed against the low ceiling. "Okay, I'll give you that one. And what's this?" She angled her body toward him and pulled her jacket open, showing him the T-shirt underneath.

Felix was appalled to feel his face heat at the way her chest jutted forward. He hoped the fluorescents washed him out enough that she didn't notice him blushing like a teenager. "A hexagon with a twenty inside it," he said, his eyes darting back to her face.

"Hm." Jo let her jacket fall closed and uncinched her drawstring bag. She dumped out a handful of sparkly red plastic shapes—a cube, a pyramid, a diamond, plus a few more he couldn't readily name—and reached across the table to place one of them near him. Felix picked it up and examined it. White numbers were etched onto each triangle-shaped face.

"It's a d20," Jo explained. "A twenty-sided die that's used for most of the rolls in MnM. The hexagon is how it's represented in print, like you're looking at it from above."

Felix rolled the die between his thumb and forefinger until he found the "20." The shape on Jo's shirt suddenly made sense. He nodded. "I see."

Then—because why the hell not?—he shook the die in his palm and rolled it on the table.

"Don't!" Jo cried, lurching to her feet. She splayed herself over the table and tried to grab the die, but it was too far away for her reach. The d20 came to a stop. "What did you roll?" she groaned.

Felix managed to peel his gaze away from the woman lying prone on the table. "A three."

"Damn it—you jinxed it." She didn't sound angry, but she plopped into her chair and held her hand out. He gave the d20 back. Cradling it in her palm, she looked down on it like it was a naughty puppy. "Are you going to be good, or do I have to put you in jail? You're the only one I've got tonight, but there's plenty more back home to replace you if you don't behave."

Felix blinked at her absurdity. Was she... *talking* to a die?

What the fuck had he gotten himself into?

JO ROLLED HER d20 and sighed in relief when it landed on sixteen. "Thank you," she murmured as she set it down with the rest of her multi-sided dice. With the twenty facing up for good luck, of course. Granted, if no one else showed up to play, she might not be rolling dice tonight at all.

Felix, it seemed, had never met a dice gremlin before. He was staring at her with wide, dark brown eyes, his heavy, black eyebrows raised in what looked a lot like concern. Leaning back in his seat, he folded his arms across his broad chest. The fabric of his plum dress shirt bunched up and parted between his buttons.

Despite her best intentions, Jo glanced down and found herself caught between disappointment and relief that he was wearing an undershirt. She quickly refocused on Felix's face. His long, oval, deep olive face with dark stubble so thick Jo couldn't tell if he groomed it that way or if he simply had the most intense five o'clock shadow she'd ever seen. The patch below his lower lip, covering his chin, was gray. Her body ached at the sight, and Jo had never been more keenly aware that she was nearing thirty-five.

"Sorry," she said as she reigned her thoughts back in. "Some

MnM players get really particular about other people rolling their dice."

"And you're one of them, I see." His eyebrows lowered to a more neutral position. "I apologize for my faux pas."

Jo waved away his weirdly formal apology and pointed her thumb toward the door. "Are you expecting more people tonight?"

"In all honesty, I don't know what to expect tonight," he said. "This is the library's first attempt at this type of program, and hosting it fell into my lap. Our director, Warren, hoped a weekly game night would bring in some new, younger patrons... though he seemed to believe a single flyer in the lobby would suffice for advertising." He cleared his throat and ran a hand through his hair, lifting his ebony waves and letting them fall. "I apologize again. I spoke out of turn. I'm sure the director knows best."

"I don't know about that," Jo said with a grin. "How smart can he be if he put the guy who knows nothing about MnM in charge of RPG night?"

Felix puffed out a tiny exhale from between his lips, a sound that was almost a laugh. "I don't think anyone on staff knows much about this game of yours—just that it's become something of a pop culture phenomenon in recent years. And apparently, my going to a fancy, East Coast grad school was enough for Warren to think I know what 'kids these days' are into."

"Oh my God, please don't tell me he actually used the phrase 'kids these days.'"

"It was heavily implied," he said with the tiniest hint of a smile.

She laughed but couldn't think of anything else to say. Silence fell, then lingered, then drew out into awkwardness. Felix tapped his phone until it lit up and hummed in displeasure. Jo pulled out her phone too. Six forty-six. Officially late enough that it was safe to assume no one else would show up. It wasn't like this was Los

Angeles, where traffic made everyone thirty minutes late to everything.

"Is it possible to play this game with only the two of us?" Felix asked.

Jo smiled. She loved librarians—always willing to go the extra mile for their patrons. "It's possible, but not particularly fun. Especially since I brought a warlock. I'm squishy. I'll die in the first encounter."

"I see," he said, although Jo had a feeling he didn't have a goddamn clue what she was talking about. "Then perhaps we should call it a night and try again next week. I'll speak to our director about upping our advertising efforts so that you'll have some people to play with."

"That would be nice, but..."

She trailed off, unsure if her opinion was wanted. Felix hadn't asked for it. But when she didn't say anything further, he gestured encouragingly at her.

"It's just that, if you don't know how to play, you won't be able to GM," she said quickly. "To run a game, I mean. Roleplaying games like MnM need a storyteller. They guide the narrative, adjudicate rules and dice rolls, and manage combat with monsters. You could have a table full of players, and you still couldn't play without a GM."

"And GM means...?"

"Game Master," she explained. She slid into the chair closer to Felix and removed *Monsters & Mythology: Core Rules* from his stack of books. She opened to the very first page of the very first chapter and pointed to the "What You Need" heading. The very first bullet point read "Game Master (GM)" in bold, followed by a few sentences summarizing the GM's role. "It's literally on page one, dude."

She meant for it to sound joking, but Felix didn't smile or laugh. She was about to apologize, but he spoke first.

"Would you be willing to run the game, then, since you know how to play?"

And there it was. Exactly what she'd been worried about, what had kept her rooted to the spot on the corner outside. GMs tended to be in short supply at public games, and organizers were always trying to recruit more volunteers. Saying no wasn't exactly Jo's strong suit, especially when it came to MnM. It was too easy for her to dive in headfirst, overcommit herself, and get burned out.

Once, she had loved GMing as much as she loved playing. But over the last couple of years, it had begun to feel more stressful than fun. It wasn't easy writing adventures and doing prep work for multiple games, week after week. Jeremy, her ex-boyfriend, had never liked how much time she spent on MnM. So she'd quietly pulled back from gaming conventions and public events and limited herself to one game: the longstanding campaign she ran for her closest friends.

She really didn't want to fall into that old pattern again. All she wanted was to play a casual game of MnM once in a while, and maybe make some new friends in the process.

Jo swallowed her "yes" and shook her head. "I'm sorry. I have run games before, but I think I'd prefer to take a break to play. GMing is a lot of work, and I don't think I can commit to that while I'm settling in here."

"Settling in?" Felix asked, cocking his head.

"I just moved here from California. New job, new apartment, all that."

"I can understand that. I guess it's up to me then." He eyed the stack of books warily.

Jo took pity on him.

She nudged *Core Rules* closer to Felix. "Start with this. Chapters one through three are going to be the most important for you to know. Skim the rest, and don't bother reading the magic spell descriptions. That's an entire chapter, and you can look them up as needed." She pulled *Monster Compendium (Volume 1)* out of the stack next. "Familiarize yourself with how to interpret the monsters' game statistics and combat actions. You don't need to memorize any of them. Like the spells, you'll look them up when you need them, but you should understand the abbreviations and stuff." She placed her palm on the stack of supplemental books. "These are all extras. You can ignore them for the time being."

Felix was wide-eyed again, but this time it looked less like concern and more like... awe. Which wasn't quite the reaction Jo expected. She was used to MnM outsiders rolling their eyes or getting a glazed-over look when she went too deep in the weeds. But Felix did neither of those things.

"Would you help me?" he blurted, a tiny crack in his composure.

It caught her so off guard, she could only reply with a very eloquent, "Huh?"

He sighed. "I tried to read these after Warren assigned this event to me, but they don't make any sense. Even the beginning of this *Core Rules* book went completely over my head."

"But chapter one is mostly world building," Jo said. "It's not even rules heavy."

"I don't generally read this kind of thing. I don't like fantasy."

"*Excuse me?*" she cried, forgetting to use her indoor voice. Good thing this room was far away from the quiet book browsers and evening studiers. "But you're a librarian!"

"I'm aware." Felix offered her a slow nod and another almost-smile. "Luckily, there are many types of books to enjoy, and many types of librarian to be."

"Okay, you got me there. What kind of librarian are you?"

"At present? One in need of assistance." Felix's dark eyes softened, and Jo's heart did too. Just a little bit. "I understand you're too busy to GM every week. But if you're willing, I would appreciate your help—even just a few hours of your time."

Jo pressed her lips together, feeling the tackiness of her lip stain. The "yes" was already crawling up the back of her throat. But this time, it didn't feel quite like her typical kneejerk reaction. She *wanted* to say it.

Moving to Ashville was supposed to be her fresh start—for a lot of things. She never meant to leave MnM behind for good, just to find a better balance for it in her life. As she glanced around at the empty chairs, she realized that helping Felix might be the only way to stay involved with the game for now. Maybe there was a way to say yes without it becoming an all-consuming thing. Aida, her best friend back home, the paladin to her cleric, was always talking about setting boundaries "early and often." Jo had never been particularly good at that either, but...

Fresh start, Jo. No time like the present.

"Yeah, sure," she said, and Felix smiled. Actually smiled, for the first time since she'd walked into the room. Jo did her best not to be distracted by how that beaming grin sent sparks dancing over her skin. "I can help for... an hour a week for the next six weeks." Admittedly, she pulled the numbers out of thin air, but they sounded reasonable. An hour a week wasn't overdoing it, right?

"Thank you," Felix said, his eyes soft and warm and genuine.

The kind of eyes someone could get lost in.

"Can I make a suggestion?" Jo said, hurriedly glancing down so she didn't stare too long and make it weird.

"Please do."

"If someone does show up and there's no one else here, they might not be inclined to come back," she said. "I've seen it happen before, where public game programs die before they can get off the ground. If you can get your director to agree to more advertising, maybe you could do a grand opening of sorts in a few weeks. Build up enough excitement to make the first week... not this." She waved her hands at the empty room. "One big event, and you'll have people coming back for more."

"That's a good idea. Thank you. I'll see if Warren agrees," Felix said, getting to his feet.

Jo's mouth went dry. Holy shit, how tall was this guy? And how did a librarian get a body like that? She'd noticed his broad chest already, but the man was seriously built more like an athlete than the bookish type. Not that they were mutually exclusive, but *Jesus*. Those charcoal slacks barely contained his thighs.

Felix stacked the MnM books neatly on top of the others. He picked up the whole lot with ease, even though they were an unwieldy size and weighed at least a couple of pounds each. His biceps shifted under his sleeves. Jo scrambled to pull her phone out of her pocket to give herself something else to stare at. Thank God there was a text from Aida to distract her.

Aida

How's it going?

Jo started typing a reply.

Jo

Long story, but okay, I think? I'm the only—

"Jo?"

Her head snapped up. Felix stood by the door.

"Are you coming?"

"Oh, shit, yeah, sorry." Jo shoved her phone in her jacket pocket and dumped her dice loose into her purse, along with their bag and her pencil. She folded her unused character sheet and pocketed it next to her phone, feeling Felix's eyes on her the entire time. She mumbled another apology as he stood aside to let her through the door first. He caught up with her by the time she reached the bottom of the stairs. Okay, yeah, he was tall. Easily six foot two. Maybe three.

"The library closes early on Fridays, at six o'clock," he said. "Perhaps you could come then to show me how all of this"—he hefted the rulebooks in his arms while Jo diligently ignored his biceps— "works."

"Bold of you to assume I don't have plans on Friday nights."

"Do you?"

"Um. No."

He flashed her another smile, and Jo had to grip the railing for balance. "Then I'll see you Friday."

FELIX WHEELED THE bin of overnight returns to the front desk and stacked the books to check them in. He loved this part of the morning shift, the peace and quiet of the library with no patrons or co-workers yet. Just him and the methodical refrain of scanning each book, confirming where it belonged, and sorting it onto the proper reshelving cart.

Unfortunately, the night's returns were minimal, and he was done in under ten minutes. He put his hands on his hips and surveyed the carts. He contemplated doing the shelving next, but that was one of Peggy's favorite tasks, and she'd be arriving any minute. Instead, he checked his email and then the library's general inbox. He fired off a polite response to someone asking about voter registration forms and forwarded two emails to Emma, the children's librarian, with questions she'd be able to answer better than he could.

Ah, the glamorous life of a public librarian.

Felix sighed and sipped his vanilla café con leche out of an old, faded, blue travel mug, dutifully sealing the lid as he set it down. Though Warren didn't have a rule against open containers at the front desk, three semesters of special collections courses at Rutgers University had ingrained certain habits into Felix. Of course, he wasn't allowed to bring *any* liquids into the archives, but even in regular lecture rooms, beverages were required to be sealable. An archivist-in-training could never be too careful. And while Felix might not be an archivist yet, there was no reason to let himself get sloppy.

He glanced around for something to keep him occupied. Two enormous books stared back: *Core Rules* and *Monster Compendium (Volume 1)*. After saying good night to Jo the previous evening, he'd returned most of the Monsters and Mythology books to their shelf and checked out the two she suggested he start with. He hadn't brought them home; they were still part of a work assignment, after all. They were still sitting exactly where he'd left them, tucked under the monitor of his usual computer station.

"Might as well," he murmured. He flipped *Core Rules* open.

"GREETINGS, ADVENTURER," yelled the first line on page one. Felix cringed but gritted his teeth and soldiered on. He had made it to the end of page three when the front door offered him a reprieve.

"Mornin', Felix," Peggy called. "Any patrons yet?" She was a lean white woman somewhere north of fifty with a spiky, highlighted haircut that screamed "early 2000s mom." It suited her to a tee. Today's cardigan was deep blue and covered in embroidered cherry blossoms. In the nine months they'd been working together, Felix had never seen her repeat a cardigan. He had to admire her commitment.

"Good morning, Peg. Not yet."

She came around the desk and deposited her purse on the open office chair beside him. "Oh, you're a peach. You left the returns for me!"

"Of course," Felix said with a smile. "Though before you get started, I have a question for you."

"Sure thing." She cocked her hip and rested her hand on it, the other hand draped on a cart.

"Just between us?"

"Ooh, that sounds juicy."

Felix exhaled a breathy laugh. "It's not, really. Just work stuff."

"Everything okay, kiddo?"

At thirty-six and on his second career, Felix was hardly a "kiddo," but Peggy's mom energy was powerful enough to make the nickname feel completely natural. And since Felix had barely seen his own mother in recent years, he didn't really mind it.

"I'm fine," he said. "Thank you for asking."

"Well, I'm great at keeping secrets, so lay it on me." Peggy scooped her hand toward herself in an encouraging gesture.

"What do you think about Warren's insistence on making the library more, as he puts it, 'youth-friendly' with this game night?"

Peggy regarded him for a moment before answering. "It's a good idea. Emma's up to her eyeballs with all the kids' program-ming, and the retired crowd keeps our romance, mysteries, and thrillers on constant rotation. But we've lost a lot of the young folks without kids. We used to get students from the community college who would stick with us after graduation. A few years back, the college completely renovated their bookstore and added a huge study space. And they have a café. A *café*, Felix. We can't compete with that, so why not try something new and different? Something the college doesn't offer."

"I can see the logic in that."

"And then there's the whole budget thing to consider," Peggy said with a sigh.

That got Felix's attention. "What budget thing?"

"Oh, did I say something about the library's budget?"

He laughed, even though his pulse spiked with anxiety. "What was that about keeping secrets?"

"This isn't a secret." Peggy set her fists on her hips defiantly. "Not really. Warren just hasn't made any staff-wide announcements about it yet. It's all public information. On the Butler County website." She nodded toward the computer monitor in front of him with a meaningful look on her face.

"I see," he said deliberately. "Well, if Warren hasn't addressed it, I certainly won't ask you anything more about it."

Before she could respond, the front door opened. And, speak of the devil, Warren stepped inside. Peggy caught Felix's eye and subtly shook her head. Felix winked to indicate he understood. He was on his own to research the county's budget, and that would have to wait.

"Good morning, Felix, Peggy," their boss said, smoothing his hand over his tie. Warren was in his early sixties or so, a white man with impeccably gelled gray hair and a work wardrobe that consisted of nothing but white shirts, black trousers, and solid-colored ties. "How was last night's event? Good turnout?"

"Not exactly," Felix admitted as Peggy slipped away with one of the returns carts. "Do you have some time this morning, Warren? I was hoping to talk to you about some game night ideas from a new volunteer."

JO WAS SEATED at the front desk of White Hills Senior Living and Care Center with a notebook perched on her knees and her glasses sliding down her nose. She usually preferred wearing contacts at work, but some days her eyeballs needed the break. She pushed her glasses back into place, scribbled the words "find an optometrist" in the margins of her notes, and then went back to jotting down the running commentary of the receptionist, Leo.

As a nurse in the skilled care wing of the facility, Jo would only need to cover the front desk if there was a staffing emergency. But her floor lead, Lucille, believed in a thorough training schedule. Nothing wrong with being prepared, of course, but Jo would rather be getting to know the elderly residents in her charge. Two and a half weeks into the job and she still hadn't learned all their names.

Leo, a bespectacled, sandy-haired white man with a smattering of freckles, was describing the check-in/check-out system when the front door opened, bringing with it a blast of damp springtime air.

"Mr. Ortiz, good morning!" he greeted the forty-something Latino man who walked in.

"Hey, Leo. Checking out my dad for his oncologist appointment," Mr. Ortiz said.

"Good timing!" Leo crowed. He tended to speak in all exclamation points with residents and their families. Thankfully, he wasn't like that with co-workers or Jo might have screamed five minutes into training. "I'm showing our newest nurse here how checkouts work! Would you mind if I used you and Mr. Ortiz Sr. as an example?"

"Fine by me."

Jo took notes while Leo paged a nurse, and Mr. Ortiz entered everything into a tablet bolted to the waist-high counter. While they waited for the elder Mr. Ortiz, they made polite small talk about the weather. There was a classic Midwestern rainstorm expected that afternoon, same as the last five days. Jo really needed to buy an umbrella.

It wasn't long before Vanessa, one of Jo's skilled nursing co-workers, wheeled Mr. Ortiz (Sr.) into the lobby. Vanessa was a pretty, tanned white woman in her twenties wearing maroon scrubs and bright white sneakers laced with black-and-yellow shoelaces. Her long, dusty blonde hair was pulled back into a high ponytail that swayed behind her like a pendulum, and her bangs were expertly curled and swept to the side. With a peppy greeting, she handed off the wheelchair to Mr. Ortiz (Jr.) and pushed the automatic door button. Then she, Jo, and Leo all stood around waving goodbye as father and son left.

As soon as they were out of sight, Vanessa leaned heavily on the front desk. "Ugh, I need caffeine. You wanna grab a coffee, Jo?"

"Oh, um... I don't know if I'm done yet." Jo turned to Leo.

"That was the last thing I had for now," he said. "They'll be back around one, so come by then, and I can show you how we do check-ins."

"Sounds good. Thanks." Jo stood and addressed Vanessa. "I'll get coffee with you. Is there a Starbucks nearby or something?"

Vanessa clicked her tongue off the roof of her mouth. "Aw, California, you're cute. I was talking about the Keurig in the break room."

Jo laughed at herself, hoping to save face in front of her new co-workers. "Oh, well. That makes more sense, since I haven't actually seen a Starbucks anywhere. But my answer hasn't changed! Let's do it."

Vanessa led Jo to the break room, stopping to say hello to the residents they passed and introducing them to Jo. "She's from *California*," Vanessa said to every single one, with a teasing look at Jo each time.

"You're never going to let me live that down, are you?" Jo asked as they entered the stale-coffee-scented solace of the break room.

"Which part?" Vanessa said with deadpan seriousness that still managed to be playful. "The being from California part, or the part where you thought we could swan off in the middle of our shift to this town's one-and-only Starbucks? Which, by the way, is *waaaay* out by the expressway."

"My God, I haven't heard someone say 'swan off' since my great-aunt was alive," Jo teased.

"I work with old people, California," Vanessa said as she futzed with the Keurig. "All of my idioms are from the forties."

"That's what the internet is for. Keeping your vocabulary up to date."

"Huh." Vanessa cocked her head like she'd been given a new insight on life. "I thought it was for swiping on cute boys who live in Kansas City and trying to decide if it's worth a two-hour drive to get laid."

If Jo had made her drink first, she would have choked on it. Instead, she made a strangled sound in the back of her throat.

Vanessa grabbed her cup from the machine and moved aside to let Jo in. "Sorry, too much? I pretty much turn off my filter when I'm not with the residents or Lucille. It's the only way I keep my head on straight sometimes."

Jo shook her head as she pushed the button for hot water. Tea was definitely preferable to single-serve coffee from a machine that probably hadn't been cleaned in six months. "You're good. Just took me by surprise is all. So does that mean there aren't really any guys in Ashville?"

Jo only asked to make conversation. Part of the whole "fresh start in a new state" thing was figuring out her life on her own. Getting tied to someone, so soon after moving here, so soon after Jeremy, would make things too messy. And yet, as soon as she asked the question, a pair of dark, soulful eyes above a handsome smile flashed through her mind. She tried to focus on dunking an English breakfast tea bag into her water.

"Oh, there are plenty of guys," Vanessa said, nodding toward a table where they sat down. "But I went to high school with all of them and have either dated them already or know they're bad news." She pointed her finger at Jo. "You get asked out by anyone who graduated from Eisenhower High around 2016, you come to me first. I'll tell you who's worth your time."

Jo laughed, but at the same time, a warm feeling spread through her. She could hear the sincerity in Vanessa's offer, a fierceness that reminded her of the way her best friend Aida always stood up for people.

"I'll keep that in mind," she said. "But I'm thirty-four. I should probably skew a little older."

Vanessa made a face. "All the over-thirties in Ashville are married or losers. Or both."

Is Felix married? a small voice in Jo's head asked.

Jesus, Jo, she chastised herself.

Suddenly, Vanessa scoffed. "Oh my God, I can't believe we're *those* bitches talking about boys over break-room coffee. Please tell me something, anything, about yourself. What brought you to this place from the land of movie stars and Starbuckses on every corner?"

Jo winced. "Not a great question if you don't want to talk about boys."

Vanessa, to her credit, winced too. "Oh, shit, I'm sorry. Bad breakup or something?"

"Yeah. I needed to get away, start somewhere fresh where I didn't know anybody."

"Halfway across the country?"

"Well, I couldn't afford California rent on my own," she shrugged, defaulting to the simple explanation, the one fit for co-workers and acquaintances. "It's definitely cheaper out here."

"Cheaper, maybe, but way duller. You got any hobbies to keep the mind-numbing, small-town boredom at bay?" Vanessa asked, skillfully steering the conversation elsewhere. Jo felt a rush of gratitude toward her.

In answer to the question, though, only one thing came to mind—the hobby that had spent years taking up space in Jo's brain. "Well... are you familiar with the game Monsters and Mythology?"

To Jo's surprise, Vanessa nodded. "I know of it, but I've never played. You play?"

"Yeah, I've been playing since college. People around here don't seem to know it, though. How'd you hear about MnM?"

"My dad's a big ol' nerd," she said. "He used to play, mostly back in the eighties. He always wanted me to start a group at ACC—Ashville Community College—but I was a different kind of nerd." Vanessa swiveled her hips and kicked up both feet around the edge of the table. Jo squinted until she finally parsed the golden-yellow pattern on her shoelaces.

"You're a *Star Wars* fan?" Jo asked, breaking into a huge grin.

"All the *Stars. Wars* and *Trek* and *Gate*," Vanessa replied, lifting her coffee cup in salute. "Thanks, Dad."

"My mom's the one who got me into fantasy," she said. "The *Earthsea* books are her favorite, and she took me to all of the *Lord of the Rings* movies on opening weekend."

"I love that."

There was a lull in the conversation as they both sipped their drinks. Jo nudged up her glasses and swirled her teabag around a couple of times.

"We should get back," Vanessa grumbled.

"Yeah, I'm supposed to check in with Lucille," Jo agreed. "And, hey, if you ever want to try MnM, the library is starting a game night soon. I went last night, but I was the only one there. I think they're going to launch again in a few weeks, after they advertise a bit more." She offered Vanessa a smile. "Something to keep the small-town boredom at bay."

She grinned back. "That's so cool. Let me know when they start it. I'll come with you."

It wasn't until hours later that Jo realized that maybe inviting Vanessa to join her wasn't the best way to balance MnM in her life. What if she ended up having to teach Vanessa the game too? Or showing up to play when she needed a night off because Vanessa expected her to be there?

Well, shit. What if she had already fucked up her fresh start?

THAT EVENING, FELIX delved into the Butler County website, scouring meeting minutes and long-winded proposals. "Fuck," he said for at least the eighth time in the past hour. Why the hell hadn't Warren said anything about this?

The Board of Supervisors was recommending a twenty percent reduction in the county libraries' operating budget to reallocate funds to public safety: a thinly veiled euphemism for throwing more money at law enforcement. The budget wouldn't be finalized until September, but if the proposal passed, it would be in place for the next three fiscal years.

Leaving his laptop on the couch, Felix strode down the hall to the guest bedroom he'd been occupying for nearly a year. His button-down shirt landed on the bed, leaving him in his undershirt, and he changed into sweatpants and tennis shoes. He filled a water bottle at the kitchen sink and headed down to the basement, flipping on the lights and the fan as he went.

He needed to punch some shit.

But first, music. He pulled up a playlist on his phone, set it to shuffle, and connected it to the speaker on the wall. The blaring guitar-and-synth opening of "Somebody Told Me" by The Killers did its best to drown out his thoughts.

Then, warm up. He jogged ten clockwise laps around the basement, turned, and did ten more counterclockwise. Jumping jacks, squats, budget cuts. *Shit.* He shook out his hands and stretched his forearms, wrists, and fingers while he jogged in place.

Next, hand wraps. He hooked the starting loop over his thumb and wound the length of fabric over his knuckles, around his wrist, between each finger. Over and over, an intricate pattern that was second nature to him. *Twenty goddamn percent.* He wrapped his other hand and flexed his fingers in and out of fists, checking the tightness.

Finally, gloves. He didn't always wear them to work out, but he had learned the hard way not to go bare knuckled when he was stressed. *Damn sheriff's office lobbyists.*

Felix rolled his neck once and charged the punching bag suspended from the ceiling. He was supposed to start slow and work up to full-force punches, but fuck that. Rihanna shouted at him to "Shut Up and Drive" as he attacked the bag with jabs and hooks. When his arms grew heavy, he shook them out and hopped from foot to foot to keep his heart rate up.

Twenty percent was a county-wide cut. El Dorado, the county seat, had three libraries. They'd lobby to hold on to as much of their budget as they could. Which meant Ashville was going to get screwed. Felix knew from his previous career in corporate vendor procurement that salaries and benefits were the most expensive part of any budget. He'd also been around enough layoffs to know that first on the chopping block was *always* the new guy. Which, at Ashville Public Library, was him.

He hit the bag so hard he grunted. He did it again. And again.

Grad school wasn't cheap. He had nearly six figures of debt to prove it. Most of his small salary went toward his loans since he was lucky enough to live rent-free here in Tito's house.

Tito.

"Fuck. Fuck. Fuck." Each word was punctuated by a punch.

Like hell he could leave his grandfather all alone at that retirement home. Like hell he could pick up and move if he lost his job. Lita hadn't even been gone for a year. His parents sure as hell weren't doing anything to help Tito deal with the grief.

He'd have to get another job in town, then, and whatever he found would probably do jack shit for his brand-new career. He'd *finally* gone back to school to pursue the dream he'd had since he was a teenager, and now it was in danger of being ripped away from him. Never mind special collections, *any* library job was hard to come by. Finding one in tiny, out-of-the-way Ashville, right when Tito had needed him here, was practically a miracle. And if he lost that job in a few months? A year at a tiny public library and then a string of minimum wage jobs wasn't exactly how an aspiring archivist built up a resume.

Felix's shoulders burned. He didn't slow down, didn't stop. His arms were full of lead, but will.i.am, et al. were convincing him to "Pump It," accompanied by a trumpet and also, for some reason, surf music? Whatever. If Peggy's hair could be stuck in the early 2000s, so could his taste in music. They both made it work.

He pushed himself through the song, his face pouring sweat and his arms screaming for relief. He was relentless, punishing, brutal. On the final downbeat, he let out a sharp yell and shoved the punching bag away with both hands. He hopped to the side so it wouldn't hit him on the return swing and doubled over, panting heavily, his arms dangling toward the floor.

"*Fuck.*"

The incomparable Britney Spears, begging "Gimme More," washed over him as he caught his breath and came down from the adrenaline. He pushed his gloves off and rolled out his hands and wrists, stretched his arms, back, and chest.

In the post-workout clarity, one truth made itself abundantly clear. Felix needed to keep his job. He could see two potential roads to make that happen. He could either build up a roleplaying game program that brought a crowd of young people into the library, or he could work so hard in the attempt that he proved himself indispensable to Warren.

Only hours ago, he'd convinced his boss to pull game night off the schedule until they could launch it with a big event. Warren had put the launch on the calendar for mid-June and made MnM night part of the library's summer programs. That gave Felix six weeks to learn that goddamn game backwards and forwards. Which he would. He would even figure out how to advertise it properly.

And then, by the end of the summer, by the time those final budget meetings rolled around, they'd have enough ammunition to show the board their importance in the community. They would hold onto their budget. They had to.

"Thank God for Jo," he muttered before pouring a glug of water down his throat. He had yet to make it past page three of the Monsters and Mythology rulebook, and he had a feeling he'd be shit out of luck without her help.

Felix lifted the hem of his sweat-soaked T-shirt. As he closed his eyes to wipe his face, he saw a pair of dark red lips, parted in surprise, with a hint of a smile turning up their corners.

3

AIDA MAHMOUD, JO'S best friend since the seventh grade, couldn't seem to stop laughing. Jo had already turned down her phone's volume once, and she bumped it down another couple of notches.

"Are you done?" she asked, giving Aida a blank look over the video call.

"No!" Aida wailed and cackled again. Her sleek, jet-black ponytail swung forward as she doubled over. When she sat up, she wiped a knuckle under her hazel eyes. Was she actually *crying* from laughter? "It's just so fucking *you*, Jo. You're spending your Friday night at the library! Doing MnM stuff!"

"Only for an hour!" Jo tried to sound incensed, but she was touched how Aida knew that, all things considered, her ideal Friday night would include some combination of books and MnM.

"And then what? Go home and watch that one episode of *Bridgerton* for the zillionth time and then jack off and fall asleep by nine?"

Jo was no longer touched that Aida knew her so well. "I'll have you know that I'm perfectly happy with my vib—"

"I don't actually want to know that level of detail, babe."

"I was going to say 'my life choices,'" Jo fibbed.

"Sure you were."

"Hold on, did you say 'jack off' at work just now?"

"My office door is closed, it's fine." Aida waved an amber-brown hand set off by square green nails and a gold engagement ring. "I can't chat long, though, so any other updates besides 'I'm sitting in my car in my scrubs on a Friday night, waiting to go into the library'? How's the Goober settling in?"

Jo smiled. The only other person in the world who had a nickname for Jo's cat was Aida. "He's okay. He... misses Jeremy."

"You better not be projecting right now, or I will get on a plane tonight."

"I'm not, I promise," Jo said, holding up her pinky in sight of the camera. Aida held up her pinky too. It was as good as their middle-school pinky promises, a system they'd developed in college when they were thousands of miles apart for the first time in their friendship. "I'm not projecting. I don't miss him. Merry, however, stands on the empty side of the bed and screams for an hour every night when I turn off the lights."

"Aww, Goober," Aida pouted. "I bet he misses Pippin, though. Not the asshole."

"He is an asshole, isn't he?"

"Who splits up pair-bonded cats?" Aida cried, as if that was the most blasphemous sin of them all.

On the list of Jeremy's shortcomings, it was certainly up there. He and Jo had adopted the littermates as kittens. When they broke up, Jeremy had insisted they each take one, and Jo hadn't known how to say no. Aida had been livid. She still hadn't forgiven him.

"Assholes, that's who," Jo declared.

"Damn right."

"Hey. I love you."

Aida smiled softly. "I love you too, babe. Let me know how to-night goes, okay?"

"Always. Good luck with your meeting."

Her best friend rolled her eyes. "Ten bucks says it could have been an email."

"You don't get to complain. You have an office."

"And you have a hot librarian to go meet." She made a shooing motion with her hand.

Jo blushed. "I never said he was hot."

"Come on, Jo. I could hear it in your voice. Now go. I have to run too." The camera jostled as she stood up and started walking. "I'll see you in three weeks."

Jo's entire face brightened in the thumbnail of her own camera view. "Oh my God, you're right. Only three more weeks until Indi-Con!"

Aida gave a soft cry of joy. "Aah! Okaylreallygottagoloveyou-bye."

The call disconnected. Jo's phone declared it one minute after six. She checked her teeth in the rearview mirror, then grabbed her purse and the empty takeout bag from the mediocre carnitas burrito she'd scarfed down before calling Aida. She tossed the bag into the trash and headed toward the library door on the corner. Luckily, the afternoon's rain had let up, so she didn't have to walk through a drizzle. The air smelled pleasantly of wet concrete and soil, and Jo took a deep inhale. That fresh, clean smell was rare in southern California, but here in Ashville, she got to enjoy it al-most every day. Maybe those Midwestern storms weren't so bad... though she still hadn't gotten an umbrella.

Felix was waiting for her on the corner. His dress shirt today was pale gray, and he stood facing away from her with one hip out to the side and his hands in the pockets of his navy slacks. In the slanted evening light, the shadows emphasized how well the fabric hugged his ass. Jo forced herself to look at the back of his head, where his loose, dark waves fell slightly past his ears.

"Hey there!" she called.

Felix turned around and offered her a small, polite smile.

"Sorry I'm a couple minutes late. I was on the phone."

"No need to apologize," he said. "I haven't been outside since lunch, so I thought I'd get some air after the last patrons left."

"Oh," Jo said, strangely disappointed that he was *not*, in fact, waiting for her. She brushed it off and jerked her thumb over her shoulder. "Want me to go around the block a few times so you can smell the petrichor a bit longer?"

Felix's grin was genuine this time, and Jo's heart went all aflutter. "Kind of you to offer, and excellent word choice, but we can head inside. I don't want to keep you longer than an hour."

He held the door open for her. Inside, she waited at the top of the stairs for him. Except he didn't follow her. He stayed by the door and pulled a set of keys out of his pocket.

Her pulse once again beat a little faster, for an entirely different reason. She shifted her weight onto her back foot, her hands clutching her purse strap. "You're locking the door?"

"Yes, the library's clo—" Felix stopped short, his eyes glancing over her body language. His face paled. "Oh *fuck*, I'm an idiot. This was a terrible idea. Do you want to leave? You can leave."

He moved behind the front desk to clear her path to the door. The desk was waist-high on the customer side and chair-height on the employee side, effectively putting a barrier between them. Felix dropped the keys on the desk. He started to tuck his hands into his pockets, then stopped and slowly pulled them out where she could see them. "I'm so sorry, Jo. We can reschedule for when there are other people around."

His horrified reaction went a long way in reassuring her that Felix meant her no harm. His face was still pale, and she doubted even the best actor could pull that off without makeup. "I'm okay," she said slowly. "Maybe you could leave the door unlocked, though?"

Felix winced. "I'm sorry, but Warren would have my head. He knows I'm working with a volunteer after hours, but it's still protocol to lock up on time. It has to do with insurance liability. I can give you the keys, though. Would that help?"

Jo pressed her lips together. She wanted to trust Felix, but she reminded herself she didn't really know him. They'd only spoken once before tonight, and not even for a full twenty minutes.

"There are cameras," Felix added when Jo didn't say anything. He pointed to the devices mounted on the ceiling, one pointed toward the front door and one toward the desk. "We can sit here at the desk, and we'll be filmed the whole time."

Jo furrowed her brows. "Oh, right. I guess I forgot that we could sit up here. I was feeling weird about being alone in that meeting room downstairs."

"We were alone in that room on Tuesday," Felix pointed out, relaxing enough to slide his hands into his pockets. One thing, at least, Jo was certain of. He didn't have a weapon in either pocket. She would have seen the outline of it against his thick thighs.

She lifted her eyes away from where his knuckles created ripples in the navy fabric. "But if I'd screamed on Tuesday, someone would have rushed downstairs, even if it was just to tell me to be quiet in the library."

Felix laughed, a high-pitched chuckle that didn't really match his tall, broad stature and his baritone voice. The tension between them eased. "Surely you don't think so little of our librarians that you believe *that* would be their priority if someone screamed?"

"No, of course not," Jo said with a smile, "and don't call me Shirley."

Felix cocked his head. "What?"

"Never mind. Movie reference."

"Ah," he said. "Are you saying you want to stay? I meant it when I said we could reschedule."

"I'll stay," Jo said, approaching the desk and resting her hands on it. "I've actually been looking forward to this all week. Sorry I freaked out a little."

"Truly, do not apologize," Felix took one hand out of his pocket, showing her his palm in a placating gesture. "I owe *you* an apology. I should have asked someone else to stay late with me."

"It's all good," Jo said. She came around one side of the desk while Felix went around the other, scooping up the keys on his way to lock up. Jo sat in the chair closest to the door and slipped her phone from the pocket of her scrub top.

Jo

> Sorry, I know you're in a meeting but I'm alone in the library with this guy and he has to lock the door or his boss will be pissed. I don't feel unsafe, but also maybe if I don't text or call by 7:15 my time, call the Ashville sheriff?

> No wait, call me first. If I don't pick up after three tries, then call the sheriff.

Aida

> WTF???

> Fine, I trust you.

> 7:15 EXACTLY, though.

> Make good choices.

Felix cleared his throat behind her, and Jo hurriedly turned off her screen. He was holding a small ring of keys out to her.

"The front door is this one, with the tiny G stamped on it. I don't know why it's a G."

How had he known she was just wondering that? Their fingers brushed as she took the keys from him, and he quickly withdrew his hand. Jo bit her cheek to keep from smiling and set the keys on the desk next to her.

"Did you text someone that we're here?" he asked as he went the long way around the desk to the other chair.

"Yeah, my best friend Aida." Jo left out the part about Aida being fifteen hundred miles away.

Felix nodded. "Good, I'm glad. Shall we get started?"

She cracked her knuckles, wiggled her fingers, and rolled out her neck. The familiar excitement of teaching someone to play MnM filled her to the brim, dissolving the last of her worries. "Let's do it."

STILL FEELING LIKE an idiot, Felix dragged the two rulebooks over, and Jo opened *Core Rules*. He sat up straighter, a librarian working with a volunteer. Professional. Helpful. Polite, but not overly familiar.

"Did you have a chance to read any of this?" she asked.

"Yes, the first two chapters. I skimmed chapter three, but I ran out of time to read it closely. I'm sorry I'm not fully prepared; I didn't realize that chapter was seventy-eight pages long."

Jo looked at him through round, tortoiseshell glasses, which she hadn't been wearing the other night. They brought out darker flecks in her pale brown eyes that he hadn't noticed before. Her short hair was uncurled and pulled back into a ponytail, and Felix realized for the first time how round her cheeks were. Like apples. Or, with her pinkish complexion, maybe peaches were a more apt comparison.

"You counted the exact number of pages?" she asked with a smile.

"It was simple subtraction," Felix replied.

"Basic math. A good skill for a GM."

Felix had the distinct feeling that a joke had gone over his head, but she didn't give him time to dwell on it. She gestured to the book in front of her and got to the matter at hand.

"I thought tonight I would walk you through building a character, since that's how any new player who comes in would start," she said. "Making your own character is one of the best ways to learn the setup and fundamentals of the game."

"All right," Felix said, trying not to look pained as he ran a hand through his hair. Playing make-believe wasn't his ideal way to spend an evening, but he'd survived worse work assignments.

"Before we jump in, did you have any questions about what you read? You seemed confused by the world building before." Jo rummaged in her purse and pulled out the same things she'd had on Tuesday: a mechanical pencil, a drawstring bag that rattled with dice, and a folded piece of paper. She unfolded it to reveal a blank version of the paper she'd tried to hand him the other night, a template with nothing handwritten on it yet. She smoothed it on the desk, and Felix was briefly transfixed by her hands, her thin fingers tipped with short, neat fingernails.

"I understood it better on a second pass," he said. "I prefer things that are grounded in reality, so I tried relating the fantasy concepts to the real world. The pantheon of gods, for example, isn't too far off from Greek and Roman ones."

"It's almost like 'mythology' is in the title of the game, huh?" Jo said with a teasing grin, which Felix couldn't help but return. Make-believe or not, at least he could count on Jo to keep the evening interesting.

She handed him her pencil. He took it, careful not to brush her hand again. She turned to chapter three in *Core Rules*, titled "Archetypes."

This is for my job, he reminded himself. *For me and for Tito.*

"It's good to have a party—a group of characters adventuring together—with a diverse set of skills and abilities," she began. "For example, my warlock has a high score in charisma. She's good at talking to people, bewitching enemies into thinking they are friends, that kind of thing. But warlocks don't wear armor, so in combat they're easy to hit and easy to kill. Squishy."

As she spoke, she flipped back and forth through the pages with an expert hand, pausing to point out different pictures and rules. She showed him an illustration of a robed warlock and the words "Armor: None" from a long list of "Archetype Features." This was already so much easier than attempting to figure everything out on his own.

"I'm following you so far," he said.

"So if you were going to make a character to complement my warlock, they should be able to take a lot of hits and do a lot of damage." She turned to the beginning of chapter three, where there was a list of the archetypes and a one-sentence description of each. "Your best options for that are going to be a fighter, a paladin, or a barbarian."

She angled the book toward him to let him read over the

descriptions. He nodded as he recalled some of what he'd skimmed over his lunch break today.

"A fighter sounds the simplest," he said, thinking about the boxing gym in his basement.

"Sure, that's a really good starter archetype." She reached across the book and tapped a blank line at the top of his paper labeled "Archetype."

As he wrote down "Fighter," he asked, "Is there an option to be a boxer?"

Jo's face lit up as she turned a few pages. "Actually, yeah. The fighter has a pugilist subtype. You'd do more damage unarmed than with a weapon."

How the hell did she know where every single page she needed was? As he stared down at an illustration of a shirtless, pointy-eared man with incorrect hand wraps, Felix's first thought was that Jo was like magic. Clearly, he'd already been at this fantasy stuff too long.

Hand wraps aside, though, the pugilist was pretty well grounded in his reality. "Where do I write that down?"

"You don't, not yet," Jo replied. "You pick a subtype at level three, after you earn experience points by playing the game. We're only doing level one today."

"Ah," he said, trying to keep his voice neutral. He wasn't actually going to be *playing* with this character, was he?

Jo proceeded to walk him through the "Fighter" section of the chapter and showed him where to write everything down on his character sheet. Then they rolled some dice to determine scores for his abilities: strength, intelligence, and so on.

"All right, so your race is next before we can finalize those scores," Jo said, turning to chapter two. "You've got your Tolkien standards: elf, dwarf, halfling, orc. And then—"

"Could I just be a person?" he cut in.

Jo broke into a grin. "Felix, in this world, they're all people."

He suppressed the urge to groan. He liked pedantry as much as the next librarian, but even he had his limits. "A human, I mean."

"You want to play a human fighter?" she asked with barely concealed laughter. It was so infectious that Felix couldn't help smiling.

"Is that bad?"

"It's only *the* most basic option you could choose."

"Well, like I said, I prefer things grounded in reality."

She pulled her shoulders all the way up to her earlobes in the biggest, cutest shrug Felix had even seen. "Felix, the whole point of this is to give you an idea of the options in MnM so you can help other newbies."

"Fine, I take your point," Felix said with an exaggerated sigh. He ignored Jo's smug smile. "What should I pick, then?"

She flipped pages again before stopping abruptly. "How about a dragonkin? You'll get a boost to your strength, which is good for a fighter. And you also get the ability to breathe fire and ice so you can attack more than one enemy at a time."

Felix had seen this illustration of a red-scaled reptilian creature, fully clothed and on two legs, when he'd paged through the book earlier. But this time, something new clicked into place. "A dragon is a person in this game?"

"It's not a full-blooded dragon, it's a dragon*kin*," Jo explained. "The actual dragons are in the *Monster Compendia*. This is a humanoid descended from a dragon way back in their ancestry."

Felix narrowed his eyes, unsure whether he should be amused or concerned by that concept. "I don't really want to know how that happened."

"Welcome to Monsters and Mythology, dude," Jo laughed. "People will try to fuck anything that can consent."

Well, that settled it. Felix was by no means a prude, but this was his *workplace*. His family-friendly workplace, at that. He pushed his chair back from the desk and looked at Jo with all seriousness. "Jo, please don't tell me this game is about people playing out their sex fantasies."

The smile fell from her face. "It's not meant to be, no. Sometimes people get weird about trying too hard to seduce a barmaid, or even a dragon or a vampire. Especially newbies who don't know the boundaries of roleplaying games yet. It's your job as the GM to decide whether or not you allow that at your table."

"Absolutely not," he said without hesitation.

"For a public event, that's a good call," Jo said with a nod. "People will often flirt with or charm the NPCs—non-player characters. That's okay within reason. Interacting with the world and the people in it is part of the game. But you can, and should, shut it down if it goes too far."

It was bad enough that Felix had to learn this entire fantasy world and all its rules. Now he had to chaperone people from being overtly horny at a public library? This was getting ridiculous. There must be something about this game that he was missing, something that drew people to it that he couldn't see.

He set his pencil down and raked his hands through his hair. "I think I need some help here, Jo. Can you explain to me why people do this? I don't get it."

Jo leaned away from him and averted her gaze.

"I'm sorry, did I say something wrong?"

She didn't reply. Her eyes glazed over as she stared at nothing.

"Jo?"

4

I DON'T GET IT.

The words rang in Jo's ears, echoing back through months, through years.

A memory from over a year ago surfaced. In her mind, Jeremy's voice was as clear as day. *Damn it, Jo. I already told my friends we'd be at their barbecue this weekend. You signed up for another fucking convention? I don't get it. Why are you so obsessed with this damn game?*

Another memory, another time—maybe three or four years ago. His voice was low and sultry now, as if he were whispering in Jo's ear. *I don't get it, baby... but, fuck, I love it when you play an elf for me. What's your name tonight?*

Then, she and Jeremy were younger, both of them still in their mid-twenties. Things between them were new and fresh and fun. They were willing to try things for each other. At least, Jo had thought they were. *I tried your monster game once, okay?* His tone teetered on a knife's edge between exasperated and callous. *Please get off my back about it. I don't get it, and I never will. Have fun with your friends, just leave me the hell out of it.*

"Hey. Jo?"

A gentle voice pierced through the haze of memory. She blinked and cleared her vision. Felix's dark eyes, wide with worry, were the first things she saw. He was leaning forward in his chair, his hand suspended in midair, as if he'd reached out to touch her but had thought better of it. What with the whole being-alone-behind-a-locked-door thing.

"You with me, Jo?"

"Yeah, yeah," she said, jamming her glasses onto the bridge of her nose. "I'm here, sorry. Got lost in thought."

Felix eyed her for a moment, then seemed to decide not to push it. He redirected his hand to the pencil on the desk. "It was dragon-kin, right?"

"Right," she said. She watched him write the word in precise uppercase letters on the "Race" line. Then she made a decision of her own. "Do you want me to answer your question? About why people do this?"

Felix looked at her with a tenderness Jo hadn't seen in... well, a long damn time. "Only if it won't upset you."

"It won't," she assured him.

He put his pencil back down and swiveled to face her, giving her his full attention. The weight of his gaze was like staring into the sun, but he was so earnest she couldn't look away.

"You like things that are based on reality, right?" she said. "For some people, reality sucks. MnM can be an escape, a safe place. The game has always prided itself on being inclusive. There's a whole section in chapter one about how MnM worlds don't have the kinds of stigmas or prejudices around race, gender and sexuality, or disability that our world has. I've known so many people who find that incredibly freeing. My friend, Young, discovered they were non-binary because they played a non-binary dwarf in one of my games a few years ago and felt more like themself than they ever had in their life. Can you imagine?"

Jo swallowed the lump in her throat. Felix reached under the desk and pulled out an unopened water bottle from God knows where. She thanked him and paused for a sip.

"Sometimes it's good and healthy, *necessary* even, to play out fantasies when the real world tears you down or tells you that you can't be yourself," she continued. "I don't know what your politics are, Felix. But if you're going to be a GM for a game with a core tenet of inclusivity, you need to know that you can't question a trans kid or a closeted twenty-something playing a character that they wish they could be in real life."

Felix shook his head, his mouth slightly open. "I would never."

"I'm glad to hear it," she replied.

"Was it like that for you?" he asked, tentative and careful.

Jo smiled to herself. "Not exactly. I'm white and able-bodied, and I'm not queer. In a completely different way, though, I learned what kind of person I want to be through MnM." She turned to page seven in *Core Rules*. She read aloud from the text under the "Welcome to the Sibylline Wastes" heading, easily slipping into her narrator's cadence.

"'The Sibylline Wastes are in need of heroes. Monstrous creatures ravage the lands. Giants lay waste to crops. Gods kidnap people as servants for their temples. Corrupt rulers levy heavy taxes and oppress their citizens. You (yes, *you*, adventurer) have a calling to be a hero. To stand up for what is right, even to the point of death. To fight for justice and freedom for all peoples in all lands. To sing on behalf of those who cannot speak up for themselves. Will you take up your calling? Will you be the hero the Sibylline Wastes need?'"

Jo leaned back and blinked away the tears those words always brought to her eyes. Felix was gazing at her as if seeing her for the first time.

"That was written in 1979 when Monsters and Mythology was first created," she said. "It's been printed, unchanged, in every single Sibylline Wastes book since then. Even the novels."

"Wow," Felix said under his breath.

"I went to a convention once where every gaming session was opened by someone yelling, 'Will you take up your calling?' Hundreds of people yelled back, 'Huzzah!' I got chills every time. People have tattoos of that line. I've got one that says, 'yes, *you*, adventurer' to remind myself that it's my job to keep fighting the good fight every damn day. That it's possible to win with nothing but unshakeable belief and a good group of allies."

There was a heavy pause. Felix and Jo stared at each other until Jo's cheeks warmed.

Then he said, "I get it."

Jo took a long drink of water, tipping her head back so Felix wouldn't see the fresh tears that had gathered in her eyes at those words. Perhaps he saw them anyway, because he chose that moment to excuse himself to the bathroom. She composed herself and checked the time on her phone, disappointed to see that their hour was nearly over. While she waited for Felix, she texted Aida.

Jo

> Not dead yet. Will text again when we're done, but this guy actually has some emotional intelligence.

Aida

> Still locked in with a stranger, dumbass

Jo

Can you say something about
boundaries? I only gave him an
hour and it's almost up but I kind of
want to stay?

Aida

I shouldn't need to say anything about
boundaries, because you are LOCKED
IN WITH A STRANGER

DUMBASS

But here: Make good choices, which
includes keeping the boundaries you
set because you are worth taking care
of, especially by yourself.

Jo

Does taking care of myself also
include jacking off to Bridgerton?

She tucked her phone into her pocket as Felix reentered the lobby. "You need a name for your character," she declared, attempting to lighten the mood as they wrapped up. "And I swear to God if you suggest 'Felix,' I will be furious."

Felix laughed and leaned his elbows on the counter, his hands clasped together, and his sleeves now rolled up. Jo did an actual, literal double take.

Jesus Christ. Those forearms. Jo had never seen someone with such definition in their *forearms* before. She could count three individual cords of muscle running up the tops of his arms under dark hair.

"Will you come up with a name for me?" Felix asked.

Jo tore her attention away from her momentary muscular fixation to look him in the eye. "I will do no such thing. Your character's name should be something you like, since the GM will use it to refer to you during games. Even pre-generated character sheets have blank names so the player can come up with their own."

"Do you have any suggestions, then? I don't know what a dragon's name should sound like, but I'm guessing 'Steve' or 'Debra' would be a bad choice."

Jo grinned. "Technically, you can pick any name you want. But the *Core Rules* has a list of name suggestions under each race."

He reached for the book. Jo handed it to him, keeping her focus on Felix's face and not the underside of his arm, which was almost as corded as the top. Who the hell worked out their forearms that much?

Felix turned to the table of contents, ran one long finger down the page until he found the "Dragonkin" page number, and opened to it. Jo added another item to her mental list of things to teach him next time: sticky notes to mark each section for easy reference during games.

"That's your homework," she said, standing up and tapping the page Felix was perusing.

Felix glanced at the clock, which showed two minutes past seven. "You're giving me homework?" he said with a playful lilt to his voice.

"Oh, there's more," she said as she gathered her things. "I know I said to skim the chapters after three, but I want you to go through the equipment chapter and pick out what you want your fighter to start with. You're not a pugilist yet, so you'll at least need armor and melee and ranged weapons. Your archetype gives you starting gold—we wrote that down—so that's how much money you have to spend."

He stared at her. "I'm sorry, you've lost me."

"Here, give me your number," Jo said, offering him her phone. "You can text if you have questions."

He glanced down at the phone without taking it. "I can give you my card. Email me what you just explained, if you don't mind, and I'll write you back with any questions."

"Sure, whatever works." Jo kicked herself. First, she openly ogled the man's arms, then she tried to wrangle his phone number out of him. Jo wasn't locked in here with Felix. He was locked in here with *her*!

He rounded the desk and dug out a business card that read:

FELIX NAVARRO, MI

JUNIOR LIBRARIAN, GENERAL SERVICES

"Thanks," Jo said. Felix nodded and slid his hands into his pockets. After a moment, she inclined her head toward the door. "You want to let me out?"

"Fuck, I'm sorry." Felix reached across Jo for the keys. He'd been so careful not to touch her all night, but now his chest brushed against her shoulder, warm and firm. Startled, she moved back and immediately regretted it. Felix either didn't notice or chose to politely ignore it.

He unlocked the door and stepped outside, holding it open for her. It was drizzling again. Jo followed him out and paused under the concrete overhang that kept them dry.

"Thank you for your help tonight. Are you going to be all right getting to your car?" he asked, professional and courteous once more. If she was being honest, Jo preferred the version of Felix that swore and had soft, kind eyes, but she liked this version well enough.

"I'm good, thanks. Same time next week?"

"Yes, I'll be here. If you have business at the library during the week, I hope you'll say hello."

"Of course," she said, waving goodnight. "Don't work too late!"

He raised a hand in farewell as Jo jogged through the feather-light dusting of rain. She glanced back before turning the corner of the building to see Felix watching her with an easy smile. Her heart fluttered and kept on fluttering until she was inside her car.

She pulled out her phone to text Aida that she had survived, and her stomach plummeted. A text notification, plainly visible on the lock screen, read:

Aida

> That or the hot librarian

"Oh my God," Jo muttered. "Oh my fucking God, I handed him my phone."

Was the screen on? Was the phone unlocked? No, no, she definitely remembered *not* unlocking her phone, which in retrospect was pretty fucking stupid of her. But had she bumped the power button and turned on the screen while it was facing him? What if the notification popped up at *the exact moment* she handed him the phone?

"Oh my Gooooood," she wailed. What time had she handed Felix the phone? Sometime right after seven? Aida had texted at seven-oh-three. And he had glanced down. He had definitely glanced down at her phone as she held it out to him. And then gave her his email address instead of his number. "Nooooo!"

She didn't even bother texting Aida. She called her. As soon as the ring cut off, Jo blurted out, "He might have seen your last text."

Aida gasped and gave the exact right response. "Oh my God!"

Jo gave her the rundown of her last five minutes with Felix, corded forearms and all. "I have to fix this, Aida. Felix seems like a genuinely good guy, and I don't want him to think I'm a total creep."

"Okay, babe. Here's what you're going to do," Aida said in her no-nonsense, project-manager-for-seven-figure-contracts voice. "You're going to email him and play it totally cool. Don't use too many exclamation points, treat him like you'd treat a work friend, and obviously don't say anything about the text because odds are he didn't even see it."

Jo was nodding along, even though Aida couldn't see her. "I can do that. But also, fuck you, because exclamation points are a really good tone indicator in writing."

"Work friend, Jo," she countered. "He's being all professional with you, so you match that."

Jo sighed. "You're right. Now I need to go home so he doesn't walk out here and see me watching the building from my car. Like a total creep."

From: Jolene Rainier
To: Felix Navarro
Date: Friday, May 3, 2024, 7:36 P.M.
Subject: Homework

Hey Felix,

Here's your homework. Chapter 4 of the Core Rules lists all the basic non-magical equipment characters can get. Your fighter has gold, labeled G on your character sheet. (Wait, the library key was gold! Is that why there's a G on it???) That's how much money you have to spend on your equipment. Make sure you at least get a set of armor and two weapons: one melee and one ranged. Up to you what else to get.

Let me know if you have any questions and if you pick a name!

Have a good weekend,
Jo

From: Felix Navarro
To: Jolene Rainier
Date: Saturday, May 4, 2024, 8:34 A.M.
Subject: RE: Homework

Good morning Jo,

Thank you for the information. I appreciate you taking the time to write this out for me. I doubt the G on the library's key stands for gold, but your supposition is a clever one. It made me smile before 9 A.M. on a Saturday, which is no easy feat.

I haven't picked a name for the character yet, but I decided to make him a male. Here's a question that just occurred to me.

Is male correct, or does one say "man" when the creature isn't strictly human?

Best,

Felix

~

Felix Navarro, MI

Junior Librarian, General Services

Butler County Library District — Ashville Public Library

From: Jolene Rainier

To: Felix Navarro

Date: Saturday, May 4, 2024, 3:22 P.M.

Subject: RE: Homework

Weirdly, there is so much drama about that. Most people say man and woman for those genders and don't think about it too much. But some players are rules lawyers (aka a**holes) who insist on using male and female for every race (even human) because that's what the original 1979 rulebook did. Honestly, I think it's dated and kinda skeevy. Just say man. He/him works too.

Can I ask *you* a question (besides this one)? What does the MI stand for after your name? I Googled it, but "MI library" and "MI librarian" just showed me all of the libraries and librarian jobs in Michigan.

You're probably at work, so don't let me take up your time.

You can tell me on Friday. I just didn't want to forget to ask. I'll see you then!

Jo

From: Felix Navarro
To: Jolene Rainier
Date: Monday, May 6, 2024, 8:43 A.M.
Subject: RE: Homework

Dear Jo,

I did some online research of my own, specifically about the type of players you called "rules lawyers." I'm inclined to agree with your assessment of them. Some insight into how to manage them as a GM would be appreciated. Let's please save that topic until we're in person, though; I think a conversation would be more fruitful than email.

I completed your homework assignment last night, aside from choosing a name. I assure you, I'll have one by Friday. I didn't have any questions, which I attribute to your excellent tutelage the other night. Thank you again for your time. I'm very grateful.

To answer your question, MI stands for Master of Information, the type of graduate degree I hold from Rutgers University. It's similar to MLIS and MLS, which are the more well-known abbreviations for librarians' master's degrees.

If questions about names are on the table, I must admit I'm curious about Jo as a nickname for Jolene. I'm sure you hear this all the time, but I would have assumed Josephine or Joanna. For what it's worth, I think Jolene suits you.

Best,
Felix

From: Jo Rainier
To: Felix Navarro
Date: Tuesday, May 7, 2024, 6:10 P.M.
Subject: RE: Homework

Oh my god, I totally forgot that my display name was Jolene. It's fixed now.

As you might have guessed, my mom's a big Dolly Parton fan. And obviously, Dolly is the queen, but there's only so many times a kid can stand having her own name sung at her when she meets someone new. I even had auburn hair as a girl. (It went more brown as I got older, but now I dye it auburn anyway because eff me, I guess.) I cannot tell you how glad I am not to have eyes of emerald green, though! But thanks for saying Jolene suits me... that's really nice.

I started going by Jo in middle school. It was my best friend Aida's idea, actually. We got paired up for some icebreaker activity, and I didn't want to tell her my name. She weaseled the whole story out of me and suggested I go by Jo instead. I loved it immediately, and Aida and I became inseparable. She corrected everyone who called me Jolene until it stuck.

And since I've written you two full paragraphs about my name, I'm going to shut up now.

I'm glad you figured out the equipment! Happy to help. Can't wait to hear that name on Friday!

Jo

P.S. Funny story. When I told my parents I was moving to Ashville, my mom literally shrieked with joy because she thought I said Nashville and she's always wanted to go to Dollywood. Like she was only excited to visit me because of my proximity to a theme park. (lol thanks mom)

5

BY FRIDAY, FELIX was exhausted. Exchanging emails with Jo had kept her on his mind all week. He couldn't stop picturing her hands, her smile, her pale eyes flecked with dark umber. He'd wanted to write her back, but he couldn't come up with anything more to say under the guise of librarian/volunteer correspondence. Even asking about her name was pushing the bounds of professionalism.

He read through more of *Core Rules* to find questions to ask her, but things were actually beginning to make sense. Once he got past the fantasy elements, he found the rules complex, meticulous, and esoteric—in the best way. Wrapping his mind around their intricacies and having things click was extremely satisfying. And since it would be rude to make up questions and waste Jo's time, he didn't email her back.

That didn't stop him from looking up sharply every time the front door of the library opened, though, hoping she'd stroll in to pick up some books. Or from thinking about her in the evenings while he lay on the couch with a book and a glass of wine. Or from hearing her booming laugh in the back of his mind as he fell asleep.

And that's why he was so exhausted on Friday. He spent every night in his basement gym, getting out the restlessness Jo stirred up in him, overworking his body as he pummeled the bag to the sounds of "Hey Ya!" and "Supermassive Black Hole" and "Work It." That last one, actually, he'd had to skip when it came up on shuffle. It didn't help matters.

He was just lonely and pent up, Felix told himself. Dating in his thirties in a town of only eight thousand people was tough. Most women his age were married with kids. He hadn't slept with anyone, or even gone out much, since he'd lived in New Jersey. He'd just started seeing someone when he got that phone call from Tito last June, a mere week after finishing grad school. Things weren't serious enough for them to want to try long distance, and since then, there hadn't been anyone Felix was interested in pursuing.

But now, here was Jo. Funny and cute and passionate about something she loved. Charming him with an abundance of parenthetical statements in her emails. Willing to help him out and asking nothing in return. And, as a bonus, if that text was any indication, she apparently thought he was hot.

There was no denying how good that felt.

"Hey, Peg?" Felix said when his co-worker came back from her lunch break Friday afternoon. "May I ask a favor?"

"You still owe me a dollar from the last time you wanted a pop," Peggy retorted with a smile.

He chuckled. "Not that. Are you free to stay late tonight? For about an hour?"

"What for?"

"The volunteer I'm working with on the game night launch is coming at six," he said. "She's a woman. Last week I didn't think about the fact that we'd be alone in here. And I had to lock the door after hours."

Peggy grimaced. "Ooh, honey."

"I know. I feel awful about it." Felix ran a hand through his hair and felt the dull burn of a tight muscle deep in his shoulder. "It turned out okay, but she was understandably nervous at first. I think she'll be more at ease if someone else is here."

"Well, you know me," Peggy said with her best customer service smile. "Always glad to help out with volunteers. I'll be here."

"Thank you, Peggy."

A few hours later, right before six, Jo arrived. She was in scrubs again—navy blue pants and a top with a blue-and-white paisley pattern. Her denim jacket was over her head, her glasses dotted with rain from the downpour outside. On her shoulder was a yellow tote bag, emblazoned with the words "There's a non-zero chance this bag is filled with dice." She beamed at Felix across the front desk, and he grinned and gave her a polite wave.

"Hey, sugar, we're closing in a few," Peggy said as she came around the corner from the reading room, where she'd made the same announcement.

"Oh, I'm here for Felix," Jo replied, pointing at him. Felix's heart leapt, despite his head knowing that she didn't mean it the way it sounded.

"Peggy, this is Jo, our volunteer for game night," he said, standing up. "Jo, my colleague, Peggy."

"Great!" Peggy said with a double thumbs-up. "Sorry about that, sugar. If you two want to go get started, I can watch the desk."

Jo glanced between them and furrowed her brow.

"Peggy's going to stay tonight," Felix jumped in. "I thought you'd be more comfortable that way."

Jo's jaw dropped in surprise. "You—oh. That... that was thoughtful of you. Thanks. And thanks, Peggy."

"No trouble at all, Jo. We like to keep our volunteers happy." She waved in the direction of the reading room. "You kids go on. Plenty of space available."

Jo gave Felix an eager grin, which did more funny things to his heart. "Ready when you are."

As they headed off, Peggy called after them, "Holler if you need me!"

"You betcha!" Felix replied with an exaggerated Midwestern accent. He and Peggy both smiled at the inside joke, and he caught Jo smiling too.

They picked a large, round table and began laying out books and papers as the last few stragglers filed out.

"Before we dive in..." Jo rubbed her hands together excitedly. Then she turned her palms up, cupped her hands, and motioned her fingers toward herself in a "come here" gesture. "Lay it on me."

"Uh, what?" Felix said, his mind spiraling to very work-inappropriate places.

"Your name! What did you pick?"

"Oh, of course." He opened the manila folder he'd put his character sheet in. He wanted to get it right. "Graxalos. Grax for short."

Jo's eyes shone behind her rain-speckled glasses. "I fucking love it."

THE HOUR WITH Felix flew by. Jo covered as much ground as she could, starting with how to handle rules-lawyer players and then moving on to combat rules: rolling initiative and turn order, monster actions, and how to track damage and health points. She had brought her own copies of the rulebooks so they could reference multiple things at once, and the large reading-room table was perfect for spreading out.

Peggy walked by the open doorway a couple of times, first pushing a cart full of books, and later with some cash in hand that was replaced by chips and a soda on her way back. She never looked into the room, and Jo got the feeling she wasn't checking up on them so much as reminding Jo she was in a safe space. Truly, librarians were the best.

When their time was up, Felix relaxed into his chair. He interlaced his fingers and rested his hands on his head. His lips tightened, and his face scrunched up momentarily, like he was in pain. Not the first time he'd done that tonight, she'd noticed.

"Any homework for me this week?" he asked.

"I'll go over spellcasting with you next week, so maybe read through that part of the rules. Chapter nine. You can email me with any questions. I also want to do a trial run game with you. Something quick that we can do in about thirty minutes."

"That's a good idea," Felix said. "I'm still a little fuzzy on how everything fits together."

Jo bit her upper lip and fiddled with her pencil. *Just say it, Jo. Just ask. You'll feel better if you do.*

"Hey, speaking of email," she blurted unceremoniously, "I hope I didn't come on too strong or something."

She'd been beating herself up about it for days. She had tried—really tried—to keep things work-friend level, but then he'd asked about her name. It was impossible for her to talk about that without making it personal. It was all her awkward childhood memories and the way she met her best friend wrapped up in a single word. And Felix hadn't written back. She'd checked her email every morning, every break at work, every night, and nothing. Normally, she'd keep quiet about this kind of thing, but Felix was starting to feel like a real friend, not just a work friend. (A very hot friend whose shirt buttons were currently straining against his broad chest, but still.) If she'd made it weird, it would be better to clear the air and move forward. Get a fresh start.

"What are you talking about?" Felix asked, his voice gentle.

"You didn't email me back, so I thought my story about my name might be too personal for our..." Jo gestured between the two of them with both hands. "Our working relationship. If it was, I'm sorry."

"It's your name, Jo," he said, slowly lowering his hands to his lap. "Of course it's personal. I asked, and you answered. I didn't respond because your email ended with something about seeing me Friday, which seemed like the end of the conversation."

"Oh."

"And I didn't have any questions for you, so I didn't start a new one."

"Oh," she said again, not sure what else to say. It was so obvious now, and she felt stupid for assuming the worst.

"I'm sorry my silence troubled you."

"No, it's all good," Jo said, shaking her head. "I kind of got in my head about it, you know? Trying to make friends in a new town, good impressions, all that."

Felix tilted his head and smiled. "You want to be friends? What happened to 'our working relationship'?"

"¿Por qué no los dos?"

Felix's eyes lit up as he raised his eyebrows in delight. "¿Hablas español?"

"What? No. Sorry, it's a meme," Jo said in a rush. "You speak Spanish?"

"I *am* Spanish." He seemed more amused than disappointed, which Jo took as a good sign for the whole "let's be friends" thing. "'Why not both' is a meme?"

"Yeah. I thought... I mean... Can't we be both?"

He nodded, a slow, steady drop of his chin until he was looking up at her from under his brows. "I'd like that."

Christ, his eyelashes. She was almost jealous of how long and thick they were. Jo had never met a man who made hair—all hair, everywhere—look so good.

"Cool," she managed to say.

Felix stood to pack up and winced again.

"You okay? You look like you're in pain. We could have canceled tonight if you're not feeling well."

"I'm just sore," he said. "I worked out a little too hard this week."

"What do you do to work out?" Jo asked.

"Boxing, mostly."

Her jaw dropped as the pieces slotted into place. "Oh my God, of course you do, Mr. Grounded-in-Reality. A real-life pugilist."

Felix grinned shyly. "Not really. I don't hit people. Just a punching bag in the basement."

"Still cool."

"Thank you."

In the lull that followed, Jo and Felix did nothing more than stare at each other.

"You kids about done?"

Jo jumped. She'd forgotten Peggy was here.

Felix tapped his phone screen. "Fuck," he muttered, then he raised his voice. "Packing up now, Peg—sorry! Sorry to you too, Jo. I kept you five minutes over."

"That was friend time," she replied, "not work time."

"Except for Peggy."

"Yeah, oops," Jo said, shoving books and dice into her tote. "Thank you again for doing that. It, um, it means a lot."

"Peggy's good people."

You are too. Jo barely had time to bite back the words. Maybe she shouldn't have. Maybe it would have been a nice, friendly compliment. But it felt way too intimate a thing to say to someone she'd spent less than three hours with, during which she'd mostly talked his ear off about Monsters and Mythology. So she held the words inside, where they settled, warm and solid and true, near her heart.

He let her go ahead of him into the lobby, where Peggy was standing near the door, library key in one hand and car key in the other.

"Thanks for staying, Peggy," Jo said. "You don't have to next week, though. I feel comfortable here." Out of the corner of her eye, she watched a gratified smile appear on Felix's face.

"Are you sure, honey?" Peggy said. "I really don't mind. I'm just starving. I can bring dinner next time, and I'll be less inclined to holler." She winked.

Unable to stop herself, Jo glanced over at Felix. "I'm sure."

Later that evening, Jo curled up on the couch in her one-bedroom apartment on the top floor of a fourplex. She was in her pajamas, aimlessly scrolling through random videos and posts on her phone, while Merry, her brown tabby, snoozed on her feet. Her ankle was quirked at a weird angle, but she knew better than to disturb a sleeping cat. If she'd thought ahead, she could have grabbed her library book off the nightstand—the one Leni had recommended to her. But she hadn't thought ahead and, again, sleeping cat. She was trapped.

Bored of cycling through the same three social media apps, she switched over to her texts. Aida was out with her fiancé, Trey, tonight, so Jo pulled up the dormant group text with her California MnM group. The group included Aida, of course, but hopefully someone else would be around to respond.

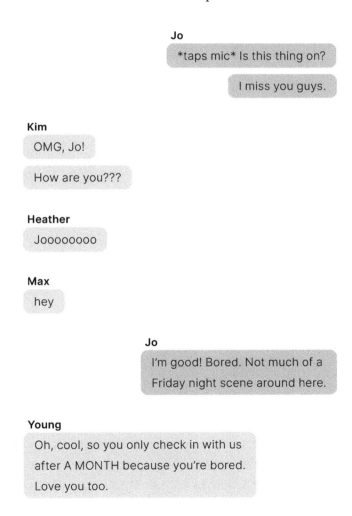

Jo
taps mic Is this thing on?

I miss you guys.

Kim
OMG, Jo!

How are you???

Heather
Joooooooo

Max
hey

Jo
I'm good! Bored. Not much of a Friday night scene around here.

Young
Oh, cool, so you only check in with us after A MONTH because you're bored. Love you too.

> J/K, moving sucks and it's always
> busier than you think it'll be.

David

> Hi, Jo. Miss you. We're starting up the
> new campaign next week. Mind if I pick
> your brain about GMing some time? I
> don't know how you did this much prep
> every week.

Jo

> It's a lot! It's easier once things get
> rolling. But yeah, text me any time!

Max

> speaking of mnm

> INDI-CON

Kim

> Two more weeks!!

Heather

> Indi-Con, baby! Kim, remind me to ask
> you about cosplay stuff.

Jo smiled as excited messages poured in, fast and furious. With each new text, excitement stirred within her too. Indi-Con was going to be her first gaming convention in almost two years. She'd said no at first, months ago, when the group decided to make the trip out to Indianapolis for the biggest MnM con in the country.

It was only after she and Jeremy broke up and she made plans to move to Kansas that she changed her mind, mostly for the excuse to see Aida and everyone else.

Now, though, her excitement wasn't just about seeing her friends. Jo could practically hear the buzz of the crowded gaming hall and the clatter of dice. She could picture the bright green Indi-Con banners and the enormous exhibit hall packed with vendors and artists. She could feel the electric energy of meeting gamers from around the country and the delirious high of running on barely any sleep for an entire weekend.

Young
Let's make sure we get in a game together.

Kim
Yeah! Can we all play our characters from our last campaign?

Max
Lyric, bard extraordinaire, shall rise again

David
Signups are open online. I'll see what's available.

Several minutes later, they had all signed up for the same Saturday morning game. Jo navigated back to the main Indi-Con webpage and scrolled through the schedule. Lots of games still needed GMs, including the giant Legendary event, her favorite part of any convention. She tapped on one of the open Legendary tables, and her finger hovered over the "Join as GM" button.

"What do you think, Mer-bear?" she asked her cat. His ear rotated toward her, but he was otherwise disinclined to provide any guidance. "You're hurting my ankle you know, you big dingus."

Merry didn't even dignify that with an ear turn.

"You're no help at all."

Jo took a deep breath and tapped the button. She watched the page reload. "Game Master: Jo Rainier," it said. Tears filled her eyes, and she smiled to herself. She couldn't fully explain it, but it felt like a victory, like returning home.

She didn't want to bother Aida, but she wanted to tell someone what she'd just done. And the person who came to mind, even ahead of her friends in the group chat, was Felix.

Which was ridiculous, of course. He wouldn't understand. He probably wouldn't even care. There was no reason to tell him. She only thought of him in the first place because they were officially friends now.

Jo's smile grew. She was friends with Felix.

Felix, who listened to her and absorbed all the information she threw at him. Who made sure she felt comfortable around him. Who wrote overly formal emails but said "fuck" like he meant it, all breathy and low and dark.

Her phone buzzed in her hand, startling her out of her thoughts. The Indi-Con conversation had moved on to finding a place to get dinner together on their first night in town. Jo sent a message casting her vote for whatever was closest to the hotel.

She shifted her foot, and Merry popped his head up and glared at her with sleepy eyes. "I'm sorry, sir, did I disturb you? We should go to bed soon anyway, so you might as well get up."

Merry stood and arched his back, vibrating all over as he

stretched. Jo scratched his shoulders, which was her first mistake. Her second mistake was not moving her feet as soon as Merry released her. He turned in a tight circle and flopped back onto Jo's ankle, lying on his opposite side.

"Buddy, nooo," Jo nudged him with her foot, but Merry just side-eyed her and put his chin on his paws.

From: Felix Navarro
To: Jo Rainier
Date: Saturday, May 11, 2024, 8:26 A.M.
Subject: Advertising for MnM

Good morning Jo,

I've given some thought to advertising the library's MnM launch event. I don't believe I've mentioned this yet, actually: Warren Riggs, our director, has set the launch date for Tuesday, June 11th. One month from today, in fact. Game night is now one of the library's summer programs and will run through the end of August.

My thinking is that, if the objective is to bring a younger age bracket into the library, we should be advertising around Ashville Community College. Tonight, I plan to head to Stan's, a popular bar near ACC, to see if they are interested in partnering with us. Since you know MnM much better than I do, I'd appreciate your help talking it up. I understand that this goes beyond the hour per week you agreed to volunteer for the library, so please feel no obligation.

<u>Here is a map link</u> to Stan's location. I'll be arriving around
9:00 P.M. this evening.

Best,
Felix
~
Felix Navarro, MI
Junior Librarian, General Services
Butler County Library District — Ashville Public Library

From: Jo Rainier
To: Felix Navarro
Date: Saturday, May 11, 2024, 9:44 A.M.
Subject: RE: Advertising for MnM

Oh god, you want me to show up somewhere at 9pm? A
college bar on a Saturday night, no less?? I'm almost 35,
dude.

(I'm in.)

Jo

6

FELIX STOOD OUTSIDE Stan's, rocking from foot to foot, doing his best not to obsessively check the time on his phone. He raked his fingers through his hair, damp at the roots from his shower.

After work, he'd spent time boxing in the basement, trying to get out his... *energy* before meeting up with Jo. Unfortunately, he was still sore and had to take his workout easier than he'd planned. So he'd taken matters into his own hands (so to speak) in the shower, struggling to keep his mind blank. Getting off to thoughts of Jo felt wrong, but, in the end, it was a losing battle. He came, hard and loud, when an image sprang to mind of her eyes behind glasses beaded with water droplets. In the reading room the previous night, it had taken almost ten minutes before she thought to wipe the rain off those fucking glasses. He'd been distracted the entire time, wanting to take them off her, clean them for her, hand them back, and watch her bite her lip and smile and say thank you. Felix didn't quite know how to feel about that urge, but his dick was apparently into it.

"Hey there!"

Felix turned toward her voice. She was dressed much like she had been the night they met. Instead of leggings, Jo wore black, high-waisted skinny jeans that emphasized her ample hips. Her cropped T-shirt was pale pink with a faded screen print of a cat napping on a stack of books. And, of course, there was that denim jacket that Felix was starting to associate with her as closely as her smile, her eyes, her sense of humor. Jo's hair was down and curled, and she was wearing her glasses.

"Hi," he said. Fuck, did his voice crack? Did she hear it? *Get it together, man. This is not a date. You are friends. You are not that douchebag who can't tell the difference.*

"You look nice," Jo said. "I've never seen you outside of work clothes."

"Oh, thanks," Felix said, running a hand self-consciously down his torso. He'd kept it simple with dark wash jeans, a plain black T-shirt, and a maroon zip-up hoodie with the Rutgers "R" embroidered on the chest. Hardly "nice" clothes, but he appreciated her kindness anyway. "You too. Cat person?"

She glanced down at her shirt. "Yeah. Library user, MnM player, cat person. I'm a triple threat."

Felix laughed and gestured toward the door. "Do you have any?" he asked while the bouncer carded them.

"Two—nope, I have one cat. Merry."

"I'm sorry, did you lose one?"

The bouncer waved them in. A blast of electronic music rattled Felix's eardrums as he followed Jo inside.

"Kind of?" Jo shouted, leaning closer to be heard. "I... I broke up with someone before I moved here. He kept our other cat."

"That's rough."

Jo shrugged.

"Let me guess," Felix said. "Is the other cat Pippin?"

She rocked onto her back foot and looked up at him, impressed. "You said you don't read fantasy!"

"But I do watch Oscar-winning movies on occasion." They squeezed up to the bar between two groups of tipsy twenty-somethings. Felix bent closer to Jo's ear. She smelled like something fruity, something just shy of cloying, a scent that plummeted right into the depths of him. "Was I right?"

"Yeah," she said, flashing him a quick smile. "I miss him. The cat, not the guy."

Felix nodded, unsure how to follow up that comment. A bartender, a white guy with a shaved head and two full sleeves of tattoos, made eye contact with him and gave a "be right there" nod.

"Are we drinking?" Jo asked. "I don't really know your plan. I'm following your lead here."

"I'll probably get a beer or cider or something. I planned to talk to the manager about advertising here."

"On a Saturday night?" Jo scoffed, waving broadly at the packed bar. "Good luck. You should have come at, like, five o'clock."

She had a point.

"Well, fuck."

Jo spun to face him, and her hair hit his arm. When he glanced down toward the unexpected touch, he spotted a flash of midriff between her cropped shirt and jeans. Fuck. *Fuck.* A sliver of skin should not be that successful in undoing him. He really needed to get out more.

"Can I ask you something?" she said.

Before he could respond, the bartender appeared, leaning on the bar with his tattooed arms spread in a wide V. "What'll it be, folks?"

They ordered—wheat beer for Felix and gin martini for Jo— and paid, and then Jo pointed out an empty high table along the back wall. With the blaring music, it wasn't much quieter there, but at least the cacophony of the bar top was farther away.

"What's your question?" Felix asked as soon as they were seated.

"I'm confused about something," she replied. "Most of the time you seem pretty buttoned up and reserved, and your emails are the most formal ones I've ever gotten. But then something will slip out, like a 'fuck' or a dig at your boss or a joke with Peggy. It throws me off a little."

Felix took a sip of beer before responding. "You're in medicine, right?"

"Yeah, I'm a nurse."

"Did you ever go to grad school?"

Jo sat up straighter, and her entire body tensed. "No," she said defensively. "I didn't need to."

"I'm not suggesting you did. I merely meant to establish a point of reference," he said. She relaxed, but she didn't quite look at him as she sipped her martini. "I don't know the medical field, really, but I know there are aspects of it that are very competitive. Libraries are the same way. Getting into grad school is extremely difficult, let alone getting into your chosen specialty and finding a job on the other side. I got lucky: a couple of months after I moved to Ashville last year, a librarian retired. When Warren saw that he had a Rutgers MI in the candidate pool, someone who was already in town and didn't need to be convinced to move to the middle of nowhere, I was a shoo-in."

"You only moved here last year? You're not from Ashville?"

Felix shook his head. "I'm from Tulsa originally, and then I spent several years on the East Coast. Jersey, most recently. I moved here when my grandma was dying so my grandpa wouldn't be alone. Tito is one of those heart-on-his-sleeve old timers who'd been married so long he was incomplete without his wife. If I hadn't come, and stayed, we probably would have lost him, too, after she was gone."

He paused and drank deeply from his glass, remembering how hard those last few weeks of Lita's life were.

"I don't know what to say to that except I'm sorry about your grandma," Jo said after a moment.

"Thanks." He sniffed and cleared the lump from his throat. "Anyway, yes, libraries are competitive. And I eventually want to work in special collections at a university, which is even more insular and elite. I'm starting later in life than some people, and I never landed an internship, so I'm already a few steps behind. I need to be exceptional at my job to get glowing references and work my way up to where I want to be."

"Hence the formality."

"Exactly." Felix raised his beer in mock salute. "I also can't afford to lose my job. I can't leave Tito, and there aren't any other libraries in town."

"Why would you lose your job?" she asked. "Based on the way you've treated MnM night, you seem very dedicated."

"Because the county is considering pulling some library funding to put more cops on the street."

Jo let out a "boo" so long and loud that people at other tables looked over at her.

"My thoughts exactly," Felix said, unable to stop himself from smiling.

"Seriously, fuck that," she said vehemently. "Is there a petition or something I can sign?"

Felix shrugged one shoulder. "I don't know about that, but my hope is that MnM will help the library become more relevant to the community and allow us to push back on the county's recommendations. So thank you for your help there."

"Oh, I can do better than that," she declared. "We're making MnM night the coolest place in town. It's time for some guerilla marketing."

"What—?"

Jo was on her feet before he could get another word out. She swept over to the table next to theirs. "Excuse me, have you heard of the game Monsters and Mythology?"

"Um, yeah, I think so?" said a very confused, pink-haired girl.

Jo launched into a spiel about the library's upcoming event, making up details on the spot that Felix did his best to commit to memory so he could try to deliver on them. Then, she stood there and waited for the four people at the table to enter the information into their calendar apps. The last thing she said before she left them was, "I'll see you there! I'm Jo, by the way. That's Felix; he'll be there too."

Felix gave the table a wave and what he hoped was a friendly-looking smile. Jo hopped back up onto her stool and grinned at him. He opened his mouth, but all that came out was a sound so small she probably couldn't hear it over the music. He didn't know whether to be impressed or slightly terrified.

"What?" Jo asked, all wide-eyed, adorable innocence.

"I..." Felix racked his brain for something to say. "Weren't you following my lead on this?"

"Shit, you're right," Jo said, instantly deflating. "Sorry, did I embarrass you?"

"No, God, I was joking," Felix said. "That was incredible. Maybe we need to come back with flyers and do that for real."

Jo grinned shyly and finished off her drink. "Oh, I have another question for you."

"Shoot." Felix took a long drink to bolster his courage for whatever was going to happen next. Nothing about tonight was going as he'd expected, but fuck if he wasn't having the most fun he'd had in months.

"Do you ever slip up and call your boss 'Roarin' Wigs'?"

Beer almost shot out of Felix's nose. He managed to swallow before coughing into his elbow. Jo leaned forward and laid a hand on his forearm.

"Sorry, you okay? Do you need water?"

Felix nodded and coughed some more. Jo disappeared into the crowd and returned shortly with a small water glass in each hand. He took one and drank deeply.

"Run that by me one more time?" Felix asked, his voice rough from almost choking to death on alcohol and carbonation.

"Roarin' Wigs," she repeated. "Like, if you accidentally switch up the sounds. What's that called?"

"Spoonerism," Felix coughed.

"Yeah, that's it. Fucking librarians, of course you'd know," she said, and the affection in her voice nearly killed Felix all over again. "When I read your email this morning, I thought it would be an easy mistake to make. Also, 'Warren Riggs's Roarin' Wigs' would absolutely be the name of a disguise shop in MnM."

"I do not understand how your mind works," Felix said with a shake of his head.

Jo winced and shrank back. "Sorry."

"It's a compliment, Jo," Felix said. He leaned forward and rested his forearms on the table, his tight shoulder muscles stretching as they shifted. He knit his brow and regarded her closely. "Why do you keep thinking I'm insulting you or belittling you tonight? You're the most creative person I've ever met. I'm so impressed by how you come up with examples of MnM stuff on the fly. And the way you make connections between things is wonderful. You know that every time I use my library key, I smile about that stamped G meaning 'gold'?"

Jo was staring at him without blinking. Her eyes were big, as round as her cheeks, and shiny in the dim bar light. They'd looked like that before, when she'd teared up last week talking about what MnM meant to her.

"You think I'm creative?" She asked it as if she didn't believe it, as if she didn't know it to be true.

But of course it was true. It was one of the truest things Felix had ever known. As true as the sunrise. As true as Tito and Lita's love. As true as his own heartbeat.

And she didn't know it.

Holy fuck. Someone had really done a number on her. Or maybe, somewhere along the way, she'd done it to herself.

Felix reached across the table and grasped Jo's shoulder. He would have rather taken her hand, but he didn't want her to mis-read his intention.

"Yes, Jo. I do."

She made a little O with her mouth and breathed out in a long, slow exhale. She didn't say "thank you," but Felix didn't need to hear it. He squeezed her shoulder before sitting back. After a mo-ment, he said, "For the record, no, I have never called my boss Roarin' Wigs. But if I do now, it will be all your fault."

She laughed in that quick, sharp way of hers, and Felix's entire chest caved in on itself.

"I will take full responsibility, so you don't lose your job."

"Thank you. Now, I have a question for you," he said.

"Go."

"At Warren Riggs's Roarin' Wigs, do the wigs actually roar?"

Jo went bug-eyed. "Shit, you're a genius. I was thinking that the wigs are a fun time, like rip-roarin'. There's got to be an en-chanting spell for that, though."

Her eyes darted back and forth in thought. She pulled out her phone. As he finished off his pint, Felix watched her open a note titled "Campaign Ideas." She scrolled down a long list of bullet points that moved too fast to read. At the bottom, she'd already written down the name of the shop. She added another line, indented it, and typed "Make them actually roar (credit: Felix)."

JO RETURNED HER phone to her jacket pocket. Felix was done with his beer. She'd successfully managed not to break down in tears in front of him. Now what?

"Do you want some more water?" she asked.

"Yes, but I'll get it this time," he replied, on his feet before Jo could protest. When he returned, he gave her back her glass but didn't sit down.

"I'm going to ask about talking to the manager," he said, leaning into her space enough that her breath caught. "I'm sure you're right that it's a long shot, but I did come here with a purpose. I might as well try."

"Want company?"

"No, that's okay. You hold our table," he said. "If it's as fruitless as you suspect, I'll be right back. If it works, I'll wave you over."

He took a big gulp of water, set down his glass, and strode across the room, half a head taller than the crowd. Jo watched him lean casually on the bar and settle his weight into his hip, ass on full display.

"Jesus," she muttered. "That thing should be illegal."

She forced herself to look around instead of gawk. Maybe she'd get lucky and spot someone wearing a "This is how I roll" shirt to tell about the launch event. But instead, as her gaze wandered, so did her mind.

Felix thought she was creative. Her dumb joke about the library key had made him smile all week. He'd been thinking about her. Thinking about her and thinking she was creative. Jo liked to believe she had her moments—a flash of inspiration about a campaign story arc, a witty retort in character, that kind of thing. But no more creative than anyone else she roleplayed with. Certainly not worthy of being "the most creative person" someone knew. Felix just hadn't met enough roleplayers yet to realize she was pretty average.

Why do you keep thinking I'm insulting you or belittling you tonight?

Oh God, why *did* she? She could see it now, looking back on the night. She hadn't even realized she was doing it. And now here she was again, doing it to herself. Why? And why had Felix's compliment made her feel like crying?

Maybe because tonight felt a little bit too much like a date. And maybe because it had been a long-ass time since someone she dated, someone she *liked*, complimented her in regard to MnM.

A wave of heat swept over Jo from head to toe, leaving goosebumps in its wake. "God damn it." She fumbled for her phone.

Jo

Help I like him

Like like him

The reply was almost immediate.

Aida

Oh damn

How do you feel about that?

Jo was scrolling through "confused" gif options for one that felt right when she spotted a maroon hoodie approaching out of the corner of her eye. She hastily typed "later" and sent it to Aida. She set her phone face down on the table as Felix slid onto his stool and held up a black business card with white text.

"Turns out the bartender who served us is the manager," he said. "He couldn't talk now but told me to call him on Monday."

"That's great!"

"We'll see how it goes."

They smiled at each other and went quiet. Jo took a sip of water. Felix drummed his fingers on his empty pint glass.

"I should've asked before I went to the bar," he finally said, "but do you want another drink? On me, if that's okay, to thank you for coming to what ended up being a complete waste of your time."

"Not a waste of time," she replied. "I got to see a new place in town. And hang out with a friend." *Because that's what you are, Jo. Friends.* "Better than falling asleep on the couch rewatching Xena for the hundredth time."

"That's high praise, I think," he said with a smile. "So, another round?"

Jo frowned. "I'd better not, actually. Sorry. I picked up a shift at work tomorrow, and I have to be in at eight."

Was that disappointment on Felix's face? It passed so quickly she couldn't be sure.

"You want to stay a bit longer or call it a night?" he asked.

Jo flipped her phone over, angled away from Felix. Nothing from Aida, but after last time, she wasn't taking any chances. She checked the time. They'd only been there for half an hour.

"We can stay," she said. "If that's cool with you."

There was no mistaking his expression now. The slow grin, the crinkled corners of his eyes, the ever-so-slight flush in his cheeks. "That's cool with me."

They talked until Jo's voice was raw from shouting over the

music and the ever-expanding crowd of drunk college students. She asked him about his time at Rutgers and why he decided to go back to school. It was a childhood dream, he explained, ever since he saw the Rare Books Collection on a field trip to the University of Oklahoma.

She asked what sorts of books he liked, since fantasy wasn't his thing. Research-heavy nonfiction, he said, which made perfect sense to Jo. What surprised her, though, was that he also enjoyed poetry. He liked the way each word had to be precisely chosen, how poems could convey beautiful imagery or depth of emotion in a few brief lines.

In return, Jo mostly talked about MnM. At first, she kept her answers to Felix's questions brief so she didn't bore him. But when he asked for some stories from her campaign with her friends, he looked so genuinely curious she stopped holding back. She told him story after story: how Max and Heather decided that their demonkin characters, Lyric and Rosalis, should be cousins because they couldn't stop bickering; how Lyric kept fucking *dying*, and Young's cleric Sierra had to bring him back to life at least a dozen times; how Kim's halfling rogue Lucas got the kill shot on the final combat of the entire campaign when all hope seemed lost. And of course, the epic love story of Kelpie and Sorn, Aida's druid and David's warlock, who pined after each other for months, finally confessed their feelings, adopted a daughter, and sailed off into the sunset as a family.

"Are Aida and David together then?" Felix asked.

"No, Aida's engaged to someone else, and David's aromantic, so he doesn't date much."

"So it's only their characters who are in love."

"Yup," Jo confirmed. "MnM is about telling stories together. Sometimes love is part of the story."

"Does that ever get weird?"

"It can," she said with a shrug. "It's best for the players to talk things through if they see the potential for a love story between their characters. Both players, obviously, need to be on board for it to happen. The GM can guide that conversation and figure out how to work it into the overall story."

"Huh," Felix said. He paused thoughtfully before he continued. "I suppose that's not much different from real life—talking through your feelings and deciding what you both want. It's hard to imagine doing that on behalf of a character who doesn't really exist though."

"When you're roleplaying, you're making all kinds of decisions on the character's behalf. This might sound strange, but it's almost like you become a part of the character and the character becomes a part of you."

"That's not so strange," he said. "Plenty of actors say things like that when they really embody a role."

"Exactly!" Jo cried. "The only difference is we improvise the script and use dice rolls to help determine the plot as we go."

A bemused grin came over his face. "And you think you're not creative."

Jo stammered a handful of sounds that didn't somehow magically turn into words.

"Thank you for telling me about your game," he said, saving her from herself. "I feel like I have a richer understanding of MnM now."

This is the part where you say "you're welcome," Jo, she told herself as a rich warmth washed over her.

"I need to pee," she yelled instead. "I drank, like, six of those tiny glasses of water." Jo grabbed her phone off the table and practically ran for the bathroom. It wasn't complete bullshit; she *did* have to pee. But she stayed in the stall for a bit when she was done.

Jo

I feel pretty damn okay about it

Aida

Good for you, babe

Send pics

If he hurts you, I will get on a plane

RIP hot librarian

Jo

I love you

Aida

Imagine me saying something about
good choices

When Jo returned to the table, Felix was already standing, his hands in the pockets of his hoodie. Their glasses had been cleared away.

"I didn't realize it was almost eleven," he said. "Shall we head out?"

Her first instinct was to apologize for keeping him, for talking too much, but she bit back the words. He *wanted* to know about MnM. He'd even thanked her for sharing. She had nothing to apologize for... right?

They shouldered their way through the sea of bodies, and Jo's ears rang with the sudden quiet outside. She pulled her jacket tighter around her to keep the cold air from creeping up her crop top. She crossed her arms under her boobs to hold the jacket closed and craned her neck toward the night sky. The number of stars visible here still took her breath away. Jo doubted she would ever get tired of seeing so many constellations at once.

She lowered her gaze to find Felix watching her curiously. "I like the sky here," she said. Before she could think better of it, she added, "And I like being friends with you."

He blinked in surprise, but then looked pleased. "Me too, Jo. It's been... a while since I've gone out with a friend. I had fun tonight. You want a walk to your car?"

Jo almost declined. The parking lot was right behind the bar, and Ashville was generally safe. But, come to think of it, Felix was probably going the same direction anyway.

"Sure. Thanks."

They walked side by side to the lot, accompanied by drunken shouts and laughter from people taking a smoke break or stumbling down the street. Jo pointed out her car, a bright blue hatchback. Felix stood a few paces away while she opened her door. She paused before getting inside, looking at him one last time, surrounded by stars that went all the way to the horizon. She tucked her hair behind her ear and said good night.

"Night, Jo. See you next Friday."

Friday. Six days away. It might as well be an eternity.

7

"GOOD MORNING, MR. NAVARRO!"

"Hello, Leo." Felix approached the front desk and tapped the large "visitor check-in" button on the tablet.

"Visiting or checking out today?"

"Signing in to visit for now," he replied as he tapped through the screens with practiced ease. "Depends on what Tito is up for."

"Great!" Leo chirped. "Just give a shout if you two decide to go on an adventure today!"

Felix's lips quirked up. Apparently, he couldn't even hear the word "adventure" anymore without thinking of Jo. He supposed it was because he'd spent over an hour the night before listening to stories about her friends and the shenanigans their campaign party had gotten up to.

"I sure will," he said and hit the "print" button. Leo handed him a visitor's badge sticker with the date and time, Felix's name, and "Guest of Manuel Navarro." No matter how many Sundays in a row Felix came to visit Tito at White Hills, it was always jarring to see his grandfather's legal name on the visitor's badge. Even

Leo, who used formal address with everyone else, called the old man "Tito."

Leo waved him on, and Felix affixed the sticker to his T-shirt as he walked the familiar path to the communal lounge in the assisted living area. Tito was sitting in his usual spot in the large, high-ceilinged room: the leftmost seat of a brown suede couch with lush cushions. He held a sudoku book up near his face with his right hand, a pencil in his left. On his lap was the library book Felix had brought him the previous Sunday.

He swore to himself, suddenly realizing he'd forgotten this week's book.

"Hey, Tito." He bent down and gave his grandpa a gentle double tap on the side of his knee. "¿Cómo andas?"

"'Ey, hijo," Tito replied with a toothy, yellowed grin. Tito had given up smoking over two decades ago, when Felix was in middle school, but his teeth never fully recovered. He stuck his pencil in the sudoku book as a bookmark and set it on the end table beside him. "Thought you forgot about me today."

"Never, Tito. I'm sorry I'm late." Felix kicked back in a matching armchair beside the couch, slouching almost to the point of reclining. He folded his hands and dropped them onto his stomach.

"Busy Saturday night, eh? Out late with your girl?" Tito's grin grew even wider under his heavy mustache.

Felix's own facial hair was thick, but he had nothing on Tito. That 'stache was dense as a push broom and black as ink. Unlike Felix's stubble, which started coming in gray a couple of years ago, Tito's mustache was as dark as it had been when the man was twenty; Felix had seen his grandparents' wedding photos to prove it. And despite turning ninety a few months back, Tito still had a full head of wavy salt-and-pepper hair. His skin tone was several shades darker than Felix's, a combination of genetics and decades of working outdoors as a cattle rancher. But they had the same oval face, the same long nose and chin, the same dark brown irises. Felix was even starting to see the same laughter lines around his eyes that Tito had.

"I keep telling you I don't have a girl," Felix said with a soft laugh. "I got a drink with a friend last night and time got away from us, that's all." As if to emphasize his point, a yawn crawled its way out of his mouth. He covered it with the back of his hand.

"This is why you forgot my book then, eh?"

Felix winced. "I'm sorry. I had a busy day at work yesterday and didn't have time to check your holds. I'll drop it off at lunch tomorrow so you have something to read this week. And I can return that one for you."

He felt bad for the white lie, but the way Tito harped on him about finding someone and settling down, he wasn't about to tell him the truth—that the idea of going to Stan's with Jo had distracted him so badly he'd completely forgotten to pick up Tito's reserved book at the end of the day. Tito handed over his current book, a thriller called *By Dark of Night*. Felix flipped the cover open to skim the description on the inside flap.

"You wouldn't like it," Tito said. "Too exciting."

"Only the most boring books for me, huh?"

"That's my boy."

Felix closed the book and wedged it between his thigh and the arm of the chair. "What are we doing today, Tito? Brunch? Walk in the park? Or you want to stay here and get your ass handed to you in backgammon?"

"You cheated last time."

"Slander!"

Tito grabbed the sudoku book and smacked Felix on the arm with it, which hurt more than it should from the pencil sticking out the top. Felix let out an indignant cry, and Tito gave him a smug look before dissolving into laughter.

And then Felix heard another laugh. Sharp, staccato, and loud enough to carry from somewhere out of sight. Felix sat up, ramrod straight. "Jo?" He got to his feet almost without thinking, driven toward the sound of her.

"Felix? Where are you going?"

"Un momento, Tito." Felix crossed the room and went through the rear doorway that led to the private residences. A hallway ran parallel to the back wall of the lounge. Felix peered left and right, looking past a few people going about their days. He didn't see Jo.

Had he imagined it? Had she become so entrenched in his mind that he was hearing her laugh out of thin air? What would she even be doing here anyway? She was supposed to be at—

Fuck, he was an idiot sometimes. Jo was supposed to be *at work*. As a nurse. He had made a completely unfounded assumption that she worked at Ashville Hospital, but it was just as likely that she worked right here at White Hills.

But then... where was she?

He stood in the hallway for an awkward moment. He couldn't wander around aimlessly with Tito waiting for him, and calling out for Jo was undoubtedly a terrible idea. Yelling for a nurse could put the whole place on alert. He was about to give up and go back to the lounge when he heard her laugh again.

To his right.

He whipped his head toward the sound. A few feet away was a corner where another hallway seemed to branch off. His feet began to move, and it took all his willpower not to break into a full sprint. He turned the corner—and had to draw himself up short. He wasn't in a hallway at all but a small alcove ending in an open door. Felix had nearly walked straight into a supply closet.

AT THE SOUND of stumbling footsteps and a hand slapping against the doorframe, Jo spun, arms out, ready to catch a falling resident. But the person stopping short in the doorway wasn't a resident.

"Jo."

"Sir, do you need assistance?" Jo's co-worker Sharon asked with urgency. "Is there a medical emergency?"

"No, I'm sorry," said Felix.

He didn't take his eyes off her, and Jo stood frozen, like an actual goddamn deer in headlights. Something in the back of her mind registered that his stubble was shorter than she'd ever seen it, shaved down to the skin but still thick and dark enough to cast a shadow over his warm olive skin. She'd never seen him in the morning before.

"What are you doing here?" she demanded. Or, rather—tried to demand. It came out more like a breathy whisper. She blamed his heather-gray T-shirt and its obnoxious ability to show off his arms. The sleeves were skin-tight around his biceps, for Christ's sake. She could not be held responsible for the tone of her voice under such conditions.

"Jo, is there a problem?" Sharon asked, looking between the two of them warily. Felix's broad, tall body filled the doorway, effectively trapping the two nurses in the closet. And Jo's stunned expression certainly couldn't be helping Sharon feel at ease.

"I don't know yet?" Jo said. Distractingly sexy arms aside, she still had no idea how Felix had found her at work.

"I heard you laugh." Felix pointed his thumb behind him, almost in a daze. "From the lounge. I'm visiting Tito."

Jo's shock transformed into delighted surprise. She noticed the name badge now, read the name "Manuel Navarro" under Felix's. "Your grandpa lives here?"

Felix nodded.

"Jo...?" Sharon said, drawing out the syllable.

"Sorry, Sharon, it's all good. This is my friend Felix." Jo put a hand on Felix's upper arm, hoping the friendly touch would reassure Sharon that all was well. And for no other reason at all. "For a second there I thought he was stalking me. I told him I was working an extra shift today, but not *where* I work."

Felix flinched back, leaving Jo's hand hovering in midair. "You thought that?"

"I-I mean," she stammered, "no, not *really*, but it entered my mind—briefly!—when you showed up in the supply closet at my job out of fucking nowhere."

"Language," Sharon warned. "May I get by, please, sir?"

With a mumbled apology, Felix moved aside to let Sharon out with a tray of supplies. Leaving Jo and Felix alone. In a closet. A big, walk-in closet, but still a closet.

"I'm sorry I scared you," Felix said quietly. "I heard you laugh."

"So you said."

"I wanted to say hi."

The sweet innocence with which he said it nearly melted Jo's heart. She gave him a soft smile. "Hi."

A matching grin came over his face. "Hi."

And then it was as if an enchantment spell broke. Felix's face fell, and he shoved his hand into his hair, gripping it in his fist, completely mortified. "Oh, God, Jo, I'm so sorry. You're at *work*. I was not thinking at all. I'll get out of your way. I'll see you later."

"Can I meet him?" she asked before he could run away. "Tito?"

Felix unclenched his hair and smoothed it out, taking a moment to respond. "Of course. If you're not too busy."

She shrugged. "Not really. I'm usually over in skilled nursing, not assisted living. My boss suggested I shadow the other team to see how they work. Sometimes we have to float back and forth if we're short-staffed. I can't take too long, but I'll catch up with Sharon in a bit."

She locked the door behind them and fell into step alongside him. Nudging his arm with her elbow, she stretched her neck up to whisper, "Question. I thought his name was Tito, but your badge says Manuel?"

Felix tilted sideways to whisper back. "That's more a statement than a question."

"Okay, um... what gives?"

"Manuel is his given name," he explained with a laugh. "Tito actually comes from 'uncle,' but it's been his nickname forever, long before I was born. I picked it up as a kid, and it stuck."

As they approached a man seated on a brown sofa, he called out to them, "You're bringing me a nurse now, hijo? Am I sick?"

"Hush, Tito," Felix said. "I'd like you to meet my friend Jo. I just found out she works here, and she wanted to say hello."

"Hello, Mr. Navarro," Jo said, extending her hand. "It's lovely to meet you."

Tito narrowed his eyes, regarding her hand with suspicion. "You're friends with my Felix?"

"Yes, sir," she said. "Felix speaks very highly of you."

"Then how come he didn't tell you to call me Tito, eh?" He pitched forward on the couch and jabbed Felix in the ribs with his index finger, completely ignoring Jo's outstretched hand.

Felix squawked and dodged the blow a split second too late. As

Tito cackled, Felix rubbed the flat of his hand over his side and said something playful in Spanish. Jo did her best not to notice the way that tight T-shirt shifted along his abs.

"Tito it is, then," she said as she smiled and lowered her hand. "How long have you lived here with us?"

Tito's brows flickered together briefly. "Almost a year now. Since mi vida, my wife, passed."

Jo's cheeks heated. Felix had said something about his grandmother dying last year, and she couldn't believe she'd accidentally brought it up five seconds after meeting Tito. She pressed her lips together and sank down on the couch next to him, perched on the edge to avoid being too familiar. She was still a nurse meeting a resident, after all.

"I'm sorry," she said. "Felix mentioned your wife last night. What was her name?"

Instead of answering, Tito slowly turned his head and raised an eyebrow at Felix. Felix ran his hand through his hair and sighed like a put-upon parent dealing with a stubborn toddler.

Jo felt like she was missing an inside joke. "Did I say something wrong?"

"Not at all, Jo," Felix said, sitting in the armchair next to Tito. He crossed his ankle over his knee and gave his grandpa an exasperated look. "Are you going to answer her, or should I?"

"María Isabel Acosta Garrido," Tito said, going dreamy-eyed and placing his hand over his heart. "Mi vida y mi corazón."

"'My life and my heart,'" Felix translated. "Maribel to her friends. Lita to me. From abuelita."

Jo knew that one. "Grandma," she said wistfully. "You both must miss her terribly. I'm sorry for your loss."

Tito nodded with a sad smile. Then he suddenly clapped his hands together. "So, Jo, how did you meet my Felix?"

She stole a quick glimpse at Felix, who was watching her with lifted eyebrows. "At the library," she said. "I'm volunteering with him to put on an event next month."

Tito returned his attention to Felix. "How come you haven't invited me to this event?"

"You wouldn't like it. Too boring."

Jo's stomach flip-flopped. "You think it's boring?"

Felix's eyes went wide. "No! That was—I was referring to something Tito said earlier." He reached toward his hip and pulled out a large, hardcover book with a dark cityscape and yellow text on the cover.

Jo wasn't sure how a book was supposed to explain things, exactly, but she had clearly misread something. Tito rattled off a sentence in Spanish, and Felix looked chagrined.

"Don't listen to my boy, Jo." Tito patted the back of her hand. "Will *you* invite me to this event at least?"

"If you'll do me the honor, Tito, it's a date," she said.

Tito shook his head and clucked his tongue. "*This* Navarro is too old for you, solete. I'll come as your friend so you can bring a real date."

Tito inclined his head toward Felix, and Jo's entire face burned.

"Tito," Felix said sharply. The blush Jo felt was mirrored on his cheeks. Tito spread his hands and looked between the two of them with a wide-eyed innocence that fooled no one.

"Come to think of it," she said quickly. "I'll probably be too busy at the event to bring a date at all. Better we all go as friends."

"If you say so," Tito replied with a shrug and a knowing look in his eye.

Before the awkwardness could fully set in, Jo pushed herself onto her feet. Felix stood up too. "I should get back to work, but, Tito, it was so nice to meet you."

"Encantado, solete," he said with a wide grin that made him look even more like Felix.

"Thanks for saying hello." Felix tucked his hands into the back pockets of his jeans, not quite meeting her eye. "I guess I'll see you on Friday."

Shit, were things going to be weird between them now? *Thanks, Tito.* Sure, Jo liked Felix, and he was the kindest, most gorgeous man she'd ever met, but he had only ever treated her like a friend and colleague. Clearly, he was embarrassed by the idea of them dating. She needed to fix this, to make things normal again. If the next time they saw each other was Friday, alone in the library after hours, with Tito's suggestion hanging over them...

"Have Leo page me before you leave," she said. "I'll come say goodbye."

Felix blinked slowly and, when his eyes opened, he was looking directly at her with such obvious relief it threatened to overwhelm her. "I will."

FELIX WAITED UNTIL Jo was out of sight, then gave it a few more seconds to make sure she was well out of earshot. He rounded on Tito and put his hands on his hips. "What the hell was that?"

"I could ask you the same thing," Tito replied, grinning and giddy. "This is the friend you had a drink and stayed out too late with? Do you not have eyes, hijo?"

Felix quickly glanced around and switched to Spanish. "I'm not doing this; I'm not talking about her here. This is your home, but it's her workplace. I'm not going to risk anyone overhearing us. Not even in Spanish."

Tito leaned back against the couch. The humor left his face, and he pointed to the armchair. Felix obeyed the unspoken directive and sat.

"You're a good man, Felix," Tito said in Spanish. "You're respectful, and I'm proud of that. I won't ask you to talk about her here. But you want to talk about her, don't you?"

Yes.

The word rang, clear as a bell, through Felix's mind before he quite realized he was thinking it. Despite living in Ashville for almost a year, he didn't really have friends in town. Like hell he could talk to Peggy about Jo. Even Peggy "Anything for a Volunteer!" Shelton would look askance at Felix for having a crush on his volunteer after less than two weeks. Because that's what this was. A crush. A big one. He couldn't deny it anymore, not after his compulsion to find her when he'd heard her laugh and his relief that she still wanted to see him after Tito had embarrassed them both.

Felix had it bad.

And thus far his only outlets had been beating the shit out of his punching bag or stroking his dick while trying not to imagine how round, how soft Jo's hips must feel.

"I haven't had breakfast." He stood and put out his hands to help Tito up. "Come on. I'm taking you to the Old Bell."

"I'm getting waffles."

8

THE OLD BELL Diner was a sprawling restaurant smack dab in the center of Ashville, on the corner where the two main roads met. There were a handful of chain diners out by the expressway, where the truckers and cross-country road-trippers stopped, but the Old Bell was for the locals. It was open twenty-four hours a day, and it had enough customers to fill every one of those hours. The hospital, sheriff's office, and fire station were all within walking distance of the place, so even at three a.m., the booths were full of people stopping by for a bite or a coffee before their shifts. And then, of course, there were the half-drunk college kids wandering over from Stan's to split a giant platter of hash browns.

One of the reasons Felix always visited his grandpa on Sundays was because Tito and Lita used to go to the Old Bell every week after mass for the senior brunch discount. In the first months after she was gone, Tito couldn't even look at the place when they drove past. Then, last fall, he had cautiously asked Felix if they might go to brunch. They'd only made it as far as ordering coffee before it was too much, and Felix had to take Tito home. They tried again a few weeks later, and again in the weeks that followed, until Tito was able to eat an entire meal there.

Now, whenever Tito was up for a Sunday outing, they came to the Old Bell. Each time, Tito paused by the enormous, seven-foot-tall bronze bell outside the entrance and lovingly ran his palm along the waist-high band that had been worn smooth and shiny by tens of thousands of hands. The bell was practically an institution in Ashville, but Tito had never touched it when Lita was alive. That had been her ritual. She was the one who had loved the sleek feel of the bronze, who had claimed one touch connected her to every other person who had ever rubbed the bell. Tito used to tease her for it, to remind her to go wash her hands before they ate. Now, he did it for her.

Sunday mornings at the diner were always packed, and that morning was no exception. It was later than Felix and Tito usually arrived for brunch, and there was a wait for a table. But the hostess shifted them up the queue with a wink so that Tito didn't have to stand in the crowded lobby for more than a couple of minutes. The other Sunday regulars waved as she brought them to a booth.

True to his word, Tito ordered waffles—apple cinnamon—along with sausage links, two eggs over easy, sourdough toast, and country potatoes, with his usual black coffee and orange juice. Felix got a Denver omelet, hash browns, and a short stack of pancakes with a cappuccino. The Navarro men knew how to eat.

Tito had the decency to wait until they had gotten their food and eaten a few bites before he broached the subject of Jo. But he didn't pull his punches.

"So," he said around a bite of sausage, "tell me why you aren't dating this sweet, lovely friend of yours."

Felix sighed and mumbled, "For a lot of reasons."

Tito raised an eyebrow at him—a clear "you're going to have to do better than that, señor" expression that Felix had seen hundreds of times. Felix shoveled a giant forkful of his omelet into his mouth and chewed slowly, staring Tito in the face.

"Cabezota," Tito muttered. "Fine. Then tell me about her."

So Felix did. He told Tito again how they met—glossing over the intricacies of MnM for the sake of simplicity—how Jo was generously helping him and, by extension, the library and the town. He told Tito that Jo made him laugh and told captivating stories, that she wore cute T-shirts and scrubs but apparently only owned one jacket, that she was clever and cared about people.

"These are all good things," Tito said when Felix had finished. "What's the problem?"

"First of all, Tito, it's not only my decision," he said. "She has to want to date me too."

"And you have asked her?"

Felix didn't respond to that, and Tito sighed resignedly. "Hijito, when you lose track of time with someone, that's a good sign. It means you want to be together. That you are happy together. You are happy together, aren't you?"

"I enjoy her company, yes. And she seems to enjoy mine. But she just ended a relationship and moved here a few weeks ago. She wants to be friends." Felix stabbed a piece of pancake with his fork. "Besides, we're working together on this library event. I can't date a volunteer. It's unprofessional."

"Unprofessional," Tito said with a *tsk*. "Always you are obsessed with this job you don't even like very much."

"I like my job fine," he said. He kept his expression neutral, though he felt a stab of dread as the thought of budget cuts loomed in the back of his mind. He knew Tito would listen if he wanted to talk about that too. But he couldn't. Not yet. Not until he knew for certain what was going to happen to his job. Tito would only worry.

His grandpa leaned across the table to grip his forearm. "Hijo, I'm doing okay now. I have friends of my own at White Hills. I'm not so lonely anymore. If you want to find another place to work, to live—"

"What? No. Stop." Felix set his fork down and closed his hand over Tito's. His rancher's hands were so small and fragile now. Felix could feel the veins bulging through his thin skin. "We're not having this conversation."

"Felix." He switched to Spanish, as he often did when his emotions became too big for English. "You uprooted your life for me. You left someone behind for me. It's because of you I'm here. Not just here in the Old Bell, but here in this world." His eyes misted over. "But I never wanted to be a burden to you. You know that— that's why I moved to White Hills in the first place. I want you to be happy. If you aren't happy in Ashville, I don't want you here anymore."

As if he'd been punched in the gut, the air flew from Felix's lungs. He knew without having to think about it that he wasn't happy here, not really. Ashville had never felt like home. It was Tito and Lita's home, the place he visited for short stints before going back to his real life. Most folks in town had grown up together, which made him feel like an outsider, even after living here for almost a year.

Felix's life in Ashville wasn't *bad* by any stretch of the imagination. His days were pleasant enough. More often than not, his work was rewarding. He was content. But not particularly happy.

Not unless he was with—

"But if this woman makes you happy," Tito continued, giving voice to what was already on Felix's mind, "chase that. Don't let go of it. It's a rare and beautiful thing to find someone who brings you that kind of joy. Who makes the sun shine brighter and the rain feel less cold and damp. Even if that person is a friend, she should be cherished."

"You should've been a poet, Tito," Felix said in English, his voice thick with emotion.

Tito grinned. "What makes you believe I wasn't? Your lita kept every letter I ever wrote her, you know."

"Sí, lo sé."

Tito squeezed Felix's forearm firmly and withdrew his hand. They resumed eating, each man occupied with his own thoughts for a long time. Felix wasn't convinced he should ask Jo out. It was still unprofessional as long as they worked together. If anything, he was reminded that friendship was just as meaningful as a romantic relationship. Crushes came and went, but Jo liked being his friend, and he liked being hers. He needed that. Maybe what they had wasn't the rare, beautiful thing Tito had described, but it was still worthwhile. Still important and good.

"You feel better?" Tito asked as he sopped up runny egg yolk with his toast.

"Sí. Thank you for listening."

"You forgot my book this week. I need *something* to keep me entertained."

Felix groaned, but it was mostly for show. "I said I'll bring it tomorrow."

"That doesn't help me today, now does it?" Tito quirked an eyebrow at Felix and then burst out laughing. Felix joined him.

JO'S PAGER BUZZED against her wrist. She peeked at the face of the watch-like device, read "Front desk: Nonurgent," and smiled to herself. She let Sharon know she was taking a short break and wound through the halls to the lobby. Felix was standing near the desk, one hand in his back pocket while he typed something on his phone with the other.

"Heading out?" Jo called.

Felix grinned and lowered his phone. "Yeah, off to run some errands."

"Where's Tito?"

"Probably sound asleep already," he replied with that high-pitched chuckle of his. "I have it on good authority that he always takes a long nap after our brunches."

"I can't wait until I'm retired," she said longingly. "Will you let me know how it goes with the guy from Stan's tomorrow?"

"Sure, I'll email you."

"Make it extra formal for me."

"As thou commandeth."

She made a face. "Oh God, I take it back."

Felix gave her a sly grin that sent her pulse skyrocketing. He backed toward the front door. "Too late, Jo. You asked for it."

"I take it back, though!" She took a few steps toward him, but he backed up faster.

"No take backs!"

And then he was out the door, jogging toward his car and glancing back at her over his shoulder. As if she might chase him. If she hadn't been at work, with Leo looking on, she totally would have.

From: Felix Navarro
To: Jo Rainier
Date: Monday, May 13, 2024, 2:17 P.M.
Subject: On the Subject of Stan's

Dear Ms. Rainier,

Pursuant to the agreed upon action item resulting from our most recent conversation, please find below a brief summation of my telephone meeting with one Mr. Charlie Ross, Manager of Stan's Bar in Ashville, Kansas.

- He said no.

- He informed me that Ashville Community College hosts periodic community outreach days, wherein nonprofit groups from Butler County, and frequently Wichita and Topeka, advertise their events and programs.

I will be investigating this potential new avenue for advertising later this week, as my bandwidth allows. If you desire, I can keep you abreast of my progress in this matter.

Sincerely,
Mr. Navarro, MI
~
Felix Navarro, MI
Junior Librarian, General Services
Butler County Library District — Ashville Public Library

From: Jo Rainier
To: Felix Navarro
Date: Monday, May 13, 2024, 5:03 P.M.
Subject: RE: On the Subject of Stan's

This is both the best and worst thing I've ever read.
Congratulations. (Looks like we're both creative, huh?)

Bummer about Stan's, but I'm still down for some guerilla
marketing. We just need some flyers and maybe a martini
for courage.

See ya Friday,
Jo

ON FRIDAY, JO was in hell. Bureaucratic, red taped, "please-wait-here-until-your-number-is-called" hell. And she didn't even have the internet to distract her. She was going on four hours of sitting in the lobby of the Butler County Motor Vehicles office, twenty miles from Ashville, waiting for her number to come up.

She had tried to make transferring her car registration and driver's license as painless as possible. She'd switched shifts at work to free up a weekday, made an appointment, gathered all the paperwork she thought she needed, and even arrived early. But she'd missed one crucial step. Apparently, out-of-state cars required an inspection before the registration could be transferred. By the time she'd driven out to the inspection facility halfway across the county, waited for her car to be checked, and driven back, there were no more appointments available. She was now at the mercy of the walk-in schedule.

Which was taking *forever.*

And to top it off, the customer Wi-Fi was down, and her phone only had one measly, flickering bar of service. She'd finished her book within the first couple of hours, and she hadn't thought she'd be waiting long enough to need a second one. She'd taken to writing notes on the back of a receipt she'd found in her purse—topics for Felix's MnM lessons, ideas for marketing the launch event, and the beginnings of a packing list for Indi-Con.

She was starting to run out of room on the receipt when an automated voice announced, "Now serving... number fifty-two."

Jo jumped up from the plastic chair, her butt numb. "That's me!"

The actual process of transferring everything didn't take very long. She showed them proof of residence, her documentation from California, and that damn vehicle inspection paperwork; took a one-minute vision test; and smiled into a camera for her new license photo.

Then—finally—she rushed out the door to hop into her Kansas-official car. She had just enough time to run home, grab a granola bar and her MnM bag, and get over to her lesson with Felix by six o'clock.

What she wouldn't have time for was a video call with Aida from the library parking lot, which had become their Friday night routine. Instead, as soon as she had signal again, she called her best friend on speaker and stuck her phone in the cupholder. They traded off venting about their days, and then Jo asked Aida how the first session of their friends' new MnM campaign had gone the night before.

"It's not the same without you," Aida said, "but it was really good.

Kim brought a friend of hers to try it out. She's cool, but things are moving a little slow since she's new. David's a great GM. He threw us into combat, like, three minutes in. Max almost died twice."

"Seriously? How does he keep doing that? First Lyric and now this new character."

"Andros," Aida said. "He's playing a barbarian this time. Built to absorb damage, but then he rushes in without thinking and ends up bleeding out in round two of combat."

Jo laughed and pressed a hand to her heart. "I love that dumbass."

"Me too."

"I miss playing so much, Aida." Jo turned on her windshield wipers as it started to drizzle. "Felix and I are doing a mock game tonight. It'll be super simple, but I can't wait to GM again."

"I knew you couldn't stay away for long. Cattle theft?" Aida asked, referring to the adventure Jo had written specifically for breaking in new players.

"It's a classic for a reason."

"And how are things with the hot librarian?"

Jo could feel her cheeks heat. "You know his name, Aida."

"Yeah, babe," Aida said, sounding mildly exasperated. "It's Hot Librarian. By the way, you still owe me pics."

"How exactly am I supposed to take pictures of him? You told me to treat him like a work friend."

"That was before. Now we're treating him like Jo's sexy crush."

Her heart skipped a beat. She hadn't quite thought about Felix in those terms yet. The idea made her feel all gooey inside. "Which means what? Gentle online stalking to dig up photos of him from Rutgers?"

"Rutgers?" There was a lilt of interest in Aida's voice as she latched onto that tidbit. "That's a start. What's his last name?"

"Nope."

"Babe, please. You have to give me *something*."

Jo took a slow, even breath. She wasn't planning on saying any-thing until she'd brought it up with Felix first, but... "I was think-ing of inviting him to Indi-Con next weekend."

Aida gasped. "Jo! I fully support this. This is the best idea you've ever had."

"You think so? It's not too much?"

"Of course it's too much," Aida said, blunt as ever. "Indi-Con is like drinking from the firehose of MnM. It's perfect."

"How can it be too much and also perfect?"

There was a long pause. Jo wondered if her phone signal had gone out again, but then Aida said, "Hold on. I need to close my office door."

"Okay..." Jo replied warily. While she waited, she glanced at the sky. The rain was coming down harder now. Dark, gray-green clouds were gathering ahead of her. It had been overcast at the motor vehicles office, but not like this. She seemed to driving into a storm.

Through the phone, there was the sound of a door closing. "Can you handle some real talk right now?" asked Aida.

Jo's grip on the steering wheel tightened. "Uh-huh."

"After Jeremy," Aida began, and that's how Jo knew it was seri-ous. Aida never said his name. He was always "the asshole." Her heart beat a little faster; her fists clenched a little harder. "I want you to find someone who understands you. Someone who gets what MnM means to you and why you devote so much time to it. Listen to yourself, babe—you can't wait to GM again? You swore that you were going to take a break when you moved. Now you're teaching someone how to play, inviting him to a con—which I had to talk you into going to, by the way—*and* helping launch a public game program!"

"Jesus, Aida," Jo interjected, not even trying to hide the hurt in her voice.

"I'm not guilt-tripping you, Jo, I swear. Please don't misunderstand me. I think what you're doing is awesome. I'm trying to help you see that MnM is always going to be part of you. You can't stay away from it. And you shouldn't have to. You love it. You're brilliant at it. If Hot Librarian isn't cool with that, fuck him. If he runs screaming from Indi-Con, I'd rather you know now before you go through a lot of hurt again."

Jo went quiet, digesting that as the rain pattered on the metal and glass around her. Teaching Felix MnM *had* given her a kind of joy she hadn't felt in years. It was wonderful, sharing the game with him and remembering the thrill of learning it herself back in college. It was even better to be free of the guilt and the shame that the man she loved refused to be involved in one of the biggest parts of her life.

Tears sprang to Jo's eyes as her swirling thoughts coalesced on Jeremy. What if... what if she hadn't stopped going to conventions and public games because she was burned out? What if she hadn't actually been burned out at all? What if she had stopped because it wasn't worth it anymore? Not with how much Jeremey hated them, the way he made her feel bad about wanting to go.

What if she didn't have to hold back anymore? What if she could let herself fall in love with MnM all over again?

"I forgot to tell you," Jo said quietly, blinking away her tears. "I signed up to GM a few games at Indi-Con."

"That's awesome," Aida replied. "I'm so proud of you."

"And you really think I should invite Felix?"

"I do. Not as a boyfriend test or whatever—that's gross. But if you really do like him, it couldn't hurt to learn as much about him as possible, including what he thinks of MnM on that scale."

Jo sniffed and cleared her throat to keep herself from full-on crying. What the hell had she done to deserve a best friend like Aida? "Can I ask a favor?"

"Anything."

"If Felix comes to Indi-Con, will you ask Trey to help keep him company?"

Aida chuckled. Her fiancé didn't play MnM very much, but he sometimes came to cons with the group to get in a game or two. "Are you kidding? Trey would love an exhibit hall buddy."

"You two are the best."

"I know, babe."

"And, um, on that note, I think I need to go," Jo said, looking skyward again. "I think it's starting to hail. I should focus on driving."

"Oh, damn, yes, you should. I'll see you next week at Indi-Con."

"Can't wait. Love you."

"Love you too."

Jo carefully drove the rest of the way into Ashville, keeping a close eye on the time. About a mile outside of town, the rain and hail suddenly stopped. The wide Kansan sky was still hidden behind a thick, low ceiling of cloud cover, but she seemed to have made it through the worst of the storm.

That's weird, she thought. But then again, she hadn't done much driving outside of Ashville. Maybe rainstorms here were really localized.

After a quick pit stop at home to get her things, Jo finally made it to the library with two minutes to spare. She sat in her car for a brief moment to steady herself. It had been a wild day, with wild emotions and wild weather. But now, she got to spend an hour with Felix, playing her favorite game and letting go of the stress and distractions. And at the end of their lesson, she would invite him to come with her to Indi-Con, a prospect that was equal parts nerve-racking and electrifying.

"Here we go," she muttered, stepping out of the car.

The wind immediately whipped her flyaways around her face. The hairs on the back of her neck stood up, and she found herself shuddering. She grabbed her tote bag and purse and hustled to the shelter of the library.

Felix's head snapped up when she entered. The wind caught the door, and she had to haul it closed with both hands. He was on his feet by the time she turned back around. Jesus, he looked good today. His shirt was a little rumpled, more disheveled than he usually was at work. His hair was mussed, as if he'd been running his hands through his black waves. She didn't hate it.

"I wasn't sure if you were coming," Felix said, gesturing toward the windows that framed the front door and the dark clouds beyond them. He seemed to be breathing a little heavily.

"Because of the rain?" she said with a smile. "I may be from California, but I'm not made of sugar, you know."

Felix squinted at her, looked out the windows, and back to her. "Did you get my email?"

"No, sorry," Jo replied. "It's been kind of a long day, and I didn't think to check it. Why? Is something going on?"

"There's a tornado watch, Jo."

"There's a *WHAT?!*"

Felix was kind enough not to shush her in the library.

9

"HOLY SHIT," JO breathed. She grabbed the front of her shirt in her fist, pressing her knuckles against her racing heart. "Do we need to get underground?"

"It's just a watch," Felix said, far too calmly. "That means we keep an eye on the sky and the alerts. We only have to shelter if it's upgraded to a warning."

"Okay." Jo swallowed and glanced around the empty lobby. Peggy wasn't here. Judging by the complete silence from the rooms beyond, neither was anyone else. "Is everyone gone?"

Felix nodded. "No one's come in since the watch alert went out about an hour ago, and Peggy went home early to get her chickens secured."

Jo's mind raced, flashing with images of Dorothy (and her little dog too) dashing through sepia-toned plains. "Do I need to go home? Do *you*?"

Felix walked over, stopped an arm's length away. He put his hand on her shoulder, like he'd done at Stan's last weekend. He made eye contact with the same kind of steadiness Jo had been trained to use in medical emergencies. "Do you have a basement at home?"

Jo focused on Felix's deep brown eyes and tried to recall what her landlord had told her when she moved in. There was definitely something about a designated tornado shelter, but, at the moment, she couldn't remember the details. "I don't know. I don't think so. I'm not sure where the shelter I'm supposed to use is."

"Okay, then we'll stay here," Felix said, cool as a goddamn cucumber. "Would you feel better if we went downstairs now?"

The Wicked Witch of the West's theme music was now looping like a broken record in Jo's mind. How could she have been so stupid? Sure, she'd never actually seen tornado weather before. But if she hadn't been in such a rush and gotten distracted talking to Aida about her silly boy problems, maybe she would have put two and two together. The music in her head crescendoed, mocking her. She shook her head, trying to clear it away.

Felix apparently took that for a no, but Jo could barely remember what he had even asked. He slid his hand to her upper back and murmured "okay." He guided her around the desk, where she plopped onto a chair and let her bags tumble to the floor. A male voice intoned softly from a yellow handheld radio beside her, rattling off numbers and meteorological phrases that she only partially understood.

Felix took the other chair. "May I have your phone, please?"

She blinked at him. "Why?"

"I'd like to install the Butler County Severe Weather app on it. And the NWS Mobile app."

Jo unlocked her phone and handed it over without further protest. Watching him work and listening to the steady drone of the man on the radio had a mildly calming effect. Jo's heart rate returned to something closer to normal, and her flashbacks of *The Wizard of Oz* faded away.

"Thank you for doing that," she said to Felix. Looking at the careful way he held her phone, she could almost feel the imprint of his touch on her back.

"You're welcome," he said. "Do you mind if I give you my number and text myself so I have yours? I don't think it's a good idea to keep relying on email to communicate."

"That's fine." She watched as he created a new contact for himself with his full name. *Of course*, Jo thought. *So formal.* He typed a message reading "Jo" and tapped send. Finally, he gave back her phone.

"Let me know if you need any help with the apps," he said. He grabbed his own phone to save her number. "You can turn off some alerts and sounds, but others, like tornado watches and warnings, will always push through."

"You stayed for me."

Felix froze, not looking up from his phone.

"Didn't you?" she prompted. "I never responded to your email, so you stayed here in case I showed up. Instead of going home like everyone else."

"I needed to make sure you were safe." His voice was soft as a whisper, but too rough to be called one. He lifted his chin a fraction of an inch and peered at Jo through his eyelashes. His gaze seared her skin with dark fire, her face heating from the scorch of it. Her pulse throbbed once—hard—in her temples, in her wrists, between her thighs. Felix had never looked at her like that before. No one had ever looked at her like that before. Like she was something worth keeping safe.

FELIX KNEW THE look he was giving her was too honest, too intense, too *real*. But the past hour had turned him into a wreck, and he didn't have the energy left to stop himself.

This was Ashville's first tornado watch since Jo had moved here. As soon as it was announced, he'd emailed her to make sure she had heard. Then he'd spent an hour refreshing his inbox over and over, even though it should have refreshed automatically with each new email. When he didn't hear from Jo, there was no question of whether he'd wait for her. The shelter downstairs was as safe as his basement. He would stay. He had to. He couldn't simply lock the door and walk away and hope for the best. Wait to hear from Jo on the other side of her first fucking tornado. He needed to see for himself that she was okay and give her somewhere safe to wait it out.

Jo didn't look away from his scrutiny. Her breath quickened, and some instinct within Felix told him it wasn't from fear of the storm.

"Oh," Jo finally said, all round eyes and round cheeks and round glasses. "I'm glad you're here."

Before he could respond, two klaxons of emergency notifications blared.

"Oh my God, oh my God, oh my God." Jo was white-knuckling her phone with both hands, wide eyes locked onto the screen. Felix's phone displayed the same message she was seeing.

TORNADO WARNING IN YOUR AREA. SEEK SHELTER
IMMEDIATELY. FOR MORE INFORM...

"Come on." Felix offered her his hand. She took it without hesitation. But when he pushed to his feet, she didn't move. She was still staring at her phone. He roughly pulled her up, jolting her into action. Her feet were barely under her when she started running for the stairs. Felix gripped her hand tighter and ran alongside her.

At the base of the stairs, he took control. He steered them to the large, empty room at the end of the hallway, in the dead center of the building. Once the door was securely closed behind them, Felix turned on the flashlight on his phone. He stuck it in his pocket, light facing out, to keep his hand free. Because no way in hell he was letting go of Jo.

He reached for the hook on the wall that held the portable radio. And immediately realized his mistake.

"Shit. I have to get the radio. I left it on the desk."

"What?" Jo's hand clenched even tighter around his. She grabbed at his forearm, pulling on his sleeve. "You can't go up there!"

He almost touched her cheek. At the last second, he diverted to her shoulder, chest to chest with her. "Cell service isn't reliable right now. We need that radio to know what's going on and when it's all clear. I'll come right back. I promise. Stay here."

Jo released him, hovering a breath away. "Hurry."

Felix tore himself from her side, leaving a piece of his heart behind to watch over her.

He pounded down the hall, up the stairs. The windows rattled. He didn't spare them even a glance. He launched himself at the desk, hopping up to land on his belly on the tall counter. A soft "oof" escaped him. He snatched up the radio and, in the same movement, shoved himself backward. Looping the wrist strap over his hand, he made a beeline for the stairs. Two steps down, he tripped on the carpet and had to slam against the wall to catch himself.

Fuck.

He took the rest more carefully. Nurse or not, the last thing Jo needed right now was a broken ankle—or worse, a broken neck— to deal with.

She was rooted to the same spot he'd left her, white as a sheet and clutching her phone to her chest. She hadn't even turned on her flashlight. Felix pushed the radio strap up to his elbow and took Jo by the shoulders.

"You okay?" he asked.

She stared right through his chest, eyes glazed over.

"Look at me, Jo," he demanded, making his voice deep and commanding. She started but obeyed. "There you are," he continued, more gently. "Stay with me. Are you okay?"

"No, I am not the fuck okay." Her words were flat and emotionless.

"What can I do?"

"Get me out of here. Put me on a plane back to California."

A stab went through Felix's heart. He shoved the feeling aside. Later. Later, he could process what the thought of sending Jo away did to him. "What can I do that doesn't involve leaving this room?"

Something in Jo shifted as the shock wore off. She started to shake. Her phone thudded to the floor; her palms pressed against her cheeks. Her fingers curled around the arms of her glasses, digging into her temples. She wasn't looking at him anymore.

"I-I—I don't..."

"Shh, it's all right, cariño. Come here, come sit down." He guided her to a corner and sat her on the floor. On the radio, the tornado warning was repeating over and over. Nothing about a touchdown. Not yet.

Jo hugged her knees to her chest, wedged into the space where the two walls met. Felix sat beside her and stretched his legs out long, a third wall to protect her.

"I hate this," she muttered, staring into the darkness. "I hate this so much."

"This is the safest spot in the building. We'll be okay."

"Earthquakes just *happen*. They're over before you know it.

Waiting around like this is *so* much worse. Christ, I was just starting to like it here."

She sounded more like herself, so Felix took a chance at teasing her, hoping to draw her out more. "You do know you moved to Kansas in the middle of tornado season, right?"

Jo finally looked at him, wincing. "Honestly? I didn't think about it too much. I was afraid I'd chicken out."

Well, that explained a lot. Her surprise about the tornado watch despite ominous weather, her ignorance of alert apps, her apparent lack of a waterproof jacket. But it did raise another question.

Perhaps keeping her distracted was a good idea. They might be here a while.

He shifted, angling his torso toward her. "Jo, why did you move here? Of all places, why Ashville?"

She didn't answer at first. Then, letting out a long sigh, she said, "Remember, at Stan's, how I said I broke up with someone? He... he actually broke up with me. Maybe I should have seen it coming, but I didn't, and it got messy. We lived together, and when he ended things, I floundered for a while. I didn't know where to go. It was right after the holidays, so I'd just spent a bunch of money on Christmas gifts. I didn't have a deposit saved up, and I couldn't afford rent on my own anyway. I really didn't want to do the whole roommate thing again in my thirties. Plenty of people do it, I know, but we'd been together so long—"

"You don't have to justify yourself to me," Felix interjected.

Jo knit her brow and regarded him for a moment. "Oh. Thanks. Anyway, I was crashing in Aida and her fiancé's guest room. One night, she sat me down with a bottle of gin and a laptop and told me to figure my shit out."

"That sounds harsh."

"No, that's just Aida," Jo said with a tiny laugh. "I needed a kick in the pants, and she knew it. She'd watched me wallow and fed me ice cream and Thai food for two months at that point, and there was no end in sight. Literally, the only things I did outside work were sleep, eat, and run our MnM game. I hadn't even looked at apartments in weeks."

"Then I amend my statement," Felix said. "That sounds like a pretty great best friend."

"Yeah," Jo stared at her hands, clasped on top of her knees. There was a gentle, affectionate smile on her face. Felix wondered if she ever smiled that way when she thought about her friendship with him. The way he did, especially whenever he saw the damn library key. Lately, he'd taken to running his thumb over that meaningless, stamped G.

"So what happened?" Felix prompted.

Jo's smile turned sly. "We got blackout drunk that night, is what. When I woke up, I had a hangover so epic that bards should write songs about it. And I found tabs open on my browser for"—Jo ticked them off on her fingers—"'lowest cost of living cities in the U.S.', a map of Ashville, the jobs page on the White Hills website, and my email, where I somehow already had an approved apartment application. Luckily, I didn't apply for *my job* while blacked out, but once I stopped barfing and could see straight, I decided to go for it."

Jo tipped her head back against the wall and closed her eyes. Felix allowed his gaze to wander down the line of her throat. It bobbed as she swallowed. His eyes trailed all the way down to the point of the V-neck of her sage green shirt. His lips fell open of their own accord, and sensation flooded to his dick. Jo took a deep, shuddering inhale, and Felix realized, with the same level of subtlety as being hit by a truck, that she was trying not to cry.

Fuck. Shit. Stop it.

Felix bent the leg closer to Jo and slung his arm casually over his knee. Hiding the tightness in his slacks because *Jesus Christ, man, the woman is crying. The fuck is wrong with you?*

"But it wasn't just about money," Jo continued, oblivious. "Jeremy and I were together a while. I didn't know what it was like to be me, on my own, anymore. I thought it might be good to get a fresh start somewhere, where I didn't know anybody. I wanted somewhere cheap... but also somewhere far. I don't know if I was being brave or just trying to get away from the people who looked at me with pity. But drunk-me thought we were brave, and that bitch chose Ashville. Aida and Trey gave me the money for movers, and I drove out here. Just me and Merry. God, I hope he's okay right now." She opened her eyes and met his gaze. "So that's the story. Here I am. In the middle of a fucking tornado, sitting in a library basement, with a—"

SLAM!

Jo screamed. Felix jumped and yelled, "Fuck!"

It sounded like the entire library, books and all, had collapsed on top of them. The ceiling trembled, though the walls were rock-steady. They were both frozen, waiting for the next sound and... holding each other tightly.

Jo's arms were wrapped around Felix's waist. Her grip was so strong it was a struggle to draw a full breath. Her face was buried in his chest, rapid breaths fluttering his shirt, glasses digging into his pec. Felix had somehow draped his long legs over hers. Her knees were poking the back of his thigh. His were flattening her boobs. He could feel the underwire of her bra against his kneecap. His upper body was folded over her protectively, one arm down her back and the other covering his own head and neck. He was breathing against her hair, practically tasting that sweet, fruity scent that cut right to the core of him. And, it appeared, he was clutching a handful of her thick, fleshy hip to draw her body even closer against his.

Fuck if it wasn't as soft and yielding as he'd imagined.

"Holy shit, holy shit, holy shit," Jo was saying, over and over.

Felix shushed her and said, "Radio."

"Sorry," she whispered.

They sat there, unmoving, clinging to one another, and listened. The touchdown had happened a couple of minutes ago, about a mile outside the town limits. It had lasted a mere forty-seven seconds. Felix's distraction was so effective they'd both completely missed it.

But the tornado warning wasn't lifted yet.

"There might be another one?" Jo wailed against his shirt.

"Sounds like it," he replied into her hair.

"Well. At least you smell good."

Felix's hand flexed, involuntarily, against her hip.

JO REALLY, REALLY didn't want to let go of Felix. He practically engulfed her, and she still wasn't close enough to him. Too many clothes in the way. Oh Jesus, was this that thing where people who were about to die got really horny all of a sudden? Some "we might not make it through the night, sweetheart, so let's make every moment count" bullshit?

That was the only rational explanation for why she'd blurted out how good he smelled, like cloves and coffee with a hint of vanilla sweetness. And for the way her pussy twitched when his large, warm hand tightened on her ass. Because Felix was fully grabbing her ass right now. And she did not care to stop him. She knew it was a great ass. That's why her "signature look," as her friend Kim called it, was high-waisted pants and cropped tees.

Just two people with great asses, holding each other in a dim basement, terrified of dying.

Two people who were friends. And colleagues. Fucking hell, they were at Felix's *workplace*. He'd been so considerate of her at White Hills last weekend. She owed him the same.

"I think I'm okay now." Because Jo was only human, she allowed her hands to slide along his taut waist as she released him. One of her fingers snagged on the fabric between his shirt buttons, and she heard his breath hitch. He disentangled from her quickly after that.

They sat on the floor, backs to the wall. Staring dead ahead, not looking at each other. Silently waiting for the all clear.

It came about ten minutes later. No more touchdowns were reported. The skies were clearing, the weatherman said, leaving only a few high, light gray clouds.

Felix got to his feet and offered Jo a hand up. She took it, but they both let go as soon as she was standing. She retrieved her phone from where she'd dropped it in a panic, relieved to see the screen wasn't cracked and everything worked fine.

"Shall we go see what that sound was?" Felix asked, running his fingers through his hair. Fingers that had just been on her ass.

Stop it, you animal.

Cautiously, they went upstairs.

In the middle of the children's area, they found the source of the noise that had sent them into each other's arms. The entire space was situated under a massive glass skylight, which had shattered when a tree branch ten feet long and two feet across landed on it. The branch had hit a bookshelf on the way down, toppling it and scattering books all over. Felix glanced back toward the stairs in the lobby.

"We were right underneath this," he whispered.

"Shit."

"I'm so glad that's all it was." He raked his hair again. "I-I thought the whole building had come down." Felix stared at the mess of branch, books, and glass, his eyes slightly unfocused.

"You okay?" Jo asked. He nodded distractedly. "Felix?"

He blinked his eyes back into focus and found her gaze. "I'm sorry."

She shook her head, stepping closer to him. "Don't be. This was fucking terrifying."

"I meant I'm sorry I, um..." He blushed and looked in the general direction of the floor. "I was overly familiar with you."

Jo hid a smile. She'd never heard a more polite term for feeling someone up. "Hey, I made you listen to my sad little moving-to-Kansas story, so maybe we both overstepped a bit tonight."

"You didn't—Jo, I shouldn't have—"

"It's all good, Felix, really," she interrupted. No way could she tell him she actually, kinda, really, really liked it. "If it makes you feel better, I accept your apology, but I've gotten a lot worse from guys I've liked a lot less. We were both scared. Please don't worry about it."

"All right," he said. "Thank you for understanding."

"No problem." She gestured broadly around the children's area. "What do we do about all of this?"

Felix stood a little straighter, falling back on his professionalism. He almost pulled it off, but Jo could detect the slight flutter in his voice as he took in the destruction. "Right. We have emergency protocols. I need to call Warren and the appropriate response team—likely that's the fire department. No injuries makes this simpler." He turned sharply to Jo. "You're not injured, are you?"

"I'm fine," she assured him, warmth spreading through her at his concern. "Anything I can do to help?"

"I can handle it. You should go home, make sure Merry is okay. And your car."

"Oh my God, Felix. What about Tito?"

His eyes went wide, and he scrambled for his phone. He didn't even turn off the flashlight first, just jabbed at the screen and pressed it to his ear. After only a few seconds, the jovial timbre of Tito's voice came over the tiny speaker.

"Tito, thank God," Felix said and continued in rapid-fire Spanish. He gave Jo a relieved nod, and she gave a thumbs-up in return.

She wandered back to the lobby and peered out the windows. If it weren't for the tree branches, roofing shingles, and other debris scattered around, it would have seemed like a perfectly normal Friday evening. The sky was as big and blue as could be. The sun hadn't even set yet. Strange. It had felt like the middle of the night somehow, huddled underground with Felix, safe in his embrace.

Jo shook her head at her own flight of fancy and went behind the front desk. Her books, dice, and pencils had scattered when she'd dropped her tote, so she crouched to clean up. It wasn't long before Felix joined her, no longer on the phone. He pulled a binder out of a drawer and, with trembling hands, flipped to a tab in the middle. He paused when he realized Jo was watching him.

"I'm going to run home to check on Merry," she said. "If he's not too traumatized, I'll come back and help out."

"You shouldn't clog up the roads," he said in a clipped, distracted tone. "It's not safe. There could be downed trees or power lines, and emergency vehicles need to get through. It would be best if you went home and stayed there."

She dropped her gaze, feeling stupid for suggesting it. Of course it wasn't safe to be on the roads right now. "I'm sorry," she said meekly. "I'm only trying to help."

Felix scrubbed his hands over his face, his stubble rasping against his palms. "No, *I'm* sorry, Jo. I don't mean to be rude. I appreciate the offer, but I'm just going to be waiting for other people to show up. There's not a lot for you to do."

He had a point there too, but he was clearly still rattled by what had happened. She didn't want to leave him alone like this. "I can keep you company?" she offered.

Taking a step toward her, he put his hands in his pockets. "I'd rather you get home safe tonight."

Jo moved closer still. She crossed her arms over her chest, the weight pressing down her boobs reminding her of where Felix's knees had been. "You're shaken up, Felix. Has it occurred to you that maybe I want you to get home safe too?"

From the way his face went slack, Jo was afraid she knew the answer. He had been so caring and patient with her when she began to panic downstairs. Did he really have no one who showed him that kind of concern? Her heart ached for him. Felix deserved someone who made him feel as safe and secure and seen as he made others feel. As he made *her* feel.

He leaned heavily on the edge of the desk and sighed. "How about this? You go check on Merry. Text me when you make it home safely. I'll tell you what's going on here and how I'm doing. Once Warren arrives, I should be able to pull myself together."

"Always the professional," Jo murmured.

Felix gave a sheepish shrug. "If things are really bad, or if I need something, I'll let you know."

"I agree to your terms," she said, "with an addendum of my own."

He broke into a small smile. "I'm listening."

"Either way, whether I come back or not, you text me when you get home tonight too. No matter how late it is."

"Deal."

They shook on it.

Jo

> I'm home. Car is fine and roads weren't too bad. A bunch of people were out clearing debris and stuff already. Merry is fine, the dingus. Probably slept through the whole thing.

Felix

> Glad to hear it. Warren just walked in. More soon.

> Waiting for the fire department to arrive. We're low priority because no injuries.

Jo

> The deal was you also tell me how you're doing.

> Don't make me drive over there.

I hear the roads are unsafe.

Felix

Sorry for the delay. Deputies arrived to take a report for insurance and they needed my statement. They might want yours as well. I gave them your name as the other witness but not your contact info.

I'm better. Warren took charge as soon as he got here, so I'm following his lead.

Jo

Good. I'm here if you need me.

Felix

Thank you.

Jo

I can also send cat pics.

Felix

I just got home. I'll tell you the whole story when I see you, but things went smoothly. Warren assured me everything will be fixed well before the MnM launch night.

Always yes to cat pics.

I'm getting some sleep. See you next Friday, if not sooner.

Jo

Always???

No take backs

Get ready for me to unleash hell upon your data plan

Not tonight, I'm almost asleep over here too

But soon

Felix

Go to sleep Jo

Jo

Soooooooooon

10

JO WAS GREETED the next morning by bright blue skies and fluffy white clouds. As if nothing at all had happened the night before. As if nothing had changed.

That was some bullshit. Everything had changed. Jo didn't fully realize it until now, but her dreams had made it pretty damn clear. She wanted Felix. Not just to ogle or to play MnM with or to have a moon-eyed crush on. She wanted to be with him.

She had dreamt of it—the two of them entangled together on the floor of the library basement. Instead of letting go of each other and staring awkwardly into the dark, in her mind they'd looked up at each other slowly. Felix had dipped his head closer to hers. She had kissed him, tasted cloves and coffee, and then he'd pulled her into his lap. Dream logic had kicked in and they were suddenly naked, Jo riding Felix's cock until he screamed her name, and she came so hard she woke up panting.

She'd gotten a glass of water and gone back to sleep, and this time she had dreamt of him holding her, soothing her fears with calm words, calling her something sweet in Spanish. She couldn't remember the word he'd used, but she knew it had an ñ sound that her unconscious mind had repeated back to her over and over in his accented baritone. His solid warmth and his strong arms had surrounded her. His tender words had known exactly what she needed to hear. His dark eyes had gazed down at her protectively. And she had felt at home.

So when the morning came, and Merry yowled in her face for breakfast, Jo knew.

Felix.

She wanted Felix.

The knowing thrummed through her entire body and settled as a throb between her legs. Jo rolled onto her back, sending Merry leaping to the floor. Her hand snaked its way down her stomach and tucked under her pajama pants. She bent one knee out to the side and let her eyes fall closed as she skimmed her fingers over her panties. She gasped from that light touch and urgently needed more, more, more.

Her vibrator was in easy reach on the nightstand next to her, but she used her fingers today, imagining that they were Felix's. What would a boxer's hand feel like? Would he be quick and dexterous? Or slow and gentle but *strong*? Would he pound into her with a roughness and ferocity that left her whimpering and weak?

Oh God, oh *Christ*, how she wanted to find out.

Jo circled her fingers on her clit faster and faster, arching her back off the bed. She ran her other hand over the tattoo on her chest just below her shoulder, trailed it lower, and played with her nipple over her tank top until it was a firm peak. She cried out Felix's name as she pinched it between her thumb and forefinger. His large hand would engulf her entire breast, wouldn't it? All her curves were in her hips, so he could probably palm her tits and enclose them completely.

"Yes, Felix," she whispered to no one. "Touch me."

She slipped her ring finger alongside the other two and within seconds she was coming, harder than she had in her sleep, harder than Jeremy had ever made her come. Jo buried that thought as soon as it surfaced, refusing to let her ex intrude on this moment. She said Felix's name again to solidify him in her mind. Behind her closed eyes, she saw him smile down at her, reveling in her pleasure. She smiled back.

TRAILING WARREN AND his contractor friend, Jimmy, Felix tramped over the plastic sheeting that now covered the entire children's area of the library. That had been Jimmy's idea; he'd had the sheeting in his truck and suggested they protect the area from the elements until a new skylight could be installed. As they made their way to the lobby, Warren ribbed Jimmy about the price of the quote. Jimmy quipped back, "That's what insurance is for." Over the two old friends bickering, Felix caught the sound of another voice, one he would know anywhere.

"You didn't tell me that it was a total space opera," said Jo.

"I didn't know that was a selling point with you!" came Leni's reply.

From the front desk, they both glanced toward the men entering the lobby. Leni smiled crookedly and turned back to Jo, who was holding a hardcover in her hands, her gaze locked on Felix's.

"Thanks again, Jimmy," Warren said. "We'll see you and your guys next weekend. Really appreciate you comin' out over the holiday."

"You bet, Warren. Happy to do our part."

They shook hands, and Felix forced himself to look away from

Jo to do the same. With a polite nod toward the women, Jimmy took his leave.

"Please tell me this author has more books," Jo said to Leni.

"Oh, totally," Leni said, typing on her computer. "You're cool with gay stuff, then, right? She's got this whole sapphic series set on Jupiter. *Red Storm* is the first one. Let me see if it's in right now."

Jo replied, "I can check. I was going to browse a bit anyway."

"We're only open for hold pickups right now, ma'am," said Warren. "We had an incident in the storm."

"Warren, this is Jo Rainier," Felix cut in. "She's the volunteer who was with me last night when it happened. Jo, our director R—Warren Riggs."

She stifled a laugh and waved. "Nice to meet you. Sorry, I should have guessed browsing would be off limits."

"It's here," Leni interjected before Warren could respond. Her blue-tipped hair bounced in its ponytail as she popped up onto her toes. "Put it on hold online so I can go get it for you."

Jo laughed and got out her phone.

Warren gestured for Felix to follow him around the desk, where the books that had been knocked off the shelves and smashed by the tree branch were piled into a returns bin. Most were salvageable, but some were beyond repair. Since Emma was holed up in her office, furiously rescheduling the week's children's events, Warren directed Felix to catalog the damaged books in a spreadsheet so that replacements could be purchased.

Warren returned to his office, then, and Leni headed off to retrieve Jo's book, leaving the two of them alone in the lobby. As Felix got to work, Jo sidled over to his end of the desk.

"Hi."

His heart skipped a beat. "Hi there."

She smiled, shyly ducking her head, and his heart stopped skipping and did a full-on cartwheel.

"What happened after I left last night?" she asked.

Felix explained the whole story—from Warren's arrival to the firefighters clearing the debris to the three hours spent emptying the children's area bookshelves in case of rain. Somewhere in the middle of all that, Leni returned and checked *Red Storm* out to Jo.

"Next weekend, over Memorial Day," Felix concluded, "the contractor who was just here is going to do the repairs so we can be fully open in time for summer events to start."

Jo tilted her head. "Does that mean the library will be closed next weekend?"

"We'd be closed Sunday and Monday anyway, but yes. We'll close Saturday too."

She opened her mouth and took a breath in, then hesitated. Felix gave her a questioning look over a bent copy of *Charlotte's Web*.

"So... you're free?" she said cautiously, tapping her fingers on the plastic covering her book. "Are you working Friday?"

Damn, she was cute when she got flustered. Her cheeks turned the most delicious shade of pink, like a juicy summer peach. He wanted to bite them.

"Out with it, Jo," he said with a grin.

The words tumbled out of her. "There's a convention next weekend for MnM, and I thought you might want to come and see what it's like to play a real game. If you're free. But if you have plans for the long weekend already that's okay. I was going to ask you last night, but, well. Tornado."

"MnM has conventions?"

"That's your takeaway from this?" Leni muttered, not looking up from her computer screen.

Felix ignored her. "That sounds fun. Is it in Wichita?"

"Um, no, that's the thing," Jo said, gripping her book tightly. "It's in Indianapolis."

Felix's body got very warm. Was she inviting him to a weekend away? He liked the sound of that. No. No, of course not. This was a work event. She was probably nervous because of whatever it was in her past that made her a little shy about putting herself out there. Like the way she shrank back at Stan's after getting "too" silly or "too" nerdy. A convention for Monsters and Mythology certainly sounded supremely nerdy.

Jo was still talking. "I know it's far, but it's drivable in a day. I'm already going and meeting up with my friends from California, so I can drive us. It's no problem. I looked it up, and there are still tickets and hotel rooms available. I'm going up Friday and coming back Monday."

A road trip. Convention tickets. A hotel room over a holiday weekend. None of that sounded cheap. Ever since he'd learned about the possibility of budget cuts, Felix had been as frugal as possible. His only indulgence in the last two-plus weeks was that drink with Jo. But he had some savings that weren't reserved for Tito in case of medical emergencies. And the library did have a modest budget for travel. Might as well use it while they had it, if he could get Warren to sign off on it. He could manage.

Besides, how could he say no, with Jo looking at him like that, her eyes round and expectant?

"Okay," he said.

"Really?"

"Yes, it would be good to see how MnM works on a larger scale. Maybe get some ideas for events here."

"Yeah, that's what I was thinking," Jo said, nodding and breaking into a smile. "Okay, great. Um. Okay. I'll text you to figure out the details."

"Perfect," Felix said, fighting a dopey grin that kept trying to make itself known. "Will you also send me links to book the hotel and ticket?"

"Sure, absolutely." Jo started to back away. "Okay. This is great. But you're busy. I'll leave you alone. Bye, Felix. Bye, Leni!" She vanished out the door.

Leni craned her neck toward the hall leading to Warren's office. She tapped her toes rapidly on the floor, using them to spin her chair to face Felix. She dropped her chin and raised her eyebrows. "What the hell was that?"

"What was what?" Felix asked, more high-pitched than he'd intended.

"Did your voice just crack?" Leni cried. "Oh my gods, you're so into her."

"Leni, please stop," he said, darting his eyes toward Warren's office.

"Sorry, that's fair," she said quietly. She rolled her chair closer and leaned in to whisper, "But just in case you're really dense, hun? She's obviously into you too."

Felix shook his head and focused on his spreadsheet, trying and failing to ignore the way his pulse pounded through his body.

Jo

So I'm dumb and forgot about this when I saw you this morning, but I still want to do a sample game with you. Especially if you're sure about coming to Indi-Con. Aida says it's like drinking from the firehose of MnM and she's not wrong! Maybe we could do that this week? Before we leave on Friday?

Felix

How about Tuesday at 6:30pm?

Jo

Works for me.

Can we use the library?

Felix

It's a bit cold on the main floor at night, but if you're comfortable in one of the meeting rooms downstairs, we can do that.

Jo

I'll be there. Here are the links for tickets and hotel. Get a Sat/Sun pass, since we're driving all day Fri and Mon.

Felix

Thanks. Can't wait.

Jo

> And here's Merry being a dingus.
> Par for the course for him, really.

Felix

> His tummy looks very soft.

Jo

> It's the softest

THAT TUESDAY, FELIX watched Jo unpack books and papers from her tote bag, his leg bouncing beneath the table. He was anxious to learn and do well at this sample game. She would be bringing him to a convention with all her friends from home, and he didn't want to embarrass himself, or her, in front of them.

He'd never been the kind of person, even as a kid, who imagined himself fighting dragons or being a superhero. He never wished to visit the Shire or travel through time and space. Not that he didn't have an imagination—he was very good at imagining certain things, particularly where Jo was involved. He simply didn't feel the need to escape into a fantasy world when the real world was more deserving of his attention.

But he was going to try. For Jo, for his job, for Tito, and for himself. Maybe he would fall in love with MnM; he'd never know if he didn't try.

Jo handed him a small bag of bright yellow dice and a piece of paper. The paper looked something like a blank spreadsheet, a log with many rows and several columns labeled along the top.

"What's this?" he asked.

"That's your logsheet for SWOP."

"Swap?"

"S-W-O-P. Sibylline Wastes Organized Play," she explained. "It's the official ruleset for public MnM events. Cons always follow SWOP rules and use SWOP adventures to keep things standardized. The logsheet is for tracking your level, gold, and magical equipment." With a flourish of her hand, she continued, "And since I happen to be a SWOP-certified GM, we can use this game to make Graxalos level two before Indi-Con. That way I can show you how leveling up works, and you'll have more game mechanics to try out at the con."

"I think I got all of that," he said.

"I'm also going to play my warlock, Veena, in addition to GMing. That's technically not allowed, but I wanted to give you another character to interact with and let you see how spellcasting works. Don't tell the SWOP police."

Felix watched her rearrange her papers, muttering to herself, and felt a sense of awe wash over him. "Thank you, Jo. You originally only gave me an hour a week, and this has become a lot more. I hope you know that I appreciate it."

She scoffed, barely glancing up. "I'm pretty sure Friday doesn't count. Because, you know. *There was a tornado.*"

He shook his head but let a bemused smile settle on his lips. Someday. Someday she'd accept a compliment from him at face value.

"Ready?" The glee in her voice was the cutest thing Felix had ever heard.

"As I'll ever be."

With a deep breath, she began. "Graxalos, you and your friend Veena are walking down the street. You two have been friends for a while. She's a merfolk warlock devoted to a powerful fey creature of the Undersea. The two of you have been doing odd jobs around town. The townsfolk know you to be reliable and strong, with abilities well above the average person. You're the muscle, and she's the magic."

Felix grinned. Not totally swept up in the story yet, but he could picture the scene Jo painted with words. A small town, not unlike Ashville. A main thoroughfare with small shops on either side. A reptilian biped like the dragonkin illustrated in *Core Rules* walking alongside a creature that resembled Ariel from *The Little Mermaid* (the version with legs).

"As you two are walking," she continued, "you see someone up ahead. You recognize him as Chauncey. He owns the cattle farm at the edge of town."

An image of Tito, the cattle rancher that Felix knew best, came to mind.

"He spots the two of you," Jo continued, "and runs over. 'Grax! Veena! You gotta help me!'"

He burst out laughing. Jo had suddenly become a completely different person, flailing her arms and speaking in a horrible Southern accent. She gave Felix a smile and kept going. In Chauncey's voice, she told a melodramatic story of a cattle theft the night before. Speaking as Grax but using own voice, Felix offered to help find the thieves. Jo's demeanor changed again as Veena agreed. Her voice went high and girlish, and her eyes widened like an ingenue from a classic Hollywood movie.

Felix was floored by how quickly she could switch from narrator to Chauncey to Veena and back again. How the fuck was *he* supposed to be a GM? He couldn't do character voices. He wasn't an actor. Hell, he could barely imagine the story without relying on things from real life.

Despite his doubts, he found himself relaxing into the game the longer they played. Jo made it easy, cracking jokes and teasing him as Veena as if she and Graxalos were old friends. Together, the two characters tracked the stolen herd to a hideout in the woods. Grax kicked in the back door on a room full of cattle rustlers, and a fight immediately broke out.

They rolled for initiative to determine the turn order. On Felix's turn, he had Grax punch one of the thieves who had attacked first and injured Veena. He rolled his yellow d20, and Jo declared it was high enough to hit.

"Go ahead and roll damage," she said. "That's a d6 plus your strength bonus."

Felix rolled and did some quick mental math. "Nine."

"Awesome!" Jo crossed out a line in a notebook where she was tracking combat. "That's a solid hit—enough to take him down. Do you want to describe the attack?"

Fuck it. He was invested now. Might as well go all out.

He got to his feet, describing and acting out a one-two punch: left jab into right cross. He watched Jo's eyes travel down and back up his body. She bit her lip.

Let her look, came an urge from deep in his gut. *Let her like what she sees.*

JO'S GROUP TEXT with her California friends completely blew up over the next few days. One person (usually Max) would send a random text that said "INDI-CON" with a long string of exclamation points, and everyone else would reply with whichever excited gif suited their mood. Then there were the vital discussions about which games they'd signed up for, their dinner reservation for Friday night, and, of course, Felix. Only Aida (and probably Trey, because those two shared *everything*) knew about her feelings for him, but Jo gave everyone a rundown of her volunteering and a heads-up that he was tagging along.

Everyone said all the right things about being excited to meet him, but as the day of the road trip approached, Jo couldn't stop her growing worry. Sure, Felix had seemed to enjoy their sample game once he'd gotten into the swing of things, but Indi-Con was different. She was about to throw him headfirst into two straight days of gaming, plus make him meet her closest friends all at once. What if it was too much? What if they walked into the convention center and he immediately regretted coming? What if this whole thing was her worst idea ever?

Jo did her best to keep those thoughts at bay by busying herself with preparations for the trip. On Wednesday, she went through her MnM backpack and character sheets to make sure she had everything she needed for her games. On Thursday, she treated herself to a manicure and dropped off her spare key with Vanessa so she could catsit for Merry. Then, she packed.

Jo took packing very seriously. First, her usual con attire: her softest leggings, nerdy T-shirts she'd cut into crop tops, comfy shoes and socks, and her trusty jean jacket. Into a second bag went her pajamas, hair dryer, curling iron, makeup, toiletries, emergency tampons, and extra underwear. And a book. Just in case. A few other necessities—her MnM backpack of course, plus two tote bags full of car snacks, and a flat of water bottles—and she was ready to go.

She loaded everything into her trunk to make sure there was room for whatever Felix was bringing. As long as he packed lighter than she did, they'd be good. If he didn't? God help them.

Finally, she cuddled in bed with Merry until the pre-con jitters settled. She spent the night dreaming of rolling dice, hugging Aida, and adventuring alongside a dragonkin fighter with a wicked right cross.

When she pulled up to Felix's address the next morning, he was waiting for her. A rush of relief hit her that he hadn't backed out at the last minute. He was even smiling, as if he were happy to see her. She smiled back, waving through the windshield.

His house was single story, with pale yellow siding, a bright green door, and a few stone steps leading to a fenced-in porch. A porch where Felix was standing in charcoal lounge pants, a plain black T-shirt, and his Rutgers hoodie with a backpack over one shoulder and a duffel bag over the other. He held two drink tumblers in his hands. His hair was damp, his jaw unshaven.

"Jesus Christ, dude," she murmured to herself as he jogged over. She popped open the hatchback and heard his high-pitched chuckle as he tossed in his bags.

"Think you brought enough stuff?" he teased as he settled in next to her, juggling the tumblers. Several additional swear words flew through Jo's mind as the heady scent of a freshly showered Felix hit her square in the face.

"Good morning to you too," she replied with an ease she hoped hid her sudden horniness. "Did you bring coffee?"

"I should've asked how you take yours," he said, "but by the time I realized that, I figured you'd already be driving."

"You've taken up your hero's calling today, my friend. I'll drink anything that's not plain, unsweetened black," she said.

"So regular con leche or vanilla?" he said, holding up the tumblers. "Café con leche is kind of like a strong latte."

"Regular."

"Thank God. This one's yours." He indicated the red tumbler with gold polka dots and set it in the cupholder for her. He held onto a yellow one covered in bees and daisies and put his seatbelt on.

"Last chance to back out," Jo said, resting her palm on the gearshift. Her heart clenched with anticipation.

"No way," he replied with a laugh. The click of his seatbelt in its buckle punctuated his statement. "I'm game if you are."

"Was that a pun?"

"Yes."

Her confidence renewed, Jo reversed out of the driveway and eased onto the street. Her phone chirped robotic directions to I-35 North.

"I like your place," she commented as they pulled away from it.

"It's Tito's house," he said. "And these mugs were Lita's. She adored her café. Taught me how to make con leche, americano, cortado, just about every way there is to drink coffee in Spain, plus some of her own concoctions."

Jo lifted her coffee in toast. "To Lita. I'm honored to partake of her legacy." She took a sip and caught Felix's gaze momentarily when she put the tumbler back in the cupholder. What she glimpsed there was enough to make sparks flash like lightning all over her skin. She shivered and quickly bumped up the heat so Felix would think she was cold.

"First of all, that's delicious," she said. "And second of all, can I ask you a question?"

"Sure," he said. He pulled sunglasses out of his hoodie pocket and slid them on. Jo fought to keep her eyes on the road.

"Are your parents in the picture?"

"How do you mean?"

"You've never talked about them, and when Tito needed somebody last year, it was you who showed up. I wondered if maybe your parents weren't part of your life." Suddenly worried she was overstepping, she added, "Sorry, is that too personal?"

"No, it's fine," he said evenly. "I have a decent enough relationship with my parents. A few years ago, they retired to Spain, so I don't see them much. They did come out here when Lita was sick, but they went back shortly after the funeral. They talked about taking Tito back to Spain with them, but I'd already decided to stay here. He would never leave the place where his wife is buried anyway."

"I hope I find that someday. That kind of love," Jo breathed, barely aware of what she was saying until the words were already out.

Felix turned toward her, his expression inscrutable behind his sunglasses. After a moment, he said, "Me too."

They fell quiet while Jo merged onto the highway.

"Are both your parents Spanish?" she asked, hoping to steer the conversation somewhere a little less intense.

"Just my dad," Felix said. "Tito and Lita came to the U.S. in their twenties, when she was pregnant with him. I don't know the details, but apparently it was a rough childbirth, and she almost didn't make it. They never tried for any more kids after that. Mom doesn't speak a word of Spanish, but she always thought Spain was so romantic. She and Dad went to Barcelona on their honeymoon, and she's the one who convinced him to retire there."

He paused for a long sip and said, "Your turn. You've never talked about your parents either. Or any siblings. I have none, by the way."

Jo reached for her coffee and bumped into Felix's elbow where it rested on the console between them. She muttered an apology and hoped he didn't notice her blushing. "My parents divorced when I was in high school. My mom moved to NorCal once we were all in college, and my dad is still in Garden Grove, where we grew up in the shadow of Disneyland. I'm the middle child, between two brothers."

"Are they also named after Dolly Parton hits? Let me guess: 'Nine-to-Five' and 'I-Will-Always-Love-You'?"

Jo tossed a look his direction. "You know she has a song called 'Joshua,' right?"

"Damn it," he cried, smacking his palm on his knee. "That would have been much more clever."

She reached over and patted his shoulder. Even through the thick hoodie, she could feel its firmness. "I forgive you. You haven't finished your coffee yet."

He sighed and took a long gulp. His loud swallows and the smack of his lips were probably meant to be funny, but each sound his mouth made sent a shockwave of desire rocketing through Jo's body. She bit down, hard, on the inside of her cheek. She could still smell the cloves-and-sweet-coffee scent of him and his damn vanilla café con leche. How adorable was it that Felix liked vanilla in his coffee?

Jesus fuck. This road trip was *definitely* her worst idea ever, but not for the reason she'd feared all week. Being beside Felix was like sitting too close to a fire. She was going to combust before the nine-and-a-half-hour drive was over. Maybe even before the first hour was up. At least she would go surrounded by pretty country— all these amber waves of grain, waist-high prairie grasses, and fields of sunflowers as far as the eye could see.

"I didn't expect Kansas to be so beautiful," she said. Hopefully Felix didn't mind the sudden change of subject, but she needed to say *something* to distract herself.

"Beautiful?" he asked.

"Yeah, look how green it is!" She gestured through the windshield. "All this rain you get—back home, everything turns brown in the summer. And the smog, God. The air out here is so clean you can see forever."

Felix quieted, turning away from her to look out the passenger window.

"You don't think it's pretty?" she asked.

"It's not that," he said softly, almost wistfully. "I suppose I just haven't really thought much about it since moving back to the Midwest."

"I guess if you grow up with it, you get used to it."

"Maybe," he replied. He turned back to her, and she stole a glance to see a gentle smile on his face. "But it's nice to see it through your eyes."

Jo's whole body felt even hotter. She turned the heater back down and checked the clock on the dashboard. Only nine hours and thirteen minutes to go, not including lunch, gas, and pee breaks. She was never going to make it to Indianapolis alive.

FELIX TOOK A minute to breathe in the rest stop men's room, which, given his surroundings, was not the smartest decision. They were stopped in Missouri, between Columbia, where they'd gotten lunch, and St. Louis. Four-and-a-half hours down, five to go. He was losing his mind. He was crawling out of his skin.

The night before, lying in bed at two in the morning, wide awake and horny as fuck, he'd made a decision. He was tired of settling for his hand and his imagination in the shower. Tired of making excuses about professionalism. Tired of pretending he didn't want Jo. Tired of pretending he didn't see the way she wanted him too. She'd always thought he was hot. That much had been obvious from their first Friday after hours in the library. Even without the text from Aida he wasn't supposed to see, he would have known. Jo wasn't exactly subtle about it.

But there was more to it now. They were friends, and they liked each other, and they *wanted* each other.

So he'd decided: he wasn't going to hold himself back anymore. He wouldn't admit his feelings right away. On the off chance he was misreading her, he wouldn't risk making things awkward when they were about to spend four straight days together. But he was done pretending. By the time she dropped him off at home on Monday night, she was going to know exactly how he felt about her.

He'd finally been able to sleep after that and had woken up in the morning resolved to be as kind and caring and charming and gentle as possible. Everything he wanted to be for her. Everything she deserved. He just hadn't expected that the moment he sat down in the car beside her, his insides would turn into jelly, and he'd regret making the comfortable choice to wear sweatpants.

He stepped out of the men's room into the blazing afternoon sun. Jo was standing next to her car, her legs wide, rocking side to side to stretch out her hips.

"Fuck everything," he mumbled, hypnotized by the sway of her teardrop-shaped body. No, not a teardrop—that was much too sad an image for Jo. She was a dew drop hanging off the point of a leaf on a damp morning. A bead of sweat running down heated skin. He wanted to stick out his tongue and drink her down. To take all that she was inside of him and finally, finally quench his thirst. To drown in the flood of her magnificence.

Apparently, Tito wasn't the only poet in the family.

Jo grinned at him, oblivious to the storm raging inside him, the thunder roaring in his ears. "Ready?"

"Would you like me to drive for a while?" he asked. "I'd be happy to give you a break if you don't mind me driving your car."

"Seriously? That would be amazing. Think fast!" She tossed her keys at him, and he caught them easily. She ran around to the passenger side and dove for the door, as if he might change his mind if she didn't get there first. This woman was going to destroy him.

Fuck, she already had.

Back on the highway, he said, "All right, we've talked about family, the beauty of the Midwest, childhood vacations, minor high school traumas, and your California friends. What's next?"

"Actually, do you mind if we put some music on?"

"Sure," he replied. "Here. Use my phone to save your battery for the GPS." Felix dug his phone out of his pocket and unlocked it with his thumbprint. He opened his music app before handing it to Jo. Their fingers brushed as she took it, and he didn't hurry to pull away. "Pick whatever you want."

She quietly connected his phone to the car speakers and scrolled through the app. He tried to keep his eyes forward, but her nails were painted a distractingly pretty kelly green with orange d20 shapes on her ring fingers. Suddenly, she gasped and tapped something. Before he could ask, a bass-y synth hit sounded, followed by an electronic "whoop." He'd know that intro anywhere.

"'Aughts workout mix'?" Jo said, holding up his phone as the lyrics to "Circus" kicked in. She'd found his boxing playlist.

"Don't you dare make fun of me," he said, completely deadpan. "Britney is a legend."

"Nobody is arguing that," she laughed. "It was just unexpected. Are you a 'put on a show kind of girl'?"

Felix gave her his most flirtatious smirk. He slid his sunglasses down his nose and winked. "When the mood strikes."

Her jaw slackened, and her cheeks went bright pink. Felix pushed his sunglasses up as he turned back to the road. The pre-chorus kicked in, and he belted it out. Jo laughed again, that loud sound he loved so much, and joined him. They sang every word together. As soon as the song ended, the next one kicked in. A guitar riff solo started the track, then violins joined in, then drums and synth trilling up and down the scale.

"Wait, this is ABBA," Jo said. "It's from the seventies. Why is this on here?"

"What does it say in parentheses?" Felix asked.

Jo tapped the screen to wake it up. "'A Man After Midnight'?"

"The other parentheses."

"'Original Motion Picture Soundtrack,'" she read.

"From *Mamma Mia*."

"That's not in the parentheses, but yeah."

"Which came out in 2008," he explained in a tone that would accept no argument. "It counts."

"Fucking librarians," she scoffed. "Got an answer for everything."

"Be quiet and sing."

She opened her mouth to argue with that logic, but Felix was already singing the chorus.

They passed the afternoon eating junk food and singing along to Lady Gaga, Jimmy Eat World, Flo Rida, and, of course, more Britney. Felix drove them through St. Louis, across Illinois, and over the state line into Indiana. Jo offered to take over for the last leg into Indianapolis, and he accepted. Twenty minutes past seven o'clock, she pulled up to the Hotel Paragon, a tall building across the street from a convention center boasting giant green and orange "Indi-Con" banners.

"Your nails match," Felix said.

Jo grinned. "You noticed?"

"Of course."

They parked in the underground garage, stretched their legs and backs, and loaded themselves up with their weekend luggage. Jo told him to leave the water bottles where they were. She'd grab some the next day to pass around so people didn't have to pay five bucks a bottle from the convention center vendors. Felix didn't quite have words for how much he admired that thoughtfulness of hers.

The lobby of the Hotel Paragon was packed with nerds. As he and Jo stood in line to check into their rooms, he cast his eyes around to take it all in. MnM T-shirts everywhere. Clusters of people in full costume as elves, wizards, red-skinned demonkin, and blue-finned merfolk. Folks of every race and gender and age and body type and hair color, united by their love of Monsters and Mythology. What was it Aida had said? *Drinking from the firehose of MnM.* That seemed pretty damn accurate. He only understood about a third of the conversations happening around him with all the abbreviations and jargon. He was in way over his head.

Jo is here, he told himself to calm the jitters in his stomach. *She'll help me. It'll be fine.*

"Next, please," said the woman behind the front desk. Jo moved aside to wait for him, holding her room key booklet between her fingers.

"Checking in. Felix Navarro," he said as he approached. He set down his duffel and pulled out his wallet for his credit card.

"JO!"

Two people were running in their direction. Felix recognized them from Jo's descriptions in the car. Kim Capell, a plus-sized white woman with alabaster skin, blue eyes, and freckles, was wearing her signature style of fifties vintage. From the curled jet-black hair tied up with a red kerchief to the wide-necked white top and red cigarette pants, she was head-to-toe rockabilly. Alongside her was a short, slim white man with piercing emerald-green eyes. Max Kelly, most likely, judging by the baggy jeans, shaggy teal hair, and *Super Mario Bros.* T-shirt. According to Jo, Max had never been seen by a member of their group in anything other than a video game shirt.

Jo squealed and dropped her bags to hug them both at the same time. Kim and Jo started chattering a mile a minute while Max silently grinned.

"Sir?" said the woman at the desk. "I'm sorry, could you please spell your last name for me?"

Felix did so, and the woman clicked her tongue. "That's what I have here. I'm not finding your reservation, I'm afraid. Could it be under a different name?"

"No, just me," he said.

"Do you have your confirmation number? I'll try that," she said. "It should have been emailed to you."

Felix searched for the hotel name in his email but didn't find anything. *Strange.* He searched again in the trash in case he accidentally deleted it, but there was nothing. He moved aside and told the woman he needed a moment to find it, gesturing to the person behind him in line to come forward.

"Is everything okay?" Jo asked.

"They can't find my reservation, and I don't have a confirmation email," he said, scrolling through his inbox carefully. He checked his work email and his credit card app to see if there was any evidence of his booking there. Nothing. He pushed a hand through his hair. "It must not have gone through when I booked it."

He returned to the desk when the woman was free, explained the situation, and asked if he could book a room now. She gave him a pleasant, dead-eyed smile and a speech she'd probably delivered a hundred times today. "I'm terribly sorry, sir, but we're booked up. I have vacancies starting Sunday night, but nothing for tonight or tomorrow."

Felix puffed out a breath. "I understand. Completely my fault. Thank you for your help. I'll try another hotel."

"Good luck," she singsonged as Felix returned to Jo and her friends.

"I need to try a different hotel. They're booked," he told them.

"Uh, everywhere's booked, dude," Max said. "It's fucking INDI-CON!" A few people near them cheered and huzzahed.

"I gathered," Felix said flatly.

"You could... stay with me?" Jo said, barely audible.

Felix went weak at the knees. He couldn't. Could he? He shouldn't. But what other choice did he have? He should try the other hotels first, at least. He should refuse. Definitely. Refusing was the gentlemanly thing to do.

But the look in Jo's pale brown eyes was... hopeful, almost pleading.

Fuck being a gentleman.

"Are you sure, Jo?" he asked. Gentleman or (decidedly) not, he had to be certain the offer was genuine. He watched her closely for any sign of apprehension. "You're comfortable with that?"

Without so much as a blink, Jo's gaze sharpened. She pulled one of the keycards from her little booklet and held it out to him like a precious offering. "Yes."

He reached out with both hands, enclosing them around her fingers and letting her release the key to him. He withdrew with deliberate gentleness and watched her breath catch in her chest. He inched half a step closer to her.

"You guys are joining us for dinner, right?" Max blurted.

Felix looked past Jo. Max was distracted by something on his phone, but Kim was watching closely, her wide eyes darting back and forth between them, wearing an expression that plainly said, *Holy shit, are these two fucking?*

Jo spun to face her friends as if nothing had happened. "Yup! We'll take our stuff upstairs and meet you back here in a few."

"Jo," Felix said. "I'm pretty tired. Mind if I take a raincheck on dinner?"

The disappointment on her face was a knife between his ribs.

"If that's what you want."

"I'll meet everyone tomorrow, I promise," he said quietly. "Go catch up with your friends. I'll take your bags upstairs for you."

He stooped to gather everything; he could manage it all in one trip if he planned it right.

"Okay," Jo said. "It's room eight-thirteen. I'll text you when I'm headed back."

"I'll see you in a bit." He raised his voice to call, "Kim, Max, good to meet you. I'll see you all tomorrow. Have fun at dinner."

Her eyes burned into his back all the way to the elevator. As the doors closed between them, those eyes, wide and anguished, were the last thing he saw.

"Fuck, fuck, fuck." Felix squeezed his own eyes shut so he wouldn't have to look at himself in the mirrored walls that surrounded him. "I'm sorry, Jo."

12

"ARE YOU TWO fucking?" Kim asked the second the elevator doors shut.

Jo whirled around, the blunt question distracting her from her quickly spiraling thoughts.

Max peeked up from the game on his phone and shook his faded teal hair out of his eyes. "Who's fucking?"

"Jo and that guy," Kim said, smacking him on the arm. "Did you see the way they looked at each other?"

"Um, no?"

"We're not—!" Jo cried, then remembered she was in public. She lowered her voice. "We're not fucking."

"But you want to be, right?" Kim said, looping her arm through Jo's and pulling her toward the front doors.

"I... maybe?" she admitted.

Max trailed behind them, staring at his game.

"Oooooo, you're blushing," Kim said. "Come on, I need to see everyone's faces when they find out."

"No, please don't!" Jo cried. "Felix and I are friends. I don't want to make him uncomfortable around everyone."

Oh God, was *that* why he bailed on dinner? Here she was thinking that Indi-Con had already freaked him out. That he would hole
up in the hotel room all weekend and say "fuck it" to the con, to
MnM, to everything. But maybe that wasn't it at all. Maybe he
took one look at Kim's face and realized he couldn't handle all of
Jo's friends jumping to the same conclusion she had. Just because
he'd been a little flirty today didn't mean he wanted, or deserved,
to be paraded around for their inspection.

Jo glanced back toward the elevator, wondering if she should
follow him and make sure things weren't going to be weird now.
Or would that make it worse, to admit to what Kim saw between
them? Probably best to give him his space. She could play along
with his story that he was tired. She was used to making excuses
for the man in her life.

But first, she had to deal with the person currently dragging
her across the lobby. Jo planted her feet and forced them to a stop.
"Kim, listen. There's a reason I told the group I was bringing a
friend that I'm volunteering with. I'm not ready for everyone to
know. Hell, I'm not even sure *I* know what just happened between
us. Please, for now, keep this to yourself."

"What's going on?" Max asked as he caught up with them.

"Nothing," Kim said quickly, and Jo mouthed "thank you" to
her. "Nothing's going on."

Kim, Max, and Jo were the last of their friends to arrive at
Dilley's Bar & Grill for dinner. The circle of Heather, David, Young,
Aida, and Trey expanded to include them. They practically fell
over each other trying to be the first to hug Jo. When Aida finally
made it to her, Jo grabbed onto her tightly.

"God, I missed you," Jo said, blinking back tears. Her arms fully
encircled Aida's long and lean form, made even taller by the heels
she wore. The woman seriously dressed like she was on the way to

a board meeting every day of the week: pantsuit, silk blouse, heels, full makeup and hair, the whole nine.

"I missed you too, babe," Aida said. "How was the drive?"

Jo knew what she was really asking. "Oh my God, I don't even know," she whispered. "I have so much to tell you."

"Bathroom later."

They broke apart, and Aida's fiancé, a handsome, pudgy Black man named Trey Wilson, swept Jo into his arms.

"Mojo!" he cried as he lifted her off her feet and spun her around, his long black locs fanning out behind him.

"Hey, beefcake," she said. "What's shakin'?"

"Where's your friend?" he asked as he set her down. "I'm excited to meet him."

Jo shrugged and gave a casual, practiced smile. "He was tired from the drive, but he'll be around all weekend. You'll meet him tomorrow."

"Good," Trey said. He slung his arm over Jo's shoulder as the hostess walked the group to their table. "I need someone to wander the exhibit hall with me and tell me it's reasonable to spend five hundred bucks on a replica of Sting."

"The sword or the singer?"

Trey's full-bellied guffaw carried over the noise of the dinner crowd. "Honestly, I'd take either one."

"You're not buying a sword this weekend," Aida called back to him. "We only packed carry-ons."

"Damn."

Jo found a seat at the table between Aida and their Korean friend Young Kwon. Young had gotten a new haircut since Jo had last seen them—short at the back and long on top, styled in a perfect pompadour and bleached platinum white. Their square glasses had tiny flowers on the frames.

Daisies.

Suddenly, all she could think about was Felix and his bees-and-daisies coffee tumbler. She looked around the table at her friends, ordering drinks and swapping MnM stories they'd told a hundred times. There was an empty seat at one end of the table. Jo held in a sigh as she stared at it.

Young nudged her. "What's up?"

"Nothing," she replied. "I just wish my friend had been up to joining us."

"Yeah, bummer," they said. "But so cool that you're getting an MnM scene going in Kansas. How's it been getting settled?"

Jo answered the question by talking about work, rather than MnM. Across the table, Heather Abrams, a bubbly, strawberry blonde, white woman, tuned in to their conversation and jumped in right away with questions. Heather was a nurse, too, in pediatrics, and she and Jo had bonded years ago over horror stories from college and floor training.

"Hey, Mojo," said Trey brightly, commanding the attention of the entire table. "Does everyone know about the tornado?"

Multiple pairs of eyes homed in on Jo. She had told only Aida about the tornado, everything that had happened that night, and all the things she'd felt the next morning. Yup—safe to assume that Trey knew everything about Felix that Aida did.

"The, um... the what now?" said David Espinoza with a slight Salvadoran accent. The most soft-spoken of their group, he peered at Jo from down the table through a curtain of long black hair.

"Spill!" shouted Heather, tossing her curls.

Jo couldn't help but glance over at the empty chair again. She wished Felix were here to tell the story with her. She was curious to hear his perspective of that night, especially of how they'd ended up in each other's arms. Would he gloss over that fact or make light of it? Would he play up how scared they were or shrug it off like it was no big deal?

Everyone was watching her. And Felix *wasn't* here. Fine. She'd tell the story on her own.

"So in Kansas?" she started, putting a wide grin on her face and leaning into her storyteller's voice. "They have these things called tornadoes."

Her friends were enraptured as she told the story, making it as dramatic as possible. Then she insisted someone else talk because she had barely touched her enormous Cobb salad and was starving. The conversation broke up into multiple small ones, and Jo listened to Heather and Young go back and forth about the best desserts from around the world. It was an ongoing debate between the two of them, and tonight it was tiramisu versus hamantaschen.

As people were ordering dessert (Young got the tiramisu; Heather went with crème brûlée), Aida bumped Jo's knee and stood up. Jo followed her. They ducked into a single-stall restroom.

The door was barely closed and locked when Aida said, "Talk."

Jo talked. She told Aida about everything: the café con leche and Felix's music, their laughter-filled conversations in the car, the fact that they were sharing a room, the heart-pounding moment between them when she gave him her key, and finally, why she suspected he hadn't come to dinner.

Aida steepled her fingers under her chin and paced the tiny bathroom, deep in thought. "What if—now hear me out," she finally said. "You two fuck this weekend?"

"Aida!" Jo cried. "What happened to making good choices?"

"This is a good choice," she replied. "You two clearly have the hots for each other. You need to bang it out. You either get it out of your systems and move on, or it's magic and sparks and earth-shaking orgasms, and then you can be together. Either way, it's a win-win, right?"

"Or..." Jo countered. "It becomes really awkward between us for the rest of the weekend and the *nine-hour car ride home*, and then we still have to work together to plan MnM for the library."

Aida regarded her. "I'd say you could always quit volunteering, but something tells me you don't want to do that."

Jo let out a weary sigh. "No, I can't quit. I promised to help him for six weeks. His job might be on the line, and I can't—"

"I'm not talking about 'can't,' babe. I'm talking about what you *want*."

"I want—" Tears suddenly gathered in Jo's eyes. "Him. I don't want to bang it out. I want *him*. So much it aches sometimes. Felix is... Aida, he's wonderful."

Aida pulled her into a hug. Jo fell against her and lost it. Fuck texting and fuck video calls. Jo had needed her best friend these last few weeks, and now that she had her, everything came pouring out at once.

"No one has been wonderful to me like this in years, Aida. Why did I stay with Jeremy for *so fucking long*? Why did I beg him not to leave when he dumped me? I don't even *have* Felix yet, and he's so much better to me than that asshole ever was! Motherfucker stole my cat!" She wept and wept while Aida rubbed her back and made gentle, soothing sounds.

"I'm so scared I'm going to fuck it up," Jo whispered.

"Babe, how would you fuck it up?"

Jo shook her head against Aida's shoulder. She didn't know. She couldn't put the feeling into words. But it was always lingering in the back of her mind, in the pit of her stomach, in the core of her heart. Whenever Felix was too good to her. Whenever he saw her for all that she was and didn't turn away from her. A monstrous voice inside Jo insisted she was only one false move away from everything crashing down around her ears. If it wasn't inviting him to Indi-Con that did it, it would be something else.

If Jo could explain that, if she somehow found the right words, Aida would tell her she was wrong. Aida would call her "babe" and reassure her that she wasn't going to fuck it up. And Jo would believe it. She would believe it long enough to make it through dessert with their friends. Maybe even long enough to get back to the hotel and say good night to Felix. But the feeling, the voice, would come back. It always did.

Aida didn't press her for a response. She simply held her until her sobs subsided and then wet a paper towel with cool water and dabbed the red splotches from her cheeks. "I'm so sorry you've been feeling like this, Jo," she said with eyes full of sympathy. "I know I'm usually the problem-solver, but I don't really know what to tell you."

"I guess there's a first time for everything."

Aida gave her a soft smile. "You know how much I love you, right?"

"Yeah, I know. I love you too."

"And I trust you," she continued. "You're smart, and you're braver than you give yourself credit for. You drove halfway across the country to figure out what you wanted the rest of your life to look like. Do you know what kind of balls it takes to do that?"

Jo chuckled. A snot bubble came out of her nose.

"For the record," Aida said as she wiped Jo's nose, "I'm still on Team You-Two-Should-Fuck. Which probably means you start by telling him how you feel. But whatever choice you make, I promise I trust you to make the right one." She held up her pinky. "For you."

Jo hooked her pinky around Aida's. *For me.*

"Thank you."

Aida pulled her in for another hug and kissed Jo's hair. "Do you want a minute alone, or do you want me to stay?"

"I need a minute," Jo told her. Aida squeezed her once more before she left. Jo splashed some water on her face, peed, and took several deep breaths in the mirror. Her eyes were puffy and red, but she didn't really mind if her friends saw. Knowing Aida, she had already told them to play it cool.

Jo stayed quiet through dessert and focused on her exceptional chocolate lava cake. Trey and Aida picked up the bill, because of course they did. They both made good money and were generous to a fault with it. As they all returned to the hotel together, Heather walking slightly crooked from her three whiskey sours, Jo texted Felix that she was on the way. They squeezed into one elevator, stopping for hugs and "see you tomorrows" at each of their floors, until finally Jo rode up to the eighth floor alone. She followed the corridor to room eight-thirteen and knocked before opening the door.

A light was on. From the entryway she could see the ends of two queen beds, one of which was occupied. She shut the door quietly. "Are you awake?"

"Yeah," Felix replied over the whisper of rustling sheets. As she stepped fully into the room, he sat up and gave her a soft, sleepy smile.

Oh.

Jo had had no idea, not a goddamn clue, how it would feel to see Felix in bed. He wore a loose, pale gray T-shirt with one sleeve riding up to expose his biceps and deltoid. His hair was mussed from the pillow. The white duvet pooled in his lap as he leaned against the headboard. And that smile he was giving her—Jesus. Even if he'd been standing there fully naked it wouldn't have been this intimate.

Perhaps it was that intimacy that made her feel brave.

Felix absently scratched an itch on his chest. "Did you have a nice time?"

"Why didn't you come tonight?"

His mouth fell open, and a tiny, wordless sound came out.

"I wanted you there, Felix." She kept her voice low but steady, refusing to acknowledge the part of her that was begging her to shut up, to laugh it off. "I wanted you to meet my friends."

"Jo, I'm sorry," he said. He got out of bed and approached her. His hand drifted forward, but he didn't touch her. Thank God. If he did, she would lose the last shred of her composure.

"Why didn't you come?"

"I—" Felix cut himself off with a strangled sound. He raked both hands roughly through his hair and held his head. His eyes darted back and forth between hers. Then he flung his arms wide and let them fall to his sides. Jo could practically hear him thinking, *fuck it.* "Because I was afraid of what would've happened if we'd walked into this room together."

She shifted her weight back. Her heartbeat pounded in her ears. He couldn't possibly mean... "Wh-what would have happened?"

Felix took a step, forcing her to crane her neck. His breathing had gone fast and shallow. "If I'd been alone with you after you trusted me with your room key, I would have confessed everything. Everything I feel for you, Jo. Everything I want to have with you. One way or the other, I would have ruined your night. Either by stealing your friends' thunder with the truth of how much I care about you, or... or by not being able to keep my hands off you."

Okay. So that *was* what he meant. Holy shit.

There were other words in there too. Confessions that her heart drank up like a thirsty sponge, but that her mind didn't know how to handle right now. It was easier to focus on the sexy part of what he said. The part that lit up her every nerve, sharpening her senses and kindling heat low in her belly. She tightened her grip on the strap of her purse, which she apparently hadn't taken off her shoulder yet. For a moment, it was a lifeline, something tangible to cling to while the world tilted sideways and settled someplace new.

Then Felix moved even closer, towering over her, and the ground became unsteady once more. He must have showered to wash off the grime of the road, because Jo was struck by the scent of cloves and sweet vanilla. She inhaled sharply, involuntarily. Her lips parted as she let out the breath, and Felix's eyes trailed lazily down to her mouth.

"I would have brought you into this room, Jo, and done anything you asked me to," he said, his voice deep and oh so gentle. "I would have laid you down and touched you however you wanted, for however long you wanted. I don't think I'm wrong that you want that as much as I do. Am I?"

His gaze darted back to her eyes. The intensity of the desire in those dark brown pools made her sob—a sound wrenched from deep within, where she was burning from the inside out. Felix's arm lurched forward, but he stopped himself. His hand curled into a fist. Every muscle in his arm bulged from the effort of not touching her.

"Am I wrong, Jo?" he repeated.

"No," she whispered. "No, you're not wrong."

Felix exhaled slowly. The corners of his lips lifted in a satisfied grin. Not smug. Just pleased. Happy. She'd made him happy.

"I was afraid that if I didn't put some distance between us in that moment when I wanted you so badly, I'd ruin everything about tonight—maybe this entire weekend—that you were looking forward to," he said, his smile fading. "It appears I ruined your night anyway, and I'm so sorry, Jo. I'm sorry I didn't come with you, but even more so, I'm sorry I hurt you."

Jo fought past the need that blazed through her body. This conversation was important. Before anything else tonight might bring, they needed to finish it. "I *was* hurt, Felix. And confused," she said. "But I understand now why you needed some space and why you couldn't really explain. I forgive you."

Felix released a shaky breath, relief smoothing the lines on his face.

"You didn't ruin my night. I had a good time with my friends. And..." She wrung her purse strap. Could he see how her hands shook? Could he see how he made her tremble? "The night isn't over. If we don't want it to be."

"Jo..."

"Kiss me, Felix."

13

FELIX DIDN'T NEED to be told twice. He opened his fist, wiggled his fingers, and allowed his arm to relax. He reached for Jo. Adorable Jo. Beautiful Jo. Nerdy, creative, funny, thoughtful Jo. Who wanted him to kiss her. Who admitted to wanting a lot more than that. Her eyes fluttered closed. Her face angled up toward him.

He hooked his fingers under the strap of her purse and gently tugged. Jo's brows knit together, and she blinked her eyes open.

"If we're going to do this," he murmured, "we're going to do it right. You're not going to be clinging to your purse when you could be touching me instead."

He tugged again, and she let go.

"That's my girl, Jo," he said, each word precise.

She whimpered and bit her lip. Oh, fuck, he needed to make that sound come out of her again. He pulled her purse off her shoulder and leaned over to set it on the dresser nearby. Jo's eyes followed him.

Felix took his time. He was going to savor this moment. Make her savor it too. He palmed the sides of Jo's waist under that damn denim jacket, right where her leggings met her cropped blue shirt with an illustration of a cat on its back, playing with a giant d20 as if it were a ball of yarn.

When his hands made contact, she gasped in a breath that threatened to unravel his control. Hot, heavy need flooded his body, firming his cock and urging his pulse faster. His hands slid to her back. His fingers moved under the edge of her shirt, grazing skin and the band of her bra. He fingered the clasps and slipped underneath them. She was warm, warmer than his hands. Smooth and soft. He drank in the sight of the midriff he'd revealed by hiking up the back of her shirt. He would taste her there next, after he kissed her. He'd drop to his knees and roll down her leggings. Kiss her ivory skin all the way down to her pussy. Bite into the meat of her exquisite hips. Perhaps that would make her whimper again. He licked his lips in anticipation.

He slid a longing gaze back up, over her breasts and collarbone and throat and jaw and lips and cheeks and eyes. He resisted the desire to pull Jo against his body. She would feel so good, so fucking good, against his erection, but he wanted her mouth first. Wanted to let the sensations of her body and his together ramp up gradually. In order. Hands first, then lips, then tongues, then... *everything*.

"Felix, please," Jo whispered when his eyes found hers again. Her face was still angled up at him, desperation evident in every pore.

He smiled down at her. "Do you want to touch me too?"

"Yes."

"Then do it."

Jo swallowed. Moving as slowly and carefully as he had, she rested her hands on his shoulders. Her fingers tightened. Awestruck eyes darted from left to right as she beheld the muscles he'd toned over so many years. It was worth it. Every morning that he woke up sore, every wrist sprain, every time he pushed himself a little harder, every dollar he spent on coaches when he was a beginner. It was all worth it to see the way Jo's eyes grew even rounder and needier. She looked at his body like it was a gift she got to unwrap, something she'd always wanted but never dared to ask for.

Then her gaze returned to his face, studying him, and her fingers skated up his shoulders. She skimmed the sides of his neck, and he groaned as goosebumps skittered over his skin.

"Fuck, Jo," he whispered. "Do that again."

She grinned and put her hands back on his shoulders. She ran her fingertips even more lightly over him, the sweetest tickle up the sides of his neck. He shivered and threw his head back and moaned.

"How?" he asked the ceiling. "How does that simple touch feel so good, Jo? How are you doing this to me?"

Her fingers touched his chin next, drawing his head forward.

"I like your stubble," she said. "I've always liked it. Since the first day I saw you, sitting next to that ridiculous stack of MnM books. Especially this part." She grazed her index finger over the patch of gray on his chin.

"You like my grays?" Felix asked. No one had ever told him that before. Not that he'd been gray for very long, but the women he'd been with usually liked his thick, night-black hair over the gray on his chin. Leave it to Jo, whose mind worked in mysterious ways, to pick that part of his body to compliment first.

"What can I say? I'm an old lady."

"And I'm an old man who wants to kiss you before he shuffles off this mortal coil."

"You could have kissed me at any point up to now," she said with deliberate laziness. Her finger continued to play with his stubble while her other hand rested on his cheek. "You're the one who told me to touch you first. So I'm touching you first."

"Let me know when you're done then," he said. "I'll be right here."

"Will do."

Fuck. If he'd known Jo was this much of a goddamn tease, maybe he would have moved a little faster. He gripped her back tighter, digging the pads of his fingers into her skin. She bit her lower lip, and those pale eyes with their dark flecks rolled back in pleasure. God, they hadn't even kissed yet, hadn't even taken any clothes off, and already they were falling apart under one another's hands.

"Almost," she promised. She dragged the backs of her nails over his stubble, from his chin to his temples. Prickles of electricity cascaded down his entire body.

"Oh my God," Felix breathed. "You're going to kill me, woman."

"Mm-hmm," Jo hummed in agreement. She eased her fingers into his hair above his ears and leisurely passed her eyes over his dark waves. "Soft," she murmured. "Silky."

Her eyes locked onto his, no longer lazy, no longer teasing and coy. He didn't make her ask again. He closed his mouth over hers. Jo let out a shuddering, open-mouthed moan. Their lips had barely touched and already she was inviting him in. How could he refuse such an invitation? He smelled chocolate on her breath, tasted it on her tongue. She returned that sweet pressure against his tongue and whimpered into his mouth.

There it is.

Her hands tightened in his hair, tugging, drawing him closer. Felix responded by pulling her roughly against his body. A surprised little "oh!" slipped out of Jo when his cock dug into her belly. And fuck if he wasn't right. She felt so good—shifting, friction, soft against hard. He tucked his hand into the high waistband of her leggings, lowered it to the small of her back. He could feel the edge of her panties, and he flicked it with his middle finger. Jo tensed ever so slightly in his arms, and Felix couldn't tell if it was from desire or reticence.

He withdrew from her lips and nudged her nose with his. "Tell me," he said, panting. "Tell me what you want tonight. Like I said before. However you want to be touched, for however long you want. All you have to do is ask, Jo."

A heavy pause.

"I don't—I don't know," she said. She bumped his nose, but only because she was shaking her head. "I'm sorry, Felix. I don't know."

Felix exhaled and pressed his cheek against hers, angling to avoid her glasses. He couldn't let her see his disappointment. He wouldn't put that on her. He squeezed his eyes shut and calmed his body down with long, even breaths. He withdrew his hand from her leggings and held onto her hips.

Her grip had shifted too. Her hands weren't in his hair anymore. They were holding onto the back of his neck as if he were an anchor in a stormy sea.

"I'm sorry," she said again.

"Don't do that," he said. "Don't apologize when you've done nothing wrong."

"But—"

"No." He stepped back so he could see her. His heart nearly broke when he saw the tears in her eyes. "No 'buts.' However you want, for however long you want, right? If we've reached the end of 'however long' tonight, that's your call."

"You're—I—I made you—" She looked down, where his pajama pants were doing fuck-all to hide his raging hard-on. "I should help you—"

"Jo, oh my God, stop. Please." He took her face in his hands and kissed her forehead. "Of course I was turned on by the way you touched me. That doesn't mean you owe me more than you want to give. I'm an old man, remember?" He offered her a small smile, trying to diffuse whatever the hell they had walked into. "I've been here before, and I can handle myself."

A sudden snort of laughter burst out of her. "I *bet* you can."

He chuckled and shifted to hold her shoulders. "That's not how I meant it, but I could do that, if need be. Three showers in one day, why not?"

Jo closed her eyes. She slid her hands to his chest, her fingers dancing over his muscles. "Please don't think this means I don't want you, Felix. I just—"

"You don't have to—"

"Wait, I need to say this."

Instantly cowed, he said, "I'm sorry. Please continue."

Eyes still closed, she furrowed her brow and said, "I haven't been with anyone since my ex. It's strange to be intimate with someone again. Someone new. I... I need a little more time." She opened her eyes. "Is that okay?"

Oh, God. She has to ask?

"Yes, Jo. Of course, it's okay. Don't rush yourself. I'll be here whenever you're ready."

She tapped her index finger, its nail painted Indi-Con green, against his chest. She was looking at it rather than him. "Felix?"

"Hmm?"

"Will you kiss me again? Without all the buildup. Just kiss me?"

He took her chin between his thumb and his knuckle and gently tilted her head back. He paused for a second or two, letting *some* anticipation build. That was half the fun of kissing, after all;

the breaths right before it, the moments of knowing it was about to happen.

Felix kissed Jo. Tenderly, sweetly, earnestly. Jo kissed him back. Warmly, solidly, affectionately.

After, he touched his forehead to hers, and they breathed together. His body was calmer now. The discomfort was waning, his blood flow returning to status quo.

"It might be best to sleep in separate beds tonight," he said.

"I think you're right," she replied. "And on that note, I should get ready for bed. Tomorrow's a long day."

"Oh, right," Felix said. "There's a gaming convention or some such across the street."

"That is why we're here," she chuckled.

"I thought this was all some nefarious plan to get me into a hotel room with you," he teased. "Tell it to me straight, Jo. Did you sabotage my booking?"

She gasped in mock outrage and shoved lightly at his chest. "I'm no rogue!"

"No, you're..." he thought for a moment, recalling what he knew about the different MnM archetypes. "I bet you're a cleric, aren't you? A healer, of course, and you're always looking out for people, offering support and going above and beyond in that support."

Jo blinked at him behind her glasses. "Yeah, that's right."

"Hot damn!" He pumped his fist into the air. "I'm learning."

IN THE MORNING, Jo's alarm went off before Felix's. She quickly silenced it. He stirred in the bed next to hers but didn't wake up. Jo watched him as he slept. He lay on his side, facing her, fuzzy to her naked eyes. Both arms were wrapped around one end of his pillow, which he held lengthwise against his chest as his head rested on the other end. His lips were parted, and disheveled locks of hair flopped over his forehead. Since he hadn't shaved the day before, his beard was the longest she'd ever seen it.

She felt like sighing a contented sigh, so she did. She honestly couldn't remember the last time someone made her feel the way Felix did. Maybe no one ever had. Being in his arms had felt so different from what she was used to that it had overwhelmed her, made her hesitate. Part of her couldn't quite believe that she hadn't fucked everything up. That he'd stopped at her slightest hint of uncertainty. That he hadn't said, "At least get me off first, baby."

Stealthily, Jo got up, grabbed her clothes and toiletries, and took them into the bathroom. In the shower, she let her mind wander over everything that had happened in the last twenty-four hours. By the time she was toweled off and in her underwear, she'd made a decision. She hadn't brought her phone in with her, and her hands itched to text Aida and get confirmation that this was the right next step. But she didn't actually need to. Aida had already confirmed it, with an unbreakable pinky promise.

Whatever choice you make, I promise I trust you to make the right one. For you.

"For me," Jo whispered into the mirror and finished getting dressed.

She heard Felix's alarm go off, followed by the thump of heavy footsteps. Jo called that she'd be right out and received a grunt in response. Steam poured out of the bathroom as she emerged. A drowsy, tousled, downright adorable Felix blinked at her.

"Morning," she said.

He grunted again as he dug through his duffel bag.

"You want me to go get you some coffee?" she offered with a grin.

"Hero's calling. Answered," he muttered as he pointed at her. He stumbled into the bathroom without another word, and the shower came on.

She flipped her head upside down and quickly blow dried her hair, waiting to curl it and do her makeup until she returned from her quest. Down in the lobby's continental breakfast nook, she filled two to-go containers with scrambled eggs, bacon, sausage, muffins, mini croissants, and mixed fruit that was mostly under-ripe chunks of white-green honeydew. She tossed two yogurts on top, then closed the lids and moved on to the coffee bar.

"Mojo!"

Jo grinned to herself. "Beefcake!"

From behind, Trey kissed her hair. She heard him smack his lips and turned to see a vaguely grossed-out look on his face. "Mmm, fruity."

"Shut up, at least I showered," she fired back.

Trey fell in beside her with a playful bump of his elbow. His locs were pulled back into a thick ponytail at the base of his skull today, and he wore a hunter green T-shirt with a stylized MnM logo. They made their coffees, and Jo dug through the bowl of mini creamers until she found a few vanilla ones.

"Felix joining us today?" Trey asked, a bit too casually.

"That's the idea," she replied.

He picked up his coffee and took a sip. He made a face.

"What? Too fruity?" Jo asked.

"If only." He added more cream and sugar. "Aida told me why he didn't join us last night."

She blushed. "Actually, I was wrong about that. Kind of. It's... we worked it out."

"Yeah?" Trey asked, giving her a hopeful look.

She nodded.

"I'm glad. You know I'll beat his ass if he messes you around, right?"

Jo unleashed a loud laugh and patted Trey on the shoulder. "Oh, beefcake. I would love to see you try."

The elevator dropped Trey off on the fifth floor, and he got out with a wave and a promise to see her soon. The whole group was meeting in the lobby at eight-thirty to walk over to the con, where the games kicked off at nine o'clock sharp.

On her floor, Jo jostled the to-go containers and coffee cups but found she couldn't manage them and the keycard at the same time. She kicked her door twice.

"You out of the shower yet?" she called. "Can you get the door?"

"Yeah, hang on," Felix called back.

When the door opened, she almost dropped everything she was carrying. Felix had one hand on the doorknob, and the other was busy pulling a burgundy waffle-knit Henley shirt over his torso. She got only a glimpse of his abs and the trail of black hair that ran down their center, but that was more than enough to send her reeling.

"Jesus Christ," she said out loud.

Felix, freshly shaved and grinning, winked at her. Vain bastard knew exactly what he was doing. He held the door with his hip and took the coffees from her. Jo told him which cup was his and offered him first pick of the assortment of breakfast foods as they set everything on the desk in the corner.

"Thank you for getting this," Felix said. He bent as if he were going to kiss her. Then froze.

"I wanted to talk about that," she said breathily. It was getting harder and harder not to be breathless around Felix. Especially when he did things like that.

"I'm all ears," he said. "Can we talk while we eat so we're not late?"

Jo agreed. Felix ripped off the top of one of the to-go boxes and used it as a plate, picking and choosing food from both. Including the cherry yogurt, damn him. Jo, stuck with the inferior peach yogurt, made a plate for herself and sat in the desk chair. Felix settled in the armchair in the opposite corner.

"I realized," she began, "that I never really responded to some of the non-sex things you said last night."

"The non-sex things?" he repeated and sipped his coffee. "Hey, you got me vanilla! Thanks."

"Not as good as Lita's, of course."

"Still good," he said with another sip. "Sorry, please go on."

She stared down at her makeshift plate, too nervous to start eating. "I mean the part about you caring for me and having feelings for me," she continued slowly. "You said 'everything I want to have with you.' Maybe we should talk about what that means?"

Felix swallowed his bacon and regarded her seriously. "It means I want to be with you, Jo. Not just have sex with you. I want more than that. I want to be yours, and I want you to be mine. I want all of it."

Jo's heart was lodged in her throat, making it very difficult to speak. How inconvenient. She pushed the words out anyway, expressing what she'd resolved in the shower to tell him. "I want that too, Felix. I want all of it."

He was on his feet and across the room before she could say another word. He dropped his plate onto the desk and gripped the arms of her chair, caging her in. And there she was, breathless once again. He hovered over her, and they stared at each other.

Not a hesitation, but a confirmation. A shared *are we really doing this?*

And then the answer.

Yes.

He kissed her, hard. His lips were smoky and greasy from the bacon, and she flicked her tongue out for a taste. Felix groaned and opened his mouth for her. She snaked one hand into his damp hair, held on tight, and devoured him.

He dragged her chair closer to himself, and her knees brushed the insides of his thighs. He was practically straddling her. Suddenly, he wrenched himself away from her lips, panting.

"Fucking hell, Jo, you drive me wild." He grinned wickedly. "I have to stop, or we *will* be late."

Despite his words, he leaned in to kiss her again. Their lips met, light and sweet, and then he withdrew. He nodded resolutely, as if he'd proven to himself that he could kiss her without tumbling over the edge into sheer, unrelenting desire.

Maybe he needed a bit more evidence.

Jo gave his head a gentle nudge closer. He made a feeble sound of protest but fell forward against her lips once more. She kept the kiss chaste—she wasn't a monster, after all—and released him.

"I guess you're my boyfriend now?" she said.

"Only if you're my girlfriend now."

Jo shrugged, feigning nonchalance. "Yeah, okay."

He let out a high-pitched laugh, echoing the joy that ricocheted inside her, made her want to leap into the air and never come down. He pecked her on the cheek and returned to his seat with his breakfast.

"All right, GM Jo," he said as he scooped up some eggs. "It's game time. Remind me what to expect today."

Jo

Since I know you'll want to know first

We didn't fuck, but we kissed and we talked and we decided to be together for realsies

And I'm so happy

Aida

YES YES YES YES YES

Jo

Hi, just a heads up. Felix and I are a couple now. As of this morning. Like, 10 mins ago. Be cool and don't make it weird, ya weirdos. See you soon.

Kim

I knew it!!!

Max

who?

David

Tornado guy

Max

oh yeah

nice

Heather

Someone make sure Aida tells Trey!

Aida

Already did

Young

Happy for you, Jo.

Kim

Me too!!!!!!

This is so exciting!

OMG, he's even hotter than he was yesterday!

Way to go, Jo!!!

Young

Kim, we're all together now. You don't have to keep texting the group.

Kim

You want me to say he's hot out loud?

Max

yes

Heather

Yes

Young

Kinda?

Jo

No

Aida

I'll do it if you don't

14

STEPPING INTO THE convention center was like entering another world. Felix had thought the lobby of the Hotel Paragon was
a sight to behold, but it had nothing on the foyer he was currently
gaping at.

"INDIIIII," hollered a voice from somewhere in the crowd.

"CON!" screamed back literally everyone else. On pure instinct,
Felix ducked like he was dodging a punch.

"Okay there, man?" asked Trey, who hadn't left his side since they
shook hands in the hotel lobby a few minutes ago. He patted Felix on
the back and chuckled. "This is a pretty intense choice for a first con."

Felix laughed off his embarrassment. "I guess I don't like to
half-ass things."

"Neither do they," Trey said, gesturing to the group of Jo's
friends who walked ahead of them, deeper into the abyss that was
Indi-Con. "At least we have a guide who's easy to spot."

Felix grinned toward Heather, the leader of the pack who was
in costume as her demonkin character, Rosalis the rogue. With
pink face paint, a pink wig, and a full set of leather armor with
rose gold studs, she was hard to miss.

Jo's friends were, frankly, intimidating as fuck. Kim was practically skipping in her fifties-style, dice-patterned dress—which she'd proudly declared she'd made herself. Young, with sunglasses on indoors, a sky-high pompadour, and a slim-cut yellow blazer with the sleeves rolled up, exuded cool. Then there was Aida, Jo's best friend, who walked with purpose everywhere she went and looked more at ease in stilettos than Felix felt in tennis shoes.

David was more chill, but he didn't seem to want to talk much. He had a relaxed Southern-California-surfer vibe, although maybe Felix was only getting that because of the long hair, golden-brown skin, and floral board shorts. The flower crown and the elf ears sticking out from his hair didn't seem to scream "surfer," but then again, Felix had never met one (or an elf, for that matter).

Max was harder to get a read on. He barely looked up from his phone except to check that he was still with the group and wasn't about to walk into any walls. He had greeted Felix with a chin lift and a "'Sup, tornado guy?" before fading into the background.

As they wound toward the gaming hall, another "Indi" and "Con" call-and-response rang out in the foyer behind them. Max huzzahed without looking up. Felix kept his gaze fixed on Heather's pink wig so he didn't get lost... until Jo turned around. She paused to let him catch up to her. Trey slipped away toward Aida and draped his arm around her shoulder. She caught his wrist and leaned into him in that easy way reserved for couples who'd been together forever.

"What do you think so far?" Jo asked.

Felix felt the timid nudge of her fingers on his. He captured her hand and interlaced their fingers. God, it felt so good to touch her.

"I think I'm glad I'm here with you," he responded. "And I think I'm going to need more coffee."

Jo squeezed his hand, and he squeezed back.

The wall outside the SWOP gaming hall was papered with white printouts. Felix knew what to expect here, thanks to Jo. All of this weekend's Organized Play games had been posted online for GMs and players to sign up for in advance. The printouts listed names and table assignments for each game, so people knew where to go. Jo had assured him there were always lots of spaces available day-of for people like him to sign up last minute.

Kim made it to the wall first. "We're at table twelve."

They had all signed up to play a high-level game with their characters from Jo's campaign, with Jo playing one of her own characters. Most of the group followed Kim into the hall, but David held back, reading over the sign-up sheets for the afternoon games.

"Do you want to find a game for the morning session?" Jo asked Felix.

"I'd prefer to watch first," he replied. "Is that allowed?"

"Yeah, of course. Just don't, like, hover over the GM's shoulder or anything. But if you want to play this afternoon, we can look now."

"Lead on," Felix said, gesturing toward the wall. Jo and David helped him find an intro-level game with open seats. He jotted down his name and made a mental note of the table number and GM's name.

"What about the evening session?" he asked. "Should I find a game then too?"

"Tonight's the Legendary," David said.

Felix glanced between him and Jo. "What's the Legendary?"

"All of the tables play the same adventure at the same time," he explained, "with different objectives depending on character level. What happens at one table might impact another, and everyone wins or loses collectively. It's completely bananas."

That overwhelmed feeling rose up, and Felix's stomach started to churn. "That sounds like the perfect time to check out the exhibit hall with Trey."

Jo nudged him with her elbow. "You could watch for a little bit?" she suggested. "Any event with at least five tables can host a SWOP Legendary. If the library event grows enough, who knows?"

"Plus, Jo's GMing for it," David added. "She's great at Legendaries."

"Aw, thanks," she said.

"I'll come check it out," Felix promised. Jo smiled up at him, and he steeled himself as the three of them entered the gaming hall.

"I'M GOING TO stand up on the dragon's back," Max said, hopping up and straddling his chair. He opened his hand and slowly drove his palm forward as if pushing against a heavy weight. "I reach through its razor-sharp scales to the thick hide underneath. I say, 'I've killed greater beings than you, Longfang. You're nothing but an oversized bird.' And as I touch it, I cast Bite of the Vampire at level ten."

"Ten?!" Kim yelled.

"You better fuckin' hit," said Young.

Jo bounced in her seat and cried, "Get its ass!" God, how she'd missed this. She'd almost forgotten how much Max came alive as Lyric, his bard persona.

Still on his feet, Max picked up a d20. Then he set it back down and chose a different one. He exhaled. And rolled. The die traveled to the center of the table. Everyone, even Felix and Trey, even their GM Richard, leaned in.

"Yes!" Max crowed as the entire group cheered. "That's a roll of eighteen, plus my spell bonus. Twenty-nine!"

"The dragon is hit!" cried Richard. "Roll your damage." As Max picked up a massive handful of dice, the GM narrated, "The ancient creature writhes and twists, attempting to throw the bard off its back. It's injured, badly, and it knows it." The dice clattered onto the table in front of Max, and he began to add up the total. "You see Longfang look to the skies, about to make a break for it, hoping to live to fight another day."

Heather muttered under her breath. "Don't you dare, you mother—"

"But the bard's spell strikes true," Richard gestured at Max right as Max looked up from his dice.

Max's grin was as luminous as the life-giving magic wielded by the strongest cleric. "Sixty-nine points of damage," he said.

Everyone started talking at once.

"Nice!"

"Nice."

"What, really? That's hilarious."

"Damn, son."

"That's got to be enough to kill it, right?"

"Shhh!"

Richard smiled and said, "Longfang, The Scourge of the North, The Wingèd Death, begins to screech. The Bite of the Vampire spell pierces its flesh, and its life force is drained before your eyes. Lyric, you feel the power of the dragon surge up your arm, transferring its health to you. You gain sixty-nine health."

"Nice," multiple people said.

Max nodded. "I now have seventy."

"You were at *one*?" Aida cried.

"It's fine," he quipped.

"Longfang's eyes go white and milky," Richard said. "Its jaw goes slack, and its screech dies on the wind. The wings go limp, and it is falling. Its corpse is crashing to earth, with the bard on its back."

"Teleport away!" Jo cried, unable to keep the laughter out of her voice.

"I'm out of spells!" Max shouted back.

"So am I," said Young, their cleric and healer. "So don't die."

Richard rolled a handful of dice. "Lyric takes... thirty-eight points of damage from the fall."

"I'm alive!" Max roared. The entire table applauded, and Jo's cheers were the loudest of all.

Heather, though, was still in character as Rosalis, Lyric's snarky cousin. "Every time I'm about to inherit your share of the family tavern, cuz, you ruin everything."

"Hey," Max shot back as Lyric, "if you hadn't run away when the dragon came down on us, I wouldn't have been alone to take all of its attacks. It was your fault I almost died in the first place."

"I didn't run away. I fell back to a more advantageous position," Heather-as-Rosalis argued.

Jo addressed Richard, "They're always like this. You can cut them off anytime."

"In that case..." Richard jumped in with a glance at his watch. The morning session only had a few minutes left. He concluded the game succinctly with rewards and a heroes' welcome in the town where the adventure had begun. With a final flourish, he said, "Thank you all for adventuring with me today. May your next tale be even more epic."

They all applauded politely and thanked Richard for the game. Across the table, Felix stood and came around to Jo. He and Trey had observed the entire three-hour game. For most of that time, he'd watched her. It was all Jo could do to keep her head in the game.

Now standing behind her, Felix bent and whispered into her ear. "You're incredible."

She gazed up at him. "How so?"

"You're electric when you play," he said. "I couldn't keep my eyes off you."

Jo's body flushed warm all over. She shook her head, about to remind him that she wasn't the only good roleplayer at the table— but she stopped herself. She'd accepted David's earlier compliment; she didn't need to let it feel different with Felix. "Thank you."

Felix smiled at her.

"You, on the other hand, are extremely distracting," she told him as she packed up her dice and character sheet. "Next time, sit behind me."

"Trust me, Jo," Felix said, even softer and lower than before. He brushed his thigh against her ass as it hung generously off the side of the chair. Jo's spine straightened. "I like the view from back here, but your eyes are much more fun to watch during a game."

"Well, if you're going to do that, never mind," she said airily. "That's even more distracting."

"Good." The word was guttural and raw. Less a word and more of a sound.

The muscles deep in the core of her body tightened. She squeezed her thighs together. And then, just like that, Felix was upright again, going over to Richard to ask some GMing questions.

Jo's phone buzzed in her pocket, which it had been doing off and on throughout the game. She pulled it out to find a text notification from Aida, who was only two seats over, phone in hand, chatting innocently with Trey.

Aida

> That's a point for Team You Two Should Fuck

Jo unlocked her phone to respond, only to find a whole string of texts from Aida.

Aida

He's looking at you

I've counted six lip bites so far

Seven

Is he taking notes? That's so cute.

Did you hear that little "woo" he did when you rolled a 20?

I lost count but I think we're up to ten lip bites

Babe seriously where did you find this guy?

Eleven

That's a point for Team You Two Should Fuck

Jo

Are you keeping score?

Aida

If every lip bite is a point, I'm totally winning

Aida stood smoothly. "Where are we getting lunch?"

They decided to split up, since they only had an hour until the afternoon session. Every lunch place within five blocks was about to have a line out the door. Hand in hand, Jo and Felix headed toward a deli the next block over.

Holding hands with him felt as natural as breathing. His was large and warm compared to hers. Comforting. Strong. She'd never held hands with anyone whose palm muscles bulged with each twitch of a finger. Without warning, her mind conjured up the memory of the morning after the tornado, when she imagined what Felix's touch would feel like on her body. A shiver ran down her spine, even as they walked through the early summer sunshine. She could feel the ghost of his fingers against her skin, right under her bra, where they'd been the night before. Without thinking, she arched her back and rolled her shoulders.

"Do you have an itch?" Felix asked.

"If I say yes, will you scratch it?"

"Only one way to find out."

"Then yes."

Felix let go of her hand, slowed his pace, and touched her upper back lightly. Soft and sultry, he said, "Tell me where."

"Lower."

His hand shifted, and sparks glittered over every inch he touched.

"Left, and down a little more."

Felix obeyed her directions and ran his nails back and forth at the base of her shoulder blade. The sparks intensified. Not only over her skin, but deeper, into her muscles. They spread from that one spot and cascaded across her body. Even her scalp tingled.

Jo hummed in delight. "Right there."

"Can you even feel me through that denim jacket of yours?" he asked. "Or should I slip underneath?"

Oh, you'd like that, wouldn't you?

"I feel you just fine, thanks," she said, light and breezy.

"You really are going to be the death of me, you know."

She grinned at him. "A little to the right, please."

Felix groaned through closed lips, but he continued to scratch her back all the way to the deli.

AFTER LUNCH, FELIX sat at his first MnM table without Jo. He could hear her laugh from halfway across the hall where she sat ready to GM a game. Felix had taken a seat facing away from her to keep the distraction to a minimum, but that laugh sure did carry. His girlfriend's laugh. Felix smiled like a teenager with a crush, all goofy and lopsided. He was thirty-six, for crying out loud. He should not be this dopey over having a girlfriend.

He turned to look over his shoulder and spotted Jo in the crowd, loose auburn curls bouncing as she stood up to adjust something at the center of her table. One of her MnM books was open and pressed against her chest. Felix found his attention glued to the hint of green and orange on her hand that was splayed over the book's spine. The touch of those hands had lit such a fire in him—he'd never felt anything like it. He wanted to feel it again.

His thoughts were interrupted by his GM, a young white woman named Grace, arriving. They introduced themselves, and once the table filled up, the adventure got underway. The din of the gaming hall built up to the point that Felix couldn't hear Jo anymore. That was probably for the best since his mind tended to wander whenever he did.

Someone else caught his attention, though. Trey and Aida were playing at a table nearby, and Trey was doing some bizarre character voice, like a child actor rejected from playing a street urchin in an *Oliver Twist* adaptation. There was also a lot of meowing involved, which made Aida crack up every time.

At Felix's table, the story followed a format similar to the sample game Jo had run for him. Grax and his party were hired by a small-town mayor to investigate some strange noises in the local copper mine. The whole thing was rather *Scooby-Doo*-esque, with fake ghosts, crotchety old landowners, and an actual line about meddling kids. Jo would have played up the comedy of the adventure, Felix thought. She would have had the entire table rolling with laughter as she embellished the silly parts rather than skimming over them as Grace did. Grace was a fine GM, but she seemed more interested in keeping the game moving than anything else. Felix wouldn't put it past Jo to also add a Great Dane with a penchant for snacks into the mix.

When the game wrapped up, Felix noted the details on his SWOP logsheet and thanked Grace and the other players. He stood, and his eyes instantly found Jo, still in the thick of her game. Before he could decide whether to head over there, he heard his name. Aida was waving him over. She and Trey were the only ones left at their table.

"How was your game?" he asked as he sat alongside them.

"Great," Aida replied. "We killed some ghosts and saved a temple from a necromancer's evil schemes. You?"

"Sadly, all of my ghosts were merely illusory diversions. Which made them very hard to hit with a sword."

"*He* gets a sword," Trey said indignantly.

"It's an imaginary sword, T," Aida said with a long-suffering sigh. "It doesn't count."

"Trey, I have to ask," Felix jumped in, "what's with the meowing?"

"You heard that?" Aida asked with a laugh.

"Oi, guv, that's jus' Jolly," Trey said, returning to his god-awful Cockney. "'E's a li'l catfolk tryna be a wizard is all. Jolly loves castin' spells, wot?"

"God, I love Jolly," Aida said, covering her face with her hand. "It's so dumb, but he makes me laugh every time."

"Why do you think I bring him to every convention, lovey?" Trey said in his regular voice. He uncovered her face and pecked her on the cheek.

"So, Felix!" Aida said brightly. She angled toward him and leaned back against Trey's shoulder.

"Here it comes," Felix said with a knowing grin.

"You and Jo, huh?"

"Me and Jo," he confirmed. "Are you going to ask about my intentions toward your best friend?"

"We'll see," Aida said. "Thoughts on cats?"

"Slight preference for dogs, but I like cats too. I had both growing up."

"Coffee or tea?"

"Coffee. Con leche. And vanilla."

"Why boxing?"

"Because it's a good stress reliever, I enjoy the discipline it requires, and it makes me look really good."

"Why Ashville?"

"My grandpa lives there, and I didn't want him to be alone."

Aida paused and cast her eyes around like she was thinking. Felix was mildly surprised she didn't have a list of questions memorized.

"What do you think of MnM?" she asked.

"The jury's still out, but so far it's been pretty good."

"What do you think of Jo?"

"She's amazing and funny and cute as hell, and I love being around her."

"Right back atcha," said Jo from directly behind him.

Felix jumped. Jo was smiling down at him with her backpack slung over one shoulder and her tote bag over the other.

"How long were you there?" Felix asked.

"Not long," Jo replied, sliding into the seat next to him. "Jury's still out on MnM?"

"Yeah," Felix said, a bit disheartened. "My last game wasn't nearly as fun as playing with you or watching this morning. But I did make it to level three."

Jo gasped with delight. "Congrats! You're officially a pugilist. Do you need help leveling up?"

"I'd like to try it myself first, but thank you for offering. I'll let you know if I have trouble."

Jo clapped for him, and Felix felt a rush of pride.

"Sorry the game wasn't great," she said, a look of concern washing over her features. "That happens sometimes at cons. Not as much character interaction playing with strangers, and the hard time limits can stifle creativity. Was there anything memorable that stood out?"

Felix smiled. "Probably when I attempted to stab a ghost, and it turned out to be an illusion. The GM said I ran right through it, ate shit, and dropped my sword. I was already in a *Scooby-Doo* mindset, so imagining it in that old seventies animation style was fun."

"See, if Veena had been there, she would have given you so much shit for that," she said, and then her eyes flashed with realization. "Wait, we haven't signed up for a game together. Let's come a little early tomorrow to make sure we find a table."

"Absolutely," Felix agreed. "Grax and Veena are a good team."

Jo grinned and leaned in. "I think so too."

Felix met her halfway and kissed her. Sweet and simple. Easy.

"Gross," said Aida.

"Get a room," Trey added.

"Way ahead of you," Felix said with a wink.

15

FELIX HELD A T-shirt against his torso.

"Yup, that's the one," Trey said.

"Yeah?" he replied. "Not 'Things Are Getting Dicey'?"

"It's too generic," Trey said with a shake of his head. "Get the fighter one."

"Maybe I'll get the dicey one for Jo, though. I think she'd like the pun."

"She does own more dice than anyone I know. When Aida and I helped her pack for Kansas, we filled an entire box with dice. Those sons of bitches get heavy."

Felix chuckled and found a dice shirt that looked Jo-sized. He paid for the shirts, ignoring the twinge in his stomach at spending the money. It would be fine, he told himself. Sharing a room with Jo meant this trip would be significantly cheaper than he'd anticipated. And it would be worth it, to see the look on Jo's face when he surprised her by wearing an MnM T-shirt.

He and Trey continued to wind through the sprawling exhibit hall, where big-name companies and an official MnM merch booth were nestled alongside independent artisans, authors, and game developers. The two of them set a leisurely pace, stopping to admire everything from art prints to handmade tote bags, from gaming accessories to jewelry. And dice. So many goddamn dice.

Felix picked out a new, cheap dice set for himself, since he only had the one set of yellow dice Jo had given him. Trey splurged on a large d20 made out of moonstone for Aida and bought himself a hammered silver tankard with a hinged lid he could open and close with his thumb. He also made Felix take pictures of him with all the replica movie swords he could get his hands on. He texted every single one to Aida.

Eventually, after looping through each aisle, they started back toward the gaming hall to catch the last hour of the Legendary event.

"Thanks for showing me around," Felix began, trying to find his way to a topic he'd been wanting to bring up. "I appreciate you helping me feel a little less lost."

"Don't mention it, man," Trey said, gripping Felix's shoulder as they passed through the exhibit hall doors. "I'm usually only good for one or two games anyway, so it's nice to have someone to wander around with."

Bless you, Trey. That was probably the best opening Felix could have hoped for. "You only play occasionally, right? Not with the weekly group?"

Trey nodded. "Yeah, just at cons a couple times a year."

"With a catboy wizard."

"*Catfolk,*" Trey corrected. "Catboy is a very different thing."

"I'll take your word for it," Felix said. "So... you play for Aida? To make her laugh?"

Trey gave him an appraising look before answering. "Not only for her. I like MnM well enough, but it's more fun for me when it's rare. If I played every week, I'd run out of stamina and creativity pretty quick." He paused and tilted his head toward Felix. "Now, do you want to tell me what you're really getting at?"

"Am I that transparent?" Felix asked with a self-deprecating shrug.

"I'm that perceptive," he responded. "I'm also a great listener."

Felix sighed and let his concerns tumble out. "I was barely even aware MnM existed until a few weeks ago. I started down this path because my job required it, and now it's all jumbled up with Jo and how I feel about her. I love how much she loves MnM, I really do. It clearly makes her happy, and I like seeing her happy. But... does she expect me to become as enmeshed in this world as she is?"

Trey shook his head gently. "I'm not sure I can answer that for you."

"I know; I don't expect you to. I guess I'm thinking out loud." Felix paused, uncertain if he should even ask his next question. It sat there, on the tip of his tongue, as they walked. They'd almost made it to the gaming hall when it finally slipped out. "Did Jo's ex play MnM?"

Trey looked uneasy. "No. But I'm not answering any more questions about him. Jo should tell you all that herself."

"I know," he said again as guilt crept in. "I'm sorry. I'm not trying to put you in the middle of this."

"Felix." Trey came to a stop in front of the wall of sign-up sheets. The racket in the hall nearly drowned him out. He rested a hand on Felix's shoulder and leaned in to be heard. "You and Jo have been together for, what, twelve hours? Give it time. You'll figure it out."

Felix combed his fingers through his hair. "I never expected this, Trey. To care about someone so deeply, so fast. I want to give Jo what she needs" —he gestured toward the hall— "even if it's something that seems frivolous on the surface. Fuck, I'm sorry, man. You barely know me, and here I am, dumping all of my shit on you."

Trey shrugged and smiled. "I told you I'm a good listener."

"You are, and I appreciate it."

"For what it's worth, Felix, I think Jo is lucky to have you. She deserves to be with someone considerate of her needs."

Something in Trey's tone made Felix pause. As if Jo hadn't had that kind of consideration before. The more he gleaned about this ex of hers, the less he liked the guy.

"I'll do my best," he said. A promise to himself—and to Jo.

Trey gave his shoulder a firm pat as there was a collective outcry from the hall. He pointed his thumb toward the doorway. "Shall we go see what that was all about?"

The hall was more crowded than it had been all day. Hundreds of people were crammed around dozens of tables—shouting, laughing, rolling dice, and having the time of their lives. Trey gave Felix a nod and went off in search of Aida. Felix listened in at a table near the door, catching the end of a combat encounter.

"And with that final blow, the chimera is defeated," the GM cried. She called for someone to make a d20 roll for a nature-based skill check. A kid who couldn't have been older than ten raised his hand and made the roll. He counted the total on his fingers.

"Seventeen!" he said proudly.

"Excellent," the GM said. "Working quickly, Ivan is able to extract a tooth from each of the chimera's three heads. Your allies will be able to use the teeth to create the potion they need to complete their objectives." She handed the boy a slip of paper. "Please take that over to table twenty-three."

The boy hopped up and took off running, beaming and giggling. Felix couldn't help but laugh too. The GM caught his eye, and they shared a quick smile before she continued with the game. He moved around the room, catching bits and pieces of the story as he went. The energy in the room was palpable, but instead of being overwhelmed, Felix just felt... excited.

Finally, he found Jo at her table. She was so invested in her game she didn't notice him at first.

"The sphinx rises on all fours above you, looming twelve feet tall at the shoulder," she was saying. "She stretches her wings, and their fluttering sends wind cascading over you, billowing your cloaks around your ankles. She leers at you and lazily says, 'What in the world could you small things possibly wish of me? Come to destroy me, perhaps? Or do you seek a riddle? An attempt to prove your worth to me and beg of me a favor?'"

"That last one," a young man at her table replied. "But we *will* kill you if we have to."

The player sitting next to him shook his head. "No, we won't. We need her help."

"Well, you should decide soon," Jo said in character. The languid, sensuous voice of the sphinx stirred a strange, startling desire within Felix.

Shit, was he into roleplay now?

"'I'm about to become bored,'" she continued, "'and you all look very much like playthings to me.' Then the sphinx lifts one of her massive paws and bats Nox on the shoulder like a cat with a spider. You aren't injured, but the paw covers you from shoulder to knee."

"Wow." The player that Felix assumed was playing Nox switched to his character voice and continued, "No, yeah, let's definitely get that riddle. No killing here, nice big cat lady."

Jo glanced down at her notes and finally spotted Felix when she looked up. She grinned, and he gave her a small wave.

"What is it that breaks once its name is spoken?" Jo-the-sphinx asked.

Felix crossed his arms and watched the players debate the answer. He stole a glance at Jo, who was staring at his biceps. He waited until her gaze shifted up to his face and winked at her. She went bright pink and returned her attention to her players.

"Time's up," she purred. "Do you have an answer for me? Or will you turn tail and run like rats? I do so love a chase."

"We're going to say quiet."

"No, silence."

"Right, silence. You break the silence when you say the word out loud."

"'My, my,'" Jo replied with a feline tilt to her head. "'What unexpected cleverness.' The sphinx folds her paws under her and curls up into a cat-like loaf, still nearly ten feet tall. 'Now, what sort of favor would you ask of me?'"

Felix blew Jo a kiss and continued his stroll through the tables. He waved to Jo's friends when he saw them. Kim and Young were at a table together, and Max was at another, once again acting out the casting of his bard's spells with a dramatic flourish. David was GMing at the table where Aida was playing, giving his players the same sphinx riddle that Jo had. Heather's rogue was nowhere to be seen. Perhaps she was there somewhere, out of costume. Felix doubted he would recognize her outside of her all-pink getup.

As the Legendary neared its end, an event administrator at the front of the room—a lanky white man with neat gray hair and a name tag that read "Matthew"—started giving a countdown in five-minute increments. Each announcement was returned with cries of anguish from all around as the players raced to complete their objectives. People were getting up from their tables and running to the front to report their successes to the admins. At that point, Felix decided he should keep the pathways between the tables clear. He watched the last ten minutes of the game from the side of the room, mesmerized.

It was pandemonium. Dice flying. Players jumping up and down at their tables. Slips of paper being passed from hand to hand. Full-on sprints to the admins. Three white boards tallying successes in different categories. GMs hurrying their players along. The countdown increasing to one-minute markers. More anguished screams. Glances at the white boards from tables that finished early. People on their tiptoes trying to count tally marks from across the room.

"Thirty seconds!"

Felix saw Jo on her feet, frantically pointing back and forth between two players. He couldn't tell what they were doing, but suddenly there was a whoop of joy, and Jo held out a slip of paper.

"Fifteen seconds!"

A player at Jo's table grabbed the slip and pelted toward the front, dodging chairs and people like an honest-to-God rogue.

"Ten! Nine!" Dozens of people—admins and GMs and players alike—took up the countdown. Felix joined them.

"Move!"

"Eight! Seven! Six!"

Jo's player slammed the slip onto the admin table, panting. A woman behind the table snatched it up.

"Five! Four!"

"Success in combat," the woman said, and a tally went on the board.

"Success in exploration," added another admin as a player thrust a piece of paper in his face. Another tally on a different board.

"Three! Two!"

"Success in social," said two admins at once. Two tallies.

"One!"

"*Successincombat*," someone snuck in. A hasty tally.

"TIME!"

A subdued scattering of applause around the room was all that met that announcement. Felix was surprised there wasn't more excitement, but then he remembered. David had said that everyone wins or loses the Legendary together. MnM wasn't typically the kind of game players win or lose; Jo had explained that to Felix early on. Telling a story together came with highs and lows, successes and failures, but that was where the concept of "winning" usually ended. The Legendary, though, was different. It had a win condition. And the group here at Indi-Con didn't know yet if they had won.

The admins hurriedly took down the white boards and turned them away from the crowd. A hush fell over the room. Hundreds of people on pins and needles. Felix, caught up in the moment, felt his heart pounding.

"Heroes of the Sibylline Wastes," shouted Matthew, the admin who had called the countdown. "Tonight, you—"

"Yes, *you*, adventurer!" half of the room supplied.

"—took up your calling. In order to win your Legendary adventure, you needed to collect forty successes in each of the three categories." Matthew gestured toward the backs of the white boards and paused dramatically. "In social encounters, you earned a collective forty-four successes."

Some cheers and applause as one white board was flipped over and held up.

"In exploration, you earned a total of fifty successes. Well done, explorers."

The second white board was turned. There were no cheers this time. The room was silent.

"In combat," Matthew yelled, his voice cracking from overuse, "which is the most challenging category, you earned... *exactly* forty successes."

The silence broke. The uproar was deafening. GMs applauded and high-fived their players. Some people actually danced with excitement. Felix had never seen anything like it. The closest comparison he could come up with was a stadium full of football fans cheering for their team's playoff win. Except, even that wasn't quite right—everyone here had participated in the win. They weren't the fans; they were the team. And unlike a football team, most of these people were perfect strangers to one another.

There was something beautiful, awe-inspiring even, about it. Felix remembered this feeling from the night Jo first explained MnM to him. Not the books or the rules or the archetypes, but what the game was *really* about. Inclusivity, teamwork, and good prevailing over evil, even if it was for pretend. The idea that, with unshakeable belief and a good group of allies, it was possible to *win*. Felix doubted that everyone in the hall tonight saw MnM that way. For most of them, it was probably just a game. For Trey, it was a way to goof off and let loose and make his fiancé laugh. For Max, it seemed to allow him to come out of his shell and become someone else for a while.

But for Jo? For Jo, it was this. This feeling of camaraderie and triumph that hummed like magic through the room.

And Felix got it.

"GMs, please distribute rewards to your players," Matthew bellowed with the last vestiges of his voice.

Players and GMs took their seats, and the noise level returned to the dull roar of conversation. When the hall finally started clearing out, Felix headed to Jo's table.

"Hey," he greeted her, leaning on the backrest of a chair.

Jo smiled at him, sending his heart into a tailspin. "Oh, good. I was afraid we scared you away."

"That was the wildest shit I've ever seen," Felix said. "And I loved it."

Jo stopped scooping handfuls of dice into her enormous drawstring bag. She stared at Felix for a long second then abandoned her side of the table and rushed him. Felix barely had time to stand up straight before she was throwing her arms around his neck. He caught her waist, hitting her butt with his bag of exhibit hall purchases. Jo didn't seem to notice.

"You really loved it?" she said in his ear. "You're not just saying that?"

"I really did. And I think I understand better why you love it too."

Jo sniffled, and Felix drew back to find her crying. He brushed her sweet, round cheeks free of tears.

"Ugh, sorry." Jo shook her head and stepped back, roughly drying her face with her palms. "I don't know why I'm crying. I'm just exhausted. It's been a long couple of days."

"You're allowed to cry, Jo."

"Over MnM?" she scoffed at herself.

"Sure, why not?" he said. "Or over your boyfriend saying something nice."

A tear slipped down her cheek. She didn't scrub it away. It trailed all the way down to her jaw and splashed on her T-shirt. "Thank you, Felix."

"I got you something," he said, opening his bag. "I hope it fits. They said I could exchange it tomorrow if it doesn't."

He held up the "Things Are Getting Dicey" shirt for her, with its bubbly font and scattered dice of every shape and color. Jo gasped and giggled.

"It's not cropped," he said.

"It's perfect," she replied, taking the shirt with both hands. "I love it. I'm going to wear it tomorrow."

She grasped him by the back of the neck and pulled him roughly toward her, kissing him soundly on the mouth. He had barely begun to kiss her back when she released him. Felix staggered back, a bit dizzy.

She reached for his bag. "What else did you get?"

"Oh, no, you don't," he said, lifting it up out of her reach. "These are surprises for tomorrow."

Jo dropped her fists onto her hips. "Just tell me you didn't buy any swords and promise to ship them to Trey."

"Now why didn't *we* think of that?" he cried.

She smacked him lightly on the arm.

JO RETURNED HER attention to her pile of GM supplies. Felix offered to help, so she handed him a stack of papers and asked him to return them to the admins. For just a moment, she stared at his ass as he walked to the front of the room.

A T-shirt. He'd gotten her an MnM T-shirt with a dumb, wonderful pun. She'd almost started crying again at the sight of it. Jeremy never would have—

Stop it, Jo, she told herself. *Don't compare them.*

It was so hard not to, when Jeremy was all she'd known for so long. And really, what was a few months broken up compared to their years together? He was still right behind her, just over her shoulder. She was driving on the highway, trying to move forward with Felix beside her yet seeing Jeremy every time she glanced in the rearview mirror. She just needed to keep driving, keep leaving him behind and holding on to the man next to her. Hopefully, with a little more time, a little more distance, it would be easier to separate them in her mind.

Hopefully, Jeremy wasn't lurking in the backseat, keeping pace with them as they went.

On the walk back to the hotel, Felix told her about the exhibit hall and his time with Trey, and she gave him some of the highlights from her Legendary table. In the elevator, Felix moved behind her and wrapped one arm around her waist, his hand a warm, secure weight against her low belly. "I liked the part of your game I saw," he murmured. "I liked your sphinx voice."

"Oh really?" she said, pitching her voice down. She'd only done the voice in the first place because she thought it was funny. It had started as a bad Lauren Bacall impression and ended up a mishmash of femme fatale caricatures. She rolled it out for sphinxes, seductive archfey of all genders, and hags in disguise luring people to their deaths.

"Yeah," Felix said. "I really did."

His breath was hot on her ear. Jo leaned her head back, exposing her throat to him. He pressed his lips to the side of her neck, and she let out a breathy moan.

"I might be persuaded to use it more often," she said in that low, lazy voice, "if—"

The elevator came to a stop, and the doors opened on their floor, revealing a well-dressed elderly white couple waiting to head downstairs. Felix quickly released Jo, and they hurried off the elevator.

"That woman gave me the dirtiest look," he said with a chuckle once they were out of earshot.

"I was avoiding eye contact," Jo replied. "But they're the ones going out at ten o'clock. We should be giving *them* the stink eye."

The moment they were safely inside their room, Felix's hand was on her stomach again, dragging her backward against his chest. "What was that you were saying? You'll use it more often if..."

"Oh, I can't remember," Jo said in her normal voice. She tapped him on the wrist. "Let me go, please, I have to pee."

Felix grumbled but did as requested. She kissed his cheek, right on the edge of his stubble, before dropping her bags and disappearing into the bathroom. Leaning back on the door, she pressed her hand to her chest.

Jo knew what she wanted now, in a way she hadn't a mere twenty-four hours ago. This wasn't just a con hookup; it wasn't just sex. They weren't going to bang it out and move on. Felix was hers, and she was his. She held his hand and brought him breakfast when he woke up grumpy. He scratched her back and bought her stupid, perfect T-shirts.

Christ, how her heart was pounding. She skimmed her fingers over the spot on her neck where his lips had brushed her skin. *More*, her body demanded. *More, more, more*, with every throb of her pulse in her clit.

It was so tempting, to fling open the door and fall into his arms and ask him to touch her and taste her and fuck her until she couldn't see straight. To give him everything he so plainly wanted. To ride him like she had dreamt about and hear the sounds he made when he came.

There was only one problem: she really was exhausted. Playing and running MnM all day, including a Legendary, had wiped her out. Her eyelids were like lead. She didn't want to be fighting off sleep their first time together. She wanted to be present and remember every detail.

Tomorrow, she told herself as a flutter of anticipation went through her. *Sleep tonight; sex tomorrow.*

As Jo readied for bed, she considered if she should tell Felix what she was planning. *Not yet,* she decided. She was already having fun teasing him. And despite (or maybe because of) his claims that he was going to die over it, she thought he was enjoying it too. Plus, they would be playing together as Grax and Veena in the morning.

Oh yes. Tomorrow was going to be so much fun.

16

"GOOD MORNING, FOLKS. Everyone excited for some MnM?"

Felix looked up from double-checking his new pugilist abilities to see a middle-aged white man with glasses and graying red hair. He had an easy smile and was wearing a bolo tie over a collared shirt with a tiny checkerboard print in white and pale blue.

"My name's Woody," he continued in his Texas drawl, "and yes, I'm a cowboy named Woody. We're here to play an adventure we call 'Why Do They Have to Be Snakes?' in tribute to Indiana Jones. Everyone in the right place?"

Felix, Jo, and the three other players at the table nodded. Woody handed out index cards for everyone to jot down their character details and prop them up on the table so everyone could remember who was who. Felix liked that idea, especially after the game he'd played the day before where the characters hardly interacted at all. He flipped over his character sheet and added a bullet point to his growing list of GMing ideas.

"You *are* taking notes," Jo whispered beside him. At his curious look, she explained, "Aida thought she saw you taking notes yesterday. She thought it was cute."

"And what do you think?" he asked.

"I think it's cute too." She bumped his shoulder with hers, and Felix grinned. She glanced down at his shirt. "You're just very cute today."

Cute wasn't exactly the sense he'd gotten from her earlier that morning. When he'd emerged from the bathroom in his new shirt—a gray tee with the words "World's Okayest Fighter" and a d20 showing the number ten—Jo had looked at him like she was about to pounce. He hadn't even had to flash his abs at her. Definitely worth the money.

"You too," Felix said, pointing with his chin at her shirt, the one he'd bought. She'd tied it up by knotting the hem at her ribs, right under her left boob. She'd also left her jacket in the hotel room. It was warm out, but Felix wondered if she'd done it to show off more of her midriff. Either way, he wasn't complaining. "I think I might win, though," he continued.

Jo's eyebrows went up. "It's a competition?"

"Yes. And I have one more surprise." He reached into his backpack.

"All right, ready to take up your calling?" Woody said with an eager smile.

"Let's do it," responded a middle-aged Black man. The index card in front of him read "Mzuzi, halfling artificer, level 4."

Felix decided to wait for a better moment to show Jo his surprise as Woody launched into the story: A village had been attacked by winged snakes that left several people injured and poisoned. The adventurers were tasked with finding out where they were coming from and putting a stop to it. Grax, the strongest character, had his work cut out for him as they headed into the jungle. He hacked through the bush, rescued Mzuzi when he fell into a pit trap, and boosted their half-elf hunter, Poppy, into a tree so she could keep them from getting lost.

When they tracked down the nest of snakes, it was time for combat. They rolled for initiative, and as Woody set up the turn order, Felix pulled his new dice out of his backpack. Jo caught his movement and watched him. Next to the yellow dice she had given him, he placed a green set with orange numbers, then he tapped the polished nail of her ring finger. The orange d20 on green. Indi-Con's colors.

Jo's eyes shone with delight. "You win," she whispered.

Poppy acted first in combat. The young white woman playing her rolled a d20 for an attack. She hit and rolled her damage, and then Woody turned to Jo.

"Veena, you're up," he said. "Poppy has injured one snake, but there are four more about to take wing out of the nest."

"I got this!" Jo said in Veena's girlish voice, then switched to her normal one. "I'm going to run over to the nest and cast Shockwave at the cluster of them."

A few rolls and calculations later, their GM declared that the snakes were agile enough to dodge the full brunt of her spell. They were hurt, but still alive. And pissed.

"And unfortunately," Woody said, "the snakes take their turns next. The four you attacked, Veena, are all going to slither into the air and strike you."

"This is fine," Jo said with a nervous laugh, already picking up her pencil to mark down the damage she was about to take. Three out of the four attacks landed, and Felix watched Veena's health drop into the single digits.

Woody pointed to Felix. "Grax, you are up next. What are you going to do to save your party?"

"I'm going to go help Veena," Felix said without hesitation. "Grax is her friend. He isn't going to let her down."

Out of the corner of his eye, he saw Jo smile.

"All right," Woody prompted. "Tell me how you're going to help her."

"I would like to punch one of the snakes." *There's a sentence I never thought I'd say.* Felix rolled his new green d20 and mentally added his pugilist attack bonus. "Nineteen to hit?"

"That hits!"

He rolled a second attack, which also hit, and then rolled the damage for both attacks. Woody took over narrating with a rich description of Grax rushing up and slamming his fists into first one snake, and then another. The other players at the table cheered as he killed them both, sending a rush of satisfaction through Felix.

But that was nothing compared to the feeling that followed it.

Because as Woody moved on to the next turn, Jo leaned over and whispered in Veena's voice, "Thanks, Grax. You're very good with your hands."

Heat pooled in Felix's gut, spread lower, made him squirm. Jo giggled and leaned away. Felix followed her with his body. Two could play at that game.

"Oh, Veena," he murmured. "You have *no* idea."

Under the table, he placed his palm on Jo's knee and slowly curled his fingers until they draped against her inner thigh. With the lightest touch, he glided them back and forth across her leggings. Now Jo was the one squirming.

"That's six points of health back to you, Veena," said the young Indian man playing Hulvin, an orc cleric.

Jo scrambled for her pencil. "Six? Thanks, Hulvin."

It didn't take long for the last couple of snakes to be defeated. Then, after some investigation, the group discovered the entrance to an underground hideout hidden beneath the nest. They wound through dark, dirty tunnels until they stumbled across a sect of dragon-worshiping cultists conducting some sort of unholy ritual. The cultists immediately attacked.

Jo sent Veena into the thick of the fighting again, and Felix sent Grax in after her.

"Stop doing that. You're squishy," he said playfully, then addressed Woody. "Grax is going to breathe fire on the cultists."

"Hell yeah!" Poppy's player cheered. "Dragon versus dragon."

Woody and Felix both rolled their dice, and Grax's fire took out two of the cultists, leaving three for them to deal with.

Jo leaned over to Felix once more, close enough for him to smell her strawberry-scented conditioner. This time, she used her own voice, not Veena's. "I guess your mouth's not bad either."

"Damn you," he whispered back, all breathy and soft while another kind of fire raged inside him. Jo chuckled in the back of her throat, which only managed to fan the flames. Felix refocused on the game, willing his body to calm down. At this rate, he would have to go back to the hotel room over lunch to let off some steam. Maybe Jo would come with him. *Fuck.* He had to cut off that train of thought before it made things worse.

Jo had mercy on him for the remainder of the game, thank God. It was a tough battle to take out the spell-slinging cultists, and Felix needed to concentrate and strategize with his party. They focused their attacks while Hulvin the cleric kept them healed up enough to just barely win the fight. That feeling of satisfaction returned as Felix and the other players exchanged smiles and high fives. Jo grinned at him, clearly pleased to see him enjoying himself.

"Congratulations, adventurers," Woody said after narrating

their triumphant return to the village, "on a job well done. Thank you all for joining me. This was a blast, and I hope you had as much fun as I did."

Echoing back their thanks, Felix and Jo began to pack up. She breezily asked where they should grab lunch. As if she hadn't just worked him into a frenzy.

He opened his mouth to make a half-serious joke about their hotel room when it dawned on him what day it was. "Actually, I should call Tito," he said. "It's the first Sunday in almost a year I'm not there to visit him."

"Of course," Jo replied tenderly. "I can pick up food for us."

They headed out into the pleasant warmth of the noontime sun, and he found a quiet, shady spot to make his call. Jo stole a quick kiss, and he watched the sway of her hips as she walked away.

"Hijo," said Tito when he answered the phone. "Aren't you too busy with your friend for me?"

"I'm never too busy for you, Tito," Felix replied. "How are you feeling today?"

"I'm always good, you know that. I wish I had waffles in front of me, but such is life."

"How about I buy you extra waffles next week?"

Tito clicked his tongue. "That does me no good today, does it?"

He then told Felix about the book he was reading—another noir thriller—and the latest gossip about two of his neighbors who were having a fling. Felix told Tito about the con in broad strokes, about meeting Jo's friends, and finally about Jo herself.

"I thought you'd want to know," he said, "that Jo and I decided to start dating."

"Felix, me alegro!" Tito cried. In Spanish, he continued, "I'm so happy you came to your senses. Are you happy too? Does she bring you joy?"

All of a sudden, Felix's heart felt too big for his chest. "Sí, Tito. She brings me joy." Even when—especially when—she was being a goddamn tease.

"Bravo," Tito said. "That is all that matters."

AS MUCH FUN as Jo was having teasing Felix, it had a side effect that, honestly, she should have anticipated. She was getting just as turned on as he seemed to be. The entire time she was buying burritos (carnitas for herself, vegetarian for Felix), her body was reminding her of the feel of Felix's hand on her back, his finger-tips on her thigh, his lips against hers. She could barely keep her hands to herself while they ate lunch on the grass.

Really, she had no one to blame but herself.

That afternoon, Jo had a game to GM, and Felix was attending panel presentations about SWOP and starting a public MnM pro-gram. She slipped her hand into his back pocket as they walked toward the gaming hall in the blessedly cool air-conditioning.

His hand moved under her backpack to the base of her spine. "Damn your lack of pockets."

"Don't blame me," she said. "Blame the fashion industry for not understanding that women deserve pockets."

"You're wearing leggings."

"And who says leggings shouldn't have pockets?"

"The fashion industry?"

"Exactly." With that, she squeezed his ass. His tight, supple, perfect ass.

He nearly choked on his own breath. "God, Jo," he murmured.

When they reached the hall, Jo pulled away and blew him a kiss. "I'll see you back here around five?"

"Uh huh," he grunted, and Jo didn't think she was imagining the fire in his eyes. It was almost too easy.

The afternoon flew by. Her table was a high-level game that had a lot of moving parts and difficult monsters, and her players were skilled enough to keep her on her toes. Thoughts of Felix faded to the back of her mind as she worked to challenge her players and improvise around their harebrained schemes. Not until hours later, when the Kraken was defeated and rewards were distributed, did she have a second to breathe.

And all those thoughts came rushing back.

And Jo was done waiting.

A quick glance at her phone told her that Felix's last panel had fifteen minutes left, so she made the most of her time. First, she stopped by the sign-up sheets on the wall to cross her name off the evening session, then she parked herself on the floor in an out-of-the-way spot in the hallway. As she scarfed down her last granola bar, she texted her friends before she went off the grid for the rest of the night.

Jo

Checking in! How's everyone's Sunday?

Heather

I regret everything.

I should not have cosplayed two days in a row

Why are wigs so hot???

I hate my life

Kim

I'm at a panel about MnM-inspired fashion and it's soooooooo good!

Young

My game is running long because this GM is so slow with combat. Ugh. Wish you were running, Jo.

Jo

So frustrating! My game just ended. It was awesome but chaotic. Underwater combat rules are way too complicated.

Aida

Trey and I took a hotel break because we are old. He's napping, and I'm watching 70s game show reruns. I'm really good at Family Feud.

Max

are we doing dinner tonight

David

I'd be down.

Young

Same

Kim

> I met a cute girl at this talk and I'm
> going to shoot my shot after so idk yet

Heather

> I need to change and shower first but
> yeah. I'm starving.

Jo

> Felix and I have plans, but how
> about breakfast tomorrow before
> we all leave?

Everyone quickly agreed. Aida offered to make a reservation somewhere, so they wouldn't have to eat stale hotel bagels for their last meal together.

"There you are."

Jo looked up to see Felix walking toward her. She started to stand, but he held up his palm to stop her and joined her on the floor. Sighing contentedly, he slouched enough to rest his head on her shoulder. Jo leaned her cheek on his silky hair as he threaded their fingers together.

On any other day, his sweetness would have warmed her heart. Today, it warmed her much, much lower.

"I was texting the group," she said. "Sorry I lost track of time."

"I found you. How is everyone?"

"Keeping busy. Except Trey, who's asleep."

"How was your game?" he asked with a laugh.

"Really good. High-level players are always a fun challenge. How were the panels?"

"Great," he said. "One of the panelists was actually a librarian at the Indianapolis Public Library. We exchanged cards afterward, and she's going to send me some of their MnM event materials to adapt."

"Felix, that's awesome," Jo replied. "I hope that makes the trip worth it."

He tilted his head back and met her eye. "It was already worth it, Jo." He squeezed her hand. Jo almost crawled on top of him. Right there in the hallway. "So, what's next? I'm not really hungry yet, but we should probably eat before the evening session. And I need to sign up for a game."

"Did you have your heart set on another game tonight?" Jo asked, giving her voice a sultry edge.

Felix tensed. "I wouldn't say that," he said slowly, carefully. "Why do you ask?"

"I thought maybe we could do something else instead." She touched the back of his hand, trailing one fingertip up to his wrist. He had an actual goddamn divot between the muscles of his forearm, and she traced her finger along it, combing through his arm hair.

He jolted upright, leaning into her, twisting to plant his free hand on the far side of her hip. With the slightest shift of his leg, he'd be on top of her. Right there in the hallway.

"You've been teasing me today, my Jo," he said, eyes alight. He'd never sounded so raw, so feral. Jo's skin was electrified by it. "And I've let you. I've liked it, even. All that wit and cleverness focused solely on vexing me. But I swear to God, if you're teasing me now—"

"I'm not," she said, fighting to control her breathing. She gripped his forearm and felt his muscles twitch powerfully under her palm. "I already took my name off the game I was going to play tonight. Take me to our room, Felix. Now."

"Get your things."

17

THE DOOR OF the hotel room slammed shut. Jo barely registered
Felix flipping the deadbolt, in too much of a rush to bother with
the "Do Not Disturb" sign. Their bags hit the floor, and then his
hands were on her, holding her face and drawing her in. Their
mouths met—hot and needy. Jesus, he tasted so good. He whispered her name over and over between each touch of their lips. Jo
had never loved the sound of her own name more.

She buried her hands in his hair and dragged him closer until
he staggered into her. She stumbled back against the wall, and
Felix's body fell onto hers. Like the other night, his cock was already hard against her stomach. Tonight, though, she wouldn't
leave him wanting. Jo moaned and arched her back, pushing her
belly forward. Felix pressed back, hard, grinding against her as he
panted. He stepped his legs apart and shifted to straddle her hip.
The pressure of his muscled thigh against her pussy was exquisite, but she craved more. *More.* She hitched her leg over his hip,
and he caught her knee.

"Fuck." The word came out of him hard and fast, like he'd been
punched in the stomach.

He raised his head, brushing his lips across her forehead. His stubble scratched pleasantly, and Jo sucked her lower lip between her teeth. Felix's thumb brushed a tender caress over her cheek.

"I don't want to go too fast," he said gently.

"I'm ready, Felix. I promise."

"I appreciate your clarity on that, but that's not what I mean." He shifted back and eased her leg down. "I mean I don't want this to be over too soon. I can't even see you properly."

Oh. That. With the blackout curtains closed, and their complete disregard of the lights, the only illumination came from the hallway light leaking under the door.

"You've gotten me all riled up today," he continued. "All weekend, really. But I want us to take our time together." He brushed her cheek again, bumping the bottom of her glasses. "I don't want a quick fuck against the wall in the dark."

He was right, damn him. As hot as the lust pounding through her blood was, as much as she was already desperate for release, there was no reason to rush. It would be all the sweeter if they eased into it.

"I don't want that either," Jo said. She fumbled along the wall and flipped the first switch she found, flooding them with light from above. She watched Felix's pupils adjust in his dark brown irises.

"That's better," he purred. His palms glided down her arms until he captured her hands. He drew her away from the wall. Jo matched him, step for step. They each toed off their shoes as they went, stopping once they stood between the two beds. The entryway light bathed the room in a pale yellow glow.

"Is this enough light?" Jo asked.

"Yes." His eyes trailed lazily up and down her body. His gaze was so intimate, she might as well already be naked. He gripped her hands tighter, settled that intense stare on her eyes. She was suddenly finding it difficult to breathe. "What I said the other night still goes. Whatever you want. However long you want it. So tell me, Jo. Tell me what you want. Let me give it to you."

Jo licked her lips. "Show me how good you are with your hands, Felix. Touch me."

He moved in closer, crowded her space. She didn't budge. The rich, spicy scent of cloves enveloped her.

"Where? Tell me where."

"Everywhere."

She wasn't surprised when his hands found her ass first. The man was obsessed. He groaned just from the pleasure of touching her there. She grasped his shoulders to steady herself, feeling the muscles shift as he moved. He dug his fingers in—groping, fondling, grabbing. As if he'd been hungering for this ever since his first taste on the night of the tornado.

"More, Felix," she encouraged. "Touch me more."

One hand stayed where it was, kneading the fullness of her cheek, while the other slid to her thigh and caressed her. If only he'd continue circling forward, moving to the front of her body and giving her pussy that pressure she'd felt from his leg. But no. He was content to keep to the outside of her thigh. He dragged his fingertips up, up, all the way to her ribs. He grasped the hem of her T-shirt, right along the band of her bra, and pulled.

Nothing happened.

"What—?"

"It's tied," she reminded him.

"Fucking..." He roughly untied the knot in her shirt. Her body jerked with the force of his actions, and she let out a small, delighted cry. Felix gave her a lopsided smirk. "You like that? When I'm rough with you?"

"Maybe a little," she admitted with a grin to complement his.

Felix kissed her cheek. "I'll keep that in mind for another time. Tonight, I'm going to take care of you."

"Oh," she breathed. Her heart fluttered in her chest. When was the last time someone took care—*really* took care—of her in this way? She didn't want to think about it too hard.

"That's what I thought," he said, reading her like a book. "You like that idea even better, don't you?"

"Yeah."

"Good. Now, where was I?"

He grasped her loosened shirt in both fists and pulled it over her head. As he let it drop to the floor, he paused and took her in, his gaze roving her body. She expected him to remove her lacy pink and white bra next so he could see her boobs.

Instead, with the tips of two fingers, he touched her left shoulder and moved her bra strap down her arm, leaving bare the tattoo on her chest. Halfway between her shoulder and breast were inked the words she'd read to him during that first MnM lesson: "Yes, *you*, adventurer." Felix ran his fingers over them as if he were touching something sacred. With care. Respect. Reverence. Her skin prickled.

"May I kiss you here?" he asked her, his eyes flicking to hers.

"God, yes."

He leaned forward and pressed the sweetest kiss to her tattoo, right over the word "you." Jo's breath caught, and tears sprang to her eyes.

"Felix." She tried to say more, but the words stuck in her throat. She swallowed and seized his head. If she couldn't tell him how much that kiss meant to her, she would show him. She ravaged his mouth with kisses, pouring every emotion that surged through her into each one. Felix took her by the hips again, holding her so tightly she might bruise. She didn't care. Let his fingerprints mark every inch of her body. Let him claim her. She would claim him right back.

She grasped his shoulders and bunched up the fabric of his new MnM shirt, hitching it up his back. "Let me see you," she begged around their kisses. "Let me see."

"Thought you'd never ask."

He raised his arms, and she yanked his shirt off, discarding it on the floor beside her own.

"Christ Almighty," she swore. He was unreal. The planes and contours of his body were superhero perfect, anatomy textbook perfect. Just looking at him made her so wet she could feel it dampen her panties. "I should take up boxing."

Felix laughed and took her by the wrist. He placed her hand on his bare chest. His heart pounded beneath her palm. She curled her fingers into his thick, dark hair and listened to his contented moan.

"What do you think?" he asked.

"Yup." Jo was nodding like a goddamn fool. "Good. Real... really good."

"Do you want to see more?" He guided her hand toward his waistband. He shuddered as her fingertips combed through his chest hair, rippled over his abs. "I'll touch you first, Jo. But I want you to take off my jeans."

Now that he'd drawn her attention downward, Jo could only stare at the bulge of his dick against his fly. She wanted to see it. Wanted it inside her. "I can do that."

"That's my girl."

Jesus, why did the core of her being melt when he said that?

Why did it make her whimper like a needy kitten? For years now, Jo had hated being called a girl, especially working in a profession where people often treated her as if she were young and naïve. But God damn it, she could listen to Felix praise her like that—warm and doting and sincere—all fucking day.

He let go of her wrist, and she eased the fly of his jeans open. She brushed his cock, drawing a guttural sound out of him. His erection was even bigger with nothing but his navy boxer briefs to hold him in. Jo pushed his jeans down and crouched to take them all the way off like he'd asked. He stepped out of them while she gazed up at him. She tossed a quick glance at his cock and licked her upper lip with the very tip of her tongue. Then, she watched the moment Felix's brain short-circuited. Jo gave him a devilish grin and slowly rose back up.

"I like your legs too, Felix."

"I'm glad," he replied. "Now I want to see you. Lie down so I can get those pants off you."

Jo glanced from side to side. She tilted her head as if confused, crossed her arms over her chest, and pointed to either side of her. "Your bed or mine?"

"Fuck, woman, I don't care. Just pick a bed and get on it."

She laughed and chose his bed. She set her glasses aside then crawled onto it on her hands and knees, giving him a view of her ass before she rolled to her back. Felix took his socks off first, then hers. He ran his hand over her body, from her throat, past the center of her bra, over her midriff, and down her leggings to stop millimeters shy of her pussy. She groaned in frustration and rolled her hips up into his hand. Felix grinned, as if he'd been waiting for her to do just that, and cupped her. The heel of his hand massaged her gently.

Christ. He felt so good already, but it wasn't nearly enough to sate the driving need inside her. "I thought you were going to take my pants off."

"I will," he assured her. "But first I'm going to tell you what's about to happen."

Jo's entire body turned white hot, centering on the lazy circles his hand was making over her vulva.

"I'm going to start off slow, with one, maybe two, fingers. I'll start to learn your body and what you like. I'll let you get familiar with my touch." He grasped the headboard and leaned over her. His hand pressed the tiniest bit harder, and Jo let out a high-pitched whine she didn't know she was capable of making. "And then I'll ramp up and give you everything I've got. I am *very* good with my hands, Jo. I have the stamina to last as long as you can. I'll make you come as many times as you want. If it's ever too much, or not enough, or if you want something different, all you have to do is ask."

"Holy shit," she breathed, trembling all over.

He reached down to brush a loose lock of hair off her forehead. "With that in mind, do you still want me to touch you, Jo?"

Jo had never wanted anything more. "Yes. Please."

The gentle pressure of his hand vanished, and he peeled her leggings off her legs. He flung them away without looking. They draped over the TV, and Jo laughed. Then he did the same with her panties, leaving her naked except for her bra.

"Spread your legs more for me," Felix said. She complied, and he knelt between her knees. He stared at her, open for him, and licked his lips. "So wet already, my Jo? Good girl."

"Oh my God," she whispered, unable to stop herself.

His first touch was divine. Two fingertips dipped into her wetness and drew slowly up toward her clit. Jo let out a soft groan when he found her favorite spot.

"Right there?" He gave her slow, steady circles, working her up with precision. His other hand glided over the dimpled flesh of her hip. "Such pretty sounds you make when I touch you. Keep letting me hear them."

The heat that enveloped her grew even stronger in her cheeks. She didn't tend to hold back when she felt good, but no one had ever *encouraged* her moans before. Letting her eyes fall closed, she gave herself over to Felix's ministrations. Soon, her wordless sounds rang out in harmony with his tender words of praise.

"Ready, Jo?" he said after a while. "I'm going to give you a little more."

His hand shifted, and his fingers slid inside her.

"God, yes. Felix. Yes."

His thumb pressed into her clit as he thrust his fingers deeper into her cunt. Jo bucked against the mattress and cried out in pleasure. She gripped the pillow tightly, needing something to anchor to.

"Do you like it, baby?"

Jo's eyes flew open. She glared at the ceiling as a pang pierced her gut, her heart, her mind, drowning out all other sensations in an instant. "Don't call me that."

"Do you like it, Jo? Do you like the way my hand feels inside you?"

Was someone touching her? She could hardly tell. Jo squeezed her eyes shut and forced herself to focus. There. She could feel it now. She squirmed. "Mm-hmm."

The hand stopped moving. Knuckles grazed her cheek.

"Hey. Look at me, Jo. Come back."

She opened her eyes. And saw Felix. She was with Felix. She

whispered his name once, twice. The tightness in her chest released, and her breaths came easily again.

"There you are," Felix said as he caressed her cheek again. "Stay with me. You okay?"

"I'm okay. I'm sorry."

"It's all right, Jo. Should I stop?"

Jo took a slow breath to give herself a second to think. No. She didn't want him to stop. She didn't want this precious night with him stolen away by her own stupid brain. Another breath. Releasing the pillow, she touched Felix's hand at her cheek. He closed his fingers around hers.

She imagined herself driving on the highway. Felix sat in the passenger seat, holding her hand like this. Gazing at her lovingly like this. She slammed on the gas pedal, leaving the past in the past.

"No," Jo said. "Please don't stop."

"I won't," Felix promised. Then, immediately, he kept his promise. His thumb swirled around her clit, and Jo gasped and dropped her head back. "Say my name again, Jo, and tell me if you like it."

"Yes. Felix, yes. I like it."

He smiled at her as he began to pump his fingers in and out of her. "That's it. Tell me as often as you want. I like to hear it."

Jo was quickly swept away by the touch of his hand. "More, Felix."

He added his ring finger and fucked her faster. She clenched onto his other hand, cool against her hot cheek.

"Hold the pillow again," he told her. It took her a moment to let go of him, but when she did, he dragged his hand down to her chest and kneaded her breast through her bra. Her nipple firmed, and she arched into his touch.

"Fuck, Felix. It's so good."

"There's more," he said, sensuous and quiet. "Do you want it?"

"Yes. *Yes.*"

"Good girl."

His hand traveled down again. Jo moaned at the loss of sensation on her nipple, and then again when he removed his thumb from her clit. "More," she whined. "Please."

The bed shifted under her. Felix's leg brushed hers as he adjusted his position. "Patience, my Jo."

She waited for the space of two thundering heartbeats. And then her body exploded with ecstasy. Three fingers pounded into her while—*holy fuck*—his other hand found her clit. Both hands were on her now, and Jo had never known anything like it. Her clit was nestled between the pads of two fingers that flew in fast, tight circles. Inside her, Felix was curling, twisting, rubbing, never doing the same thing twice as though to learn what she liked best. Jo's poor mind could barely keep up. Eventually, she stopped trying to anticipate what was coming next and simply let herself *feel.*

Words and sounds spilled from her lips as she writhed. "Felix" and "please" and "Jesus" and "yes" and "more, oh my God, more." She was losing control. She was coming apart at the seams. She was making a fool of herself.

And Felix? He kept going. He just—

Didn't.

Fucking.

Stop.

He wasn't kidding about having stamina. Not once did he slow down or readjust or pause to shake out his hands. He gave her everything he'd promised, and then some.

The pleasure began to crest within Jo, and her whole body went tense in expectation. She sucked in a breath through her teeth.

Felix noticed. "Yes, my Jo. You're so close. Let me see how beautifully you come. Don't hold back. Show me. Show me how you come. Let go."

She did. Jo screamed a short, high scream as she came so hard it dazzled her vision. Even with her eyes shut tight, she saw white. Her scream devolved into a moan that was cut off by a gasp.

"Fe—" She couldn't even get his whole name out. Couldn't beg him to stop before the pleasure destroyed her.

Because he was still going, not letting up by even a fraction. As soon as she started coming down from her orgasm, another one followed it. Jo's body spasmed and shuddered, and she released a wild yelp. She managed to unclench one fist from the pillowcase and wave her hand at Felix to stop him. Only then did he slow, deftly easing her down until he finally settled into stillness. Jo's breaths were ragged, uneven, gasping. Her body convulsed as her muscles twitched into relaxation. She peeled her eyes open and stared, wide-eyed, at the ceiling.

"Ho... ly..."

Felix's hands came away from her body, and he lay down next to her. "Breathe," he murmured in her ear. "You did great, my Jo. That was beautiful to watch. Just breathe now." His palm, as warm and grounding as his voice, rested on her stomach. She covered his hand with both of hers and felt her own wetness coating his fingers. Jo couldn't remember ever being so wet when she came.

After what seemed like hours, she calmed down enough to speak a full sentence. "What the ever-loving fuck, Felix?"

THE NEED FOR release was an insistent, nagging pulse through Felix's body, but damn if it wasn't satisfying to bring Jo to such beautiful ruin. She was so responsive, both to his hands and to his words. It made him want to touch her all night. He nuzzled his nose into her cheek and inhaled the delicious scent of her. "That's why I told you in advance what I was going to do."

"Not nearly enough of a warning." She inched her face closer, a request he answered by kissing her deeply. She hummed into his lips and rolled onto her side.

Felix slid his hand from her belly to her back, leaving a damp trail around her waist. Jo clutched at him and raked the backs of her green and orange nails through his chest hair. His skin ignited with goosebumps, and he moaned against her mouth.

"Fuck, I love the way your nails feel, Jo," he said and kissed her again. "Lower."

Her fingertips danced down his abs to the edge of his underwear. Then she dragged her nails up over his stomach, ending with a hard flick to his nipples. It made Felix grunt like an animal. Made him feel like one too. All tenderness and praise ripped from him in a moment. There was nothing left of him now but instinct and sensation and pounding, aching, unrelenting *need*. He wasn't even kissing Jo anymore. He was just lying there, aching, wound tight like a spring and ready to burst.

"Lower?" she said in that fucking teasing tone that pushed him to the brink of sanity. One hand fingered the waistband of his briefs while the other clawed at his ass. "Can I touch you now?"

Felix jerked his head in something akin to a nod. He swallowed hard and found his voice. It came out like a sob. Like a sinner begging for absolution. "God, yes. Please, Jo. With your hands or your mouth, I don't care. Just please. Please make me come."

The flash of hurt in her eyes instantly brought Felix to his senses. Fuck. What had he said wrong now?

"Make you come?" she asked hesitantly. "You don't want to fuck me?"

Oh, my Jo. He brushed back her hair. "I want to. I want to be inside you so badly. You have no idea how much. But I didn't bring any condoms. I'm clean, but I would never ask you to—"

Her soft chuckle cut him off. "Is that the only problem? I have some."

"You do?" His bewildered expression made her laugh again.

"I always bring condoms to cons," she said with a shrug of one shoulder. "People hook up at these things all the time. If my friends decide to, I want them to be safe. They all know I carry them."

"Where are they?"

"In my backpack. Under the big dice bag."

Felix pushed himself up and made for the entryway on shaky legs. He pulled her dice bag out of her backpack, and sure enough, there was a box of condoms underneath it.

Thank fuck.

He lifted the box. The very large box. "Um, Jo?"

"Hmm?" she replied lazily.

Felix returned and stopped dead in his tracks. Jo was still lying on her side, but she'd taken off her bra. Her top knee was bent forward, accentuating her voluptuous curves. One hand propped her head up, and the other draped over her waist, giving him a full view of both her hip and the gentle slope of her breasts. Her nipples were peaked into points.

"Wow," he breathed.

"Thank you," she replied. "Did you find them?"

Felix held up the box. "Jo, this is a brand new forty-pack of condoms."

"Well, you never know. Sometimes word gets around that I

have them. I've had strangers ask for some before. Better to be prepared, right?"

He shook his head at her as he popped the box open. "You are *such* a cleric."

"Good thing clerics in MnM don't have to be celibate."

Felix grabbed a condom and dropped the box on the nightstand. "Good thing this isn't actually MnM. This is you and me, Jo. Yeah?"

Jo's expression softened. She crawled over to him and knelt at the edge of the mattress. Her hands clasped the back of his neck. "Yeah, Felix. You and me. I wouldn't have it any other way."

She kissed him as he wrapped his arm around her waist. He lifted her, and she opened her legs and squeezed his sides with her knees. They fell onto the bed together, Jo fitting perfectly underneath him. She crossed her ankles at the small of his back and pressed her lips to the pulse point in his neck. Felix ground his hips into hers, barely keeping himself in control.

"Jo," he groaned at the feel of her naked pussy. His briefs were already soaked. "Jo, you're so wet."

Her breath was hot against his throat. "For you. All for you. Fuck me, Felix." She pulled back slightly. "Unless—do you still want me to touch your dick?"

Felix smiled. "Another time. Right now, I'd rather do that first thing you said. You have to let me up, though."

"Oh, sorry."

He stripped his briefs off and rolled the condom on. Jo propped herself on her elbows to watch. Her breath heaved as her gaze lowered to his cock, erect and darkened and desperate to be inside her.

"I like the way you look at my body," he told her.

"It's a good body."

"So's yours." Felix lowered himself over her. "Are you ready for me?"

"Yes." She pushed her knees wider, shifted her hips closer.

A thrum went through Felix to see Jo as needy and wanton as he was. He guided his cock to her entrance, both of them moaning when his head made contact. Then, just to see the thrill she so obviously felt when he praised her, he said, "That's my girl, Jo," and eased inside her.

He couldn't hold back once her tight heat enclosed him. He thrust, hard, into her body over and over and over. Jo breathed out a soft "yes" with each stroke. Her hand tangled in his hair and gently pulled; the other skated lightly down his spine until she grabbed his ass, nails digging in. Felix cried out roughly from those twin sensations and dropped his temple to Jo's cheek.

"Fuck. The things you do to me, Jo. You're wonderful. Your pussy feels so fucking good," he said. "Even better than I imagined."

Jo exhaled a sound that resembled a laugh. "You imagined this?"

"Yes. God, of course I did. All the time," he confessed.

"What happened to being grounded in reality?"

Only Jo. Only Jo would continue to tease him *while* he was fucking her. Damn this woman. She was going to be the end of him. But if she wanted an answer, he'd give her an answer.

"I imagined everything with you, Jo," he said around panting breaths. "This. Your body. Your beautiful pussy. But everything else too. All of it. Being with you, being yours. Imagining it is how I knew I wanted it so badly. Do you see? I needed to *make it* my reality."

Jo didn't respond. He lifted his head to gauge her reaction. She looked on the verge of tears—in a good way. She smiled, knit her brow together, brushed her fingers softly through his hair. "I'll try not to disappoint you."

"Never. You could never." Felix kissed her and swallowed her moan as he sped up the rhythm of his thrusts. Talking had split his attention and kept him from coming, but the pressure in his balls was almost unbearable. He was beyond ready for the sweet relief that was so close. So fucking close.

Suddenly, Jo pushed his head back. Their lips parted with a loud smack. "Roll over."

"Yeah."

He hooked his hands under her shoulder blades as she tucked her knees and braced him with her calves. Together, they rolled until Felix was on his back, bracketed by her legs. Jo took up his rhythm. Riding him, fucking him, undoing him.

"Can't make you do all the work," she said. She bent over him until she hovered an inch above his nose. "This is how I imagined it. Me on top."

"Fucking hell, Jo." He clung to her hips and tossed his head to the side. He wanted to watch, but he couldn't keep his eyes open because, fuck, he was about to explode. The thought barely entered his mind when the full force of his orgasm hit. Felix yelled Jo's name again, pounded his fist into the mattress, curled up toward her as she kept fucking him. The pressure that had been building inside him for hours, for days, for weeks finally, *finally* unleashed in the most intense wave of pleasure he'd ever experienced. It was like a dam bursting. Like a tidal wave slamming against the beach. He'd never come so fucking hard, so fucking *long*, in his life.

He forced himself to take smooth breaths as he descended from his peak. He heard Jo breathing deeply along with him. She was still now, resting on top of him. Her hands were planted on his stomach, and her thumbs played with the trail of hair on his low belly.

Felix opened his eyes and saw Jo grinning from ear to ear. She was the most beautiful sight he'd ever beheld.

18

AFTER THEY'D BOTH used the bathroom and cleaned themselves up, Felix turned down the bed and nestled under the cool
sheets with Jo in his arms. It was too early to sleep, so they lay
there in silence, exchanging gentle, unhurried touches. Felix
thought he could hold onto Jo forever and not tire of it. Her head
on his shoulder, her hand caressing his chest, her breath warming
his skin.

It was Felix who spoke first. "Is there something I can call you?
Like sweetheart or honey or something?"

Jo's fingers went still on his chest. "I'm sorry about that."

"You don't have to apologize. I'm sorry I called you something
you don't like."

She didn't respond.

"Shit, I'm sorry," he said again and ran his hand over her back.
"I shouldn't have brought it up. We don't have to talk about it now."

"You're good, Felix. I'm not upset," she said. "It's kind of embarrassing, is all. Why I don't like 'baby.'"

"I won't laugh. But you don't have to tell me if you don't want to."

The quiet stretched on long enough that Felix was sure the

conversation was over. He was about to change the subject when Jo took the kind of deep breath one takes to steel themself.

"My ex," she began, and dread washed over him. "He liked it when I played a character in bed. It was a joke at first. I came home from a con once in costume as a pixie character of mine. I flirted with him in character, and we ended up... anyway, he liked it, so I kept doing it."

Jo gave a small, unconvincing laugh that cut Felix to the quick. She covered her face with her hand like she didn't want him to see the way she blushed.

"He got tired of her and wanted me to make up a new character each time," she continued, her voice meeker than Felix had ever heard it. "But he could never remember their names, so he called me 'baby' the whole time."

"That sounds..." he said, searching for the right word, "dehumanizing."

Jo looked at him with something like realization in her eyes. "Yeah. That's exactly what it was."

"He shouldn't have done that to you." Felix hoped he wasn't telling her something she didn't already know. He lifted her hand to his lips and kissed her palm. Then her inner wrist. Then higher and higher, up to the crook of her elbow. "I don't have to call you anything other than Jo if that's what you prefer."

She pressed her lips together thoughtfully. "You called me something in Spanish during the tornado. What was that?"

"I don't know," Felix admitted. "I don't remember calling you anything."

"I think it ended with -iño?"

He racked his brain, but only one word came to mind. The only reason he'd call her something that ended in -iño instead of -iña. "Cariño?"

Her eyes lit up with recognition. "Yes! What does that mean?"

"It's like darling or sweetie," he explained, a little breathless. Had he really called her that? "Cariño" wasn't a term he used casually, or something he'd ever called a friend. It must have slipped out in the heat of the moment.

Jo gave him a warm smile. "I'd like that."

"Cariño mío Jo," Felix said, the words rolling off his tongue as if he'd been waiting his whole life to say them. He touched her cheek and drew her in. "I like it too."

He kissed her, pulling her on top of him as he settled deeper into the pillows. Jo slid her knee between his legs and cuddled closer, her entire body flush with his. Her thigh brushed his dick, and he groaned.

She grinned. "Already up for round two?"

"Not yet, I'm afraid," he chuckled. "Old man, remember?"

"Is that what I should call *you*?" she teased, kissing him again. "'Old man?'"

"I'd prefer 'hot librarian.'"

She planted her hand by his shoulder and pushed herself up. She stared down at his amused face, horrified. "Oh my God, you *did* see that. No wonder you didn't give me your phone number."

Felix, distracted by the way her hair fell along her blushing cheeks, didn't quite follow her. "What?"

"That night!" she cried, gesticulating with her free hand. "That first night alone in the library. I was all horny for your arms, and then I told you to give me your number while there's this 'hot librarian' text from my best friend on my phone. I was so worried I'd creeped you out."

He grinned, a slow, sly grin. "You were horny for my arms?"

"You *had* to notice me notice them."

"Well, they're extremely noticeable." He raised his arm, tucked his hand under his head, and flexed. Jo's eyes darted over. "See?"

"They're extremely attractive is what they are."

"That too." He dropped the playful tone. "Jo, the reason I didn't give you my number that night is because I thought email would be more respectful of your time. You were already offering to go above and beyond the one hour a week we agreed to. I didn't want to text you a question at lunch or late at night and have you think I expected an answer right away. Email was meant to let you respond whenever was convenient for you."

"Well, shit."

"What?"

"That's even more attractive than your arms." And she kissed Felix with such ferocity it took his breath away.

"THIS PLACE IS seriously called Grinders?" Kim asked on Monday morning as everyone entered the breakfast spot Aida had found. "What the *actual* fuck?"

"It started out as a coffee shop," Aida explained.

"I think it's cute," Heather declared in that way of hers that indicated it would be pointless to disagree.

"A grinder is also a sandwich, right?" Young asked from behind their sunglasses. "Isn't that what they call subs in the Midwest?" They looked to Felix.

"Uh, no," he said. "I mean, yes, a grinder is a sub, but that's not a Midwest thing."

"Where do they call them grinders, then?" Young asked.

"New England," Max said. He waved his phone. "Just looked it up."

"So I can't get a sub here?" Young asked.

"Literally none of us have been here before, Young," Trey said. "How would we know that?"

Young shrugged. "Online menu?"

"On it," Max said.

"My dude, they are about to hand us menus," Kim said, flailing both arms toward the host stand where Aida was checking them in.

"Now I want a sub," David said.

"It's not even nine a.m.," Heather retorted, scandalized by the thought.

"I'm going to miss you chucklefucks," Jo said with melodramatic longing.

"Aw, Jo," Kim cried. She folded Jo into an almost-painful hug from the side, pinning Jo's arms down and squishing their cheeks together. "I'm going to miss you too. When are you coming to California to visit?"

"I don't know, probably Christmas?" Her voice was muffled on account of her cheek being pressed against her teeth.

"Not til Christmas?!"

"No subs," Max reported. "But they have a Reuben and a French dip. And burgers."

David lit up. "Ooh, that means fries."

"Again. Not even nine," Heather said.

"What's the difference between fries and hash browns, though?" David argued. "Same concept."

Aida spun on her heel, grabbing their attention. "Come on, kids, breakfast time."

Kim finally released Jo and scampered after the host. Felix came alongside Jo and slipped his hand in hers. She mouthed "sorry" to him.

"Don't give me that, cariño," Felix whispered. The new nickname made her smile. "Your friends are great."

"Let's see if you still think so after they're caffeinated, hot librarian," she said.

Breakfast was about as chaotic as Jo expected. Felix mostly observed the overlapping conversations, chiming in occasionally between bites of chicken and waffles (and the fries David ordered for the table). But Jo noticed him smiling the entire time.

Their goodbyes in the parking lot were even more chaotic, with handshakes and tears and at least six hugs between Jo and Aida. All too soon, Jo climbed into her car beside Felix and set her GPS for his address. Waving through the windows, they set off for Kansas. For home.

THE DRIVE TO Ashville went by far too quickly for Felix's liking. He and Jo talked about books and movies and their families. They sat in companionable silence and watched the plains, which really *were* quite lovely, go by. They sang along to his playlists and shared some of their favorite songs with one another. They played the alphabet game with license plates. They tried turning on a podcast, but couldn't agree on what to listen to, so they went back to music.

And then, just like that, they were back.

It was nearly eight o'clock by the time they pulled into the driveway at Tito's house. Felix put the car in park but didn't turn off the engine. He was just getting dropped off, after all, and then Jo would go home. She was probably excited to sleep in her own bed again after three nights away. Felix sensed her watching him and turned to her. She was smiling gently. He wasn't quite used to her looking at him like that, like she couldn't believe her luck. His heart squeezed with some emotion he couldn't quite name.

Jo hooked a finger into the hem of his shirtsleeve. She pulled him in as she leaned closer, and their lips met tenderly above the cupholders. He wasn't ready. He didn't want to watch her drive away.

He held her face and ran his thumb over her cheek, pink from driving in the sun all day. "Are you working tomorrow?"

"No, I took an extra day off."

"I don't start until noon," he said. "Stay. Please."

"Felix..." She kissed him again, harder and deeper. Her lips parted, and Felix drank her in. He pushed his hand to the back of her head and slid his fingers into her hair. Jo took off her seatbelt and leaned in even farther, clinging to Felix with both hands. He trailed kisses along her jaw. She moaned next to his ear, sweeter than any sound he could imagine.

"You probably have to get home to take care of Merry," he said.

Jo moaned again. "Do you have any idea how hot it is that you care about my cat?"

"He's part of your life, cariño. That makes him important to me."

"Jesus Christ, Felix. Just fuck me already."

He chuckled and nipped at her earlobe. She inhaled sharply. "Is that a yes to staying over?"

"Yes," she said. "Vanessa fed Merry dinner a couple of hours ago. He'll be fine until the morning."

Felix didn't know who Vanessa was, and he didn't really care at the moment. He'd ask later. Right now, they needed to get inside. He returned to Jo's mouth and kissed her with the promise of more, much more, to come.

They unloaded the car and hurried up the porch steps. Felix

fumbled with his keys in his excitement. He'd never brought someone over to this house, and the fact Jo was the first, hopefully the only, was—

The only?

Slow down, man, he told himself. Not just about getting the key in the lock, but about that wild thought. Where the fuck had that even come from? Three days after their first kiss was a little early to be contemplating long-term commitment.

Finally, he got the door open and let Jo go in first. They set their bags on the floor between the burgundy armchairs where Tito and Lita used to watch TV together. Felix never sat there. Jo ran a finger over the leather arm of one. Slowly, she spun in a circle and took in the rest of the room: the brick fireplace with the life-sized wooden ducks on the mantle, the wall-mounted TV surrounded by dozens of family photos, the burgundy couch that matched the armchairs, the blue and goldenrod floral rug that covered most of the hardwood floor.

Something about her standing there, that sweet smile curving lips still swollen from his kisses... For the first time since he'd moved to Ashville, this house felt like home.

She indicated the wall of photos with her head. "Are there any of you?"

He took her by the hand and showed her the photos of him growing up. Photos from the backyard of his home in Tulsa; from family trips to the Alamo, Walt Disney World, and New Orleans; from his childhood soccer team that his grandparents had insisted on calling a football team until it became a running joke. One of the largest ones was his senior picture from high school where his stubble was already so thick he looked about twenty-five. He showed her wedding photos of Tito and Lita, of his parents, of his second and third cousins in Spain. Jo held his hand

and listened to him talk and asked thoughtful questions to draw out more stories.

When they reached the end, she wrapped her arms around his neck. "Thank you for sharing your family with me," she said.

"You owe me now." He tucked his fingers under the hem of her shirt and traced them along her skin. "We need to go to California so I can see all of *your* embarrassing childhood photos."

"Oh, there are some choice ones at Dad's house." She twirled a lock of his hair around her finger. "I did figure skating for a couple of years. The costumes were extremely sparkly. Nothing like an eight-year-old in rhinestones and stage makeup."

"I can't wait. Christmas, right?"

Jo's eyebrows flickered together in confusion. "What?"

"This morning, you told Kim you'd go back to California for Christmas," he said and was suddenly struck by the horrible feeling he'd said too much. His whole body went ice cold, except his face, which flushed hot. "I mean—that is, if we... if we're still—"

She pushed up onto her tiptoes and cut him off with a kiss. He pulled her tighter against his body, giving her something to balance against.

"You want us to be together at Christmas?" she asked.

"I want us to be together for a long time, cariño," he replied. "I—" There were more words inside him, somewhere deep down and tucked away, words that were too big and too soon and too terrifying to give voice to. Instead of those, he said, "I'm very into you."

Jo giggled and bit her lip. "The feeling is mutual, hot librarian. I'm very into you too."

The pressure of her fingers in his hair increased, and Felix let her lower his head. They picked up where they'd left off in the car. Hot, open-mouthed kisses. Panting breaths. Felix's mouth on Jo's neck and his hands on her ass.

He'd been telling himself for weeks that it was Jo's hips he was obsessed with. It seemed safer that way, somehow. Not as lecherous. But he might as well admit the truth to himself. It was her ass he desired. Her wide, dimpled, Rubenesque ass that begged to be gripped and spanked and maybe even fucked, if she'd let him take her that way someday. Oh, how he hoped she would. His dick in her ass and his hand in her cunt. Both hands, if he could manage it. Fucking her twice over and massaging her clit until she screamed and *screamed*. And after, holding her against his chest, murmuring gentle words, and stroking her hair as their bodies trembled with the aftershocks of pleasure.

His erection grazed Jo's belly as she slid down from her toes. She ground against him, making him hiss. "God, you're so hard already."

"Only because you know exactly how to make me feel good." He curled his hips toward her to emphasize his words.

She flushed an even rosier shade of pink and glanced away coyly. "You have a bit of a praise kink, don't you, Felix?"

"I suppose I do," he chuckled. "I like telling my partner how she makes me feel and when she does something I like. Take right now, for instance. You're so beautiful when you blush, Jo. I like knowing I'm the one who makes you turn that lovely pink." He kissed her cheek, feeling the warmth of her skin against his lips. "Is that okay? So far, you've seemed to like it, but I can stop if—"

She shook her head, cutting him off. "Don't. I don't want you to stop. I didn't know I liked it until... No one's ever talked to me like that in bed before. But it's really nice to hear."

"Then I'll keep doing it. But if you learn you don't like something, all you have to do is tell me."

They regarded one another seriously for a moment, Felix's mind casting back to the evening before, when he'd called her "baby." It wouldn't surprise him if Jo were thinking about the same thing.

"I will," she agreed. "And you should speak up if there's anything you don't like too."

"Of course." He waited a beat to see if she had more to add. When she didn't, he shifted his voice to a more playful tone. "Now, you already know how much I like your teasing, but I think we've both waited enough. Come here."

He gripped her ass, her glorious ass, and bent his knees. Jo got the drift and jumped as he hefted her up. Her legs locked around his waist. She was taller than him now, and he had to tilt his head up to kiss her. Jo draped her forearms over his shoulders, twining her fingers through his hair.

"Let me go down on you tonight, Jo," he said. "I want to know what your pussy tastes like."

"Only if I can suck your cock in return. Taste your come."

Fuck. Yes. He fought to keep his voice even, controlled, while inside he was screaming those words again and again. "I think that can be arranged."

"Thank Christ." Jo captured his mouth again and squeezed her legs around him hard enough to make him grunt. The wet spot between her legs was hot and damp against his shirt.

Felix was grateful to have grown up around his grandparents' house. He knew where every wall and piece of furniture was without needing to look. He kept kissing her as he took her into the guest bedroom, stopping only to toss her onto the bed. Jo let out a gleeful squeal as she landed. He switched on a lamp so he could watch her come and covered her body with his.

19

FOR THE SECOND morning in a row, Jo woke up holding Felix. When they were awake, it tended to be the other way around; Jo cuddled up against his broad body, his arm slung protectively around her. But sometime in the night, as they slept, she became the one who protected him. His back curled against her chest, her arm around his waist, her leg covering his hip. The big spoon to his little spoon.

Was it weird that she wanted to stay in this moment forever? That she didn't want to wake up without Felix beside her ever again? Must be some bizarre intimacy hangover from sharing a hotel room with him for three days. Sure, they'd heard each other pee through the wall and seen each other straight out of the shower, but they hadn't even gone on a real date, for Christ's sake. She really shouldn't be thinking about what it would be like to live with the man. Maybe here, in this house. With its bright green door and its cabinet full of Lita's old mugs. With the big tree in the front yard and this amazingly comfy bed. With the darling wooden ducks on the mantle and a real basement to stay safe from tornadoes in.

Jesus Christ, Jo. Stop it this instant.

Indi-Con with Felix hadn't just accelerated their relationship.

It had shoved them into a Formula One car and sent them flying around the track at hundreds of miles per hour without helmets. Jo didn't regret a minute of their whirlwind weekend together, but now that they were back... what next? If they kept going at this breakneck speed, she'd be moving in by the end of the week. No way could that be healthy. Sooner or later, they would crash.

Ashville was meant to be her fresh start. To figure out where her life would go from here. To see what it was like to be herself, *by* herself. Felix made that complicated. Jo wanted to be with him more than anything else in the world. To use his phrase, she was very (*very*) into him. But, after Jeremy, how did she know she wasn't simply grabbing onto the first man who came along who was good and kind? Who made her feel safe, and who claimed to tolerate her love of MnM?

Stay. Please.

Her arm tightened around Felix's waist, and she rested her forehead between his shoulder blades. Closing her eyes, she let herself feel his deep, even breaths. She didn't loosen her hold until he finally began to stir.

He rolled over and wrapped his leg around hers, locking their knees and ankles together. His hand splayed over her hip. Jo smiled and pushed his jet-black waves off his forehead.

"Morning," he mumbled, his eyes still closed.

"Good morning, sleepyhead."

"What time is it?"

She twisted to look at the clock on the nightstand. "Almost ten."

Felix grumbled and ran his hand over his eyes. He slowly blinked them open. "I never sleep this late."

"Cons are exhausting," Jo said. "And you drove most of the way yesterday."

"Don't forget the part where you wore me out last night."

"Are you complaining about that, old man?" She scratched her nails softly through his stubble, not unlike how she gave Merry chin rubs. Felix practically purred, a hum so deep it rumbled through his chest. He leaned into her touch as goosebumps rose over his neck and shoulders.

"Not at all."

He scootched his head forward and kissed her.

As soon as they got up, real life would kick in. Felix would go to work and Jo would go home to feed and cuddle Merry. She'd go grocery shopping and soak off her nail polish and put away her MnM stuff. She'd do laundry and go to bed early for her morning shift.

And maybe, just maybe, she'd rein herself in a little bit. Think of Felix more like the new boyfriend he was rather than fantasize about moving in with him. Keep having the best sex of her life, *obviously*, but make sure she slept in her own bed more than his. She could do that.

Probably.

But not yet. All of that could wait a little longer. She kissed Felix back. She drew him against her body, and she held on tight.

From: Felix Navarro
To: Jo Rainier
Date: Tuesday, May 28, 2024, 4:50 P.M.
Subject: Advertising at ACC on Sunday

Dear Jo,

Ashville Community College is having their community outreach day this weekend dedicated to advertising summer programs throughout the county. Leni and I plan to attend on Sunday afternoon to hand out flyers about the library's programs, which, of course, include MnM night. After hearing about Indi-Con this weekend, Leni wants to be more involved in the launch event.

Might you be interested in joining us this Sunday at the college to hand out flyers and answer questions?

Best,
Felix
~
Felix Navarro, MI
Junior Librarian, General Services
Butler County Library District — Ashville Public Library

From: Jo Rainier
To: Felix Navarro
Date: Tuesday, May 28, 2024, 5:07 P.M.
Subject: RE: Advertising at ACC on Sunday

Leni's on board! That's so exciting. She's the coolest.

I'd be happy to join you at ACC this weekend. Let me know what time to meet you there. Or if you're interested in carpooling, I'd be up for that.

Jo

Jo

> I've seen your dick, dude. I think you can do better than "best" to end an email.

> Even a work email

Felix

> Hmm... how about "warmly"?

Jo

> Much better.

Felix

> Noted.

> On another subject, may I take you to dinner on Friday after our MnM lesson?

Jo

> Hell yeah

"SPILL IT, CALIFORNIA," Vanessa said at lunch on Wednesday. "Who is he?" She reached across the break room table and stole one of Jo's tortilla chips.

"Who is who?" Jo asked around a bite of turkey sandwich.

Vanessa's expression practically screamed, *are you kidding me?* "Whoever's had you grinning like a loon all day! I know what that look means."

She hesitated. Felix wasn't a secret, of course, but with Tito living here, she had hoped to be a *little* discreet at work.

"If you found someone in this town, you have to tell me," Vanessa said. "My hunting grounds have completely dried up."

"Hunting grounds?" Jo asked.

"I calls 'em as I sees 'em. C'mon, Jo! Let me live vicariously for a sec."

She gave in. "He's the librarian I've been working with on the MnM event," she said, avoiding Felix's name in case anyone could overhear. "He came with me to Indianapolis this weekend and... a lot happened."

Vanessa smiled and clapped her hands. "I'm going to need *way* more details than that, California."

"Some of us still have a filter at work, you know," Jo replied and went back to her sandwich.

"You're the *worst*. We're going out tonight so you can tell me everything." Before Jo could respond, Vanessa added, "Or we can talk about it now in terrible euphemisms. Did the train enter the tunnel?"

Jo coughed and tried not to choke on bread and mayo.

"Did the early bird get the worm? Was the banana—"

"Stop, stop, oh my God!" Jo laughed. "Fine, we'll go out tonight." Vanessa cackled in triumph.

After work, she took Jo to a cocktail lounge called The Gandy Dancer, which she claimed was "the only upscale establishment in Ashville." She explained that the name came from an old slang term for a railroad worker, which fit with the exterior aesthetic. The lounge was on the main street that ran through the middle of Ashville, where all the buildings were from the late nineteenth century. They were generally well-maintained, but they had a distinctly old-timey charm.

The interior, however, was another story. Dark walls, dim light-ing, and low suede couches made Jo feel like she'd stepped inside a modern speakeasy. Back in Orange County, this kind of place would have been noisy and crowded, even on a weeknight, but here it was almost a respite.

Over craft cocktails, fancy sliders, and truffle fries, Jo told Vanessa about Felix. Once she got going, safe from the ears of eavesdropping co-workers, it was surprisingly easy to gush about him. It was nice—being fully honest about her boyfriend, not hav-ing to make excuses for his behavior, not having to leave things out for fear of someone giving her an odd look. Though she left out the specifics of the nights she and Felix had spent together, she told Vanessa just about everything else, including that his grandpa lived at White Hills. She didn't even have to ask for discretion; Vanessa promised it immediately.

When she was done, Jo ordered them another round of drinks. Then, it was Vanessa's turn to lament her own dating woes, which managed to upset her enough that Jo let Vanessa talk her into doing a shot of tequila together.

After that, the conversation somehow shifted to black-and-white sci-fi B movies they both loved, which lead to nerdy TV shows and then to Jo telling Vanessa that she absolutely *had* to watch *Xena: Warrior Princess*. Vanessa was just as adamant that Jo needed to watch something called *Mystery Science Theater 3000*.

By the time they were on their third (or maybe fourth? did the shots count?) round, splitting a peach crumble, and playing Fuck Marry Kill with *Star Wars* characters, Jo was having the time of her life. The work-friends wall between them had crumbled to dust, and she only wished they had done this sooner. Even if the woman did think it was acceptable to fuck Greedo, marry Yoda, and kill Chewbacca. Who the hell killed Chewbacca?

Jo didn't check her phone until they were getting the bill, and she realized she had no idea what time it was. Her stomach dropped when she lit up the screen. She had a missed call and a text from Felix, both from almost two hours ago.

Felix

> Do you want to come over tonight? I miss you, cariño.

Jo dropped her credit card on the table, grabbed her purse, and excused herself. She made her way outside. Definitely not stumbling. Tipsier than she expected, but *not* stumbling. Heart pounding, she fumbled with her phone until she managed to call Felix.

He answered on the first ring. "Hey, J—"

"I'm sorry! Vanessa and I went out for drinks, and I guess I never took my phone off silent after work, so I just saw your message. I'm sorry. I promise I wasn't ignoring you. Should I come over now?"

"Cariño, hey, it's okay," he said soothingly. "I'm not upset."

"Are you sure? I'm so sorry."

"Of-of course I'm sure." He sounded confused, but sincere. "Why would I be upset? I figured you were busy or working late."

Jo pressed her palm to her sternum, breathing deeply and blinking fast to keep from crying. *He's not upset*, she reassured herself, over and over. *He's not upset.*

"Jo?" Felix said when she didn't respond. "Are you okay?"

"Yeah," she croaked.

"You don't sound okay. Do you need me to come get you?"

"I don't know?" Jo was drunk. That was pretty goddamn obvious now. Her vision was swimming, and in the quiet street she could hear how slurred her words were. Plus, she still really, really felt like crying—always a sure sign she'd had too much.

Vanessa was younger. She could probably hold her liquor better. She might be okay to drive. She could take them back to White Hills, where Jo's car was parked. Jo would just have to work really hard to sober up before they got there.

The front door slammed open. "Where'd you go, California?" Vanessa yelled, clutching Jo's credit card in an unsteady hand. She gasped and pointed at the phone. "Is that your boyfriend? Hiiiii, Jo's boyfriend!"

Felix's voice reached Jo through a cloud of tequila and shame. "Where are you?"

"The Gandy Dancer."

"Don't get in a car. Either of you. I'll be there in five minutes." The phone blooped. He'd hung up.

"He's going to pick us up," Jo said. She took her card from Vanessa and stuck it in her bra.

And then she burst into tears.

FELIX PULLED UP in front of The Gandy Dancer, relieved to find Jo and a blonde woman, both of them in scrubs, sitting on the curb. Thank God they hadn't tried to drive themselves anywhere. The blonde waved wildly at him with both arms. Jo's face was in her hands, her elbows on her knees. As he hopped out of the car, she looked up miserably and started to cry. He resisted the urge to sweep her into his arms and kiss away all of her tears. He would do that as soon as possible, but Jo wasn't the only person who needed a little help tonight.

"Vanessa?" he asked the blonde.

"That's me." She scanned him up and down, her entire head bobbing. "God *damn*, you're a tall drink of water."

He chuckled. "Thank you. I'm Felix. May I give you a ride home?"

"Hell yeah."

Felix offered her his hand when she struggled to get up on her own and helped her into the backseat of the car. Then he reached out to his teary-eyed girlfriend. "May I give you a ride home too, cariño?"

A silent nod, and Felix repeated the process of helping her into the car. Vanessa gave him loud, drunken directions to her house just a few blocks away. When they arrived, he verified that she had a way to get her car in the morning. She mumbled something about her sister as she climbed out and said good night to Jo. Jo gave a half-hearted wave in return.

He waited until Vanessa was safely inside her house before he reached for Jo. He kissed her hand, but she only stared listlessly out the side window. "I don't know where you live."

Jo sniffed. "Can I still come over?"

"Of course." He kissed her hand again and carefully set it down in her lap.

The drive was silent but mercifully short—one of the benefits of a small town. Inside, Jo flopped onto the couch and buried her face in a throw pillow. Felix fetched a glass of water and a sleeve of crackers. He sat on the rug and offered them to her, but she shook her head without looking at him.

What the fuck had happened? It was eating him up inside to think he might have upset her without knowing it. He ran his hand up and down Jo's back, letting her know he was there whenever she was ready. Finally, she sniffled and turned her face away from the pillow. Her puffy, bloodshot eyes pierced a hole clean through Felix's heart.

"Cariño mío," he whispered. "Please talk to me. Did I do something wrong?"

Fresh tears welled in her eyes. "Oh, Felix, no." She grabbed a fistful of his shirt and pulled him closer. She touched her forehead to his chest, and he put his arms around her. "It's me. It's my stupid brain. I'm sorry. I was so relieved you weren't mad at me that I lost it, and I'm too drunk to stop crying."

Felix racked his brain for something—anything—he had done that would lead Jo to believe he'd be angry at her for ignoring a text for a couple of hours. He came up blank.

"Just so we're clear, Jo," he said. "You don't have to respond to me immediately. You're not beholden to me. You were out having fun with a friend. Getting completely hammered. On a Wednesday." He injected some levity into his voice and was rewarded with a tiny laugh. Jo's fist loosened around his shirt.

"I'm so sorry I worried you," she said.

"It's all right. I'm just glad you're okay," he said. "Besides, I think the hangover will be retribution enough."

Jo groaned, low and drawn out. "Is that water still around?"

He kissed her forehead, helped her into a sitting position, and handed her the water. She gulped half of it down in one go.

"Thank you for coming to get me," she said. "And Vanessa."

"You're welcome." He climbed onto the couch and put an arm around her. She leaned against his side. "I guess my next hero's calling is taking you to work tomorrow, huh?"

"If this water doesn't do the trick, I might call in sick."

In response, he handed her the crackers. Jo gave him a grateful look, tore the sleeve open, and ate two of them at once.

JO DIDN'T CALL in sick, but the ache behind her eyes that lasted well into the afternoon made her regret that decision. Despite Felix's gentle prodding, she hadn't been able to haul herself out of bed in time to stop at home on the way to work. She kept extra scrubs in her locker in case of any bodily fluid accidents from the residents, so at least she had clean clothes. But she still felt gross all day. Vanessa, the young whippersnapper, was fine—and, luckily, completely nonjudgmental about Jo's teary sidewalk breakdown.

"We've all been there, California," is all she said about the matter.

Jo managed to make it through the day and dragged herself home to a cantankerous Merry. He yowled the entire time she fed him and cleaned his litter box. "I know, Mer-bear, I'm sorry," she told him. "At least you didn't have to wear yesterday's underwear."

After a long, hot shower, she made herself pasta with pesto and more parmesan than she could safely endorse as a medical professional. She curled up on the couch and found an episode of the show Vanessa recommended streaming online. She proceeded to watch a man and a couple of robot puppets make fun of a terrible movie from the fifties about giant killer crickets. Partway through, her phone chimed with Felix's text sound.

Felix

How's the head? Did you survive the day?

She smiled and paused the show to give him her undivided attention.

Jo

> Alive. Pasta is helping. And clean underwear.

Felix

> I'm glad to hear it. Pasta solves all manner of problems, I've found.

Jo

> Speaking of food, I'm excited for our date tomorrow.

Felix

> So am I. What do you think about going into Wichita? There's a place there I'd like to take you.

Jo

> Totally. I'd love to see the city.

> Should I dress fancy?

Felix

> Up to you, but I won't complain if you do.

Jo

> Gotcha.

> I need to figure out what to teach you tomorrow.

For MnM, I mean

Not for the date

Anything you want to focus on?

Felix

How about I run a short game for you?
I've got less than two weeks to
practice my GMing.

Jo

Great idea! Would Leni be down to
join so it's more like a real game?

Felix

I'll ask, but I wouldn't doubt it. She said
she found one of those online MnM
shows last night and loved it. She
already made a paladin.

Jo

How is she so cool???

Felix

She named him Spanky.

Jo

Amazing

Grax might have some competition
for Veena's BFF.

Felix

Grax isn't worried.

So if you *were* going to teach me something for the date portion of our night, Jo, what would it be? What do you want me to learn how to do to you?

Jo

You're already very good at a lot of things.

Felix

So are you, cariño. Especially with that lovely mouth of yours.

Jo

I feel like I need a better name for you than hot librarian. It doesn't really roll off the tongue in a fit of passion.

Felix

You're changing the subject, Jo. What would you teach me?

Sorry, are you uncomfortable with this? I can stop.

Jo

No, I like it.

But I need a good nickname for you so I can tell you better.

Felix

You can use my name for now. I like it when you say my name.

Jo

Well then, Felix

I have this vibrator

Felix

I like where this is going.

Jo

And it has like 10 different settings

Felix

I bet you know exactly how to make yourself come with it, don't you, my Jo?

Jo

Oh, I have my favorites.

But I would let you try them all on me, Felix.

And learn which ones I like best by the way I moan for you.

Felix

Fuck

Teach me

Jo

Have patience, hot librarian

It's not date night yet

Felix

I can't wait

Jo

Until then, go take a shower and imagine it

Felix

I might not make it to the shower. Might start imagining it now, from my bed.

Jo

Send me a picture, Felix

Send me as many as you like

Felix

As you wish, my Jo

Will you send me some in return?

Jo

Deal

20

THE PROSPECT OF GMing Monsters and Mythology was more
nerve-racking than Felix expected. He found a short SWOP adventure online and read it over three times on his lunch break on
Friday. It had seemed simple enough over his PB&J, but by the
time six o'clock rolled around, he was a bundle of nerves. Walking
into the reading room behind Jo and Leni, Felix didn't just have
butterflies in his stomach. He had a damn colony of wasps in
there with nothing better to do than sting his insides.

Jo gave his elbow a reassuring squeeze. "You'll do great," she
whispered.

Felix smiled to himself. Her faith in him didn't completely
banish his anxiety, but it helped. It really fucking helped.

Over the next hour, he did his best to guide Spanky and Veena
through the adventure. Jo offered suggestions with a kind, easy
manner. Enough of her comments were directed toward Leni that
Felix didn't feel singled out. Somehow, he didn't think that was an
accident. He might be the one running the adventure, but Jo set
the tone for the game. She made it fun, simply by being herself, by
bringing her thoughtfulness and zeal for MnM to the table. There

were no words, in English or in Spanish, for how grateful Felix was that she was here.

When the first combat encounter came up, his nerves ratcheted up a notch. As a player, he only had to keep track of his own character during combat. But as a GM, there were multiple monsters, each with their own abilities and health points to track. There were strategic decisions to make, too, to keep the players challenged while not killing their characters outright. Every dice roll had the potential to change the fight and force him to switch tactics. To keep it all straight, Felix had to be focused, meticulous, and exact. And... those were all things he was good at.

Had he really gotten so wound up about GMing that he'd forgotten his own strengths?

Once he settled into the flow of it, he found combat far more interesting than the storytelling side of the game. Felix didn't have any illusions about his skills, though. Thinking through all his options made the combat slow, rather than fast-paced and exciting. And his improvisation definitely needed work. His brain seemed to lock up whenever one of them (usually Leni) proposed an idea or asked a question that the adventure didn't provide guidance for. Jo helped where she could, but sometimes Felix had to say no and move on. Luckily, Leni didn't seem to mind; for her, simply coming up with the ideas seemed to be the fun part.

And at the end of the hour, Felix wrapped up the story and gave out rewards, and Leni burst into applause. "This was so much fun, Felix. I can't wait to play again."

"You did a great job," Jo added. "Both of you." She looked back and forth between them, her gaze lingering on Felix a beat longer.

"Same time next week?" Leni asked as she gathered her things. "I want to try casting spells now that I'm at level two."

"Works for me," Jo said.

"Definitely," Felix agreed. "I'm going to need another go at this before I'm set loose on the unsuspecting public."

Jo slipped off to the bathroom while Felix unlocked the front door for Leni and shut down the library for the night, running back over the game in his mind. When he returned to the reading room to pack up his MnM things, Jo wasn't back yet. He furrowed his brow, wondering if he should be worried about her.

"Ahem."

He turned, and there she was. In the doorway of the reading room, transformed.

They had texted about her getting dressed up for their date. He'd forgotten all about that once their conversation went to more interesting places and pictures became involved. Now, he remembered, and his eyes trailed over her.

Jo wore a white sundress patterned with bright yellow lemons and pale green leaves. It was low-cut, sleeveless, and fell to mid-thigh, showing off more of her skin than usual. Her tattoo peeked around either side of the shoulder strap. Felix saw a glimpse of what looked like white, lace-edged bike shorts peeking out from under the flared skirt. On her feet were strappy yellow sandals with heels, and she wore a chunky bright teal necklace and matching bracelet. Her hair was down and straight, her glasses were nowhere to be seen, and she'd touched up her makeup. She'd added lipstick, the same dark red one she'd been wearing the night they'd met. Those lips had haunted him for days afterward. No doubt they would again.

"You're so beautiful, Jo," he breathed. "You look amazing."

"I clean up nice, huh?" she said, twirling as she came into the room. Her skirt lifted, granting him a better look at those cute shorts that hugged her form.

He slid his hand around her waist, and she leaned into him.

She was taller in heels, naturally. He liked it. It would make her that much easier to kiss. "Now I feel underdressed. I should have brought a tie."

"No, you look perfect." Jo smoothed her hand over the collar of his forest-green dress shirt, stirring his blood in his veins. Then she stroked his cheek, her thumb on the gray stubble on his chin. "You're always gorgeous."

Something else, something fathomless and unnameable, stirred within Felix at her words. He bumped her nose with his. "I don't think I've ever been called that before."

"Well, it's true. You're the most gorgeous man I've ever known."

"Tell me something, Jo," he said. "Will I smear that wicked lipstick if I kiss you right now?"

She shook her head. "It's lip stain. It'll—"

Felix didn't wait to hear what it would do. He kissed Jo with all the affection and all the aching hunger inside him. She curled her fingers around his neck. Her thumb brushed the shell of his ear, sending tingles down his spine. Fuck if she didn't always know exactly how to touch him to give him the most magnificent shivers. Places he didn't even know he liked to be touched until Jo was the one doing the touching.

Her lips curved into a smile against his. "We're at your workplace, gorgeous. I hope there aren't cameras in here."

Felix sighed through his nose. "I like that. 'Gorgeous.'"

"Then I'd better keep saying it."

"You're right, though." He released Jo and missed her warmth immediately. "Shall we go to dinner?"

"I'm famished."

On the forty-minute drive to Wichita, they talked about MnM. The sight of Jo in that dress had thrown him for a loop, but there were some questions still on his mind. Felix wasn't sure he'd be able to fully relax and enjoy their date until he hashed through them, and Jo assured him she didn't mind. He asked her about what she would do in certain situations, beginning with tonight's game and then expanding to some of the things he'd seen at Indi-Con. She gave him long and detailed answers, apologizing more than once for going on and on. Each time, Felix told her it was fine, that she didn't need to be sorry.

And each time, his chest ached to hear her second-guess herself, to assume that he didn't care what she had to say, even when he was asking her direct questions. It reminded him of that night at Stan's, back when they were first getting to know each other. Felix had thought they'd moved past this trepidation of hers. After weeks of MnM lessons, after Indi-Con, after he'd met her friends from California, how could she still think she needed to hold herself back from him? There were no traces of apology about her when they were with Leni, but now that they were alone, something had changed.

Felix would have bet Tito's house that it had something to do with her ex. Trey had told him the guy didn't play MnM. The hard, flat "no" Trey had given him made Felix believe there was a story there. One that, by rights, was Jo's story to tell. How would he even broach that subject? He certainly wasn't going to bring it up now, mere minutes from the restaurant on their first official date.

Should he even bring it up at all, though? He didn't want to force Jo to talk about her douchebag of an ex. Again. Even if the other times hadn't been intentional, he'd asked uncomfortable questions with uncomfortable answers. Most couples didn't talk about their past relationships, especially the shitty ones, so soon. There had to be a better approach, a way to remind her that he wasn't that guy. A way to help her trust him.

When he parked at the restaurant, he angled toward her. "I

hope you know how much I love listening to you talk about MnM. I appreciate how passionate you are about it, and I'm in awe of how much you know every time I ask you questions."

Jo fiddled with the lace on her shorts, staring at her hands. He willed her to look at him, but she didn't.

"I know," she whispered. "Sometimes I forget that, but I know."

He couldn't take it any longer; he touched her chin and turned her to face him. Her eyes shone in the orange lamplight. He glimpsed uneasiness there for just a moment, then it melted away. Jo mouthed the words "thank you." Tension he hadn't realized he was carrying loosened from his shoulders. He leaned over and kissed her cheek.

"So, where have you brought me, gorgeous?" she asked, blinking her eyes clear.

"Have you ever had tapas?"

A radiant grin spread across her face. "I *love* tapas."

Jo's radiance only grew in the golden light inside the restaurant. Her gaze wandered around the Spanish decor, the dark flecks in her pale eyes accentuated by her deep red lips. Sitting across the table from her, Felix was enraptured. He was lost. He was *hers*.

He didn't demur when she asked him to order for both of them. He picked out all his favorites, fully in Spanish just for the hell of it (and definitely not because he was showing off). They feasted on calamari, patatas bravas, gambas al ajillo, crab cakes, stuffed sweet peppers, and paella Valenciana. They drank wine from Madrid and, for dessert, shared a flan dripping with caramel. They talked and laughed and joked and held hands across the table when they weren't busy gorging themselves.

It was one of the best nights of Felix's life; certainly the best since he'd moved to Kansas.

On the drive back, surrounded by dark fields and few street-lights, Jo kept leaning forward in her seat to get a better view of the stars through the windshield. It was all Felix could do to keep his eyes on the road; he loved seeing how enraptured she was by this place in the middle of nowhere.

A few miles outside Ashville, he took her hand and asked, "Shall I take you back to the library for your car?" He kept his tone casual and breezy, despite the desire that had begun to pulse through him as they got closer and closer to home. Jo might have been merely teasing him with those texts of hers, but, oh, how he wanted to make them real.

"If you'd like," she said, matching the lightness of his voice. Her thumb swept across the back of his hand. "But then I think you should come over. You haven't seen my place yet or met Merry."

His fist tightened around the steering wheel. "I'd love to."

"And, if you're not too tired..." There went her thumb again, shooting tingles all the way up his arm. "I do have something to teach you."

Felix swore under his breath and pushed on the gas pedal. Jo's laugh boomed as the speedometer ticked up. She picked up his phone and changed the soft, acoustic music to his early 2000s mix. Missy Elliott's encouragement to "Get Ur Freak On" accompanied them all the way into Ashville.

An eternity later, Jo stood in front of him at the top of the staircase outside her building, unlocking her door. He hooked his arm around her waist and kissed her neck. Fuck, she smelled so good. Like a piece of strawberry candy. He wanted to hold her on his tongue until she melted. He closed his eyes and inhaled, let-ting his exhale warm her skin even as the breath came out ragged.

"Relax, gorgeous." Jo nudged him back with her hip, knowing

full well she was brushing against his cock. He groaned into her hair. Without a backwards glance, she stepped delicately out of his grasp and into her apartment. "I have a cat to feed first."

She switched on a light, and movement from the couch caught his attention. A tabby was curled up on a fleecy, orange blanket. He lifted his head, ears folded back, and blinked in the sudden brightness.

"Hi, Merry." Felix waved. "Nice to meet you."

"He says it's nice to meet you too." Jo deposited her purse on a hook beside the door.

"I'm honored."

Merry responded by yawning hugely and tucking his face under his paws.

Jo turned toward Felix. She undid his collar button, then the next one. He had no doubt that she'd stop and tease him about his eagerness again if he so much as reached for her. So he stood there and took it, watching her fingers move deftly down his shirt. Jo untucked it from his slacks and then unbuttoned his cuffs, one at a time. He remained motionless as she pushed the shirt off his shoulders, leaving him in his undershirt.

"Take this off," she said, glancing down at his chest, "and wait for me in the bedroom."

Felix whipped the shirt over his head. Startled, Jo shifted back, her pupils going wide as she passed her gaze over his bare chest. Did she honestly believe he'd wait until he was in the other room, without her, to undress? Where was the fun in that?

Without a word, he winked, tossed his shirt aside, and went down the hallway, finding her bedroom easily. He lay on her bed, and oh, Jesus, her pillows smelled like her hair. It was almost too much, all of a sudden. He was in Jo's bedroom, in Jo's bed, and he could hear Jo tending to Merry, murmuring gentle words. It was one thing to have her in his room in Tito's house; to be in her home was something else entirely. He was reminded of the way she'd given him her hotel room key in Indianapolis. No hesitation, no distrust, no worry. Just wanting him to be near, to share her space.

His eyes wandered, taking in Jo's overstuffed bookcase, her dresser topped with discarded clothes and makeup, various MnM-inspired artwork, a massive photo collage of Jo and Aida over the years, and... her vibrator. It was just sitting there on her nightstand. Hot pink, with a wide, rounded tip, molded to fit perfectly in one's palm. Was it always there, or had she left it out for them? Had she sent him in here alone knowing he would find it?

He knew that woman.

Of course she had.

He picked it up and turned it on. It buzzed. Loudly.

"I hear that!" Jo called from what sounded like the bathroom. There was no mistaking the glee in her voice; he'd played right into her hands.

"I'm waiting, cariño, don't worry. Just seeing what my options are." He clicked through the different settings, the vibrations reverberating through his hand in all sorts of interesting patterns. Slow, fast, long pulses, short pulses, mixes of various speeds. The sheer number of them boggled the mind. It made sense—everyone was different and liked different things—but Felix had never given vibrator options much thought before. A major oversight on his part, really. One he was only too willing to correct.

He turned off the vibrator, and the light clicked off too. Jo's silhouette moved through the room, outlined by the nightlight in the hallway. She opened a dresser drawer and began pulling things out. A match was struck. She lit a few candles and set them on the dresser, shoving clothes onto the floor, away from the open flames. She turned in profile, pursed her lips, and puffed out the match, an act which had no right to be as sexy as it was.

He watched her skirt sway as she brought one of the candles over to the nightstand. A light, citrusy scent wafted over him, mingling with the sulfurous smell of the match. Jo's auburn hair was the deep, rich red of pomegranate seeds. Her pale skin glowed as if lit from within with the same burning desire that coursed through him.

"Unzip me?"

Felix sat up on the edge of the bed. Inch by precious inch, he lowered the zipper of her lemon-patterned dress. He kissed along her spine as he revealed her skin, then set to work on her undergarments. When she stood naked before him, her entire body gleaming in the candlelight, he guided her to sit on his lap. Her weight sank into him, solid, soft, and warm.

He ran his hands over the lush rolls of her low belly and brushed the back of her shoulder with his chin. "I've never done this with someone before."

"Neither have I," she said over her shoulder.

Felix gauged her expression for any uncertainty or nervousness, but he saw only eager anticipation. Her breath fluttered when Felix kissed the top of her spine. She shifted from hip to hip, her tailbone skimming deliciously against his hardness.

"Let's learn together, cariño mío." He picked up the vibrator and traced its tip up her inner thigh without turning it on. Jo sucked her lower lip between her teeth. "Where do you like it best? Inside or on your clit?"

"On my clit."

"Lie down for me."

She lay on her back, and Felix stretched out next to her. Jo guided his hand where she wanted it and nodded. The instant he turned on the lowest setting, she moaned. Her head fell back against the pillow. She nudged his hand a little higher and cried out, writhing against him, her thigh granting him the sweetest friction against his dick. He pushed his hips forward for more as Jo buried her face in his neck.

"Right there, gorgeous," she panted against his skin. "Don't move."

How he loved being called that. Felix had been called a lot of flattering things before—hot, sexy, handsome. But he'd never been called gorgeous, or even beautiful. Words like that carried a deeper meaning to him, spoke to him of something beyond the way he looked. And the way Jo called him "gorgeous," with the same devotion with which she said his name, made him believe that's how she meant it.

What an intoxicating thing, to be considered gorgeous by Jo. Jo, whose wild, creative mind had chosen that word for him. Jo, who liked the grays on his chin even more than his abs. Jo, whom he admired, whose opinion he respected. Jo, whom he—

Oh.

Jo, whom he loved.

He loved Jo.

There had been hints of it before, dancing around the edges of conscious thought. But the depth, the magnitude, the *certainty* of it was undeniable now. Felix loved Jo. With all his heart, with all that he was. He loved her.

"Turn it up," Jo moaned.

He didn't react. Couldn't. His heart had overruled both his brain and his cock, and all he could do was stare into the flame of the candle on the nightstand.

"Felix, please," Jo begged, clawing at his chest. The scrape of her nails brought Felix back to the moment with a gasp. He pressed his cheek into Jo's forehead to ground himself here, with her, not lost to his own unfettered feelings. He clicked the button on the vibrator. She arched her back and whimpered.

"You like this one, cariño?" he asked, centering himself on Jo's pleasure. That was what mattered right now. She nodded wildly. "I can tell."

"Felix, I'm—" Her words cut off as she started to shake.

"Already, my Jo? Fuck, that was fast. Look at you, coming so sweetly in my arms."

All Jo's cutest features twisted with pleasure. Her lips, stained dark red even after their meal and their kisses, were wide open and round. Felix kissed the upturned corner where they met as Jo convulsed against him, her legs twitching.

Finally, her body began to relax. "Lower," she said desperately, and he shifted the vibrator lower. "No, turn it down."

Felix murmured an apology and clicked back to the lowest setting. Jo's shallow breaths eased.

"It's too much," she explained. "Right after. I need a minute."

"Take all the time you need." He kissed her temple, her cheek, her hair. He couldn't seem to stop kissing her. "You're impossible. I can't believe you came so quickly."

She grinned with those sinfully red lips. "I can't believe you're still clothed."

"I can fix that. Take over."

Jo took the vibrator from him. He rolled off the bed and got naked as quickly as possible. He retrieved the condom he'd stashed in his wallet that morning and tossed it onto a pillow. They watched each other the entire time, Jo breathing heavily as she rubbed the vibrator against her clit. A tiny (minuscule, really) part of Felix wanted to stand there and watch her make herself come over and over. Every other part of him, from head to toe, inside and out, wanted to be the one to do it instead.

As he lay back down beside her, Jo rolled onto her side away from him. Arching her spine, she pushed her ass back.

Felix laughed. "You read my mind, cariño."

"It's very easy to read sometimes. Particularly where my ass is concerned."

He dragged his fingers along her hip, watching the way her flesh yielded to his touch. "Not my fault you have a perfect ass."

"You're one to talk," she said. "Yours is pretty fucking spectacular too, you know."

"I know. Now come here." Felix spooned her, tucking his biceps under her head and nestling his shaft along the slit between her cheeks. He rolled his hips to feel the caress of her body and groaned into her hair. Jo chuckled and wiggled her hips, eliciting one more groan from him. He wrapped his arm around her waist and took back the vibrator. "Tell me when you're ready for more."

21

"I'M READY NOW," Jo breathed, resting her hand on Felix's fore-arm. He turned her vibrator up to the higher setting that never failed to hurtle her toward the peak of pleasure. Jo's breath flew from her lungs, and she squirmed against the secure circle of his arms.

"I know you like this one, cariño," Felix murmured. "I'll come back to it if you ask, but I want to see what the rest do to you."

"Yes," she gasped. "Let me show you."

Texting Felix about her vibrator was by far Jo's best idea ever. It had been the first thing that came to mind when he'd asked her that sexy question. Since he seemed to like it when she followed her creative whims, she'd decided not to overthink it. And now, it was perfect. She'd never felt so naked in front of a man before, showing him something she'd only ever reserved for herself. The intimacy of it, the trust she gave him to see her so vulnerable...

"Moan for me, my Jo. Let me hear the sounds you make when you're alone."

Oh, God. There was nothing in the world like this feeling. Jo was sure of it. She gave herself over to it completely.

Felix went through every setting on her vibrator with painstaking precision. As if he were memorizing what each one did to her. Which ones made her muscles twitch, which made her cry out, which made her bite her lip and dig her nails into his forearm, which made her thrust her hips for more.

And, most importantly, which ones made her come.

There were a few settings that were usually good for that, and Felix found them all. With their bodies connected like this, he couldn't help but be completely in tune with the minute changes that signaled her next orgasm was close. Every time, Felix gave her little nudges of sensation until she tipped her over the edge— pinching her nipple or nipping her shoulder, running his foot up her calf or tickling her ear with whispers that carried beautiful, filthy words. He made damn sure that, when it really came down to it, *he* was the one who made Jo come, and she adored him for it.

"God, Jo, I could watch you come all night," Felix said after a while. "Do you want to keep going?"

"You're overdue for your turn, gorgeous."

How long had it been since they'd started? She had no fucking idea. Long enough that his erection must be getting uncomfortable, but he shook his head against her hair. Jo's heart melted. He was too much sometimes. Far more than she deserved.

"You're giving me everything I need." As if to emphasize his point, he rocked back and forth along her ass crack, moaning as his tip brushed bare against her pussy.

But, oh, she wanted to give him so much more.

"I need a break anyway," she said honestly. She wrapped her hand around his and guided his thumb to the off button. Her body sagged against him, her pussy tingling as they eased the vibrator out together.

Felix nuzzled her cheek. "Mi hermoso cariño."

She turned her head to look into his eyes. "I love it when you say such wonderful things to me."

"You deserve them all."

"Oh, I don't know about that," she said with a modest smile.

"I do."

Suddenly, there was a fierceness in his eyes that Jo had seen only once before. The night of the tornado, when he'd stayed at the library to wait for her.

I needed to make sure you were safe.

She touched his jaw, whispered his name, and raised her head to kiss him. As he opened his mouth to her, desire asserted itself within Jo. It made her want to be assertive too. They could either lie there and whisper sweet nothings to each other, or they could get the hell on with it. Her vote was for the latter option.

She dropped her vibrator onto the nightstand and rotated in his arms until they were face to face. Taking his cock in her hand, she began to caress him, even as she continued to press forward. She gave him no choice but to roll onto his back. He breathed out a curse as she got to her knees and straddled his thighs. With steady strokes on his cock, Jo coasted her free hand down Felix's abs. She raked her nails over his skin the way he liked and listened to his sharp hiss. He arched his back.

"Jo, God, again." He grabbed the hand she had on his dick and moved it to his chest. "Harder. *Hard.*"

With both hands now, she clawed him, harder than she'd ever touched him before, hard enough to leave marks. Felix cried out and scrunched his eyes closed, glorious agony in every line and crease on his face. His cock twitched and leaked pre-come, without her even touching it. His hand flew to his head, making a fist in his hair. Jo watched his every reaction, wide-eyed, fascinated.

"Do that while you fuck me," he begged.

She would do almost anything he wanted if it made him feel that good. Her blood was singing in her veins, thrilling at the sight of Felix completely at her mercy. The stark white lines on his skin had already turned a vivid pink.

She couldn't resist teasing him. Just once more. "I guess I wasn't giving you everything you need after all, hmm? Ask me to my face, gorgeous. Tell me what you need."

"*Unh*, God," Felix complained. His eyes flew open. The depraved longing Jo saw there was so blatant, so indecent, she blushed. But she held his gaze, caressing his stomach with her palms.

"Please, Jo." His voice broke over her name. "Please. You ride me so well. Fuck me and scratch my chest. Hard. Mark me as yours. You know I already am."

"There," she said. She had to draw on all her acting experience from MnM to make her voice light and playful. It was nearly impossible when her entire body was shaking with desire. "That wasn't so hard, was it?"

"*Please.*"

Jo got the condom on him as fast as she could. He moaned when she rolled it on and again when she lowered herself onto him. She rode him and dragged her nails across his pecs, over and over, until he was shuddering. His fist in his hair tightened, and the other one clamped around Jo's arm, just above her elbow. Anchoring to her without restricting her movement.

"More, more, more."

It wasn't long ago that Jo had first dreamt of riding Felix, but never in her wildest imagination was it like this. Her eyes fell on the nightstand, and an idea wilder still sprang to mind. She lunged for her vibrator.

"You want more, my gorgeous man?" She buried her nails in his chest as she sank the vibrator between her labia, pressing it firmly just below her clit. She waited until Felix raised his head, waited long enough for him to stop her if he wanted to.

His mouth fell open, and he whispered, "Holy shit." His gaze darted between her hand and her face.

Jo cocked her head and smiled.

"Do it."

She turned it on, and they both contorted in ecstasy.

"Fuck. *Fuck,* I feel it," Felix panted. "I can feel it."

"Can I turn it up?"

"Ye-yes."

She clicked it to her favorite setting and tossed her head back. Drowning in pleasure, she pounded their bodies together, flesh slapping against flesh. Her hand on his chest jerked into motion, all the way down to his stomach and back up again. Felix howled so loudly Jo was sure her neighbors heard it. Hell, half of Ashville probably heard it.

Her orgasm ramped up so fast it took her by surprise. She gasped as her whole body lurched forward. Her cunt clenched around Felix's cock. He screamed her name, his hips driving upward as he came along with her. Jo grinded into him and gave him another scratch, pulling her arm down, hard, in one long stroke.

A guttural sound came out of him as he collapsed against the mattress. Jo's orgasm lasted a second or two longer than his, and he grunted as her pussy spasmed one final time. She switched off the vibrator, lifted off of Felix, and tumbled down next to him, utterly spent.

"Jesus," she sighed.

"Yeah." There was a long pause while they both caught their breath. "Have I told you lately how much I love the way your mind works?"

A giggle bubbled up out of her. "Tell me again."

He cupped her cheek and smiled. "I love the way your mind works."

Jo reached out and rested her hand on his chest. It was warm and flushed, with raised lines crisscrossing over it. "Did I hurt you?"

"No," he said. "You were perfect, my Jo. You *are* perfect."

Even as his praise washed over her, a pleasure as rich as her orgasm, Jo chewed on her lip. She ran her palm over him, soothing the places she'd scratched to hell. "Can I check anyway? If I made you bleed, we should put something on it."

Felix's expression went soft. He nodded. "Let me take care of the condom first."

"Washcloths in the top drawer," she told him with a kiss.

LATER, IN THE quiet darkness of Jo's bedroom, Felix skated his fingers along her upper arm. They lay with their foreheads inches apart, and he listened to her breathe. Her eyes were closed. His were wide open.

His heart thudded beneath the adhesive bandage she'd insisted on putting on him. One tiny nick in his skin from the corner of her nail, and she'd treated it with all the seriousness of applying a tourniquet. Her fingers had been gentle and dexterous as she'd dabbed antiseptic on him and covered the cut with the bandage. Then she had leaned in and kissed it. She didn't apologize, which he was grateful for. He didn't want to have to remind her that she didn't need to. He'd asked for it, and he'd loved it. He wanted her to do it again (and again and again) and didn't want her to feel guilty about it. But there was no apology. She just took care of him, made sure he was safe.

Felix hadn't planned on telling her. They'd only been together *for a week*, for fuck's sake. It was ludicrous, the way he felt. She almost certainly didn't feel the same way about him.

But then she'd kissed his cut. She'd kissed his cut and chosen not to apologize for giving him what he wanted and gazed up at him with a protective tenderness that Felix had never seen in a woman's eyes before. And suddenly nothing else mattered. It didn't matter that it had only been a week. It didn't matter that sometimes she was still anxious about being herself around him or that he saw uncertainty in her eyes when she thought she talked about MnM too much.

The only thing that mattered was that she knew the truth.

"Jo?" he whispered into the darkness.

She stirred under his gentle touch. "Hmm?"

"I need tell you to something."

She shifted again, closer to him. "What is it?"

His hand went still on her arm. "I'm in love with you."

Jo's breath caught. Her fingers slid into his chest hair. His skin tingled where she touched the scratches she'd left on him. Marks on his skin to match the ones she'd already carved on his heart.

"Really?" Her voice had been sleepy until now, muffled and soft and low. Now, she sounded wide awake.

"Yes."

Her arm looped over his shoulder, and she dragged herself against his body. She buried her face in his neck. "Felix. Say it again." Her voice was breaking; her body was trembling. "Please, please say it again."

Felix wrapped her in his arms. He cradled the back of her head. He closed his eyes and felt every inch of their joined bodies. "I'm in love with you, Jo. I don't expect you to say it back. I know it's... it's so soon. I just needed you to know." Tears welled in his eyes, and he tightened his grip on her. Jo squeezed tighter too.

"I wish I could," she said. "But not yet."

Yet.

His heart leapt at that beautiful, hopeful word. "I know. I under-stand."

They clung to each other, neither one willing to let go. Soon, Felix could sense Jo fighting off sleep. Her breathing would deepen, and her body would relax, then she'd stir and redouble her effort to hold him close. After the third time, Felix kissed her temple and whispered, "Go to sleep, cariño. I'm not going anywhere."

THE DAYS THAT followed were some of the happiest of Jo's life. June was just beginning, but even the sweltering humidity couldn't dampen her spirits. It did, however, dampen her scrubs, mostly in her underboob and between her thighs. Even the brief-est walks to and from her car left her clammy and in want of a shower. It would take some getting used to, but it was worth it. Because, while Ashville, Kansas, might have god-awful humidity, being here meant being with the man who loved her.

Felix loved her, and he even seemed to love all the nerdy, over-the-top parts of her that she was slowly learning to love again herself. In those last ten days leading up to the game night launch, Jo lived and breathed Monsters and Mythology in a way she hadn't in years. Immersing herself in it, with Felix alongside her, was like learning to fly. No, it was like remembering that once upon a time she had *known* how to fly and realizing she still had wings.

Both Jo and Felix had long since given up pretending that she was volunteering at the library for only one hour a week, so most of her free time was spent helping with final preparations. On Sunday afternoon, they met up with Leni at Ashville Community

College for the summer outreach event. The three of them spent hours handing out flyers and talking up the library's programs. Felix and Leni discussed the programs as a whole, changing up their pitch depending on what each person was interested in. Jo, on the other hand, had no qualms about giving every single person the hard sell about MnM. If she was going to be out there getting sunburned in the sticky heat, she was going to get some new gaming friends out of it, damn it.

To help, she had brought twenty sets of dice that she wasn't terribly attached to. She hung a sign on the front of their table reading "Free Dice!" and gave them away to the first twenty people who signed up for the library's e-newsletter and put the MnM launch in their calendars.

The dice were gone within thirty minutes.

"How are you so good at this?" Felix asked her after she handed off the last set to a student in a *Minecraft* T-shirt.

Jo smiled and sketched a bow. "You, sir, are looking at the 2009 to 2011 Social Coordinator for the Sigma Theta Tau International Honor Society of Nursing, Gamma Tau at-Large chapter."

He stared at her. "I know some of those words."

She laughed, a big, boisterous sound that carried across the quad. "The first rule of advertising to college students, Felix? Give them free shit."

"All of the library's programs are free," he said, clearly puzzled.

"Which you should be leading with, by the way," Jo said. "It's an obvious selling point."

Leni piped up. "Should we take the sign down now that the dice are gone?"

"No, no," she replied. "Tell people they just missed the giveaway, but there will be more freebies at the MnM launch, and to sign up for the newsletter for more info."

"We're giving away freebies at the launch?" Leni asked, turning to Felix.

Jo answered her first. "We are now."

By the end of the afternoon, Jo was a living, breathing puddle of sweat, all the flyers were gone, and over fifty people had signed up for the newsletter. Not bad for podunk little Ashville. Ecstatic, Felix called Warren on the spot to let him know how well it had gone, giving Jo all the credit. She grimaced and tried to mime to him to stop, but he only winked.

"Aren't you supposed to be saving your job?" Jo asked him after he'd hung up. "I don't mind if you and Leni take credit."

"Skilled volunteers are hard to come by. We'll take the credit for finding you; you take the credit for doing the work."

"All right," she relented, wiping her forehead with the back of her wrist, "I can live with that."

The rest of the week was a blur. At work, Jo reminded Vanessa about the launch and helped her make a character over lunch—a druid with a crow companion named Tom. On another day, she used her break to call up a local bakery and paid out of her own pocket to order three dozen cupcakes decorated with the MnM logo.

Her evenings were spent at the library, or wherever else she was needed. She drove all around town to put up flyers in every place she could think of, including the Starbucks out by the highway. She showed Leni where to order dice sets in bulk to give away. She helped Felix punch up the newsletter copy so MnM night, and all of the library's programs, sounded more enticing.

After hours, she stationed herself at Felix's dining room table, creating half a dozen starter characters for people to choose from if they didn't have their own. Felix sometimes sat with her, making his way through a thick book about the transcontinental railroad.

(Jo called him a nerd for that, and he fired back a very mature "look who's talking" that sent them both into a fit of giggles.) Otherwise, he was down in the basement, boxing and blasting his favorite pop songs. When Felix returned upstairs, shirtless and glistening with sweat, he would offer her his hand and ask her to join him in the shower. Jo always said yes.

And every day, she thought of the words he had whispered to her in the dark. Words he repeated often. Words that ran through her mind like a refrain from the most beautiful song in the world. *He loves me.*

When she woke in the morning to find Felix sound asleep, with tousled hair and Merry curled up behind his knees—*he loves me.*

When they took Tito to brunch together, and Felix blushed at the embarrassing stories his grandpa told about him—*he loves me.*

When he kissed her and touched her until she fell apart in his arms. When he called her a good girl and let her tend to him afterward—*he loves me.*

When she got her period and he brought her dinner, made her herbal tea, and cuddled with her and Merry on the couch to watch their favorite comfort movies—*he loves me.*

Jo never said it back. There was a part of her that wanted to, but her feelings for Felix were unlike anything she'd ever known. How was she supposed to classify them as love or lust or infatuation or just plain desperation if she had no point of reference for them? She knew Felix wouldn't wait around for her forever, but she couldn't say it. Not yet. Not until she was certain.

And then, of course, there was that deep-seated voice that still wormed its way in, trying to convince her that she was going to fuck it up. She talked things through with Aida more than once, but even her best friend's reassurances never lasted long. More often than Jo cared to admit, that voice, a voice that sounded an awful lot like her own, clouded her happy, sunny days, coiling like a knot in her stomach.

It doesn't matter if he loves you, Jo, it whispered, countering that lovely refrain. *Jeremy loved you, and he got sick of you and your obsessions eventually. Felix has only known you for a few weeks, after all. It's only a matter of time...*

22

BEHIND THE FRONT desk at the library, Peggy swiveled her chair to face Felix. "Nervous?"

He paused mid-stride and chuckled. "What gave it away?"

"Oh, I don't know," she mused, "maybe the endless pacing? Or the fact that you've run down to the room to check on 'one more thing' fifty times since lunch? Or, speaking of, maybe it's that you skipped lunch, which I've never seen you do before." She lowered her chin and put on her sternest mom face. "You need to eat something before people start showing up, kiddo. Can't have you fainting in front of a dozen patrons."

"I'm fine, Peg, really," he said with a wave of his hand.

She gave an "mm-hmm," opened her desk drawer, and fished out a granola bar. Without a word, she held it out to him.

Felix sighed and took it. "Thank you."

"Don't mention it," she said with a wink.

It only took a single bite for Felix to realize how ravenous he was. He swallowed his pride and dove into his own desk drawer for the sandwich he'd been too anxious to eat at lunch. This was it. Everything he'd been working toward for the last six weeks came down to tonight. Jo would be here any minute. Leni and Warren, too, followed by... well, hopefully enough people to run an MnM game. He choked down his sandwich, peanut butter sticking in his throat.

Keeping an eye on him to make sure he ate, Peggy asked, "Did I tell you my kids are coming tonight?"

"All the way from Kansas City?"

Peggy's twins, Madison and Denver, both went to college at the University of Missouri.

"Yessir. They owed me a visit anyway, so I made them come for launch week. Mad's excited. I guess she's got some friends who play the game."

That's two more, he thought hopefully.

Moments after Felix finished eating, Jo and Leni arrived. They were each lugging a giant pink box, like the kind donut shops used. Felix spotted them through the windows and jogged over to open the door.

"Here," Jo greeted him, shoving her box at him without even stepping inside. "Sorry, I probably should have asked, but I wanted it to be a surprise. I'll be right back, I have more in the car."

"More what?" Felix called after her. She merely grinned over her shoulder.

He looked helplessly at Leni, who shrugged. "I don't know, hun. I just ran into her in the parking lot. She said to take these downstairs."

By the time they made it back to the lobby, Jo had returned. Tito was on her arm.

"Tito! ¿Qué haces aquí?"

"You forgot about me, ey, Felix?" Tito retorted with a twinkle in his eye. "Your girl invited me to your big event, remember?"

"Sí, I remember." Felix ran a hand through his hair. *Now* he remembered. How could he have forgotten the awkward conversation they'd had the day he ran into Jo at White Hills? And why hadn't either of them said anything? He wasn't going to worry about it now. Tito was here, and Felix was glad to see him. "Thank you for coming, Tito."

"I wouldn't miss it!" Tito crowed. "Whatever 'it' is."

Jo laughed and guided him toward the elevator. "Do you want me to explain it again?"

"No, solete." He patted her arm. "I'll just be watching anyway."

Before following them downstairs, Felix detoured back to the desk to double check that he wasn't forgetting anything.

"We've got it, Felix." Leni pushed on his shoulders, nudging him in the direction of the stairs. "Peggy and I will send people down as they show up. When foot traffic slows, I'll join you to help you and Jo get people settled."

Felix nodded, more to himself than to Leni. It was fine; it would be fine. Everything would be fine. With Peggy's kids and Vanessa, that was at least three players—plus Jo and Tito to round out the headcount. They only needed a few additional people for the event to be well-attended. They might even end up with enough to split into two tables. Wouldn't that be something? They'd planned for that, just in case. Jo was ready to jump in and GM a second table at a moment's notice.

The front door opened as Felix hit the stairs. Leni called brightly, "Hi, hun. Are you here for Monsters and Mythology?"

"Uh, yeah," the person replied. "I got this flyer at ACC?"

Felix's heart stuttered and then skipped a beat. He couldn't tell if he was more nervous or excited. Leni started chatting with the patron about MnM, and he sent her a mental *thank you* for buying him time to get downstairs and pull himself together.

Here goes nothing.

THE PRIMARY THOUGHT in Jo's mind was *holy shit.* Twenty-three people showed up at the Ashville Public Library on a Tuesday night to play Monsters and Mythology. Twenty-fucking-three. Nearly three times the number they'd hoped for. They had so many people that they overflowed to a second meeting room, and Leni had to be recruited to GM her first-ever game.

"Put me in, coach," she said when Jo approached her with the idea. Jo handed over a copy of the same adventure Felix had practiced with them a few days earlier. Jo crossed her fingers that combat wouldn't be *too* much of a shitshow. She had faith in Leni to at least make the game fun, regardless of how loose she was with the rules.

Seated at Leni's table were Vanessa and her dad, a late-fifties white man with a beer belly and a bushy, gray beard. Vanessa had mentioned that he might tag along, since he'd been a fan of MnM since the eighties. He was one of the few middle-aged people in attendance. Everyone else—aside from one set of parents with their two children—looked to be college age or a little older. Exactly what Warren wanted.

By the time the first dice began to roll, over half of the cupcakes were gone, the "Free Dice" raffle bowl was stuffed with slips of paper, and Felix's smile was bright enough to put the sun to shame. Jo wished she could stay and watch him GM, but she had volunteered to take charge of the overflow room so neither he nor Leni had to be alone. Among her eight players was the pink-haired young woman who'd been at Stan's the same night Jo and Felix were, when Jo had guerilla marketed the launch to a table of twenty-somethings. None of the other people from that table had come, but, hey—one out of four wasn't bad.

Jo did her damnedest to show her players a good time. She used all her goofiest character voices, leapt to her feet during combat to keep the energy up, and encouraged people to speak in character and describe their actions. She had people laughing and trying out character voices of their own, cheering for one another and yelling in frustration when dice rolls didn't go their way. When she brought the game to an end, all eight players applauded so loudly Jo was sure they could be heard upstairs.

Jo brought them back to the main room for the raffle just as Felix was wrapping up his adventure. Leni descended on them, armed with a smile and a big, pink box. Jo snagged a cupcake and took the opportunity to glance around. Vanessa and her dad were cracking up over some shared joke. Tito sat in a far corner, smiling broadly at Felix from behind his thick, black mustache. Warren was in another corner, hands behind his back, observing. Jo gave him a quick smile when she caught his eye, and he nodded in acknowledgment. She watched his eyes dart over her group, as if counting. He must not have realized there was an overflow room. A wave of smug satisfaction washed over Jo. She hid her smile behind her cupcake.

Felix switched gears the moment his game was done. He grabbed the raffle bowl and thanked everyone for coming as he stirred up the papers inside. Leni quickly replaced the cupcake box in her arms with a basket full of dice sets. They'd planned for three winners, but with so many people, and plenty of dice to go around, they bumped it up to five. The woman from Stan's was one of the winners, and Jo cheered as she chose a set of pink dice to match her hair.

"Let's hear it once more for our winners," Felix said, leading the group in a final round of applause. "We hope to see you all at Monsters and Mythology night next week. Every Tuesday, all summer long, we'll be here."

"The library's open until nine if you'd like to browse!" Leni called, bouncing on her toes. "MnM books are in the sci-fi and fantasy section."

"And take cupcakes on the way out," added Jo. "Please don't make me take these home."

As the din of conversation rose, Jo noticed Warren pull Felix aside. Leni stood near the door, offering cupcakes as people slowly filtered out. Jo decided to check on Tito.

"What did you think, Tito?" she asked. "I hope you weren't bored just watching."

"Solete, I'm so proud of my Felix," he replied, his eyes shining. "It feels good to see him happy again. Thank you for bringing me."

Jo's heart melted. "I'm so glad it went well. Did everyone in here have a good time?"

"The best time. Including me." Tito took Jo's hand and kissed her knuckles.

"Stealing my girl, old man?" Felix said. He sauntered over to them with his hands in his pockets and a winning smile on his face. Jo looked him up and down, enjoying the way his slacks tightened over his thighs with every step. The sight of his approach would probably never cease to make her shiver. She leaned back against the wall so she didn't lose control and pounce on him.

Before she or Tito could respond, though, Vanessa's dad stood up from his table. He and Vanessa were the last two attendees left in the room.

"Excuse me, sir?" he asked, glancing at Felix's name tag. "Are you in charge?"

"I am," Felix said, instantly switching back to his professional demeanor. He extended his hand to the man. "Felix Navarro. What can I help you with, sir? Did you enjoy the event this evening?"

"Greg Pearce." He shook Felix's hand. "My daughter, Vanessa."

Felix nodded at Vanessa, who waved from behind her dad's back. Jo slipped away to help Leni clean up, both of them doing a terrible job of pretending not to eavesdrop.

"I had a great time. We both did," Greg continued. "I was wondering if you need more volunteers to GM. I've been playing MnM off and on for decades. I used to organize SWOP events at a game store in Wichita, but they shuttered about a year ago. I know a bunch of the people who played there. I bet they'd make the drive a couple times a month for the chance to play and GM again."

"That sounds incredible," Felix said. Jo could hear the barely restrained elation in his voice. She and Leni shared a smile. "To be frank, the turnout tonight was higher than anticipated, so more volunteers are sorely needed. I'd love to set up a time to connect. Would you mind emailing me about this? Let's head upstairs, and I can give you my card."

"Be glad to. Thanks for bringing MnM to Ashville."

While Felix was upstairs, Leni and Jo packed up, reset the tables and chairs, and escorted Tito to the elevator. He peppered them with questions about dragons and dice, trying to get a better grasp on what the heck he'd just witnessed. Leni was only too happy to oblige. When the elevator dinged on the ground floor, she took his arm and walked him over to the fantasy section, book recommendations falling from her lips one after another.

Jo trailed after them, but switched directions when Felix came around the corner from the reading room. She watched him walking toward her again, giving him another, less subtle once-over.

Felix's eyes sparkled, but he kept his voice polite. "The library is closing in five minutes, miss. May I help you find something?"

"No, thank you," Jo said softly, gazing up at him. "I have everything I need right here."

A slow smile spread across Felix's face. His eyes crinkled in the corners. "You know tonight never would've happened without you, right?"

Jo scoffed lightly and looked down at her hands. "I don't—"

"Stop." Felix touched her chin with the tip of his finger and tilted her head up. His dark brown eyes smoldered. Jo had never had someone smolder at her before, but seriously, there was no other word for it. "Don't do that. If you hadn't walked into my life six weeks ago, none of this would have happened. You did this, Jo. All of it."

Jo opened her mouth to say something. What to say, she didn't know. She wanted to remind him that she didn't do this alone. He and Leni had done more than their share of the work. But, God, the look in his eyes halted all of the words on her tongue. She could tell Felix didn't want to hear any of that. Another time, maybe. Right now, he seemed to want Jo to accept his words. To feel appreciated and acknowledged and *seen*.

"Th—"

A quiet laugh around the corner broke the moment. Felix took a large step back, turning toward the people exiting the reading room and wishing them a good night. Jo pressed her lips together and veered toward the front desk, her heart pounding against her ribs. After the patrons were gone, he moved behind the desk to shut down the computers for the night.

"What did Warren talk to you about?" she asked.

Felix grinned. "He congratulated me, and by extension, Leni and you, for the wildly successful event. He wants to meet tomorrow to talk about the game night program for the rest of the summer."

"What about it? Isn't everything all set?"

"He didn't say specifically. But he sounded excited, so I hope it can only be good news."

"Fingers crossed." Jo said, making the gesture with both hands. "I need to get home to Merry soon, but do you want to come over?"

He winced and gave her a remorseful look. "I'm sorry, cariño, I'm exhausted. I need to crash as soon as I drop Tito off. Where is he, anyway?"

"In sci-fi-fantasy. Leni's turning him into a nerd," Jo said. They shared a laugh even as guilt pricked at her. "Do you want me to take him home? I didn't mean to give you one more thing to worry about tonight."

"I appreciate the offer, but I don't mind. I've barely spoken to him tonight." His brow furrowed, and he cocked his head at her. "How did you even get him here? Only family can sign residents out."

"Ah, ah—not just family," Jo said, shaking her finger at him. "It's anyone designated by the resident."

"Which is me. And my parents, who, as far as I know, are in Barcelona."

"And me. Tito added me last week."

"Last..." He put his fists on his hips like a stern parent. "And neither of you thought to mention that at brunch on Sunday?"

"We wanted to surprise you?" Jo spread her hands helplessly as Felix unleashed a dramatic sigh. "It was Tito's idea!"

He scrubbed his hands over his face. "I never should have introduced the two of you. You're both menaces to society."

She braced her forearms on the desk and leaned forward. "Yeah. But you love us."

"Yes, I do." Felix mirrored her, hands flat on his side of the desk, torso pitched toward her. Jo recognized the look in his eyes and flicked her gaze toward the camera above the desk. He frowned and leaned back. "How about I come over tomorrow night, cariño mío?"

"Tomorrow it is. I'll make us dinner to celebrate tonight's success. Which I made possible." It wasn't anything like the heartfelt "thank you" she'd planned to give him earlier, but he looked pleased to hear her take credit anyway.

"Sounds perfect," he said. "Now where's that old man? Tito! Library's closed!"

"Sorry!" Leni called back. "We're coming."

She entered the lobby a minute later, Tito on one arm and a stack of urban fantasy under the other.

23

AFTER WORK THE next day, Felix knocked on Jo's door and was greeted by a string of curse words.

"Hang on!" she yelled. "Shit-damn-it-fuck."

"Take your time!" he responded with a laugh. When she wrenched the door open, a tantalizing aroma of garlic, onion, and roasted chicken hit him square in the face. His mouth watered.

Jo was pink-cheeked, barefoot, and wearing a lavender tank top and cobalt blue scrub pants. Her hair was pulled back in a loose knot, the baby hairs around her forehead sticking up. She was devastatingly adorable.

She didn't move from the doorway. "Can you go get me a quart of milk? Mine boiled over."

"Yeah, sure."

"Whole milk, please. Door'll be unlocked."

With that, the door closed in his face, and Felix fell a little bit more in love with Jo. "Text me if you need anything else," he called, then he traipsed down the stairs along the wall of her building.

Smiling to himself the entire time, he picked up some milk at the nearest store and soon returned to her apartment. He knocked again as he let himself in, holding up the milk in triumph. Jo whirled around from her spot at the stove, gratitude evident on her face.

"Have we done the 'hero's calling' joke to death yet?" he asked. "Or may I still say it?"

"You saved dinner," she said. She took the carton and popped up on her toes to peck his cheek. "You can make any joke you want."

"It smells wonderful," he said as she poured milk into a measuring cup next to the stove. "How can I help?"

Jo laughed—a sarcastic "ha!"—and plopped a hunk of butter into a wide pan. "Gorgeous, do you see the size of this kitchen? It barely holds one person. You can keep Merry company." She waved vaguely in the direction of the couch, where Merry was stretched out on his favorite orange blanket. "It'll just be a few more minutes. The sauce comes together fast as long as I don't get ambitious and heat the milk on the stove first."

Felix rolled up his sleeves as he joined Merry on the couch. The cat stirred and glared at him, tail flicking. Felix apologized for the disruption. He caught Jo grinning at them as she stuck the milk carton in the fridge. Merry's eyes drifted closed again, the feline equivalent of forgiveness. Felix scritched him behind the ears until he purred.

True to her word, Jo had dinner on the table in short order: pasta primavera with chicken in a creamy, garlicky sauce; toasted focaccia drizzled with olive oil and balsamic vinegar; spinach salad; and Felix's favorite pinot grigio. Felix also spotted a tray of fresh brownies on the kitchen counter. He busied himself with opening the wine and pouring them each a glass while Jo dished up pasta and salad.

"Here's to the successful launch of Monsters and Mythology

night," Felix said, raising his glass. "And to the amazing people who made it happen."

"Cheers," Jo said and clinked her glass against his.

They sipped their wine and dug into the exceptional food. Felix groaned at the first bite, making Jo giggle and blush. They talked about her day, including her lunch break with Vanessa. Apparently, her co-worker couldn't stop talking about how much fun she'd had at Leni's table. Felix had been pretty focused on his own game, but he hadn't been able to ignore the other group's raucous laughter that frequently drowned him out. He wasn't that kind of GM; he didn't inspire such reactions from his players that way Jo and Leni did. He'd even caught a couple of people glancing over at Leni's table enviously when that laughter erupted over and over again. Disappointing patrons like that really bothered him, but luckily, he wouldn't have to worry about it for much longer.

"How was your meeting with Warren?" Jo asked as she refilled their wine.

"It went great," he replied. "He's convinced that MnM night will be the perfect talking point when he speaks to the county's budget committee in September. He invited me to join him at that meeting."

"That's wonderful," Jo interjected. "That reminds me. Vanessa said she took some pictures last night. Can I have her email them to you? For the newsletter or the committee or whatever?"

"Absolutely. That's brilliant," Felix said, helping himself to more salad. "Warren also wants to expand to two nights a week instead of one."

Jo grimaced. Not the reaction he expected. "I wouldn't do that. You'll just split the attendance. And if the games don't look well-attended, fewer and fewer people will keep showing up. You need to—" She cut herself off and shrank back. "Sorry, you didn't ask what I thought."

She wouldn't meet his gaze, but the apprehension he could read on her face twisted his stomach. *Don't do this to me, Jo.*

"You know I value your opinions about MnM," he said softly. "Please continue. What do we need to do?"

She still hesitated. Felix held in a sigh and waited for her to be ready. She nibbled at her bread before responding. "It might be worth suggesting to Warren that you build up a core group of regulars first, see who shows up again after the first week or two. Last night went really well, but there are bound to be people who won't come back."

Felix pictured those jealous, dissatisfied players at his table again. Hopefully his piss-poor GMing hadn't ruined MnM for them completely.

"There may be a couple of people," Jo continued, "who commit to coming every week. But in my experience, most SWOP players show up once or twice a month. Try not to change anything until you know what to expect each week. Besides, GMing once a week is hard enough. Trust me, you don't want to prep multiple games a week."

She made excellent points. She had to know that, didn't she? Felix reached across the table, palm up. Jo set down her fork and took his hand. "Thank you, Jo. I'm sure you're right. I'll pass that along to Warren."

A relieved smile flickered over her lips. She gave his hand a quick squeeze and returned to her meal. They ate in silence for a moment before Felix spoke up again. "I had another meeting to-day."

"With who?"

"Vanessa's dad, Greg."

She cocked her head. "I'm surprised Vanessa didn't mention that."

"It all happened rather quickly," Felix said. "He emailed me, and when I called him to set up a meeting, we ended up talking things over right then. He wants to sign on as a weekly GM for us."

"Fantastic!" she cried.

"It is," he said. He paused before continuing, weighing the best approach for what came next. "Jo, would you consider GMing weekly too?"

Jo's brow knit together. "Why?"

"I know you said no the night we met because you wanted a break from MnM. But you've been so happy these last couple of weeks, both at Indi-Con and helping with the launch. I wanted to ask again in case you changed your mind."

"But why do you need me to GM at all?" she asked with a shrug. "Like I said, you aren't going to have two dozen people every week. You and Greg will have it covered. You don't need me."

Felix's mouth went dry. He licked his lips, which didn't help since his tongue felt like sandpaper. He took a swallow of wine, but even that was dry. "Warren and I agreed that I would take on more of an organizer role for game night. I won't be GMing anymore."

"Oh." She frowned. "I'm sorry he made you change roles. That sucks. Is it okay if I think about it first?"

Shit, she misunderstood him. He couldn't blame her; his phrasing was pretty damn cagey. He took another stab at it. "He didn't make me change roles, Jo. It was my idea. I... I don't particularly like GMing, and I'm aware it's not my strong suit. It does our patrons, and the program, a disservice to have me run a bad game every week."

"Felix, what are you talking about?" Jo's breath quickened, and his chest went tight. She shook her head vehemently. "Maybe you need a bit more practice, but you're not a bad GM. And you like running combat—you told me so."

"I do like combat, but the things I like aren't conducive to running a compelling, fast-paced game," Felix explained. "No one wants to sit around and watch me strategize about monster attacks. Especially not when Leni is right there, acting out a sword fight between a rogue and a pirate and making people wish they were at her table instead of mine. My games aren't *fun* the way yours and Leni's are."

Her round eyes widened, offended on his behalf. "Yes, they—"

"Jo, it's okay," he said gently, holding up a hand to stop her. "I'm not upset about this. I don't need you to reassure me, though it's very kind of you to try."

She deflated, slouching against her chair. "Are you sure?"

"I'm sure, cariño." He took her hand across the table once more and offered her a soft smile. "I'm relieved, honestly. I didn't become a librarian to play games with the public. It's been fucking exhausting doing all of this advertising and talking up MnM when I'm not even really that much of a fan." He laughed lightly but stopped abruptly at the shock on Jo's face.

Shit. What the fuck did he say it like that for? *Shit, shit, shit.*

JO BALLED HER hand into a fist around the napkin in her lap, fighting the panic that was rising up the back of her throat. The blood pounding in her ears drowned out everything except that wretched voice inside her.

This is it, Jo. You pushed him into MnM too hard. He tried it, and he hates it. Just like Jeremy.

She started to pull away from Felix, but he held onto her.

"Jo—"

"You could have told me that you hated MnM this whole time," she breathed, unable to control the tremble in her voice.

"That's not what I said."

"Then maybe you'd better tell me again."

Felix took a deep breath and pushed his hand through his hair. "I like playing MnM with you. And I love watching you play and GM. You know that. But without you, it's not the same. I don't like MnM nearly as much if you're not there. That's all I meant."

Some small corner of Jo's heart stirred at those words. There was something sweet about that sentiment—that her presence made MnM worthwhile to him. Except... it didn't quite add up. Hot tears burned the backs of her eyes. "But I *was* there."

Felix leaned forward, pushing his half-eaten plate out of the way to rest on his forearms. "Cariño, what do you mean?"

"I was there, Felix!" she yelled, wrenching her hand out of his. "These last two weeks. At the library, at your house, at the god-damn college. I was there the whole time, and it was 'fucking exhausting' for you."

She shoved away from the table. Merry streaked past, retreating into the bedroom. Jo desperately wanted to follow him, to hide under the bed and not come out until morning. Instead, she stalked into the living room. Felix's chair scraped back, and his footsteps followed her.

"I'm not explaining myself well tonight, Jo. I'm sorry," he said. He stood several feet away from her, his arms held away from his sides in a posture of surrender.

Jo swiped a tear off her cheek and crossed her arms. She didn't trust herself to speak, afraid that the vitriol running through her head would come pouring out of her mouth if she dared to say another word. Felix—patient, gentle, loving Felix—didn't deserve such vicious words. At least Jo had the presence of mind to realize that.

"Let me try again," Felix said with forced calm. "Enjoying MnM with you as a hobby isn't the same as making it my entire job. I wanted to do what I could for the library—for a lot of reasons. Now that the program is launched, I'm taking a step back from MnM itself and focusing on game night more programmatically. I hope we can continue to play MnM together, Jo, at conventions and such. I like us as Grax and Veena, and I want to support you in something that you love so much."

He almost had her. She knew it wasn't fair to expect Felix to center his whole life, or even his whole job, around a silly roleplaying game. He still wanted to play with her, and isn't that all she really wanted?

But then he'd said those last few words. Words that rang in her ears, so similar to ones from years ago.

Sure, baby, I'll play a game with you. You know I'll always support you in the things you love.

And then, mere weeks later—*I don't get it, and I never will. Have fun with your friends, just leave me the hell out of it.*

How long would it take for Felix to follow the same path Jeremy did? If she was lucky, maybe she'd get the rest of the summer. But then MnM night would end, and Felix would be relieved, like he was relieved about being off the hook for GMing.

"Jo?" Felix took a tentative step toward her, concern etched in every line on his face.

She stepped away, maintaining the distance between them. In the back of her mind, she registered the hurt in Felix's dark, warm eyes. She shut it out. "You'll support me? I've heard that line before, Felix."

Something in him seemed to snap at her icy tone. His calm vanished. Sorrow and concern transformed before her eyes into anger. Not directed at her, but anger all the same.

"From who, Jo?" he demanded, flinging his arms out wide. "Who fed you that line? Some douchebag who got off on making you role-play for him? On making you be someone you're not?" His hands slammed against his chest. "I'm not that guy, Jo. I'm not him!"

His words cut deep, and her hackles went up. "You didn't know Jeremy. He wasn't like that at the beginning. He was just as understanding and supportive as you. He—" Her voice was cut off by a new wave of tears. "He loved me too, Felix."

"*Fuck*," he spat. He shoved the heels of his hands against his eyes. "Jo, I've been trying not to bring him up, but we have to talk about this. I can't keep doing this." Felix collapsed onto the couch, forearms braced on his thighs. "Will you sit with me, cariño? Please?"

He wanted to talk. Jo could do that. She could talk. Talking meant getting things out in the open, clearing the air, setting boundaries. All those necessary, healthy things Aida always encouraged. Jo dried her cheeks and sat next to Felix.

He sighed, dropping his head into his hands and clutching his hair. "How long were you and Jeremy together?"

"Almost ten years."

He swore again, then raised his head and regarded her with red-rimmed eyes. She expected to see pity there. Pity she could handle; she'd gotten it before. Instead, she saw only tenderness and love. Softly, he said, "I think he fucked up your expectations of what a relationship should be."

A searing spike of rage lit up her entire body. "Do you think I don't know that?"

"No, of c—"

"I know he fucked me up. I *know* he did. But I don't know any other way to *be* in a relationship." Jo pushed herself off the couch and paced, fury and indignation fueling a need to move. She wrapped her arms around herself, as if she could shield herself from the past, from the too-honest way Felix was looking at her, from the storm of emotions whirling through her like a goddamn tornado. "Before Jeremy, I didn't really date. He's all I ever had until I met you. So I'm sorry I'm like this, okay? This is all I know how to be. You deserve better, Felix. I'm trying to be better for you, but it's so hard. It's so fuck—"

Her throat closed around her words. The trickle of her tears became a torrent, so insistent it dropped her to her knees. Felix dove for her, not quite catching her before she collapsed. Loud, ugly sobs racked her body as she curled in on herself, throwing her glasses down so she could cover her face with her hands. He dragged her into his lap, stroking her hair and whispering her name as she cried and cried and cried. She cried until her temples pounded and her nose was clogged with snot. Until Felix was crying too.

When her tears finally subsided, he grasped her hand in both of his and kissed it. He touched the back of it to his cheek, scratchy stubble and salty tears running across her skin.

"You made yourself small for him, Jo," he said. "I don't know the half of what he put you through, but I know that much. I don't need you to be 'better.' I just want you to be *you*, the real you, not a shadow of yourself." He sniffed and cradled her hand against his chest. Jo could feel his heart racing. "If... if it's too hard for you to be yourself around me, maybe you shouldn't be around me."

She jolted off his lap, kneeling in front of him and pressing her palm into his chest. Her heart was racing faster than his now, cracking down the middle, even as her mind refused to accept the implication of his words. Her eyes darted over his face, trying to read his expression. He just looked sad.

"Felix, what are you saying?"

"Cariño mío, I love you so much." Tears lined his eyes, matting his long, beautiful eyelashes. "But I haven't forgotten what you told me during the tornado. Coming to Ashville was your chance to learn who you are on your own. I've fucked that up for you, and maybe I moved us along too fast. If I'm not good for you because you're struggling to fit into some kind of girlfriend box you think you need to fit into for me, I—" He swallowed and blinked back tears. "I don't know if we should be together."

Jo dug her fingers into his shirt to pull him toward her. She cupped his cheek and touched their foreheads together. "That's all very noble of you, gorgeous, but you don't get to decide what's good for me and what's not."

"I know I don't." He shifted, planting his feet on either side of her, knees bent upward to cage her in, keep her close. His trembling hands splayed on her shoulders. "I misspoke. This is a decision we need to make together."

"I know my decision," Jo said without a second thought.

Felix shook his head, his forehead rolling against hers. "Jo, please. I'm asking you to think about this. Really think about it. Don't answer now, but… do you honestly believe you can be yourself around me and that I'll love you no matter what?"

Jo pressed her lips together to keep from blurting out the *yes* on the tip of her tongue.

Are you sure about that, Jo? whispered the voice slithering through her mind—the voice that was her. A small, mean part of her that she could never seem to silence. Jo's blood ran cold as doubt followed in its wake.

"I need to be honest with you," Felix continued. His fingers tightened on her shoulders. "Sometimes I feel like you expect the worst of me. Sometimes you can't even look at me. And then when you do, I see this trepidation in your eyes. Like I'm the enemy, like you're waiting for me to be cruel to you, and it hurts." His voice broke. "It hurts to keep reminding you that you don't have to apologize for being *you*. I can't second-guess everything I say and constantly reassure you that I'm not trying to hurt you. I never, ever want to hurt you, and I don't know if you truly believe that, deep down."

Jo was crying again. She pulled away from Felix so she could look him in the eye. She'd never seen him so miserable. Her cracked heart splintered and shattered into pieces. This was all her fault, and she was desperate to make it better. To shower him with kisses and shout words of love from the rooftops. To hold him and dry his tears and echo back the wonderful things he always said to her.

Except none of that would actually make it better. He had told her what he needed for that: he needed her to think about it. To figure out if there was a way forward without them repeatedly hurting one another. To be certain.

Okay, then. That's what she would do. For Felix. For herself. For them.

"I'm sorry, gorgeous," she said simply. "I didn't know I made you feel like that."

He leaned into her hand on his cheek, and she scrubbed at his stubble with her thumb. "That's why I'm telling you. I know you don't want to hurt me either."

"I don't, I promise." Jo kissed his forehead. "This is why you want us each to decide, isn't it? Because I'm not the only one who's struggling. We're both hurting each other, and maybe hurting ourselves."

"Yeah. Will you think about it?" Felix's teary eyes landed on hers, more serious than she'd ever seen him.

In the silence that followed his question, the full weight of what they were about to do seemed settle over both of them, threatening to crush them. Jo pushed through it, forcing out a single word.

"Yes."

Felix exhaled a slow breath, as if he'd been holding it in. "Maybe we shouldn't see each other for a while. So we can decide on our own what we want."

Well, that sounded like the worst fucking idea ever. Which probably meant it was the correct one. "For how long?"

"As long as it takes," he said. "Whoever is ready first will reach out. Then, with no rush, no expectations on timing, whenever the other person is ready, they'll respond. And we'll get together. And talk." He spoke haltingly, as if he were making up the rules for this breakup or hiatus or whatever the hell it was on the spot. What he was saying made sense, though, and Jo didn't have any better ideas.

"'As long as it takes' is kind of a scary thought."

"It scares me too," he admitted. "But I don't want to rush this. For either of our sakes."

"I know. I get it." She wrapped her arms around Felix and buried her face in his chest, leaving tearstains on his shirt. "I'm really going to miss you, gorgeous."

Felix embraced her, with his arms and his legs. "I'm going to miss you too, cariño." He rocked them back and forth, balancing on his hips, which took the kind of core strength that Jo could only dream about. Jesus, thinking about Felix's abs right now was making this a thousand times worse.

"Can we start tomorrow?" she asked, not bothering to keep the desperation out of her voice. "I don't want to let go of you yet."

She expected Felix to argue, maybe spout some bullshit about clean breaks, but all he said was, "Okay."

They stayed on the floor until their muscles cramped up. Slowly, reluctantly, they unwound themselves and helped one another to their feet. Neither of them was in the mood to finish the dinner she'd made, so she shoved the leftovers in the fridge to deal with later. Without discussing it, they drifted into the bedroom. Jo changed into pajamas, and Felix stripped down to his boxer briefs and undershirt.

They climbed into bed together, despite the early hour, and wrapped themselves in each other's arms again. They didn't have sex. They didn't let their hands wander. They didn't even kiss. They only held each other close, silent and still. And slept.

In the morning, Felix put his pants on, and Jo saw him to the door. She didn't make him coffee or blow him a kiss and wish him a good day at work. He didn't say goodbye to Merry or sweep Jo off her feet just to hear her laugh. Instead, she held the door open for him as he wordlessly walked out. At the bottom of the stairs, he looked back, and they exchanged hollow smiles. She shut the door.

Jo managed to hold herself together until she walked into the kitchen. The tray of brownies she'd made sat there on the counter, untouched. She hadn't even gotten the chance to cut them. She sank to the floor and stared at the wall, silent tears sliding down her face. Her alarm went off in the bedroom, and she let it chime until Merry complained. She went through the motions of feeding him and cleaning his box and then finally picked up her phone.

Before she could talk herself out of it, she tapped a couple of icons and held the phone to her ear. It rang a few times before the call was answered.

"Babe?" came the half-awake voice on the other end. "What's up? You okay?"

"Aida." Sobs finally overwhelmed her. She could barely get the words out. "I need you to get on a plane."

24

AIDA ARRIVED AROUND midnight. Jo ran out to her rental car and tackled her as soon as she was on her feet. She blubbered out a thank you and held tight to Aida's neck. They clung to each other as if it had been years, not weeks, since they'd seen each other.

"Come on, babe, let's go inside," Aida finally said.

Jo buried herself in her nest of blankets and pillows on the couch, where she'd wallowed ever since she'd gotten home from the slowest, most painful workday of her life. Right there in the living room, Aida dropped her suitcase, took off her pantsuit, and changed from a flowy turquoise blouse into a ratty T-shirt of Trey's bearing the faded words "Kidz Can Code 2013." She didn't bother with pants.

"Did you eat dinner?" she asked, hands on her hips atop her long, bronze legs. Jo listlessly shook her head, and Aida marched to the kitchen and started poking around.

"I don't want the pasta," Jo said.

"Can *I* eat the pasta?"

"Okay."

Aida peered into the freezer. "I'm making you chicken nuggets."

"Okay."

When their food was heated, Aida brought over plates and glasses of water. She'd added some wilted leftover spinach salad to Jo's plate. Jo ate that first so she didn't have to look at it.

Aida wriggled her way under the blankets and propped up her plate on a throw pillow on her lap. "Start from the beginning."

Jo had told her the basics on the phone, but now she went through everything from the last two days. Aida listened without commentary and scarfed down pasta primavera. Good. Aida could eat the whole damn pan for all Jo cared. She never wanted to eat pasta primavera again.

When Jo was done, Aida was silent for all of half a second. "I told you once that I wouldn't bring this up again, but fuck that," she said. "I want you to talk to someone about this."

Jo grimaced. "I'm talking to you about it."

"Come on, Jo," Aida said, rolling her eyes. "You know what I mean."

She groaned, pulled her comforter over her head, and shoved a chicken nugget into her mouth. "I don't want someone to criticize me for the last *decade* of my life, Aida. I know how pathetic I am for putting up with the asshole for so long. I don't need a professional to tell me that."

"Babe, you're not pathetic, and that's not what therapy is for." Jo felt Aida's arms encircle her—blankets, nuggets, and all. "If a therapist does that to you, find a different one."

She scoffed. "Sure, because quality therapists are growing on trees in Ashville, Kansas."

"Online visits are a thing. You're just making excuses. Which means you know I'm right."

"When's your flight home again?"

"Fuck you too, babe. Come here." Aida scrabbled at the blankets until she revealed Jo's head. She held Jo's face between her hands, her hazel eyes earnest. "Just because Jeremy criticized you for years doesn't mean that everyone else will. Not me, not Felix, and not a good therapist. That asshole robbed you of so much joy already. I don't want the specter of him to haunt you forever."

"That's more like a revenant than a specter."

"Jo, God damn it," Aida scolded, but the laughter in voice betrayed her. "Are you hearing me?"

"I hear you, Aida. I'll think about it."

"Thank you." Aida smoothed Jo's disheveled hair and cuddled against her shoulder. She kicked at the blankets until her feet were exposed. "It's fucking hot under here."

"Sorry. My AC isn't great, and it's too humid to open a window."

"At least tornado season is over, right?"

"Yeah."

They grew quiet as Jo ate another nugget and thought about tornadoes. And shelters. And Felix. Being in his arms. Feeling safe. She sniffled.

Aida took her hand and weaved their fingers together. "Tell me."

"I wish... I wish I had told him I love him."

"*Do* you love him? Or do you just wish you'd said it?"

Jo didn't answer right away, giving the question the thought it deserved. Loving Jeremy had been hard sometimes. A *lot* of the time. Loving Jeremy had meant making excuses for him and laughing off his shitty behavior. It had meant chipping away at herself and constantly apologizing and giving up the things she loved to go along with what he wanted.

Being with Felix wasn't like that at all. Maybe that was what made it so hard to recognize that what she felt for him... was love. She loved his smile and the gray in his beard. She loved the way he laughed at her jokes, that high-pitched chuckle such a stark contrast to his deep voice. She loved his body and the way it made her feel. She loved how kind he was, how hardworking and thoughtful and meticulous and patient. She loved that he dove headfirst into Monsters and Mythology and gave it his all and was honest about his opinion of it. She loved watching him with Tito— their affectionate gibes, the gentle way they spoke about Lita, how Felix had dropped everything to be with him when his world came crashing down.

Loving Felix was easy. It was the easiest thing in the world. Now that Jo finally saw it for what it was, it was undeniable.

"I love him, Aida. I love Felix."

"Of course you do, babe," Aida said with a soft smile.

Jesus Christ, even her pragmatic best friend had figured it out before she had.

"So does that mean you're ready to talk to him?" Aida asked.

Ah, there was that pragmatism again. Thank God. Jo would be lost without it.

She shook her head. "I think—" Tears welled up in her eyes. Why was it so hard to say out loud? There was no shame in it, of course, and Aida wouldn't judge her. (It was her goddamn idea in the first place.) But there went that voice in her head, the part of her that expected to be ridiculed and let down, warning her to be careful. And that, in and of itself, was enough to prove that this was the right choice.

Closing her eyes, she said the words that needed to be given voice. "I think I need to talk to a therapist. I need to figure out some things for me before I bring Felix back into my life."

Aida pulled Jo in for a bone-crushing hug. The last two nuggets slid off Jo's plate into the mass of blankets, never to be seen again.

ASHVILLE MEMORIAL PARK was quiet that Sunday. The late-morning air was muggy and close, stirred only by the occasional breeze. Felix and Tito sat side by side on a shaded bench overlooking a small pond in the middle of the cemetery. Lita's grave, freshly adorned with the orange and yellow gerbera daisies they'd brought, was to their right.

Tito gripped Felix's hand tightly, his eyes following the birds that flitted down to cool themselves in the pond. When Lita was alive, their backyard had been filled with bird feeders and bird baths. She had stood on the back porch every day, drinking her morning café and counting the different birds who visited. Tito had chosen this spot for her so she would always be near the creatures she had loved so much. It was eleven months to the day since Lita's death, and Felix hadn't needed to ask to know how Tito wanted to spend their morning together.

"La echo de menos, hijito," Tito whispered. "I miss her so much."

"Yo también." Felix draped his arm across Tito's thin shoulders, and Tito rested his palm on Felix's knee. Silence wrapped around them, broken only by birdsong and the rustling of leaves.

"Thank you for this," Tito said after a while. "And please thank Jo for me for giving us some time alone today."

"Oh, well..." Felix hesitated, staring out over the water. "We're not seeing each other right now."

"What? Felix, what happened?" He shook Felix's leg. "Why didn't you tell me?"

"It's not important right now. It's Lita's day."

"Of course it's important. Your lita wants you to be happy, just like I do. She won't mind if we talk about it." He turned toward Lita's headstone. "¿Verdad, mi vida?"

Felix smiled fondly.

Tito looked back at him. "She doesn't mind. What happened with Jo?"

He shifted uncomfortably. What could he say that wouldn't violate Jo's privacy? He loved Tito, but the man wasn't exactly tactful. As long as Jo worked at White Hills, he needed to watch what he said. He finally settled on, "We took some time apart to decide if we really want to be together. Things were moving fast. Too fast, and she just got out of a relationship."

"What's wrong with fast?"

Felix gave his grandfather a wry grin. "Says the man who took one look at Lita and told his friends he was going to marry her."

Tito's eyes took on a dreamy, faraway look as he gazed toward the pond. In Spanish, he said, "She was so beautiful, my María Isabel. I didn't even know her name. I just saw her smile and knew I wanted to be the one to make her smile for the rest of her life."

Felix replied in Spanish. "Except it doesn't work like that for everyone. You two got lucky."

"Lucky?" Tito shook his head. "Luck had nothing to do with it, besides putting us in the same plaza on the same afternoon. Luck didn't make me go talk to her. Luck didn't force her to agree to dinner with me. Luck didn't make us get married or bring us to America or bless us with your father. Those were choices we made for each other, Felix. To work hard and give one another the best life we could." He broke into a smile, his wrinkles deepening, and his eyes narrowing into slits. "You want to know a secret, hijito?"

"Of course I do."

"Maribel was the third girl I told my friends I was going to marry that summer. She was just the first one who said yes to a date."

Felix laughed so loudly he startled the birds. "You little shit!" he cried in English, giving Tito's shoulder a gentle shove. "All this time, you made me believe it was love at first sight with you and Lita."

Tito shrugged, grinning unapologetically. "Maybe it was. It felt like it. But love is about the choices we make, Felix. Not only the way we feel. You must know that."

"I do," he said. He plucked a long blade of grass and absently wound it around his fingers. "It's good to be reminded, though."

"So," Tito said, nudging his knee, "was fast really the problem?"

"I don't know. Maybe. I've never fallen in love so quickly, Tito. Maybe I haven't given Jo enough time to trust me. Maybe I'm putting too much on her too soon."

Tito was quiet, letting him stew on that. Felix couldn't deny that he was the one who had moved things along so quickly. He'd only wanted to be honest with Jo about his feelings, but he hadn't fully understood what her ex had been like.

Ten years. *Ten fucking years* of Jo being treated poorly by the person who claimed to love her. He was sick to his stomach thinking about it. She'd only been away from him for a few months. Three weeks with Felix wasn't nearly enough time to heal from such prolonged hurt.

It wasn't always easy, supporting her and caring for her through that kind of healing. He'd never done that for anyone before, unless he counted helping Tito through the grief of losing Lita. But grief and trauma weren't the same, and Felix had no idea if he was helping Jo or hurting her. If he was going to do this, if he was going to make the choice to love her and walk alongside her through this, he needed to learn how to do it right.

The blade of grass was shredded into pieces, and his fingertips were stained green. An image flashed through his mind: Jo, driving her car, gesturing at the landscape around them on I-35, adamantly declaring, "Look how green it is! The air out here is so clean you can see forever."

Felix smiled to himself, brushed off his hands, and rested his elbows on his knees. "Tito?"

"Mm?"

"When did you actually know you wanted to marry Lita?"

Tito's bony elbow poked him in the ribs. "Marriage already, eh? You going to go propose?"

"No," he chuckled. "I was just curious, since apparently it *wasn't* when you first saw her smile." He poked his grandpa in return.

Tito swore in Spanish and rubbed his side theatrically. Felix rolled his eyes, but he grew serious when Tito took a moment to respond. His eyes got that faraway look again, as if he were seeing a plaza in Cáceres rather than a pond in Kansas. His brow wrinkled, and tears lined his eyes.

"When I realized that the days without her were unbearable compared to the days with her. Being apart from Maribel was like being without my own arm. I almost lost her when your father was born. That would have killed me too. I never took another day with her for granted. Even seventy-one years was not enough time." Tito paused and looked at Felix. "She really was mi vida."

Felix gathered him into an embrace. "Te quiero, Tito."

"Te quiero, Felix."

Neither of them moved for a long time. Finally, Tito clapped Felix on the back, and they broke apart. Tito sniffed and dug his knuckles into his red eyes. Felix squeezed his shoulder.

"I'll give you and Lita a minute," he murmured and stood to take a stroll around the cemetery. He always gave his grandparents some time alone on these visits.

As he ambled among the graves, his gaze kept returning to the grass-stained tips of his fingers. He ran his thumbs over them, remembering that moment in the car again—the moment he had let himself see Kansas the way Jo did. He raised his eyes, past the headstones and the pond where Tito sat, and turned toward Ashville. The cemetery was on the outskirts of town, on a low rise. From here, he could see almost the entire town laid out before him under the brilliant blue sky.

For the past year, Felix had been sleeping in a guest bedroom in a house that was not his, using his dead grandmother's mugs for his coffee. The only place he'd considered his own was the dingy basement where he boxed. He'd plodded along, somewhere between happy and unhappy, getting the work experience he needed and making sure Tito survived from day to day.

Ashville wasn't a home. It was an obligation.

Until Jo.

These last few days without her had been miserable. Felix dreamed about her at night and woke up cold and lonely. He scrolled back through their texts and the sexy pictures they'd exchanged, aching to touch her and feel her touch in return. He couldn't even listen to his favorite workout playlist without being reminded of her.

But it was more than that.

It wasn't only Jo's presence that he missed. It was the way she'd opened his eyes to everything he had right in front of him. Jo had embraced this town—its places and its people—with open arms, while he had held everyone at arm's length. She'd created a community out of thin air and brought him along for the ride. And now, for the first time, he was starting to picture what it might look like to build a life here.

Felix looked out over Ashville. He could see White Hills and the library, Stan's and the Old Bell Diner, the community college and The Gandy Dancer. He even spotted the damn grocery store where he'd bought her a carton of milk. This town had her fingerprints all over it.

He wanted to fall in love with it, to be truly happy here. He wanted to make it his home. And, if Jo would have him, if he could learn to love her how she needed to be loved, he wanted her there beside him every step of the way.

JO RAPPED ON the open door of an office she'd never had cause to visit before. The middle-aged white woman inside peered at her over reading glasses, her hands coming to rest on her keyboard. She wore a sunshine yellow cardigan over a black blouse with white polka dots. She was one of the few doctors on staff at White Hills who didn't wear a white coat.

"Yes?" she asked. "Do we have an appointment?"

"Um, no," Jo said, clasping her hands in front of her. "Dr. Andrews, I was hoping to speak with you personally, if you have a minute."

Dr. Andrews glanced at the clock on her wall. "I have about ten minutes. Have a seat while I finish this email."

Jo thanked her and went inside, closing the door behind her. She folded her hands in her lap so she wouldn't wring them. Her heart was beating so frantically she was sure Dr. Andrews could hear it despite that being medically impossible.

"Okay, thank you for waiting," Dr. Andrews said momentarily. "What can I help you with"—her eyes darted to the badge clipped to Jo's breast pocket—"Jolene?"

"It's just Jo," she muttered.

"Jo, then." She leaned back in her cushy desk chair and crossed one knee over the other.

"Well, um, first, I apologize if this is unprofessional, but I didn't really know where else to go."

The doctor said nothing, regarding Jo with an open, patient expression.

"I need therapy," Jo blurted. "I know you're the psychiatrist for residents, not for staff, but like I said, I don't know where else to go. I was hoping you could point me in the right direction."

"I see," Dr. Andrews said in a clinical tone. "Have you contacted our health insurance provider?"

Jo nodded. "I started there, but there's a three-month wait for even a phone screening, and this is a little urgent."

"Jo, if you're having a psychiatric emergency, you need to call—"

"No, no! Sorry, no," Jo cut in, her cheeks feeling hot. Christ, she was fucking this all up, wasn't she? This had seemed like such a good plan last night, after she'd spent four hours on the phone with her insurance and gotten absolutely nowhere. "It's not that kind of urgent. I'm not in danger, I assure you. I just want to talk to someone as soon as possible."

"I see," Dr. Andrews said again, as stoic as before. Jo waited, but the doctor apparently had nothing to add.

She gave it one last shot. Sitting up a little straighter, she made herself sound as professional as possible. "I've been feeling like my life is on hold until I can talk through some things, and I'm ready to move forward. If you have any advice or suggestions for finding a therapist in the near future, I'm all ears. If not, I'll let you get on with your day."

The doctor watched Jo carefully, drumming her fingers on the arm of her chair. When she finally moved, she did so decisively. She snatched a business card from the holder on her desk and scribbled something on the back of it. "This is a colleague of mine in Wichita. She's out of network, but she offers sliding scale payment. I can't guarantee that she's accepting new patients right now, but if you mention to her receptionist that I referred you, they'll probably at least squeeze in a consultation."

"Oh my God, Dr. Andrews," Jo gushed, taking the business card as if it were made of solid gold. "I can't thank you enough."

"You're welcome, Jo. Best of luck."

Jo recognized a dismissal when she heard one. She left, found a deserted hallway, and gazed down at the business card. "Dr. Sheila Duncan," the back read, along with a phone number. She pulled her phone out of her pocket to text Aida the good news before her lunch break ended. Aida responded right away.

Aida

I'm making you call tonight

And I'm proud of you

Jo

Thanks. Couldn't have done this without you, friend

How's Merry?

Aida

Goober keeps butting into my video meetings.

Literally. Showing the camera his butt.

My clients adore him.

Jo

> Guess you're going to have to move
> in so they can see him all the time,
> huh?

Aida

> I've already sent for Trey. He'll be here
> tomorrow to join our little hobbit hole
> triad.

Jo

> Damn it, that makes me Frodo

Another text notification popped up on the screen. Jo's body flushed hot, then cold, then hot again, and her legs began to quake uncontrollably. She only read the first few words before the notification vanished, so she clicked over to that message thread and read the entire thing. Twice.

Felix

> Hi, Jo. I'm sorry if this catches you at
> work, but with MnM tonight I wanted to
> make sure I didn't text you too late
> afterward. I'm ready to talk whenever
> you are. Please don't feel rushed. Take
> all the time you need. I just want you to
> know I'm here. I hope you're doing well.

Jo had to lean on the wall to keep herself upright. He was ready. It had been less than a week, and Felix was ready to talk. She read over the text a third time to reassure herself there was no rush. She could take her time; she could trust Felix in this. Even if it *had* taken months for her to get a phone screen for a therapist, he would have given her whatever time she needed.

Luckily, they didn't have to wait that long.

She opened her phone's keypad and typed in the number Dr. Andrews had given her. A chipper voice greeted her on the other end. Five minutes later, Jo had an appointment to meet with Dr. Duncan on Friday morning. She was in luck, the receptionist told her; they'd just had a cancellation. She hung up, then leaned her head against the wall and took a minute to breathe. She had done it. She hadn't even needed Aida's encouragement (or nagging).

Her lunch break was definitely over by now, so she'd have to wait to tell Aida until she got home. But she had one more text to send before she clocked back in.

Jo

> Thanks, Felix. I'll let you know when I'm ready. Have fun at MnM tonight. Whenever we see each other, I hope you'll tell me all about it.

25

FOR THE SECOND time in one day, Felix was at the Old Bell Diner. He'd had Sunday brunch with Tito in the morning, and now, midafternoon, he was back. Bouncing from foot to foot on his toes, sweltering next to the giant bronze bell that radiated the sun's heat.

Waiting for Jo.

She'd texted him the night before. Two short words: "I'm ready." He had nearly dropped his phone into a sink full of dishwater in his haste to respond. Their back and forth was brief. Enough to determine a time and place to meet, but not enough to give him any indication of what she was thinking.

Felix chewed the inside of his cheek and scanned the packed parking lot—again. There. A flash of red-brown hair. It weaved through the cars, shining like a beacon. He hadn't seen Jo in seventeen-and-a-half days. But she was here now, and he couldn't look away. His eyes burned in the bright sunlight, watering profusely as he barely dared to blink. She came around an SUV and spotted him. Felix's heart melted as a slow, beautiful grin lit up her face.

Jo started to run. So did he.

In an empty parking space, between a minivan and an ancient pickup truck, they collided. Jo leapt into his arms, and Felix clung to her, his hands closing around her midriff beneath her tank top.

"Jo."

"I love you, Felix. I love you, I love you."

A joyous sound fell from his lips as he buried his face in her hair. She smelled like summertime and coming home. "Jo. My Jo. I love you too."

The sun shone on them and the black asphalt all around. Sweat dripped down their faces and mingled on their cheeks. Felix didn't care. Let the sun burn all of Kansas to the ground, and them along with it. He would die happy, with Jo in his arms, loving him.

They didn't move, or even speak, until they heard a honk. A sedan had its turn signal on, the driver gesturing impatiently at them through the windshield. Jo laughed, a sound he had been bereft without. She shouted an apology to the driver. Felix adjusted his grip on her and carried her to the sidewalk.

"We should talk," Jo said as he set her beside the bell. She slid her hands into his and squeezed, as if proving to herself that he was really here. He squeezed back, and her pale brown eyes shone with joy behind her glasses.

"I agree," Felix replied. "May I buy you a coffee?"

"Oh, shit, you didn't tell me free coffee was part of the deal!" she cried, and he laughed and kissed her cheek.

Had her cheeks always been so round and soft and pink and perfect? He kissed the other one, for good measure. Keeping one hand in hers, he led her into the oasis of the air-conditioned diner. While they waited for a table, she asked him how MnM night had gone the past two weeks.

"It's incredible, Jo. We've had about a dozen people each week," he told her. "Leni and Greg are running the tables. Greg is a pro at GMing, and Leni is picking it up quickly. I've stepped in to help with combat a couple of times, but she's doing great. And we've had seven people sign up for new library cards."

"That's wonderful," she said, gripping his forearm. His muscles flexed at her touch, and a glimmer of heat flared in her eyes.

Soon, cariño. He couldn't wait to get those clothes off her and touch her again. He knew he was getting ahead of himself, but hope stirred within him that this would go well. She loved him (holy *fuck*, she loved him), and he loved her, and she was holding onto him like she never wanted to let go.

"Are you enjoying being the organizer?" Jo asked as a host led them to a booth.

"I am," he said. "It's a much better fit for me, and Warren is thrilled to have me focused on the program as a whole."

"I'm so glad," she said with genuine warmth. "I'm... I'm hoping to come play this week."

"I hope you do. Warren agreed to your recommendation, by the way, to keep MnM once a week."

Jo blushed, but she looked him in the eye. "Thanks for telling me. I'm glad I could help."

Felix smiled at her, pleased to hear her take credit for herself. "So am I," he said.

She smiled back, tentative but proud, as they sat down across from each other.

JO ORDERED COLD brew with cream and sugar, and Felix chose an iced vanilla latte and a slice of apple pie à la mode with two forks. After their server left, an awkward moment passed between them.

Felix was the one to break the silence. He leaned forward, arms on the table and hands lightly clasped together. "Do you want to go first, or should I?"

"Me first," she said, before she could lose her nerve.

"I'm listening."

Christ, how she had missed his beautiful face. Her eyes ran over his features, snagging on the soft smile on his lips. She wanted him to kiss her cheeks again. She wanted to kiss him back, to grip his hair and drag him to her side of the booth and slip her hand under his shirt and delicately scratch his skin until he begged for *more, harder, please.*

"Jo?" Felix asked, shattering the image in her mind that had her pressing her thighs together. The sly grin on his face told her that he had a pretty good idea what was on her mind.

"I'm here," she said, giving him a quick smile in return. "You're very distracting sometimes."

"Oh, let me put these away," he said, moving his hands to his lap to hide his forearms under the table.

They shared a laugh, and then Jo took a deep breath. She'd practiced what she wanted to say with Aida, over the phone now that her best friend was back in California. The only problem was that the script was all jumbled up in her head. Jo had planned to work up to the whole "I love you" part, but once she was back in Felix's embrace, she couldn't hold her feelings inside. Might as well wing it and speak from the heart then.

"So I guess you know that I love you."

His grin turned adorably shy. "I thought I heard something like that."

"I think I've loved you for a while, Felix, but it was too hard for me to see it at first. Love has never felt like this for me before, but, well, I love it. I want to keep doing it. With you. Wait, fuck, that came out wrong."

Felix laughed, a hearty, high-pitched laugh that was practically a giggle. "God, I missed you, Jo."

Their server stopped by with their coffee and pie, giving Jo a second to organize her thoughts. Felix handed her one of the forks and gestured for her to continue.

"I want to stay together," she said plainly. "But first, I owe you an answer to your question. You wanted to know if I believe that I can be myself around you and that you'll love me no matter what."

"I remember," he murmured.

Jo's heart beat faster, and her stomach clenched around the single bite of pie she'd snuck in. "My answer is, not yet. But I want to, so badly, and I'm trying to learn how. I'm sor—I wish I could give you a more definitive answer, but it's not that simple right now. And I... I understand if that's not enough for you."

She was still clumsy with the phrases Dr. Duncan had suggested she use instead of "I'm sorry," but damn it, she was trying. Felix seemed to notice her aborted apology, given the way his expression shifted at that part. He looked surprised and pensive all at once. There was a long pause while he sipped his latte and Jo tried not to have a conniption.

"May I ask what you mean when you say you're trying to learn?" he finally asked.

"I've started seeing a therapist," she replied and suddenly remembered this part of her mental script. "I've only had two sessions, but I really like her. She's already been a huge help. I thought I understood all the ways that Jeremy affected me, but I'm not so sure anymore. I think I'll be able to move past him faster and healthier with Dr. Duncan's guidance."

"I'm really happy to hear that," Felix said, his eyes warm and kind.

"I know I need to work on loving and accepting the parts of me I was made to feel ashamed of," Jo continued, "and that's a lot easier when you're with me, loving and accepting every part of me already. I want to learn how to go easier on myself so you aren't stuck having to reassure me all the time. Because the truth is, Felix, even though I came to Ashville to figure out who I am on my own, being with you has shown me who I was deep down all along. That's who I want to be for the rest of my life."

The pride on his face was unmistakable. Jo felt pretty dang proud herself.

Then his expression shifted, taking on that contemplative look again. "Jo, I think I haven't been... wait, it's not my turn yet. Is there anything else you wanted to say?"

"Um, yeah, hang on." She pulled her phone out of her purse and opened her notes app.

"You wrote it down?" he asked, breaking into a gentle grin.

She smiled back. "Aida's idea."

"Brilliant," he said, dipping a large piece of sugared crust into the melty ice cream. "Wish I'd thought of it."

She scrolled through the bullet points of her script. Right. This part. "So... I'm trying to stop apologizing too much, but I do owe you an apology."

"What for?"

Jo reached for him, needed to touch him. Felix met her halfway, but she stretched her hand beyond his and clasped his wrist instead. He did the same to her in return. His pulse beat under the heel of her hand, a rhythmic thrum that steadied her.

"I know you're not him, Felix," she said, softly but firmly. "It was wrong of me to compare you, and I'm so sorry I even put you two in the same sentence. I spent so long defending him, even though he didn't deserve it, that it became second nature to me. I reacted badly when you said those things about him. Which, for the record, he *did* deserve. You were right. He's a douchebag of the highest order."

Felix lifted their joined hands and kissed the back of her wrist. He ran his lips over her skin, his stubble prickling. "I understand, Jo. I accept your apology, and I forgive you."

"I want to tell you everything," she said, blinking back tears. "Not right now, not in public, but if we stay together, I want you to know all of it. If... if you're okay with hearing it."

Felix looked taken aback. "Of course I want to hear it. Whatever you're comfortable sharing. Why wouldn't I?"

She shrugged one shoulder and lowered her gaze. "You stopped asking me about it. I assumed you didn't want to know."

Abruptly, Felix got up and came around the table, squeezing onto the bench beside her. His arms went around her, and she leaned into him. "I'm sorry, cariño. I stopped asking because it always seemed to hurt you when I brought him up, even inadvertently. I thought it would be better to make it about us and how much I cared about you, rather than about him. Clearly, I was wrong."

"Oh." A tear slipped down her face, even though she was trying really fucking hard not to cry in this diner right now. She took a couple of breaths to collect herself, smelling cloves and vanilla. "I forgive you. Your heart was in the right place."

"Maybe, but I should have talked to you about it instead of assuming."

"I mean, yeah, *obviously*." She nudged him in the side.

Felix grinned and kissed Jo's forehead, sending warmth flooding through her, all the way down to her toes.

As he returned to his side of the booth, Jo picked up her fork and speared a chunk of gooey, cinnamon-y apple. "Okay, gorgeous," she said. "Your turn."

"I WANT US to be together too," Felix said, cutting to the chase the way she had. He watched Jo press her lips together, holding back a smile that made her eyes sparkle. "But what I was going to say earlier is that I think I haven't been entirely fair to you, and I'm sorry for that."

"What do you mean?" she asked.

He blew out a breath, puffing out his cheeks. "My life in Ashville was very lonely before I met you, Jo. I saw Tito on Sundays, and Peggy and I were friendly enough, but that was it. I barely even spoke to Leni before we started working on MnM together. I was so busy with my family when I first moved here that I didn't try to meet people or keep up with my grad school friends, and next thing I knew, I had been here for months, and it felt too late to do anything about it and... that's not the point."

Felix pitched forward and met Jo's gaze, his focus solely on her. He gripped the edge of the bench to steady himself. His fingers dug in so hard he thought he might punch through the vinyl to the padding underneath. "The point is that from the night we went to Stan's together I knew that being with you was the happiest I'd been since moving to Ashville. You were the first real friend I had in this town, and I was desperate to hold onto that. I stopped caring if things were moving too fast or if I was being too honest because I was *so fucking happy* with you."

"I'm waiting for the part where this is unfair to me," Jo said breathlessly. "Because it sounds pretty damn lovely so far."

That made Felix smile, and the tension in his hands relaxed. "I'm beginning to realize that I put too much of my own happiness on you. Since you've been the only thing in my life that brings me joy, it was all the more painful when you shied away to try to protect yourself. It was unfair to put that on you, and it was unfair to ask for your unconditional trust so soon. I'm still figuring things out, but I think... I think I wanted you to believe I'll love you no matter what because it would hurt *me* less. But I can't make you responsible for my happiness, especially not while you're still getting past Jeremy. I need to slow down and let you move forward in your own time. And I need to learn how to find happiness elsewhere, not just with you."

"Wow." Jo blinked and cocked her head. "How did you get to be so introspective?"

"I've been doing a lot of reading. The library in this town has some pretty good books, you know," he said with a grin. "Actually, I'm also trying to find a therapist, but the wait times are ridiculous."

"Right?" she cried. "It's the worst. I basically had to beg the psych at White Hills for a referral without sounding like I was begging."

"Damn," Felix said. "Think I could pass for mid-seventies? Maybe I can move in with Tito and go see that person."

She squinted at him, considering. "Not quite enough gray yet, old man."

He swore again with a dramatic shake of his head. He nabbed one last bite of pie before nudging the plate toward Jo to let her finish it off. She was quiet as she dragged the tines of her fork through the softened ice cream, leaving four deep grooves behind.

"I appreciate you explaining all of that to me," she said. "There have been moments when I worried about how fast things were going, but there was a part of me that also stopped caring. That night, when you told me you loved me, I..." The emotion in her voice cut off her words. She blinked to clear her eyes and offered him a soft smile. "I guess I was pretty fucking happy too."

"I do love you, Jo," he said emphatically. "I love you, and I want you. I want to give you all the time you need and learn how to support you with your therapy and figure out how to balance my own life better."

"Felix..." His name on her lips was a whisper, a breath, a sigh.

"There's something else I'd like you to know," he said. Jo nodded for him to continue. "Ashville never felt like home to me. A lot of that was my own doing, and not just because I was lonely. I saw living here as being stuck in a holding pattern. I was glad to do whatever was necessary for Tito, but I never appreciated this town or wanted to settle down here. Not until you. The night you walked into Tito's house and asked about our family photos, and the next morning, when I woke up in your arms—that's when things began to change."

She was staring at him, unblinking, her attention rapt.

"I used to feel like I can't leave Ashville. Now... I don't want to," he said. "You and Tito are here, of course, but so are Leni and Peggy and Greg and the regulars at MnM who know me by name. I feel like my work is actually starting to make a difference in this community. I care about the library's budget not just for my own sake but also for the programs this town would lose. I still have my dreams, and I still want to pursue them. But, Jo, you made me see that I can have a life I love here and now. And I want that life to be with you."

"Okay."

"I know, I know," he said, holding up his hands in surrender. "I just talked about slowing down. I won't rush you into anything. I meant what I said about giving you whatever time you need. But what I'd like you to know, cariño, is that I'm in this for the long haul."

"Felix." Her expression softened with affection. "I already said okay."

He was so wrapped up in getting out his thoughts (he really *should* have written this down) that it took a moment for his brain to catch up. "Okay what?"

"Okay, let's do it," she declared. "I'm in this for the long haul too, gorgeous. I love you, and I love Ashville. I want you—I want *us* to be happy here. Let's make this place home."

Incandescent. That was the only word in Felix's mind when he looked at Jo's face. Round cheeks glowing, eyes sparkling, smile beaming. She was sunshine itself, burning hotter and brighter and fiercer than the light outside the window.

He pushed to his feet and leaned over the table, his shirt dragging across melted ice cream and sticky apple filling. Jo shoved their coffee glasses out of his way and raised her face to meet him. Felix cupped her cheeks, let anticipation build for a split second, and kissed her—deeper, harder, more true, more real than any other time he'd kissed her. She parted her lips, and her tongue dove into his mouth. Fuck, she tasted better than he remembered. Her fingers tangled in his hair, pulling ever so slightly and sending blood straight to his cock, which was currently pressed against the edge of the table. He barely restrained himself from groaning.

"Woo!" a voice yelled. "Get it, girl!"

Jo burst out laughing, throwing her head back with glee. Felix scanned the diner and found every single person staring at them. Even the waitstaff.

"Uh, you want to get out of here?" he muttered.

"Mmm... that shirt needs to come off," she replied in that motherfucking sexy sphynx voice he hadn't heard since Indi-Con. Her eyes trailed lazily down his dessert-covered chest. Then, in a quick, clipped tone, she added, "And go in the laundry so it doesn't stain."

"My good girl. Such a fucking tease," he whispered, low and heated, and watched Jo's pupils go wide with desire.

She leaned into the aisle. "Can we get the check, please?"

EPILOGUE

Five Months Later

THREE TIMERS WERE going off at once: the stove, Jo's phone, and Felix's phone.

"Mine's the rolls, right?" Felix asked, striding into the kitchen.

"Yup," Jo answered from the sink where she was draining the potatoes. "Can you turn the stove timer off too? That was the potatoes."

"On it."

Felix retrieved the golden-brown rolls from the oven and silenced the various timers. Jo dropped an entire stick of butter into the pot of steaming potato chunks to start it melting. She found the drawer with the potato masher on her first try and cheered for herself. She'd been living with Felix at Tito and Lita's house since her six-month lease expired a few weeks ago. She was still finding her way around the kitchen and hadn't had a chance to use everything yet. Because who the hell uses a potato masher more than this one day a year?

"Leni, you're on deck!" Jo called, setting the masher by the pot.

Leni came skidding around the corner, orange-tipped hair—

her color of choice for Halloween and Thanksgiving—swinging wildly.

"Felix, why is your grandpa so much cooler than you?" she demanded. "He read every single *Dresden Files* book in two months."

"Because he has too much time on his hands," Felix responded, loudly enough that Tito would hear him from the living room.

"Shit, the turkey!" Jo cried, cutting off any potential rebuttal from Tito. "That was the third timer!"

Felix checked the bird's temperature to make sure they didn't kill their dinner guests while Jo went over her list to see what needed to happen next. Leni slid over to the counter and stared at the butter as if she could make it melt faster by the power of wishful thinking.

As if on cue, she asked, "Is there a spell to melt butter?"

"Create Flame?" Felix suggested.

"Nature Weave would do it," Jo said as she pulled the cranberry sauce and salad out of the fridge.

"I like Create Flame," Leni replied. "More fun."

"More risk, you mean?" Felix asked.

"Same thing."

The doorbell rang.

"Who's showing up at our door *right now*?" Jo groaned. "I told Vanessa eight o'clock for board games and pie."

Felix, neck deep in the oven with the turkey, barely glanced over his shoulder at her. "Can you get it, cariño? I've got my hands full."

"Yeah, yeah. I've got it, Tito!" she called as she jogged toward the front door. Tito watched her from his armchair with a twinkle in his eye. Through the window, Jo glimpsed a dark gray coupe in the driveway, a car she didn't recognize. She put on what she hoped was a thankful-looking smile and yanked open the door.

"Aida!" she screamed, flinging herself into her best friend's arms. "Beefcake!"

"Surprise! Happy Thanksgiving, Mojo," Trey said, kissing her hair while Aida hugged her so tightly she could barely breathe.

Felix appeared in the doorway, laughing with delight. He sidled around Jo to greet Trey with a bear hug.

"Did you know about this?" she asked Felix without letting go of Aida.

"Of course I did," he replied. "Now you know why I bought the bigger turkey. You really thought I liked leftover turkey sandwiches that much?"

"How was I supposed to know?"

"Are we allowed to come in," Trey interjected, "or do we have to eat dinner on the porch?"

"It's my house," Tito said from his chair. "Get in here."

They all piled into the living room. Leni meandered out of the kitchen, waving, licking the potato masher, and introducing herself all at once. A loud yowl grabbed Jo's attention, and she turned to find Merry scampering up the hallway.

"Were you in on this, Mer-bear?" Jo asked him. "Your friend Aida is here to see you."

Merry meowed again and marched right up to Trey. Suddenly, Jo realized what Trey was holding. It wasn't an overnight bag, like she'd thought. It was a cat carrier.

"Merry must smell his brother," Trey said, setting the carrier down while Merry lost his goddamn mind—pawing, scratching, meowing to get at the brown tabby inside.

"What?" Jo breathed, barely daring to hope. Tears stung the backs of her eyes as she knelt down and saw a drowsy Pippin in the carrier. "Pip. Oh my God, *Pippin*."

"We had Boo-boo sedated for the flight," Aida said. "He should be fully awake in about an hour."

Jo unzipped the carrier and reached in to let Pippin sniff her hand. He sleepily nuzzled his striped face against her knuckles. Merry weaseled his way around her and groomed Pippin's ears, purring his little heart out. "How?" she asked, unable to tear her gaze from them.

"You think I don't online stalk that asshole from fake accounts to make sure he's miserable?" Aida said, crossing her arms defiantly.

Jo laughed. There was a tiny twinge in her stomach at the mention of Jeremy, a twinge that hadn't fully gone away. But there was none of the old embarrassment or shame that used to come with it. He was fully in her past, long gone from the rearview mirror. Now that Pippin was back where he belonged, she would have no reason to think of her ex at all.

"I saw that he was selling Boo-boo, because he's an assho—" Aida winced in Tito's direction. "Sorry, sir."

"What the fuck you calling me 'sir' for?" he retorted. "I'm Tito."

Aida's story was put on hold while Felix made proper introductions. Jo had eyes only for Pippin—and Merry, who had fully wedged himself into the carrier. When Aida got back around to the story of Pippin's rescue, she wove a dramatic tale of recruiting David's help, since Jeremy had never met him, and offering enough money for the cat that Jeremy wouldn't be tempted to sell him to anyone else.

"It's a Thanksgiving miracle!" cried Leni, potato masher aloft.

Felix crouched next to Jo and laid a gentle hand on her back. "Go get them settled, cariño. I'll take care of everything out here. Dinner will keep."

Jo took her time with her boys. She brought them into the

main bedroom she and Felix now shared. He had surprised her when she moved in, asking if she would be okay sleeping in there rather than the guest bedroom. She was, of course, and being with him in the larger room made the whole place feel more like home.

She carefully transferred Pippin onto a nest of blankets that smelled like the two of them. Merry made himself into a cat loaf alongside his brother. As Pip began to purr, Jo pressed her face into the thick fur on his neck.

"I'm so glad you're home, Pipsy. I'll check on you soon, okay?" She kissed his head, then Merry's, and closed the door on her way out so Pippin could acclimate to the new space.

In the living room, Felix had gotten everyone started with wine. He, Leni, and Aida were standing in front of the crackling fireplace, talking about Monsters and Mythology spells that could be used for cooking in increasingly elaborate ways. Trey lounged in the armchair next to Tito's, ankle crossed over knee. He had a soft, nostalgic grin on his face as Tito told the story of his and Lita's first Thanksgiving in America in 1955. Jo could tell by Tito's hand gestures that he had reached the part about how small their turkey was because they were so poor.

Jo caught Felix's eye and gestured toward the kitchen. He excused himself and followed her around the corner.

"How are the kitties?" he asked. "And do you want red or white?"

"White," she said. "They're good. Merry's in protective brother mode, and Pip's awake enough to purr."

He handed her a glass of wine. "I'm glad. Need my help with something?"

"Yeah," Jo said. "Come here." She moved closer, and he opened his arms as she fell against him. She snaked one arm around his waist and sipped her wine, then rested her cheek against his chest.

"You okay?"

"Mm-hmm," she murmured. "I wanted a moment alone with you before the chaos."

Felix kissed her forehead and squeezed her tighter. "I hope you don't mind that I invited Aida and Trey to stay with us this weekend. I wanted our first Thanksgiving here, together, to be memorable, especially since we'll be in California for Christmas."

"Good thing we have a guest room, then," she teased, even as a wave of affection filled her.

She already had so many wonderful memories from the last few months, and she loved Felix for wanting to create even more. She remembered Tuesday evenings over the summer, watching MnM night grow into the premier weekly event at Ashville Public Library. It was so successful that Warren made game night a permanent fixture, not just a summer event. These days there were at least three tables each week, with locals and folks from as far as Wichita coming together to roll dice and tell stories. Jo was there every single week, taking her turn once a month as one of several rotating GMs.

One of her favorites memories was the triumphant look on Felix's face after the budget meetings in September. With the library's steady growth in patronage, he and Warren had convinced the county board to maintain their budget for the next three fiscal years. His job was secure, and Warren was still singing his praises to anyone who would listen. That day had led to some long conversations about Felix's dreams of being an archivist and what their future might hold. While Felix wasn't in a rush to go anywhere, Jo was so proud of everything he had done to set himself up for success down the road.

A roar of laughter from Trey interrupted Jo's musings, and she grinned up at Felix. He bent to kiss her, soft and warm and loving.

She scratched his stubble, earning a rich hum of approval that sent sparks skittering down her spine.

"Hey, gorgeous?" she asked.

"Yes, my Jo?"

"Are you happy?"

Felix smiled. This was their routine of late, a suggestion from his therapist that they both embraced wholeheartedly. Jo would ask the question, and Felix would pause to think about what things in his life were making him happy or unhappy. He'd give her an honest answer, and if there was anything they needed to work through, they'd talk it out.

While he paused now, so did Jo. She listened to the voices from the other room, thought about her two cats cuddling in the bedroom, and imagined spending the entire holiday weekend with Aida and Trey.

She knew her answer.

"Yes, cariño," Felix said, giving her hip a quick squeeze. "I'm happy."

ACKNOWLEDGEMENTS

Whew, this book has had quite a journey! From the initial idea to drafting and revising, from querying and submitting to deciding to publish independently, I wouldn't be here, and this book wouldn't be in your hands, without a whole host of people alongside me.

First and foremost, I want to offer endless thanks to Saint Gibson, one of the first people to understand my vision for Felix and Jo. Thank you for being their champion and shepherd and for being my cheerleader. My thanks, too, to Alice Speilburg and Eva Scalzo for their dedication in seeing this book through.

Thank you to Nina Bodway for fixing my typos, for pointing out that one scene that really wasn't working, and for teaching me that we no longer have to put a comma in front of "too" at the end of a sentence. Thank you to Ana Grigoriu-Voicu and Alison Cnockaert for transforming this story from a Word doc and a bunch of character descriptions into an honest-to-god book that looks more beautiful than I ever could have imagined. Can't wait to work with y'all on the next one.

Now I'm gonna get sappy.

My undying gratitude to Kait Disney-Leugers for being my first reader, for falling in love with these characters as much as I did, and for your belief in me every step of the way. Thank you for only judging me a little bit when I texted you at three a.m. to let you know there was a new chapter for you to read when you woke up. Thank you for the reminder about how much the DMV sucks. The last few years talking about books, sharing writing/publishing woes, exchanging ideas, and texting about real life with you have meant the world to me. You're my hero and my reading buddy, and I love you more than words can say.

To Maria Johnson: I am honored to be the author of the first spicy books you've read. Thank you for listening to me gush, for feeding me mac and cheese, for asking about my D&D games, for your thoughtful comments and questions, and for wanting to talk about writing with me. Thank you for walking side by side with me on this journey we share. More than anything else, thank you for being my best friend for over two decades. You have shaped me in more ways than I can fathom. Thank you for your compassion, your honesty, your optimism, your generosity, your sense of humor, and your time. Thanks for... you know... (Helping you change?) Yeah, that, too.

Thank you to my beta readers for your honesty and insights, and for your encouragement that this story was worth telling: Tabitha Arment, Cielo Bellrose, L.B. Black, Zev Brook, Kait Disney-Leugers, Regan Flow, Erin Gannon, Johanna Goosen, Kassandra Holmes, Maria Johnson, Ruby Jones, Jon Maness, V.S. McGrath, and Emma Rudd. Thank you to Swati Hegde for helping me polish my querying materials; to Shirin Yim Leos, Writespace, and Editcetera for the wonderful classes on craft and process; and to The Badass Writers—Susan Lee, Megan McDonald, and Valerie Saul—

for being the most incredible critique group. I can't wait for the world to read your stories.

To the online communities that have supported and encouraged me, that have made me laugh and kept me balanced: the EnbyFarm, the HLU HarvMind, the USS Hood Friends of Desoto, and the #WritingCommunity. You are the best people on the Internet, and I love you all. HarvMind, treat every day like it's Freaky Friday. FoDs, if you find yourself a Drunk Shimoda in this book, please get in touch to tell me who it is.

Thank you to my D&D community: Jordan, Kait, Becca, Peter, Henry, Lori, and Jacob; Sarah, Kass, Evan, Forrest, Leeza, and Blake; the fine folks at Illusive Comics & Games and Game Kastle; and everyone in the Bay Area Gamer Guild who welcomed me into the world of roleplaying games, conventions, and Epics. Your love of stories and the incredible characters you create have been an inspiration to me. You make me a better storyteller, and you bring such joy to my life. Rolling dice with you all for so many years has been one of the greatest honors of my life.

Thank you to my family for their lifelong love and support and for always encouraging me to read, read, read. Sorry for all the sex and swears in here. I love you.

ELLE M. STEWART is a queer, neurodivergent author based in the San Francisco Bay Area. She lives with two cats named Fitz and Simmons, nine bags of dice (she counted), and more loose leaf tea than any human can reasonably drink in one lifetime. For over eight years, she's been playing tabletop roleplaying games and has written numerous campaigns and adventures. Her self-proclaimed crowning achievement is a one-shot romp titled "To Flavortown and Back Again," featuring villains Guy Fae-eri and his sidekick "saucerer," plus a jukebox mimic in a diner. Taking Initiative is her debut novel.

CONNECT WITH ELLE

Instagram: @elle.m.stew
TikTok: @your.bookish.friend
X: @ElleMStew
Storygraph: ElleMStewart
Monthly newsletter: ellemstewart.substack.com
www.ellemstewart.com